MURDER IN A CHELSEA GARDEN

A POSIE PARKER MYSTERY #12

L. B. HATHAWAY

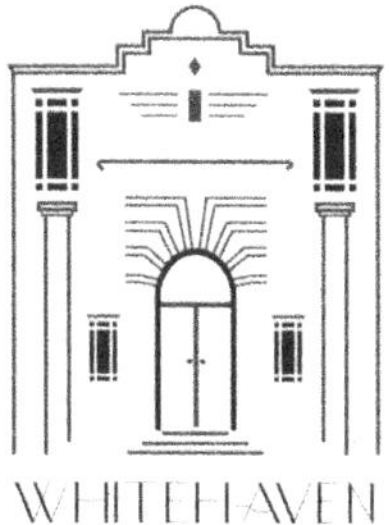

WHITEHAVEN MAN PRESS
London

First published in Great Britain in 2021
by Whitehaven Man Press, London

(http://www.lbhathaway.com, email: permissions@lbhathaway.com)

ISBN (e-book:) 978-1-913531-18-8
ISBN (paperback:) 978-1-913531-19-5

For my girls

Also by L.B. Hathaway

The Posie Parker Mystery Series

1. *Murder Offstage*

2. *The Tomb of the Honey Bee*

3. *Murder at Maypole Manor*

4. *The Vanishing of Dr Winter*

5. *Murder of a Movie Star*

(The stand-alone novella, *A Christmas Case*)

6. *Murder in Venice*

7. *The Saltwater Murder*

8. *Murder on the White Cliffs*

9. *Marriage is Murder?*

10. *Murder in the London Lights*

11. *Murder in Tuscany*

12. *Murder in a Chelsea Garden*

Prologue

The dew was heavy on the lush summer grass of the garden, and a pearly-grey dawn was stealing up the River Thames.

A salty air, thick like treacle, rolled in.

It was very early. Only four-thirty in the morning. Still pretty dark.

The perfect time.

The famous woman who owned the garden clutched a sharp knife in her hand. She had received her instructions and was acting accordingly.

Most of the residents of Chelsea – a mere mile and a half west from Westminster and central London – were still sleeping and would be for hours yet.

Chelsea was fast becoming a playground for those to whom life had invariably been kind and had no need of work.

The woman with the knife was barefoot, and she shivered slightly in her long white nightdress. She knew this garden like the back of her hand. She was, after all, a master perfumier, and this garden was her toolkit.

She walked past roses. Masses of the things. Every possible colour, every possible variety. New and exquisite roses, some created especially for her own use. But she paid scant regard to their mingled, tantalising night scents.

At the bottom of the garden was a lily pond, with a Japanese bridge built over it in the style of Monet's Garden at Giverny in France. She skimmed the pond and headed towards a thick beech hedge behind it, and then she slipped, ghost-like, through an almost-hidden hole in its side.

This was her secret garden.

Here the plants underfoot grew thick and luscious, the ground wet and mulchy from the nearby pond.

Here were black bryony, foxgloves, wolfsbane and henbane.

And every single plant was poisonous. Deadly.

A poisoner's dream.

Hurriedly pulling on her thin leather gardening gloves, the woman started to crop at a plant which was best harvested just before the dawn. Its white flowers, abundant and foamy, could be seen clearly in the grey light.

Hemlock.

It was only the leaves she needed.

The woman cut quickly, folding several of the spiky, long, dark-green leaves into a small muslin bag. She'd need to act fast; she could already smell the vapour of mulchy rottenness rising up at her from the slight crushing the leaves had suffered.

She estimated she had about two minutes, maximum. But suddenly her eye was drawn to something further on, lying half-buried in the thick foliage.

She stopped in her tracks. Stared. Something white was on the ground.

'What the…?'

The perfumier hurried over, and her heart began to beat very fast.

What she saw next, right up close, made her turn cold with fear.

A woman was lying in the undergrowth, her black hair unfashionably long, part of it trailing in mud, in water.

The woman wore a white nightdress soaked with dew. In her hands she clutched at a waterproofed black leather box. Her eyes, open and vacant, stared up at the London sky, which was growing lighter, brighter, with every passing second.

The perfumier dropped to her knees, and slapped at the woman's lovely face, lovelier than she remembered it.

'Oh! Oh! Hattie! Is that really *you*? Who did this to you?'

But it was pointless. Words and actions were all pointless. Time was no longer relevant for the woman on the ground. She had been dead for hours.

The perfumier wanted to scream, but no sound came.

This is murder. Here! In my sacred place.

Pulse racing, she turned back towards the imposing bulk of her red-brick Chelsea townhouse and she tried to run. She got past the hedge and into the main garden again. She needed to get to the telephone. To summon help.

But she never made it.

Because someone was behind her, pushing her, shoving her; hard, angrily.

Had they been waiting here for her all along? Like they had waited for poor dead Hattie?

But all she knew next was that she was falling, tipping head first into the black pond with its tangle of suffocating lilies, going under in a wave of panic and dread.

All she felt at the last was the endless, endless cold water.

And it seemed to her that there, in that final black space of unasked-for nothingness, there was, ironically, no scent at all.

* * * *

Anouk Sinne, the most celebrated 'nose' in London, flung her short dumpy legs – which she hadn't yet shaved – over the side of her eighteenth-century four-poster bed and kicked away the shrimp-coloured Egyptian cotton sheets.

She stretched and yawned, checking the small Longines carriage clock beside her bed.

It was already half-past eleven in the morning.

She'd slept late, and dreamt terrible things, like she had done for two weeks now, since finishing her latest, most ground-breaking new perfume. It had been that same awful dream.

But she couldn't afford to let the memory of it weigh her down, and she tried to ignore the nauseous feeling in her stomach, and hoped she wasn't coming down with a bug. That would be most unfortunate.

Today was a hugely important day, for her and her perfume house, the famous 'House of Sinne'.

There was a knock at her bedroom door.

'Yes? Come in if you must.'

Anouk turned quickly. 'Oh, it's *you*, Lucy.'

A slender, very blonde girl with bobbed hair stood there, holding a silver tray with a pot of tea on it, together with a pre-warmed cup and saucer, the milk and sugar separate. Also on the tray were some very bright, artificial-looking yellow cakes, and some paperwork. The girl stood on the edge of the room, as if fearful to come in properly.

In truth, Anouk's bedroom was a complete mess. Scarves and expensive velvet gowns were tossed everywhere: dresses thrown off willy-nilly in mounds all over the floor; a symphony of blacks with occasional ripples of silver.

One wouldn't even know where to start clearing it all up, or to even dare, come to that.

Lucy Reeble was Anouk's Personal Secretary, concerned with the business side of her employer's life. She was definitely *not* a maid, but on the days when Anouk slept in, Lucy tended to try and make the start of the day as easy as possible for her employer.

'Madam, I brought the morning's post through. In case it was urgent.'

'Thank you.' Anouk rose and kicked her way through the discarded clothes and took the silver tray, which she put down on a small ormolu side-table.

She sat down at the matching chair, poured the tea and sipped it thoughtfully. 'Lapsang? Well, I suppose it *is* after eleven. What a treat.'

She then bit into one of the yellow cakes, artificial cream spurting from her mouth, which she dabbed at hurriedly. 'Is everything in order for this afternoon, Lucy?'

'Yes, Madam. The regular team of housemaids cleaned the house at eight this morning, including the guest apartment upstairs. It was empty, as Count Anatole and his mother breakfasted early and went off into town somewhere. Tom is, as we speak, making sure the garden is absolutely perfect. The drawing-room already looks immaculate. You're sure you don't need me to help with anything further?'

Anouk Sinne shook a few crumbs from her lap. 'No, I need no help until the event actually starts. You have the list of guests who are attending this afternoon? Including my "special" guest? And the man accompanying her?'

'Of course.'

'Keep those two apart from the rest of the party. Put them straight in the drawing-room. Got it?'

'I understand.'

'And I told you already to box up one hundred bottles of the brand-new fragrance as samples?'

'Yes, Madam.'

'They're ready and waiting in the downstairs office, already sealed with wax. There are two of our signature black bags to pack them into. You'll need to fill in all the normal dreaded forms. Boring, I'm afraid…'

'No matter, Madam. And do I need to organise the delivery of these hundred samples? Are they going to Harrods? Or Fortnum's?'

'No. They will be collected in person. Oh! One more thing...' Anouk Sinne reached across the ormolu table, and from under a black leather box, she pulled out a sealed pink envelope, the sort she used for her own private correspondence. It was stamped already and bore a London address.

'Send this later today, will you? In a second-class postbox.'

'Very good, Madam. Shall I go and make a start on packing those bottles? It will take me some time.'

'No. Do it later. Open the mail for me now, will you?'

Anouk Sinne rose, teacup in hand. She walked to the floor-length windows in her white nightdress, flung back the shutters, and stood by the Juliette balcony, drinking her tea. Outside, her garden was basking in the flat, baking light of a perfect English summer's day. It was already slightly too hot, if anything.

Faithful old Tom Bowley, her jobbing gardener since the very start, was picking up stray leaves from the exquisite lawn, that narrow acre of grass which ran towards the Chelsea Embankment like a fresh green ribbon.

Lucy Reeble was busy ripping envelopes open, reading and assimilating information. 'No, there's nothing important in this one, Madam. Oh, wait a minute! *This* looks familiar...'

Then the sound of ripping came again. Hurried, this time. Then an aghast exclamation: 'Oh! Oh, dear, Madam. It's as I thought!'

Anouk whirled around, almost in a panic.

'What? Has someone cancelled for this afternoon?'

'No. No cancellations, Madam. Another horrible note. Posted like the others from Victoria Station. Here...'

The secretary passed across a neat typewritten postcard to her employer, who read it quickly.

Anouk carelessly tossed the postcard on the bed, although she shivered very slightly. 'How very boring! Too, too dull. Ghastly time-wasters!'

But suddenly the perfumier seemed to be wracked by a much stronger shiver, and Lucy Reeble stepped forward, concerned.

'What will you do about it all, Madam? About these notes? I think it's dangerous, if you don't mind my saying so. Will you cancel the event today, Madam?'

'Of course not!' The perfumier took another sip of her tea. 'No. *I* am about to get dressed, Lucy. But *you* are about to go downstairs, to the office, and telephone someone for me. Someone who knows exactly the right person to sort this mess out. Here are their names…'

Anouk Sinne spoke aloud two names, and her secretary wrote them down obediently.

'Very good, Madam. Oh, one other thing.' The girl's pleasant, young face was suddenly shadowed by confusion. 'It's about your cat, Julius. I haven't seen him this morning. Is he still at the vets? You told me yesterday he had gone.'

Anouk Sinne nodded. 'That's right. The procedure was more complicated than they first thought. But he'll be back tonight. And thank goodness! I'll want Julius with me tomorrow, in Mayfair.'

'Naturally, Madam. Do you need me to do anything for the Embassy Club luncheon tomorrow in Mayfair? I'm conscious I haven't helped you at all. I didn't even send out the invitations.'

'Well, the Embassy Club did that all for me, Lucy. And no, I don't need your help for tomorrow.'

Anouk shrugged slightly impatiently. 'That's just my way, Lucy. I do pretty much everything myself. And now, please leave me.'

'Of course, Madam.'

The perfumier stared out of the window again, listening to her secretary's retreating steps, the low heels of her brogues tap-tapping down several flights of marble stairs.

Another roll of shivery fear passed over Anouk Sinne.

What was it? The memory of that horrid dream? The

harsh reality of the powerful note she had just received? The heat? Sickness?

Outside the window, old Tom Bowley was still busy in the garden.

As she watched him, Anouk suddenly felt desperate for a cigarette. She felt it keenly, like an ache inside.

For years, she'd not allowed cigarettes in the House of Sinne, or in its garden. She hadn't smoked since her twenties. The profession didn't allow it. But now she felt desperate for the quick relief the nicotine would bring.

She walked over to the black leather box, created by the same expert company who had manufactured the safe downstairs; checked it was locked. She'd get dressed quickly, and go out and ask Tom Bowley for a lend of his spade.

She needed to dig. And Tom never asked any questions, thankfully.

Anouk shivered again. *That beastly dream.*

The important thing was that there was no sign of Hattie lying out there, out in the garden, down in the undergrowth by that lily pond.

Thank goodness.

It seemed that the body was quite gone.

For now, anyway.

****

PART ONE

Inside the House of Sinne
(Monday 15th June, 1925)

One

The office on Grape Street was very hot and lonesome.

Loathsome, too.

Posie Parker, London's premier female Private Detective, stood with a cup of horrid lukewarm tea in the empty client's waiting room, fidgeting with her short, sticky, dark-brown bobbed hair.

She languidly watched the dust-motes dancing in the air, which was heavy with a summer laziness. She played with her favourite necklace of pale-pink Murano glass beads, as was her wont, pulling at the string until it almost broke.

Then, out of sheer boredom, she walked over to the open sash window, and looked out over a traffic-heavy Shaftesbury Avenue, where grit was hanging in the smog which seemed to be a constant feature of Bloomsbury this summer.

Beyond the busyness was the white splendour of the British Museum. Not that *that* provided any consolation today. Crowds and yet more traffic were massed in front of it.

Len Irving, Posie's professional partner, was ensconced in his own hot office, and he had Sidney, the teenage office boy, in with him, both frantically working on a big case.

There was no time today for a cosy shared tea break. And Prudence, their secretary, was away on a much-anticipated honeymoon.

This eerie and uncompanionable silence in the office was not at all what Posie had imagined.

Posie had only just re-jigged her career. At her own insistence, she had organised with her husband, Richard Lovelace, Chief Commissioner of New Scotland Yard, that she would work only two days per week at the Detective Agency. The rest of the time would be spent with their children, whom lately she had been feeling she didn't see enough of.

This was her first day back under these new self-imposed terms, and it was a colossal disappointment.

Posie had imagined a frantic whirl of activity: trying to fit five days' work into two; with endless telephone calls to answer and dashing out to meetings and assignations; feeling full of importance, and fuelled by a breezy professionalism. Summer was usually one of Posie's busiest times.

But not this year, it seemed.

Not one new case had crossed Posie's desk in weeks.

Even Posie's fairly new dog, her Yorkshire terrier, Patsy, was quiet. The heat was too much for her today, and she lay dreaming, curled up in her basket under Posie's desk.

There was a knock at the door and the cheery bottle-blonde secretary from the office below stuck her head in.

'Lunchtime post for ya, Miss Parker. Here you go! Lumme! It's blimmin' hot in 'ere, ain't it? You goin' to get yerself an ice-popsicle for lunch, Miss? I fink you'll need it! Where's that sweet little doggie of yours, Miss?'

'Sleeping. Sensibly.'

Posie took the mail and sifted through it quickly.

There was absolutely nothing for her.

'Why is business so bally slow?' she muttered to herself testily. 'Perhaps I'm losing my touch.'

She sat down heavily in Prudence's chair, petulantly sorting the mail into two very boring piles: Len's mail, and office bills.

Dull, dull, dull.

As the years had passed since 1921, when Posie had set up the Detective Agency, the sad, strange letters from broken-hearted women who had lost men out in the muddy killing fields of the Somme and Passchendaele were growing fewer; their requests for Posie to 'search' for these missing men – as if they had chosen simply to disappear, rather than die – were coming less often. Even two years back, there had been at least a request of this type twice a week.

Now it had been months.

Well, the fact they had dried up was something, at least.

Posie had never taken those cases on anyway, choosing to write carefully instead to each and every woman, explaining that it would be a waste of everyone's time and money to take on the job. They were hopeless cases. No point prolonging the agony. Or the hope.

Posie glanced at the cover of today's copy of *The Times*, usually intended for the client's coffee table, but as yet still not put out. Good job Prudence would return next week from Skegness. Things were going to pot in the office without her.

The front page of *The Times* was filled with a picture of the Prince of Wales and his bored, beautiful face; his haunted, glassy eyes. He was on a lengthy tour somewhere in Africa and was obviously growing tired.

Further down the page as a separate story was a smaller photograph of a dark young woman, whose beauty was adorned by many sumptuous jewels. She was pictured getting out of a small aeroplane, waving at waiting admirers.

Posie read the caption: 'PERFECT PRINCESS PRIYANKA TOUCHES DOWN AT CROYDON!'

This was the glamorous but tragic Maharani of Gwilim,

Princess Priyanka Lashari, whose family had all perished in a fire at their lavish fort in India about a month ago, leaving Princess Priyanka the sole survivor of the dynasty, which, as she was female, was now declared null and void.

Her plight and her beauty had touched the world, and great futures seemed to be planned for her. It seemed she was travelling about the world, searching for an occupation. There was talk of Hollywood, and acting.

Just about to read the short story which accompanied the photograph, Posie was interrupted by the telephone ringing on Prudence's desk. The Operator asked if Posie would accept a call from Pavilion Road in Chelsea.

'Of course. Please make the connection.' Posie's spirits were suddenly lifted: this call meant that Dolly, Countess of Cardigeon, had returned.

Dolly was Posie's closest friend, and she had been away in the north, for what seemed like weeks, at Rebburn Abbey, that old wreck of a mansion which was the Cardigeon ancestral home. Dolly had even been absent from Posie and Richard's double christening for their babies, Kit and Katie. The absence had been sad and odd, and rather out of character, actually.

A crackle carried along the line. 'That you, Po? I'm just back into town.'

'Dolly. How lovely to hear your voice! I've missed you. Things are dashed quiet at this end. And Richard's involved with a huge court case, so I barely see him at the moment. Do you fancy lunch later this week? We could go to Kettner's in Soho and eat fishcakes, for old times' sake.'

But Dolly seemed distracted, not lingering over niceties, or details, or fishcakes. She sounded on edge. 'You free, Po? This afternoon?'

'I *can* be. What's so urgent? Are you going to make my day and tell me you've got matinée tickets to see *No, No, Nanette*? I can almost see the queues snaking around the block from the Palace Theatre to here! You can't get to that show for love nor money at the moment.'

'Nah, sorry, lovey. Can't help you. This is important: it's about work.'

'Work? What sort of work?' Posie frowned, but she suddenly felt excited, as if all her efforts to come to the office had been for something after all. A Christmas-anticipation-type-feeling.

'Work for *me*?'

'That's right. What do you know about perfume, darlin'?'

'What a funny question!' Posie laughed down the telephone wires.

'I don't know much, really. But I know what I like. I always order a big bottle of custom-made Parma Violet perfume twice a year from Garlands, on the High Street in Norwich. I've done that since I was eighteen. Fairly cheap, and it smells like *me*, even to myself. And as for Richard, I buy him a great big bottle of "Blenheim Bouquet" from Penhaligon's in Covent Garden for Christmas, and it lasts all year. When it comes to scent, both of us are rather predictable, I'm afraid.'

'Well, you're goin' to have to *pretend* then, Po, aren't you? You're goin' to have to pretend to understand the fanciest, darkest, costliest perfumes being made in the world right now.'

'Sorry? I'm not following you. Who wants me to work for them? One of the French Perfume Houses? Golly gosh, how exciting! Is it *Coty*, or *Caron*? Or *Guerlain*? It's not Coco Chanel herself, is it? Have I got to go to Paris?'

The note of yearningly hopeful excitement in Posie's voice was obvious, even to herself.

'Nah.' Dolly sighed, all the way over in Chelsea. 'It's funny you should mention Paris, though, lovey; it's been on my mind a lot lately. But you're stayin' right here in London.'

'Oh! Well, is it Penhaligon's, then? Or Floris, or Yardley?'

'Nah, I said 'darkest', didn't I? Think again.'

Dolly harrumphed at her friend's silence. 'Don't tell me you've never heard of the House of Sinne?'

'Anouk Sinne?' Posie drew in her breath. 'The perfumier with the famous cat? I *do* read the news, you know! Her perfumes have a sort of cult following, don't they? *Very* art-deco, and achingly fashionable, aren't they?'

'I dunno about that, Po. All I know is that Anouk wants to see you this afternoon.'

'Me?'

'Yep.'

This was intriguing.

Anouk Sinne had set up her eponymous perfume house in fashionable Chelsea before the Great War. She was rumoured to be one of the finest 'noses' in the world.

The perfumes themselves were eye-wateringly expensive, each small bottle costing around forty or fifty pounds, the equivalent of two months' salary for a qualified clerical worker in London. They were musky and sensuous creations, with each new blend being given a simple number instead of a name, letting the purchaser themselves conjure up their very own stories to accompany the scent on their skin.

The House of Sinne perfumes were stocked in the very best Department Stores in London: on the gleaming counters of Harrods and Fortnum's and Selfridges.

Posie had never stopped in front of those particular counters, never having felt the need to purchase a bottle of such edgy charm; never having wanted to blue so much money on a treat.

Anouk Sinne's short, stout figure was often to be seen in the pages of magazines, snapped by journalists as she tottered around London on ridiculously vertiginous high heels, her plump, doughy face still captivating even in her late forties, her painted lips always pouting.

Usually, she was photographed clutching her cat, or walking it on its glittering lead. It was an entirely bald creature, most similar to the Sphynx cats of ancient Egypt. This cat was a peculiar mirror of its owner: cross-looking, but beautifully and expensively adorned.

Anouk Sinne was well connected, even perhaps a close – *a very close?* – friend of the gorgeous young bachelor Prince of Wales himself, who, it was widely known, enjoyed the company of older, not entirely beautiful ladies.

Posie suddenly remembered that there had been a slightly intriguing photograph the year before of the Prince of Wales with Anouk Sinne outside the doors of the Kit-Kat Club on Piccadilly: he'd been whispering in her ear, and Anouk had been listening, one painted eyebrow raised, a slightly proprietorial hand resting on the Prince's jacket. The photograph had suggested intimacy, and had been re-printed by newspapers for months afterwards.

But above all, Anouk Sinne was famous for being a prickly character, for working alone. She was also famous for possessing her own extensive garden in which she grew everything she needed to create the House of Sinne perfumes, making her entirely self-sufficient.

Posie pulled herself back to the here and now.

'She wants to see *me*? But why?'

'Your guess is as good as mine, lovey. But I've been rung up and told to get you over to the House of Sinne for half-past three today. Blimmin' cheek of it! I feel like a flippin' messenger boy!'

Posie was confused. 'But why wasn't I rung up directly? Why did *you* have to be dragged into it all?'

There was a split-second of silence. 'It's a bit of a long story, darlin'. Let's jus' say, she obviously thought you'd come if I did the askin'. You see, Anouk Sinne and I know each other. Of old.'

'Really? I had no idea you two were friends.'

'Pah! Well, "friends" is not how I'd describe our relationship. Not on your nelly! Nor would Anouk claim *me* for a friend. Which makes this little invite all the more intriguing. But the polite little secretary girl made it sound *urgent*. It seems there's goin' to be a little private gatherin' at the House of Sinne this afternoon, to which we are invited.

Ain't we the lucky ones? Goes without sayin' it's all top-secret. And the dress-code is "tea-party". Can you go home and change, Posie, or have you got some glad-rags which might do the trick there in the office?'

'Of course. Right here with me, in fact.'

That was a lie. All Posie had in the office were evening things; heavy, sombre, blackest black.

But if she rushed out now, during her lunch hour, five minutes up the road on the bus, up through Oxford Street, to Selfridges, which Posie adored, she could pick up something off-the-peg which would more than suit the occasion of a tea-party.

She'd been going to treat herself to a new summer tea-dress anyhow, and this was the perfect chance. She fancied being *bold* today.

'I'll wait in Chelsea for you,' said Dolly, wearily. 'Truth be told, I'm still recoverin' from the long journey home yesterday. It's almost one o'clock, and I'll have a little sleep. So why don't you come here at three o'clock? We can travel over to Anouk's place in our car, with my driver Paul.'

Dolly seemed to remember something suddenly. 'Oh, and Posie?'

'Yes?'

'Come unscented.'

Posie didn't know if she'd heard correctly. '*What?*'

'Thought you'd like that! Accordin' to the secretary, no-one is even allowed to enter the House of Sinne wearin' any sort of perfume, not even one of Anouk's own. *All* scents are banned. I'd wash your special Norwich violets right off. And don't even bother with any Yardley soap. She's always been a funny one for smells, has Anouk. They get her goin' somehow. There's a list of other things we can't do. For example, I'm under strict instructions not to smoke inside the house, would you believe it?'

Dolly made to ring off, but evidently thought better of it. 'Oh, and Posie?'

‘Still here.’

‘Another one of the strict instructions. Don’t bring the dog. I know you’ve taken to carting her about pretty much everywhere you go.’

Posie bridled angrily. She hadn’t been going to bring Patsy, but anyhow!

The cheek!

‘My dog does not *smell*,’ she replied fiercely, loyally. ‘Poor Patsy. How rude!’

Posie heard her friend laugh. ‘Oh, that’s nothin’! If you want to see real rudeness, you wait until you meet our delightful hostess. You’re in for a real blimmin’ treat!’

And as Posie bit her lip, picking up her carpet bag, ready to step out on her frock-buying mission, she was more intrigued than ever.

* * * *

Two

They drew up outside the long terrace of tall, red-bricked town houses on Embankment Gardens in Chelsea.

Each house was imposing and immaculate, white-piped with fancy stonework around the windows and doors, and boasting spotless marble doorsteps and shiny, black-painted doors.

Paul, the Cardigeon's driver, pulled the navy Rolls-Royce up smartly outside Number 11, which was the terrace right at the end of the row. A bronze plaque over the number of the house read 'THE HOUSE OF SINNE', and a fancy crest was emblazoned into it, too, the details of which were too far away to make out.

Black-and-silver flags flew outside the house ostentatiously.

Posie frowned at the whole effect: it all seemed ludicrous and in quite poor taste, as was the name of the perfume house itself. It sounded and looked like some sort of upmarket brothel.

The House of Sinne, indeed!

What on earth did the poor neighbours think? This was, after all, the most respectable of London neighbourhoods, what with the renowned Chelsea Physic Garden, and the Royal Hospital on the doorstep, and fashionable Sloane Square and the King's Road for shopping nearby.

Or maybe the neighbours liked to be within a stone's throw of Anouk Sinne's particular brand of notoriety? Perhaps it gave them something to talk about?

Posie checked her little red wristwatch. It was a couple of minutes before half-past three.

The driver drummed his hands delicately on the leather-tooled steering wheel and coughed lightly. Dolly met the anxious young man's gaze in the rear-view mirror.

'It's all right, Paul love, I *do* realise the time. You get out for a minute, won't yer? Have a ciggie or somethin'? I want to talk to Miss Parker 'ere. Private, like.'

'Of course, your Ladyship. I'll walk to the corner, see if I can catch sight of the river.'

They watched Paul jump out, stretch his legs, grab a thermos flask, and walk away.

Dolly immediately lit up one of her usual black-and-silver Sobranie cigarettes, inhaling the smoke greedily.

'Better have one of these, or maybe the whole blimmin' pack, while I'm still allowed. Eh?'

Posie licked at her carefully-applied coral-pink lipstick and watched her friend, who looked rather washed-out today.

Dolly was wearing a primrose-yellow *crepe-de-chine* dress with a matching buttermilk-coloured lace bolero, the exact colour of her peroxided hair. On her head she wore an expensive but plain cloche hat in yellow, pulled far down over her eyes.

Only Dolly's great dark-brown, luminous eyes gave her any colour today. But they didn't sparkle with their usual mirth, even though Dolly had added a layer of bright-gold paillettes in a sequin-sparkling arch under each eye, like some exotic butterfly. She'd also painted her lips into a tight cupid's bow with bright, almost fluorescent lemon-yellow lipstick, which made her look like a sick canary.

None of this boded well.

And had it been Posie's imagination, or had she smelt

strong alcohol on Dolly's breath as her friend had joined her – several minutes late – as Paul had sat with the Rolls-Royce's engine already running, in the cobbled enclave of Pavilion Road, just behind Peter Jones on Sloane Square?

Dolly hadn't even apologised for keeping Posie waiting.

Posie lightly touched her friend's arm. 'What is it, Dolly? You haven't said much since we met up. Something's wrong. But what?'

A horrible thought struck Posie. Dolly was fragile and had always suffered from coughs and chills, with the result that she was packed off for a rest-cure to sunnier climes every winter. Had Dolly had bad medical news? Of the worst possible sort?

'Is it your health?'

'All fine.'

'The children? The twins, Bunny and Trixie? Little Raymond?'

Dolly nodded, a slight smile playing across her scarily-yellow lips. 'Perfect. Well, you know how it is…almost perfect.'

'Rufus, then?'

Rufus, the Eleventh Earl of Cardigeon, was Dolly's husband, and Posie had been responsible for bringing the couple together. Rufus had been Posie's brother's best friend at school. And despite her brother's death in the Great War in 1917, Posie had never lost touch with Rufus.

Dolly shrugged. 'Rufus is Rufus. We're all right, as much as any marriage *can* be after four years, anyhow. But lawks, "ever after" is a long time to promise someone, innit?'

What was that meant to mean?

Better not dig too far here, unless information was offered up readily, thought Posie to herself, making a show of studying her own lollipop-pink painted nails.

Was there another man?

Did Dolly have suspicions that Rufus had met someone else? Someone who was significant? But Dolly would say so, wouldn't she?

'So, what is it, then?'

A silence, a drag on the Sobranie.

A clock struck somewhere.

It was now exactly half-past three and Posie suddenly caught sight of a surprisingly young man dressed in butler's livery darting out of the door of Number 11, shooting an apprehensive look up and down the street. The man bit at his lip before disappearing again.

Had it been Posie's imagination or had the butler been shaking, steadying himself by holding the door-frame? It seemed ominous somehow.

He'd looked toothy, slightly scruffy, unprepossessing for sure – not what you'd expect at the House of Sinne – but it gnawed at Posie that he might have been looking up and down the street for *her* because she was about to be late.

Posie felt a jangle of nerves in her belly. She hated being late. Even by just a couple of minutes.

'I'm scared, Posie.'

Dolly flashed her huge eyes towards the building they should be stepping inside right now.

'Sorry?' said Posie, completely thrown. 'Why on earth are you scared?'

'Look, lovey, I've had lots to deal with since I got back home yesterday. Various odd calls to take. All draggin' up the past. But this one, about comin' *here*, well, I confess, it's given me the chills. I've managed to avoid Anouk Sinne for years; I've not seen her since 1913. Glad of it, too. She's like a plague. Things have a habit of turnin' out badly when she's involved. I have a bad feelin' about this afternoon.'

This was odd. It was downright unusual to find Dolly so fearful.

'What *exactly* happened between you two, Dolly? And whatever it was, you're a Countess these days, for goodness' sake! You trump Anouk Sinne massively in the social stakes. She's *got* to be nice to you, and if not, to at least be courteous.'

Posie studied her friend's curiously blank, pale face. 'Dolly! What is it?'

'It was more than twelve years ago, lovey. A lifetime ago.'

'Time to let bygones be bygones then?'

But before Dolly could properly answer, *if* she had been going to answer, Posie saw in the rear-view mirror the reflection of a familiar figure lolloping along the street. He was looking sweaty and harried, with a big box camera slung about his neck and pulling a heavy suitcase behind him.

'It's Sam Stubbs!' exclaimed Posie.

As they watched, Sam Stubbs hurried up the steps to Number 11, checking his wristwatch in a worried manner. As if he, too, had been summoned here.

But why?

Sam was a reliable contact of Posie's, a friendly journalist who had risen quickly through the news-floor ranks to become editor of the *Associated Press*. He often let Posie use the archive of cuttings and photographs at his newspaper's offices on Fleet Street.

Posie frowned. 'What on earth is Sam Stubbs doing here? He barely leaves Fleet Street these days as he's so grand! And why has he come alone? I thought you said this little get-together was top-secret, Dolly? It looks like he's playing at being photographer and journalist rolled into one today, eh? Unless his photographer cancelled on him? Golly gosh, it looks like he's lugged all that equipment from the Underground at Sloane Square, and in this sweltering heat! Shall we join him?'

But Dolly stayed silent. She continued to smoke, almost angrily, then ground out her cigarette.

Behind them a small brown van suddenly drew up; it looked like a delivery van for groceries. A small man in tobacco-coloured overalls and with a thick, wintery-looking grey tweed cap got out and was whistling loudly.

Posie watched as the delivery man brought a huge black box up the steps to Number 11, and the nervy-looking butler appeared again, signing a chit in receipt for the black box.

'Whatever Anouk Sinne is up to, it's some sort of devilry,' Dolly muttered. 'You wait, Po. Something is afoot.'

'Well, even devilry won't wait, though, will it? And sometimes devilry pays the bills.'

Posie leant over her friend and opened the motor-car door, effectively forcing Dolly out onto the pavement.

Posie took a second to smooth down her newly-acquired pink-and-blue polka-dot tea-dress, and she patted at her matching hot pink hat with its tiny navy veil. She'd brought along her old and beloved carpet bag, as, despite the fact it was almost threadbare, she'd not found anything better to replace it with. And not for want of looking.

As they walked up the steps to the house, the glistening black front door opened as if by magic. However, it wasn't the young butler who invited them inside, but a slender girl in her twenties, with blonde hair, dressed in a boy's sailor suit of purest white, clutching at a clipboard. The effect was of androgynous, sophisticated youth.

She made Posie feel suddenly and instantly very old.

'Miss Parker? Countess? I'm Lucy Reeble, Miss Sinne's Private Secretary. Thank you so much for coming. This way, please.'

The room they entered right off the vestibule was a vast, grand, white entrance hallway with immensely high stuccoed ceilings and a plain tiled floor, like you might find in an apothecary. There was absolutely nothing in the room except a telephone on a small glass table. Three identical, white-painted doors led off the room.

But Posie had missed the artful conceit of the room. Because, although it was bare, there *was* a presence here.

A masterpiece, in fact.

A huge oil painting took up a whole white wall, around

twelve feet by twelve feet in its frame, and it was vastly impressive.

Out of a dark-blue bubble, the size of a real-life automobile, a dark, cross-looking plump woman had been painted, stepping out, her small eyes intense with what looked like a pent-up rage, fury almost. A bald cat on a glittering collar and lead crouched in the bottom left-hand side of the painting, snarling. But the focus of the painting was a bottle: in the painting the woman was holding aloft a turquoise bottle of perfume, like a sword of truth, and out of this all the light of the painting radiated, in vast triangular beams.

The piece was astonishing, pure art-deco. The most modern thing Posie had seen in a while.

Posie stopped the girl in white beside her, who had been about to march them off, fast.

'This is a portrait of Miss Sinne, isn't it? A Tamara de Lempicka, unless I'm much mistaken?'

'Sorry, Miss Parker? Oh! Oh, yes. Miss Sinne sat for it a couple of years ago. With Julius, her Sphynx cat, of course. It was before I started working here. It's beautiful, isn't it? Worth a fortune, of course. You're lucky to see it, actually. It's about to go off to the National Portrait Gallery.'

Posie looked appreciative. 'How nice that the public will be able to see such a wonderful piece. It's a rare talent Miss Lempicka has, for sure.'

'Oh, yes,' agreed Miss Reeble in a slightly fawning manner. 'And it's a painting *of* a rare talent, too. Miss Sinne is the talent, I mean. Speaking of whom, we need to go down to her, immediately. I was told it was vitally important, Miss Parker.'

Miss Reeble smiled at Dolly, before continuing, all in a rush: 'Jenks, the butler, will return in a minute for you, Countess: I'm not quite sure where he is, but he'll show you through to the gathering.'

Dolly smiled graciously. 'Of course.'

Dolly suddenly sniffed, rather rudely. 'But what's that smell, Miss Reeble? It smells like somethin' is on fire. Toast, is it? An illegal ciggie?'

Posie suspected her friend was badly craving another cigarette and was irritable because of it.

'*Smell?*' Lucy Reeble looked askance at this apparently forbidden, ugly word. 'The *scent*, you mean? It's a clear note of blackest carbon. One of Miss Sinne's most popular items at perfume counters across London. It neutralizes the air and banishes negativity. Quite "the thing".'

'How novel,' murmured Posie, throwing a warning look at Dolly, who had rolled her eyes heavenwards. But the butler suddenly appeared, and up close he was even more frazzled and dishevelled-looking than he had been from afar. He had mud on his black jacket, and his hair was all over the place.

Jenks had left the middle white door open through which he'd come, and Posie had a tantalising glimpse of a conservatory leading to a lawn. A few people, holding drinks, milled about in the glass room.

A flustered-looking Sam Stubbs was messing about with a camera, trying out flash-lights.

Nearer, with his back to them, was a dark-haired, tall young man dressed in a navy blazer and flannels and no hat. He was holding a champagne flute and speaking in urgent whispers to a much older woman in a white-ruffled blouse with a prominent beige cameo brooch pinned upon it. She was wreathed in strings of thick black funereal Edwardian pearls, like something from a much earlier, more conservative age.

They were not at all the sorts of people Posie had expected to find inside the famous House of Sinne.

Rather regretfully, Posie watched Dolly leave with the shabby butler and Posie followed the secretary obediently through the third white door.

They walked down a narrow, tiled corridor, everything clinically white, then down a circular, tiled staircase.

The two women walked in silence, suddenly stopping in front of a huge cast-iron door, rubber-sealed all around. It was the sort of thing you might expect to find on board a Royal Navy vessel; an entrance to a watertight and fortified strong room.

A place of submerged secrets.

Miss Reeble rapped on the door rather nervily with the metal clip of her board.

And just then the huge door was unsealed, and the powerful dark vision from the Lempicka picture upstairs was revealed; the painting made real, brought to life.

The tiny perfumier – so familiar from newspapers and magazines – was wreathed in a huge scarf of swirling silver chiffon, scattered with embroidered stars, and underneath it was a dress of silver-and-black lamé. The perfumier wore matching black patent Mary-Jane shoes with exaggerated high-heels, decorated with silver grosgrain bows. The effect was of some ethereal, darkly magical sprite, got out of its hollow.

Even with the heels, Anouk Sinne was a good head and shoulders shorter than Posie, and Posie felt uncomfortably like a gawky, towering giant.

Anouk Sinne had extremely short, cropped hair, shorter than was fashionable, and it was very black, probably artificially so. Her face, surprisingly lovely, was a make-up artist's delight: a confection of pan-stick and magenta blush, with silver lipstick aplenty. There was glossy wet eyeshadow on her eyelids, too. A whole pot, by the looks of things.

But it was Anouk Sinne's actual eyes which struck Posie as the most curious thing of all, and she had to stop herself from gasping aloud.

The perfumier's hazel-brown irises were almost obscured by staggeringly huge, dilated black pupils. Perhaps it was just a trick of nature? But probably, and more likely, a chemical compound had been used to create this 'novelty' effect.

Her eyes make me want to shiver, Posie thought to herself with some surprise.

It's like I'm looking at her, and she's dead.

'Miss Sinne? I'm Posie Parker. You asked for me?' Posie extended her hand, smiling politely, trying not to stare at those black, bottomless eyes a moment too long and thus appear rude.

But the perfumier didn't take Posie's hand. Instead, she made an impatient shooing motion towards her secretary.

'Go away, will you, Lucy? Check the room is ready for the "reveal". Not a hair out of place, eh? Check people are where they should be, please.'

The voice was clipped and slightly nasal, authoritative.

'Of course.' The girl immediately retreated.

What on earth was the 'reveal'? Posie wondered.

But then Anouk Sinne was motioning Posie inside, bolting the big iron door shut behind her, and a dark, low-lit long room was thrown open to scrutiny.

It must once have been some part of the kitchen, or the servant's quarters – a cook's flat, perhaps? – but there was no natural light in here at all. What was possibly a set of French doors in the far wall were heavily swathed in dark velvet drapes. Huge circular fans whirred overhead.

A roaring fire was burning in a fireplace at the very end of the room, and because of this, despite the overhead fans, the room was utterly roasting on such a warm summer's day. The scent of 'carbon' back in the hallway was intensified here, and its smokiness and strength would have made Dolly say something. But Posie kept quiet, taking it all in, hoping her eyes didn't water too much.

'Welcome to my laboratory. Thank you for coming. Dolly Price always could be relied upon to do my bidding.'

But then Anouk Sinne added in a quieter, subdued voice: 'The silly little fool!'

Posie fought hard not to reply, biting her lip.

Whatever bad blood had passed between Dolly and

this woman was obviously still flowing. The assumption Posie had made that the perfumier would accord Dolly all the proper reverence due to a Countess was obviously far off the mark.

Never mind.

These are not my battles to fight. I'll get down to business and finish up as quickly as I can.

Posie looked about. The place was full of bottles and jars and glass-fronted cabinets running from floor to ceiling as far as the eye could see. This room was a cave of particular, specialised delights.

Here were specially-built, tiny rubber-sealed drawers in tall wooden cabinets, each drawer carefully labelled with a typewritten card and locked with a tiny golden padlock.

Here were the perfumier's tricks of the trade, her own store of private alchemy. Posie read the ingredients nearest her quickly:

OUD, ORANGE BLOSSOM, IRIS, FREESIA, AMSTERDAM TULIP, JUNIPER EXTRACT, TUBEROSE, MINT, CORIANDER, CARROT SEEDS, QUINCE EXTRACT.

And so on.

And on.

Hundreds of labels.

Posie looked at the rest of the room. There was a long, high table of dark wood with a matching built-in bench underneath it, running the length of the room. On this table was all manner of apparatus: test-tubes and Bunsen burners, and bottles of stoppered liquids of different colours and gloopy thicknesses.

There were books stacked high, all over the place, about flowers, gardening, and botany.

On the right-hand wall was a thin, 'floating' glass box, lit inside with turquoise and pink lights. The lights illuminated a series of identical turquoise-glass carved bottles, each one stamped in gold with a title.

Here were 'Sin 1' and 'Sin 2' and so on, up until 'Sin 12'. And then there were a few smaller turquoise bottles, more intricate, labelled with different titles: 'GOLDEN SIN', 'BEAUTIFUL SIN'.

The perfumier watched Posie's rapt gaze and smiled indulgently. 'You've noticed my display cabinet. You know, I'm almost ashamed to admit this, but it's a mere vanity.'

As she spoke, Posie saw a slight tremor roll across the woman's shoulders, and Anouk Sinne clutched herself tightly, as if very cold. But how could she be, in this stifling fuggy room?

'Those bottles are only filled with water, Miss Parker. The real fragrances, and the instructions for their composition are normally kept in my safe, under my own watchful eye. These bottles are simply my way of showing off to myself: a row of trophies. But I do not think you are the type for one of my perfumes, are you, Miss Parker?'

Anouk Sinne grinned mischievously and put her head on one side like a small cheery sparrow.

'Women - and men - buy my perfumes because they want to invoke a dream version of themselves, which they can carry about, bottled. Perhaps they want to wrap themselves in the scented whispers of a Rajasthani Garden at twilight? If so then they will choose 'Sin 6', and smell of resin and spice, cut through with quince and the heaviness of a damask rose.'

There was another great shudder, quickly hidden. 'Or maybe they want to smell of pure desire? And then they will choose 'Sin 1' and cloak themselves in trails of amber and cedarwood, evoking the heat of hot skin on leather. That first fragrance is a progressive, controversial choice; even too much for me if I'm honest.'

Anouk Sinne's hands were shaking violently and she stuffed them under her shawl, as if for warmth.

'My most popular scent, however, is 'Sin 2', which is a deceptively complicated concoction of white musk.

Perfume-counter girls tell me that their repeat-customers claim 'Sin 2' is like wearing a journey to the moon and stars, every single day.'

'That sounds, er, adventurous.' Posie smiled tightly, hoping she looked receptive to these rather wild ideas. 'Great fun, perhaps?'

'But not for you, Miss Parker. Let's be honest: none of those perfumes encapsulate *you*, do they? Because your tastes run far purer, don't they?'

'I'm sorry?'

Anouk Sinne was standing several feet away from Posie but she closed her eyes and made a show of taking a big, deep inhalation of air through her nose, her nostrils flared dramatically.

'Violet! That's your favourite, isn't it? Parma Violet!'

Posie, who had meticulously washed off every last dab of her usual perfume, grinned, impressed at the woman's olfactory skills. 'I say! Yes. That's absolutely right.'

'It's always been my least used ingredient. I believe the noses at the House of Worth in Paris are working on a violet concoction, but I've had no success with it at all. Which is a shame, as it's cheap and powdery and popular. It's secretive, strong, resilient. But I find it works best alone. Perhaps like *you*, Miss Parker?'

Posie hardly knew how to take this. Was it *praise*?

'Er, well…'

'Oh, take it as a compliment, won't you? That's why I've called you, and not the police. I feel I can rely on your discretion. Sit on the bench if you like, Miss Parker. I don't keep tea in here, but I *do* have a pitcher of plain water if you'd like a glass. I confess I have had a raging thirst all day long.'

Any wonder, in this heat!

'I'm fine, thank you.'

'As you wish.'

As Posie put down her carpet bag and climbed rather

uncomfortably onto the hard wooden bench, careful not to tear her polka-dot tea-dress, Anouk Sinne was digging in a copious pocket of her lamé dress.

She had pulled out a few white standard-issue Post Office postcards, a frown etching itself deeply into the overly-made-up face. Another juddering shiver gripped the woman, but she shook it off like you might flick away a fly, or a mosquito.

From the edge of her vision Posie made out that the postcards seemed to have typed words on them.

The perfumier waved these all in Posie's direction.

'I need your help. Just send me your bill at the end of this, do. Now, read these while I go and stoke the fire. All were sent from Victoria Station by the early post on the days in question, arriving by coffee-time. Have a good look. You'll see I have a massive problem on my hands here.'

* * * *

Three

Posie looked obediently at the postcards. They were the sort you could buy at any London kiosk, or newsstand. There were three of them.

The first, from two weeks ago, read:

NICE BUSINESS YOU HAVE HERE. YOU'LL WANT TO KEEP IT THAT WAY. KEEP YOURSELF ALL IN ONE PIECE, TOO.

IN ORDER TO DO SO, DELIVER £1,000 IN BANK NOTES TO LOCKER NUMBER 56, VICTORIA STATION, MONDAY 8 JUNE, 4.30 PM SHARP.

(COME ALONE. NO FUNNY BUSINESS. NO AUDIENCE. NO POLICE.)

Posie looked up briefly, but Anouk Sinne was stabbing at the fire, busy.

She read the next note, dated last week.

YOU DIDN'T SHOW. WHY?

THIS IS A WARNING. COME TOMORROW, FRIDAY 12 JUNE, 4.30 PM SHARP.

SAME AMOUNT, SAME PLACE. OTHERWISE, YOU WILL REGRET IT.

And the last postcard, with today's date on top of it.

IF YOU DON'T DEPOSIT THE MONIES REQUESTED, TODAY, MONDAY 15 JUNE, SAME ARRANGEMENTS, YOUR LIFE IS IN VERY GRAVE DANGER.

Posie puffed out her cheeks, exhaling rapidly.

Well, she'd wanted a case, hadn't she? And now it seemed she had one on her hands. Of the urgent variety.

A horrible hot mess of blackmail: the asking of a simply *huge* amount of money, combined with a threat of – well, what exactly? Kidnap? Or worse? Murder? Professional ruin, too?

She watched the tiny woman at the fire, and then pulled out one of her usual silver notebooks and a matching pencil from her carpet bag.

'I take it you didn't go, Miss Sinne? On one of the first two dates? Not even to hide and see who might be hanging about locker 56?'

'Of course not! I'm a very busy woman, Miss Parker. This is not some elaborate game. These fools could be extremely dangerous.'

'But you didn't take any note of that danger? Didn't follow their requests? Until now?'

'That's right. I hoped they would back off. Desist. Besides, a thousand pounds is a lot of money. It's around half of my annual salary, as it happens.'

Posie stopped herself from looking shocked just in time. *Two thousand pounds as an annual salary!* It was a staggering amount for one person. Ridiculous.

Even for someone famous.

'You didn't inform the police, Miss Sinne?'

'No.'

'Have you shown these postcards to anyone else in your household?'

'Not a soul. Well, only to my secretary, who you've already met. And that's only because she opens the post. Not because I actually *wanted* to show her.'

'I see. And have you any idea who could be sending these? Someone you *know*, perhaps?'

Posie let the full import of the word 'know' linger in the air a few seconds. Would it be enough for this strange and not-altogether-likeable woman to confess to some spurned lover?

The small dark woman came striding back from the fireplace. She checked the locks on a couple of drawers, closing padlocks with tiny golden keys.

Posie saw she had a series of perhaps thirty or more tiny, identical-looking keys on a dainty, highly expandable golden bracelet. The keys were as miniscule as charms, the whole bracelet as gorgeous as any piece of Cartier jewellery.

Out of the corner of her eye, Posie also saw a notepad and a pen, and five pink envelopes on the table, some open, some closed. It looked as though the perfumier had been attending to these before Posie had come in.

Posie urged her on. 'Do you suspect *anyone*, Miss Sinne?'

'I honestly haven't a clue, Miss Parker. I wish I did.'

Anouk Sinne closed a drawer shut with a big bang. 'Forgive me doing this, while you are here, but I work entirely alone, and some of these ingredients are worth a fortune. Orange blossom, for example. In its purest form I can expect to pay Two to Three Hundred pounds per ounce. And Oud is eye-wateringly expensive, too: costs three times the price of purest gold per ounce.'

'Gracious!' Posie was startled.

'Quite. So, before I go anywhere, even just upstairs, I always have to make sure I've got everything locked up and secure.'

The perfumier came and sat on the high bench next to Posie. She crossed her arms defensively and looked Posie square in the face.

'There's no-one serious in my life, Miss Parker, which is what you are politely hinting at. I have always, for a very long time now, lived quite alone, in a self-contained flat upstairs. I have no dependants, no husband and no children. My days are spent here, although I often go out at night, which is when I am photographed. But I admit, the thrill of sparkling London is waning, even for me. I could give it up in an instant! Photographs and appearances in general, you know, can be very misleading. When one is well-known, you find yourself in a peculiarly powerful position: on the receiving end of great generosity and trust, but also subject to great jealousy.'

'Jealousy, yes. I can imagine.'

Posie was remembering the snaps in the newspapers. Of Anouk Sinne and the Prince of Wales.

That whisper. The hand on the jacket.

'So there's no truth in those rumours? About the, ahem, the Prince?'

Anouk laughed, almost maliciously. 'Gracious, no! He's a client of mine, that's all. I make him a bespoke sandalwood cologne, nothing controversial there: nothing hinting at the raptures of "Sin 1", or anything exotic. All very staid. Besides, I'm almost old enough to be his mother, although apparently that's what he likes. No, he's very wrapped up in his own little mistress, Freda Dudley-Ward. And good luck to them, I say. Although I must admit I received a fair amount of horrible letters from poor, deluded love-struck women when that completely untrue story broke last year.'

Posie raised an eyebrow. 'Could *these,*' and she shook the postcards, 'have come from one of those deluded women, do you think?'

But even as Posie spoke, the unreality of what she was proposing hit her.

No, these were the work of an insider. For sure.

Someone who knew the woman had ready money, and wealth.

Or else, it was someone who held a secret in their armoury. A secret which could bring Anouk Sinne and her perfume house tumbling down. Although, peculiarly, there was no mention of unleashing any sort of secret in the demands.

But everyone has secrets. Some more than others.

'Is there someone else whom you have disagreed with, Miss Sinne? Professionally, I mean? An employee? A client? Someone who is a rival?'

Anouk Sinne looked affronted. 'I run a highly professional – and solitary – business, Miss Parker. I work alone. I have a minimal staff: secretary; butler; jobbing gardener. True, I do have some clients who commission me to create perfumes purely for them, like the Prince, but I enjoy excellent relationships with them all. And as for rivals, pah! Everyone knows I am the best "nose" in this business. All the big houses have nothing on me. But that doesn't mean we fight! Far from it. Some other "noses" are my friends. Each perfumier, like any great artist, is individual, and lauded for that. We do not go around threatening each other. What a thing!'

Posie was noting this all down, slightly incredulous. 'You don't even have a housekeeper?'

Anouk Sinne shook her head once. 'I clean this laboratory myself. I am paranoid about my formulas and inventions being stolen; I cannot risk anyone ever coming in. I have treated you as an exception. I *do* have a team of housemaids who come to clean and tidy the house for special occasions, like today. But generally, I can't stand people intruding. It's irregular, I know, but I'm hardly someone "normal", am I?'

Posie looked up, smiled, saw the slight sparkle in the dreadful eyes.

'What is special about today, Miss Sinne? Dolly – the *Countess*, I mean – told me you had a gathering here.'

Anouk Sinne got down from the bench, and she was scrabbling with yet another golden key. From a drawer she brought out one of the now-familiar turquoise bottles. Stoppered, closed. Sealed with a ribbon and a pearly sort of iridescent wax seal.

'This is for you, Miss Parker. *This* is what is happening today.'

The bottle was banged down unsteadily on the wooden bench right in front of Posie.

Posie saw that gold art-deco letters on the bottle curled into the legend 'THE ULTIMATE SIN'.

'Er, I don't quite see…'

'*This* is my new perfume. This will be revealed today, but privately. At four-fifteen. Only to a select group of people. Tomorrow lunchtime is the very big launch, at the Embassy Club in Mayfair. Most of fashionable London will be there. It's my most important perfume to date.' Anouk Sinne closed her eyes, as if conjuring up the scent from memory, and she stroked the air with silver-tipped fingers.

'And what is this one evocative of?' Posie asked, hoping she sounded genuine, and interested, but feeling slightly ridiculous. 'India? Lust? Outer Space?'

Anouk Sinne looked at Posie very seriously. 'It represents the beginning of everything, and yet the end of everything too. It is an ode to the fall of man. A perfume built around the top note of a fresh apple, plucked from the Garden of Eden, lying on a tea-infused heart note of crushed white tea-roses. And the base note takes this scent to a whole new level. The purity of a summer day, an innocence. All lost! Thrown away!'

Posie looked slightly incredulously at the woman. *The fall of man!*

What a load of nonsense! But the thought sent a shiver right down her spine.

The perfumier turned again to Posie. 'This perfume took me two years to develop. People have had to be patient. But, in fact, it was only very recently, only a couple of weeks ago, that I hit on the perfect formula. Enough has been made only for today and tomorrow's events, and then…'

'And then?'

Anouk Sinne smiled tightly, the silver lipstick cracking at the sides. 'More will be wanted, that much I know. It will be coveted. Legendary.'

Posie started to pull at the ribbon of the bottle, more out of politeness than real curiosity. She didn't really want to smell like a chemically-created apple, after all.

A bad apple: a rotten apple from which all evil had stemmed.

Anouk Sinne gave a trilling laugh: 'Oh, Miss Parker. Do save that bottle for yourself. Put it in your bag. There will be plenty of chances to experience the perfume upstairs.'

Posie felt relieved. 'As you wish. Tell me, do you think there is a link between the "reveal" upstairs today, and this third, brutal demand for money? Or is it just a coincidence?'

But Posie didn't like coincidences. Not one bit. It was something she shared with her husband, Richard. A coincidence jumped out from a case like a pulsating red beacon or a flare for both of them.

It was always a warning of sorts.

Anouk Sinne shrugged: 'Why would the person writing the notes have a clue what is happening here today? Today is a secret. All those invited here have been sworn to secrecy.'

The perfumier walked over to a small table near the fire, took a glass, poured water from a jug there, and drank thirstily, then re-filled and drank again. Then she pulled out what looked like a black canvas weekend bag from over near the velvet curtains. It was embroidered with a white shield, with a big snake on it, its body forming the 'S' of the word 'SINNE'. This must be the crest which also featured on the plaque outside and on the flags. It was tasteless and showy.

The bag looked heavy.

Anouk Sinne was trying to drag the bag across the floor.

Posie reached for the white postcards, left in a neat fan on the table.

'Can I keep these for now?'

'Be my guest.'

Posie put them quickly inside her carpet bag. All the while she had the sense that she was not quite seeing everything. Posie had the sensation – uncomfortably – of sand running through her fingers, a feeling of grasping at facts. And failing.

This busy, famous, mysterious woman was an enigma in herself. But did she realise she was in danger? Was she taking it seriously? Or was it a kind of joke to her?

Did she, despite her protestations, know who the author of these notes was? Her behaviour towards them so far, over the last two weeks, seemed remarkably cavalier. Dismissive.

What was so different now? What had made her call in Posie today, and not earlier?

'What would you like me to *do*, Miss Sinne? I would urge police intervention. I am a Private Detective, for sure, but…' – she checked her wristwatch, which read ten minutes to four – 'I am not a magician. And it seems your persecutor expects their money in less than one hour's time. I cannot hope to find out who this person is in such a short space of time. So if *that* is what you wanted of me, I cannot accept your case.'

'Of course you can.'

The small woman stood upright and wobbled on her heels for just a second. Suddenly, in a flash, she opened the thick black velvet curtains and Posie was blinded by the strong, sudden, and almost unbearable sunlight.

'Heavens! Hey! I say...'

Blinking, shielding her eyes, she saw that the part of the room formerly hidden by the curtains was actually a complete glass side, and the laboratory led right out onto the garden.

And what a garden.

Posie walked to the glass and saw that outside was a riot of colour, as far as the eye could see. The many, many borders were immaculate, full of carefully-planted sections of roses, in every imaginable colour.

And on and on, an immaculate English lawn, leading down to a hedge and London plane trees, and to a pond, nearer in size to a small lake.

It seemed impossible to think that Posie was still in London!

But now she noticed people walking about outside.

And then, *Oh horror! The ultimate disaster!*

There was another woman wearing the exact same pink-and-navy polka-dotted dress as Posie was sporting, paired with exactly the same hat which the salesgirl had convinced Posie to buy!

Distinctive. Bold.

Unfortunate.

Posie gulped. She had no other change of clothes with her. Well, Posie and the woman in the identical dress would simply have to brazen this out, and laugh it off, *if* indeed Posie was expected to stay and mingle.

Anouk Sinne was looking out, clutching her water again, oblivious to Posie's fashion mishap.

'You asked me what I want you to do? I want you simply to stay, Miss Parker. I do not believe that any of the guests here today wish me harm or are in any way connected with these postcards. But better safe than sorry. I want you to use your famous observational skills. Watch and see if any of my guests are behaving oddly, especially at half-past four. And I want you at the Embassy Club tomorrow, at my side. Like a limpet.'

'I'm not a bodyguard, Miss Sinne. I'll come, of course, but I advise you to involve the police. It sounds as if tomorrow's event is going to be big, and it will be difficult to make sure you are safe.'

The perfumier took another sip of her water, shrugged in a resigned fashion. 'As you advise. Perhaps you could telephone to your esteemed husband and ask him to make the necessary arrangements for tomorrow? Although I'm hoping to be safe by then. Because of *this*.'

Anouk Sinne kicked at the black bag by her foot.

'Oh? What's in the bag, Miss Sinne?'

Posie drew closer. The top of the holdall was unzipped and crisp white bundles, each tied together with a loop of bank-fresh elastic, were stacked atop of each other.

'One thousand pounds, Miss Parker. In notes, as requested. I'm going to get my secretary to deliver this to Victoria Station at four-thirty. I've a new perfume to launch, Miss Parker. I've decided to pay up: I simply haven't got time to die.'

* * * *

Four

This altered things.

Of course it did. Posie felt a sense of relief, but also of complete confusion.

By giving in and paying the thugs who had written so menacingly, was Anouk Sinne opening the floodgates to yet more demands? To yet more danger?

Posie needed to speak to Richard. Get help. Advice at least. He was in Court today, at the Old Bailey, but she'd probably be able to get a message through to him.

'Can I use the telephone, Miss Sinne?'

'Of course. It's in the small office next door to this laboratory. It's not locked, or private, unlike in here. Excuse me, but I must go up and start to mingle.'

'Oh, but wait. Tell me, who are these people you have invited today? Are they special friends of yours?'

'Sort of.'

Anouk Sinne pointed at the woman in the identical Selfridges dress, now in clear view: ginger-haired and in her mid-forties, the woman had a good figure, but she was no beauty. Under the hat she was over-rouged and puffy-cheeked, like a marmot, and her head was much too big for her body. She seemed nervy and was pulling at her wedding ring distractedly.

The red-haired woman was standing next to a well-preserved man in his very late fifties, with a leonine mane of thick white-blonde hair. He was very handsome, wearing full black-tie, which looked odd in the bright light of daytime, but he had the air of a preoccupied man, eyes roving the place. The pair were loitering at the edge of a rose border, not talking to each other.

'That's Hubert Pring, Viscount Effington, and his wife, Lady Clare.'

Posie nodded. She had heard of Pring and knew that he was involved in a good deal of governmental work about criminal reforms.

He was not a well-known figure nationally, and it was only through Richard's work that Posie knew of the Viscount. The two men often met on committees, and Richard regarded Hubert Pring as a well-meaning but interfering do-gooder, whose vast, frequent financial contributions to charitable causes, often concerning children and women's rights, made his interference just about bearable.

'Are they friends of yours, Miss Sinne?'

'Oh, much more than that,' said the perfumier airily. 'Well, he is. *She's* a bit of damp dishcloth. But Hubert and I, well: we go back a long way.'

'Is Hubert Pring something to do with perfume, Miss Sinne?'

Posie must have looked confused, for her hostess laughed.

'Not as such. But he's ridiculously rich. Hubert is my sponsor: always has been. Been in this with me from the start. I invite him to all the "reveals" and launches I have ever done: it would be rude not to. He set me up in the beginning, just before the Great War. Funded literally everything. Hubert always believed in me; he still does. It's been a long time since my last scent, but he never complains about anything. For example, Hubert still purchases the ridiculously expensive ingredients I have to order from abroad, like the orange blossom I told you about. But keep this all to yourself, Miss Parker. It is widely assumed *all* of the ingredients for the House of Sinne perfumes are grown here and that they are not imported. Our reputation would suffer if these things got out. I have your word?'

'Of course.'

Anouk waved a hand around the laboratory in a slightly dismissive way.

'Actually, Hubert owns this house and garden, the whole of Number 11, Embankment Gardens. Although I think my name *is* somewhere on the deeds as a kind of "sitting tenant", rather hilariously; it makes me sound like some kind of inconvenient old lodger who refuses to move out, don't you think? Too, too funny. But don't repeat the extent of Hubert's generosity to anyone, please. It would shatter the myth of the House of Sinne. It would be a catastrophe if anyone discovered that behind the mysterious and exclusive female-run fragrance house is this wonderful, benevolent man who is known for his support of charities.'

The word 'charities' was almost spat out in disgust.

Posie stole a quick, furtive glance at the perfumier.

Was the 'wonderful' Hubert Pring *more* than just a 'sponsor'? A love? Or a lover?

But Anouk Sinne had moved on: 'And talking of shattering myths...'

The perfumier pointed one silver-tipped finger in the direction of a big, broad-chested, ruddy-faced, handsome-as-hell, ice-blonde man in his mid-forties, who had joined the Viscount and his wife outside. But now another harsh tremble racked Anouk's body.

What was it?

Nerves? Drink?

Sickness?

Posie tactfully looked away, tried to focus on the man Anouk had meant to speak of.

He was wearing creased beige linen, playing with an old grey hat between his hands, chatting easily with Lady Clare, the 'damp dishcloth'.

'That man is Gordy Lorkinsson. He's quite something, these days. You know him? The famous gardener?'

'Oh, yes.'

Posie knew that Mr Lorkinsson was an Icelander who knew more about English gardens than the English did themselves.

She was aware he wrote several popular features for different newspapers, usually on horticultural topics so dull that Posie had never bothered to read them, not being a gardener herself, but she knew that he worked at the Chelsea Physic Garden as one of the main gardeners and he also ran the very fashionable Chelsea Flower Show, which was held in May every year.

Over the years Lorkinsson had become known for being an expert on roses; namely his own specially-created roses, which he exhibited at the Chelsea Flower Show as a highlight.

Posie said quietly, 'I suppose he works for you, does he? Here, in your perfume garden?'

This famously secret and secretive garden. Closed to all the world.

Anouk stiffened slightly. 'Well, we do have an arrangement. I'm a "nose", you understand? I know what smells right. I know about which plants go together, both in the soil and in the test tube, and eventually, what works best on your wrist. But I am *not* a cultivator of specific flowers, and Gordy is. His love is roses. Tea-roses. Once, it was me.'

The woman seemed to quiver slightly at this memory but recovered herself quickly.

'He uses my garden for free. He has done for years. As long as he lets me take enough of the roses for my perfumes, he can create whatever he likes, and can exhibit the plants, but only if he doesn't blab about the exact *location* of his plants. The arrangement has come, over time, to suit us both. He's here every day, of course. Early, usually, before he pops down the road to the Chelsea Physic Garden to do his main job; his paid job. He gets no payment at all from the House of Sinne.'

Anouk Sinne rested her forehead against the glass of the French doors, as if for relief. She carried on as if she had forgotten Posie was there.

'He told me once that as a child, growing up in an apartment block near Reykjavik, he dreamt only of growing flowers, of watching beauty push itself out from the frozen, useless, volcanic soil. He had read about roses in books. In the Bible, to begin with. But the Icelandic earth was snow-covered for most of the year. And when things *were* grown, it was vegetables, to eat. There was no space for beauty. At school, like so many other sea-faring nations, he was taught crafts for ship-building, involving metal, rope, wood: hard materials; nothing which was *alive*. He vowed to leave that country as soon as he could and move away to somewhere he could grow roses, purely for their own sake.'

'What a fascinating man,' murmured Posie, anxious to sound appreciative. She looked at the Icelander, whose face had creased in sudden smiles as an old man in loose grey flannels joined the group.

'And the old man?'

'He's my regular gardener, Tom. He'll disappear any minute now. He's in every day until four o'clock. Tidying, gathering what I need, following instructions.'

But whose instructions did Tom follow? Posie wondered. *Anouk's? The 'queen' of the House of Sinne?*

But a queen who, it turned out, did not actually own the house and garden she was known for.

And the flower garden which the perfumier was famous for was also a lie. The glories which people could only guess at were actually all down to the hard work of a paid old man, and to the accomplishments of another professional celebrity, Lorkinsson. A man who had created an 'empire' here, in a borrowed garden.

An Emperor, of sorts.

Golly, this arrangement already seemed complicated, Posie thought anxiously. And that was before the blackmail threats were taken into account.

'Does Mr Lorkinsson always attend your "reveals"?' Posie asked. 'Will he be at the big luncheon tomorrow?'

Anouk Sinne shook her head briskly. 'He won't attend tomorrow. But this latest perfume does use one of his new roses as its heart note, and so I have an obligation to ask him along today. Don't you think?'

Crushed white tea-roses.

'Mmmm.'

Posie was thinking that such a good-looking, romantic-seeming man must have many lovers, many friends, and acquaintances. Could *he* be the link which had ended with a demand for Anouk Sinne to pay one thousand pounds?

Was it not possible this big strapping man had let slip that the House of Sinne had rented out its grounds like common allotments?

But Anouk Sinne was pointing again, jabbing almost. 'And you know the Countess of Cardigeon, of course.' Anouk's voice was curiously flat and emotionless, and she motioned towards Dolly in her unflattering buttermilk-yellow ensemble.

Dolly was cloistered together with the old-fashioned woman in pearls and the dark-haired young man whom Posie had glimpsed in the conservatory earlier.

Dolly was obviously enjoying herself, despite her previous misgivings, and Posie was glad of it. She watched as her best friend cackled with laughter, looping arms with the middle-aged, buxom woman at her side, whose face was soft-looking, like a sweet pie, under her big bouffant hairstyle. The woman was laughing along with Dolly and she looked hearty and kind. And fun.

Both the woman and Dolly were holding champagne glasses, but, in addition, Dolly was holding a bottle of champagne in one hand. It looked empty, and it struck an odd, ugly note.

Dolly was tiny, like a small china doll, and alcohol went straight to her head. Posie was gripped by a sudden fear: she desperately hoped that Dolly hadn't drunk the whole bottle alone, at breakneck speed. Posie needed Dolly to be sober today.

Being drunk wouldn't help at all.

'Who are that couple?' Posie asked rather tightly, trying to keep the worry from her voice.

'They're French. Aristocrats. Old friends of mine. Mother and son.'

'Ah.'

So *this* was the reason Dolly looked so relaxed and happy.

Dolly's mother had been French, and she had raised Dolly to speak her mother tongue, despite Dolly being brought up in the East End of London. It was a language Dolly still adored. She chattered away in it to her own small twin girls, and to Raymond, the tiny Cardigeon heir, despite her husband's many objections. Dolly would speak French to whomever would chat back, and it seemed that with this big elegant bosomy woman, she had found a sparring partner.

'*She* is Duchesse Maria de Poilac,' explained Anouk crisply. 'She has a great town house in Versailles, very grand. She's a widow. Very busy. A clever woman.'

Posie wondered at the exact role of the French woman. Was she yet another sponsor?

But quite suddenly the dark-haired young man in Dolly's group turned around, and Posie almost gasped aloud. For here was a rare beauty indeed.

This man was young, twenty at most. Younger, perhaps. He was not at all obviously the son of Dolly's new pal.

Lucky genes had created something altogether more captivating in this boy: a finely-boned face with dark, high-arched eyebrows, framing large green-grey eyes, caught between colours, and deep as a foreign sea.

Posie realised that Anouk was following her gaze, almost laughing.

'That is Maria's son, the Count. Anatole de Poilac. My Godson. A charming boy, isn't he? Not at all like Maria to look at. She became a mother very late in life, and he was rather a surprise. A real gift. She adores him. He's lovely, if a little given to attaching himself to wild, dangerous causes.'

Anouk cocked her head to one side and spoke very softly.

'I think of him as the son I never had. Although he's never yet attended a "reveal" of mine. This is a first.'

The perfumier shrugged slightly. 'It seems he came to London for a different reason, but of course it's nice he could join us today. By contrast, his mother Maria *always* comes to these events. She's very loyal.'

'I see.'

Posie glanced all around the garden, saw the shaky-handed young butler, Jenks, bobbing about with a tray loaded with fresh drinks. It was painful to watch, lest he dropped everything.

Posie realised that Jenks must be one of the thousands of poor lads who had returned from the Great War with terrible damage to their nerves: 'shellshock', they called it.

And, like so many others, he was getting on with his life and incorporating these shakes alongside his daily tasks. Posie watched as Lucy Reeble, the secretary, spoke with the butler, checking her wristwatch anxiously, biting her lip, eyes darting towards the house.

As if the nerves were catching, Anouk Sinne checked her own tiny watch on the expandable golden bracelet and snapped its lid closed quickly.

'I must go out now, Miss Parker. It's past four o'clock.'

'Of course, Miss Sinne. Do you still intend to send Lucy to deposit the monies at Victoria Station? Is that wise? The note said *you* should come alone.'

'I'm sure if Lucy deposits the cash and walks away quickly, the writer of those postcards will be just as happy as if I had come in person. Don't you think?'

'I wouldn't be so sure,' Posie warned.

Anouk Sinne looked immediately sulky. 'If you're trying to get me to agree to a police guard for her, I am afraid you will fail. It will only scupper things, Miss Parker. *That* was definitely prohibited.'

It didn't seem fair at all on the secretary.

Posie would have to organise some protection, but surreptitiously.

Posie pressed on: 'Does Lucy know your intentions for her, in half an hour? Only, she looks nervous. Is it safe to trust her with all that money?'

Anouk's lack of concern for her secretary's wellbeing seemed odd to Posie, but then, Anouk Sinne *was* odd, wasn't she?

Anouk tutted. 'I haven't told Lucy where I'm sending her yet, no. But Lucy's a very capable girl. That's why I employ her. She'll just need to drop the money and return here. I'll send her in a motor-taxi, there and back. I suppose Lucy's nerves are caused by a missing guest who has probably not yet arrived; supposedly the most important guest of the whole event. Something a little "different".'

Posie was about to ask who this person might be, when she saw a man in his late fifties stepping down into the garden from steps somewhere further up on the left-hand side.

The man was immediately eye-catching, wearing a cream Panama hat and a pale pearl-grey double-breasted suit with a lurid, orange-sherbet-coloured tie. He was gloriously tanned. His suntan spoke of golf clubs and of sailing on blue sparkling seas and of expensive islands in the sun.

His utter self-possession declared that he was an American, the wealthiest and most handsome sort imaginable.

He smiled all about him, but Posie couldn't help but feel it was a calculating smile, full of too many white teeth: the smile of a man in possession of knowledge, of something slightly dangerous. His eyes under the hat were curiously dark, and he reminded Posie suddenly, and rather unfairly, of a shark.

'Is *he* your important guest, Miss Sinne?' Posie asked, her pencilled eyebrow raised.

A flicker of something strange seemed to flit across the woman's face and the eerie awful black eyes looked suddenly fearful. Was it Posie's imagination or did Anouk steal a split-second glance over at her sponsor, the Viscount, Hubert Pring? For protection, perhaps?

'No, he's not important. That's just Archie Van Dusen. From New York.' Then in a lower tone, harshly: 'But he *wasn't* supposed to be outside. Not at all.'

Expecting more of an explanation, Posie watched as Anouk picked up the poker from next to the fire, and stabbed viciously, angrily, at the dying flames.

Posie noted how white and fine the ash of the fire was, and how it looked as if paper had been burning there. Tremors from Anouk Sinne's hand were making the poker move wildly. The perfumier was certainly angry, and that anger had something to do with the American, Posie felt sure.

Feeling she had been effectively dismissed, Posie snapped her notebook shut. She pointed quickly towards the sealed door. 'I'll go and telephone, and then join your party in a few minutes?'

'Of course.' Anouk Sinne had put down the poker and was rubbing her slightly ashy hands together, sniffing at them like some kind of bloodhound on the scent of a trail.

Casting one quick glance back at the large black holdall in which all the money was held, she led Posie to the sealed door.

But seconds before she started to draw the bolts back, Anouk Sinne paused and grimaced. Posie couldn't help but notice that the woman was fingering the opaque tissue-like folds of her silver bolero, a bit like little Phyllis Lovelace did at bedtime with her favourite blankie, as if for comfort.

Posie tried her best to sound helpful. 'Is there something else, Miss Sinne? Something *beyond* these postcards, I mean? Other than the one thousand pounds? Are you, perhaps…?'

How best to word this, other than just speaking aloud the truth?

She blundered on. 'Are you afraid of something else, Miss Sinne? Something which seems strange, or unusual to you?'

There was an uncomfortable silence. The shivers had set in again for real and Anouk Sinne clamped her teeth together in a determination not to let them show.

'You're astute, Miss Parker, I'll give you that.' The woman sighed heavily. 'Lately, for the last couple of weeks, I've had this dreadful dream. Every night, I dream I come across a woman. Dead, murdered. And…'

'And?'

The strange black eyes grew even wider, agitated and angry. 'It's *me*, Miss Parker. I discover myself, my murdered self. My younger self. Here in my garden, half-hidden in the undergrowth and the seeping water from the lily pond. Night after night. And I wake in terror. I can't shake off the feeling of fear for hours.'

Posie patted the woman's arm. She wanted to be reassuring, not condescending. But it was a fine line to tread.

'Are you taking any new medicines, or tonics, to help

you sleep, Miss Sinne? Which might give you such horrible nightmares? Forgive me for saying so, but you don't seem quite the ticket today. Are you well enough for the event upstairs?'

The woman's face was, for a second, riven with fury. She looked as if she regretted having taken Posie into her confidence.

'I'm quite fine, thank you very much. Just a migraine, which I have a tendency towards. And in answer to your first question: no, *I* never take anything, Miss Parker. No drugs, no sleeping tablets. It might interfere with my sense of smell. That's always been my biggest dread. Now, you'd better get your violet-scented self away to the telephone, hadn't you? Then meet us upstairs. And go quickly, for heaven's sake.'

* * * *

Five

Stepping out into the Chelsea garden from the office some ten minutes later, Posie found she was quite alone.

Alone except for a peacock.

She found herself staring at it, and it met her gaze with its beady black eyes. It swept its magnificent blue and golden tail-feathers in a majestic arc and stalked away from her, the sunlight catching and playing on its sapphire and turquoise neck.

It glittered like a thousand jewels, more alive and beautiful than any of the gaily dressed guests in the garden had appeared to be.

'Beautiful creature. A *sad* creature somehow,' Posie muttered to herself. 'But what a lovely place to live!'

Posie breathed in the smell of freshly-cut grass, but there was something else overlaying it all, something fetid and altogether more 'London'.

It was the scent of the river, salty and briny as the sea, washed on ancient tides of history; the life-blood of London, whose glittering beauty was beguiling and ever-changing.

The conversation with Scotland Yard had taken longer than Posie had hoped.

Richard was still busy at Court, and even getting hold

of Sergeant Fox, Richard's favourite policeman of the moment, had proved tricky.

Eventually Fox had been located, and, in addition to agreeing to organise several men for surveillance at the Embassy Club luncheon the next day, Fox had promised he would nip along to Victoria Station right away, and loiter surreptitiously near to locker 56 at four-thirty, for the drop-off.

'It's lucky Victoria Station is around the corner from Scotland Yard, Miss, eh? You're not giving me much warning, are you?'

'Well, I admit it's hardly ideal. Just make sure you look authentic, Sergeant. Like you're waiting for someone. Miss Sinne wants to play according to the blackmailer's rules. She has no idea I'm asking for police involvement today. So there's to be nothing "police" about you, you understand?'

'Got it, Miss. I'll leave my truncheon and handcuffs here, shall I?'

'Very funny.'

'But seriously, Miss, what do you want me to *do*? What do I do when the low-life blighter shows up to collect the money? I've done courses on surveillance like this, you know. Very interesting, all the new techniques. Very smart stuff they have now. Gadgets. But you want him arrested?' Fox had sounded hopeful. 'Or just tailed?'

Posie hadn't actually thought that far ahead. She'd been anxious only to protect the secretary, Lucy.

'I reckon you should certainly tail the fella,' she had said decisively. 'But not if it's a gang. You might get into difficulties. Anouk Sinne is happy to pay the money, after all. It's *her* decision to play ball with the blackmailer.'

'I think she's a fool for not involving us, Miss Parker. We would have made short work of this blackmailer. Your husband is the best in the business. This would have been a routine "sting" operation for him, Miss. The more I think about it, I don't like the sound of today one bit. Such a high-profile woman, too.'

Fox had been beginning to sound as if he might have retracted his initial offer to loiter by the lockers. So Posie had charged on.

'I don't like the sound of it either, Sergeant Fox. Which is why we are doing *something*, which is better than nothing. I'm at the House of Sinne, and I feel relatively confident that Miss Sinne is safe. Watch the secretary. She's wearing bright white. Hardly inconspicuous.'

And Fox had promised he would do as Posie requested.

But now, here she was, running late.

So late that the guests had stepped inside already.

Had the 'reveal' of the new perfume happened yet? Posie felt a surprising lurch of disappointment at the thought of having missed it.

Somewhere within the house a clock was striking quarter past the hour.

Turning, running up the big, grand garden steps which she had seen Mr Van Dusen strut down, Posie entered the bright white conservatory. Like the entrance hall, this had no chairs or plants or decoration in it at all. Obviously, comfort wasn't a priority in the House of Sinne. Only the lingering carbon scent remained. There were two white doors at either end.

Standing very still, trying to get her bearings, Posie heard the sound of high, tinkly laughter, unfamiliar to her. Then came Anouk Sinne's clipped, nasal voice.

Posie followed the voice and headed to the white door on her right, which must lead to the drawing-room. She turned the polished bronze doorknob quickly, pulling the door back with more force than she had intended to.

It was hardly a low-key entrance.

Everyone inside the drawing-room turned to stare.

Posie gulped. 'Golly! I'm frightfully sorry to be so late!'

A huge, dark wooden oval table was the only furniture in the drawing-room, and all around it, tightly packed in, were seated the same people Posie had seen in the garden.

A huge electric chandelier blazed overhead with a gazillion crystals twinkling icily. The light was needed, as all the long, white-painted shutters were drawn on the summer's day outside.

For a split-second, as if preserved in a moment of time, Posie saw the horrified face of Lady Clare Pring, caught out in her identical polka-dot pink gown and neat wisp of a hat. Anger flared in the woman's rather lovely grey eyes at unwittingly finding herself wearing matching clothes to another – as yet unannounced – woman.

But there was no announcement, no introduction made. Instead, Anouk Sinne, like a squat buddha holding court at the table's furthest end, motioned silently for Posie to take the seat nearest the door she had entered by.

Posie sat down unobtrusively.

She saw how Sam Stubbs was excitedly jumping about the room with his huge black camera. He seemed to be focusing on Anouk Sinne, getting through flash-bulbs like they were going out of fashion.

Anouk had obviously been partway through a speech and she picked up the thread again as if she had not been interrupted:

'As I was saying, today it is my pleasure to hand over the "reveal" of my latest perfume. This is *not* simply a numbered perfume. This one carries a name. It is entitled "The Ultimate Sin".'

But Anouk Sinne looked ill at ease at the head of the table; she was stumbling over her words and trembling violently. *The migraine?*

Why was she handing over the 'reveal'? And to whom?

The perfumier was rubbing at her chest anxiously now, her small podgy hands making fluttering, useless movements, as if she had indigestion, or heartburn. Anouk Sinne took a sip of water from a blue glass in front of her.

Posie looked carefully about.

On Anouk Sinne's left-hand side sat Hubert Pring, his

eyebrows knitted together in concentration, and next to him sat his wife, her big face burning a hot pink to match the unfortunate hot pink outfit.

Next to Lady Clare was the young French Count, his fingers drumming on the table, obviously desperate for a cigarette; the chandelier's light reflecting off a golden signet ring worn on his little finger.

Then on from him sat his impressive mother, calm, beguiling, solid. Posie saw that the beige cameo brooch she wore on her blouse was large, antique: a carving of a peacock with its tail feathers outstretched. It looked an expensive bauble, a match for the black Edwardian pearls. But oddly, nestled behind all the heavy necklaces, was a velvet choker, on which a cheap-looking golden locket hung.

Was that really a half-heart Posie saw there? Complete with jagged, broken edges?

The kind of thing very young lovers, or schoolgirls, would give each other as a keepsake. It was at odds with the woman herself.

On Anouk's right-hand side, virtually hidden from view, sat a dark-haired woman Posie had not seen out in the garden, and next to the dark-haired woman was Mr Van Dusen, his elbows rather proprietorially resting on the table. On from him was Gordy Lorkinsson, his whole bearing one of relaxed disinterest, and then came Dolly, and then, sandwiched in tight, was the secretary, Lucy.

And when she looked carefully, Posie realised it was actually the hidden, dark-haired woman who was the focus of all of Sam Stubbs' attentions.

She was the cause of the flash-bulbs, Posie was sure of it. Not Anouk Sinne at all.

So who on earth was she?

Posie craned her neck to get more of a look, but as so many others at the table were doing the same thing, it was difficult. It was also hard to see past Van Dusen's tense, almost rigidly-held body.

But suddenly he moved.

And then there was a glimpse of unfashionably-long black hair, all swept up into a gloriously thick, high chignon. There was a flutter of a diamond-laden hand. That unfamiliar high-pitched tinkly laugh Posie had heard a few moments before, echoing down the corridors of this strange house, now issued again from this woman, who suddenly turned her beautiful, captivating head.

'Oh!' Posie almost bit at her lip to hide her own surprise. 'Goodness me!'

Here was the important guest; the reason Lucy Reeble had been so nervous out in the garden.

A famous woman whose safe and timely arrival at the House of Sinne must have been the secretary's responsibility; a task which Posie didn't envy one bit.

Anouk Sinne coughed and continued.

'And so I give you…Her Royal Highness, Princess Priyanka of Gwilim, India. She will "carry" our new perfume for us and take it to a whole new dimension.'

Princess Priyanka!

Posie watched in wonder as this film-star-in-the-making beamed a dazzling smile to all at the table.

The Princess held up a turquoise glass bottle of the new fragrance, its gold lettering catching the light of the chandelier, and the light of Sam's flash-bulbs. She posed with it: smiling; pouting; looking sultry.

Snap. Snap.

Flash-flash.

What on earth was Anouk Sinne playing at here with this handover?

Was that why the Princess had come to England – for this? Perhaps on her way to America?

And was this Princess really a good match for a perfume with a frankly slightly suggestive and dubious name? What a strange thing for the Princess to have agreed to do!

There was nothing sinful, or 'fallen' or darkly mysterious

about Princess Priyanka, was there? Of course, she did have a tragic back-story, but it wasn't an unsavoury one.

This whole 'arrangement' seemed odd.

But Posie's questions died away as she watched the girl in action, entranced. *Could such beauty really exist?*

It seemed so. No wonder she might become a film star.

The Princess had huge amber eyes, beautiful anyway, but today set off with a gleaming emerald-coloured eyeshadow. She wore a very modern and fashionable linen safari-style jacket in pure white with gold military-style buttons. The girl had dimples and looked like she might be the sort of person who laughed easily, despite what life had doled out.

She was older though than Posie had first thought, nearer thirty-five than twenty-five. Around her neck looked to be the treasure-trove of her entire lost family back in Gwilim: ropes and ropes of golden chains, and strings of huge, oyster-coloured lustrous pearls. A safe's worth of bullion, generations worth of Maharajah's treasure, right there around one slender neck.

An insurer's nightmare.

'Can you move to the right, your Highness? Brilliant! A bit more… Raise the bottle! Atta-girl!' Sam Stubbs was almost dancing. He was in his element. As he should be.

Talk about a scoop for him and his paper!

No doubt he would have exclusive rights and had been sworn to absolute secrecy. Although his presence seemed odd: why not take photographs at the big public launch tomorrow, instead?

Posie watched as the Princess obligingly posed with the perfume, holding the bottle first this way, then the next.

It was peculiar, because the Princess had not spoken once since Posie had entered the room, and yet she had the attention of absolutely everybody.

No, that was not quite true.

As Posie studied the guests at the oval table, she noticed that only the young Count and the Icelander were *not* staring at the Indian Princess. Both were instead avidly watching Anouk Sinne, who had drained yet another glass of water and was speaking again now.

'You will all experience the fragrance in a minute. And, to prepare you, I will attempt to describe it.'

Posie's thoughts tailed off. She didn't listen to what she had already heard described down in the laboratory. *That old nonsense about the apple again.*

Innocence, lost.

A load of flim-flam.

She focused instead on the young French Count, his gaze never leaving Anouk's face for a second. The son she never had, apparently. Posie was struck by the young man's face, which was restless and nervy, never still. A young man hungry for adventure, for *thrills*. Perhaps a danger-seeker?

Posie turned and saw how Gordy Lorkinsson's luminous blue gaze rested intently on the perfumier, too; how he took in her trembling. Posie saw a line of worry etch itself deeply in his forehead, and his huge capable hands were interlaced beneath the table-top, tense and restless.

Posie watched Hubert Pring, too. And that was fascinating.

She took in his confused expression and twitchy, unhappy mouth: his dark-blue eyes which moved from the Princess back to Anouk, and then back again in disbelief, eventually focusing grimly on the bottle of perfume itself. As if that one glass-stoppered chemical compound held all the answers he so obviously sought.

Because this was a new experience for him, Posie suddenly realised. A shock.

He hadn't known about the Princess.

In all the time that Hubert Pring, Viscount Effington, had been her sponsor at the House of Sinne, Anouk Sinne had never pulled a stunt like this. Posie felt certain of it.

So why was the perfumier breaking with the norm and involving the Princess at all?

But now Anouk Sinne was urging the Princess to open the bottle, and everyone waited with bated breath, Hubert Pring most of all.

You could have cut the atmosphere with a knife.

Priyanka Lashari's voice, when she spoke, was as exotic as the woman herself; beautiful, languid, her English picked out with what sounded like a French accent. But how could it be?

'It is my absolute pleasure today to give you…"The Ultimate Sin".'

There was a sound like a plug being pulled.

And they waited.

But nothing happened. There was no smell in the room at all, beyond the very slightly acrid tang of the chalky flash-lights.

Priyanka shook the bottle quickly. She splashed the liquid rather impatiently on her neck, her wrists, her bejewelled hands.

Still nothing.

And then the air sang and roared as the perfume released its magic spell.

****

Six

The scent reached the noses of everyone at slightly different times, affecting people differently.

It came in waves across the table, and for some reason Posie watched the expectant faces of the French guests first, even though they weren't nearest.

They sat as if frozen in anticipation, then they started smiling, silent throughout. As if they were in church.

But their new friend, Dolly, sitting on the other side of the table to them, was eloquent enough for everyone, which Posie found surprising, given her earlier reservations about her hostess.

'Coo-ee! It's blimmin' wonderful. Jeepers! I ain't ever smelt nuffink as good before. Lawks, I want to eat it. It's scrumptious!'

Hubert Pring had been sitting stock-still in his chair, but now he looked relieved. His investment over the last two years had obviously paid off. He banged on the table in excitement, his voice booming:

'Absolutely! I say, bally well done, Anouk old girl. A masterpiece! It's *really* a masterpiece.'

His wife, Lady Clare, inclined her head very slightly. Posie had the sudden feeling that she was there on sufferance. That these occasions were hardly enjoyable for her.

But now the scent was reaching Posie herself. She'd been determined to stay focused on the people in the room, rather than get involved in anything to do with the perfume itself, which, to be honest, she found all rather silly, but she couldn't ignore it.

The scent was all-encompassing.

Less like an apple, more like a pear. A freshness enfolding her like a just-bitten fruit on a summer's day.

But then came another hit, more powerful this time, and this was something completely different. Powdery, old-fashioned, creamy. Like the scent of a floral wedding bouquet.

Just then, at her side, Posie sensed the secretary checking her watch, and then standing, retreating unobtrusively from the room. Posie automatically glanced at her own watch, which read four-twenty-five, noting that Jenks was hovering in the hallway; his toothy mouth open in a gawping fashion. He was holding a large black bag in his arms, which looked like a heavy, dead child.

The money.

The door clicked closed. So Lucy Reeble had received her instructions, was on her way around the corner now to Victoria Station to drop off the money, as requested by the blackmailer.

But not *quite* as requested, for Anouk Sinne was still here, carrying on as normal, or what passed for normal in this strange place.

The whole thing with the money was odd, Posie thought.

If she hadn't actually seen the crisp wads of money earlier, she might think some strange charade, some sleight of hand, was occurring.

Perhaps Sergeant Fox would be able to shed a little light on *who* actually came for the bounty. Maybe he would be able to do even better than that?

And as Posie turned to watch Sam Stubbs at work, urging Anouk Sinne to stand together with the Princess and the bottle of perfume, the heavy mist of the stuff unleashed by the Indian Princess seemed to throb along the table and turn into something else. Something darker, almost deadly in its intensity.

'Oh!'

Posie had to stop herself from crying out loud. She'd been unprepared for it.

What came now, as a base note, was a sour, sharp scent, almost like decay.

A rottenness.

'Goodness!'

It really was an innocence lost, a lasting bitterness.

Not to be forgotten.

Posie glanced over at the French Count and his mother, and saw they looked uneasy.

Posie noted how the Princess was posing expertly, curling in towards the smaller, diminutive figure of Anouk Sinne, who stared fixedly ahead, her eyes still monstrously black.

'And now for the money shot!' yelled Sam Stubbs, and they were suddenly joined by the American, Mr Van Dusen, who looked around himself triumphantly, as if Princess Priyanka was an illusion all of his own conjuring.

Hubert Pring was standing up now, confusion mottling his fair face, watching the group being photographed. He was joined by his wife, who had started to whisper urgently in his ear.

But then Posie's attention was taken up with the huge, calm figure of the very blonde gardener, Lorkinsson, who had been completely silent throughout, but who now stood, chair thrown back, anger on his face.

He almost stumbled as he turned in a furious arc, pushing past Posie's chair.

She heard him muttering: 'For the love of God! It's a disgrace! She can't have used *that*! It's the devil's work!'

Lorkinsson ran to the back of the drawing-room and

Posie saw that this room, too, had its own French doors out onto the huge garden. He ran out, leaving the door swinging on its hinges, bright daylight flooding in.

Anouk Sinne acted fast.

'Oh! Enough photographs! I, too, must have some fresh air.'

Anouk Sinne broke away from the group, but not before grabbing at the perfume bottle which the Princess had been clutching, and Anouk's strangely dilated eyes were fixed on the space left by Lorkinsson.

But Hubert Pring was blocking Anouk's way out, rigid with some emotion.

Was it anger?

'Anouk, I'm not quite sure I understand. We need to talk. *Now*. What the blazes is happening?'

'I must get out.'

Anouk was a woman in flight. She rubbed at her chest in agitation. The turquoise glass bottle glittered in her hands. 'I must get into the garden, Hubert. It's that, or bed, I'm afraid. I have a migraine. I need to *breathe*. I can't breathe at all. All the excitement of the perfume, you know. You *did* like the perfume, didn't you? Let's chat in just a minute.'

But she didn't wait for an answer, turning and fleeing out of the French doors.

Posie looked about her once more – at the people standing about awkwardly in groups around the table and Sam Stubbs who was packing away – and she breathed in that strange, almost rancid base note one last time.

She decided to find Lorkinsson.

It seemed important.

He'd be out there, she knew. In his natural habitat. That fabulous, fabulous garden, which wasn't quite his garden.

And not quite Anouk Sinne's garden, either.

Out now in a tearing hurry, Posie ran down the steps to the garden. There was a sudden bright flutter of turquoise right at the end of the lawn. The peacock again.

But nearer, and more usefully, in among the roses, she saw Gordy Lorkinsson, silhouetted next to a bank of purest white blooms.

He'd thrown off his blazer and he now wore a low-slung kind of leather gardener's tool belt, with several pouches on it to hold different instruments. Posie saw him set his old grey hat upon his blonde head, protecting himself from the still-burning sun, tightening the string under his jaw in a gesture which was completely unselfconscious.

The huge man was kneeling, using a small metal atomiser, and he was spraying the blooms in front of him delicately.

Posie saw that he held tiny shears, and his actions were tender for such a big man. It felt almost rude to disturb him.

'I say! Hullo! Mr Lorkinsson?'

Gordy Lorkinsson looked up from beneath his hat, shielding his eyes from the glare. He stood and looked down at Posie from his great height as she approached.

He regarded her intently, letting his gaze wander over the pink dress, and lingering for a moment on her left hand, where she wore her wedding and engagement rings.

He smiled, but only slightly. It was lovely anyway, that half-smile, the hint of sadness there. It made his weathered face bright, and very handsome.

'Why, hello to you too. You're Miss Parker, aren't you? Posie Parker, the famous detective?'

Posie almost blushed at the description. 'You've certainly got my name right. And I wonder how, as Miss Sinne didn't announce me to the room, did she?'

'I recognise you from the newspapers. Realised who you were when you entered the room back there.'

His voice was almost entirely accent-less, but after a few sentences one started to catch, just underneath his clear, faultless clipped English, the slight guttural burr of his northern, snowy, frozen homeland.

Lorkinsson smiled. 'I'm not sure I should mention this, but, well, time *has* passed…'

'Go on, please.'

'I knew your fiancé, your fiancé *as was*, I mean. I knew him from the National Geographic Society. Alaric Boynton-Dale.'

'Ah.'

That made a sort of sense.

Although Alaric – Posie's former fiancé until his tragic and untimely death a couple of years earlier – had been a world-class explorer, he had also been fascinated by all manner of natural phenomena. It rang true that the glamorous and usually sunburned Alaric had known and perhaps been friends with the man standing in front of her right now. The two men were similar sorts: a natural fit. And the National Geographic Society would have been an appropriate homing-ground for both of them.

For a fleeting and horrible moment Posie felt wobbly, like her world was tilting on its axis, and the memory of Alaric, never far below the surface, and often rather forcibly pushed there, felt very close.

The Icelander studied his roses with exaggerated concentration. He spoke at them, rather than at her:

'Alaric told me you were beautiful. But he didn't tell me you lit up a room when you entered it; that you eclipsed the supposedly most beautiful woman of the age, that flashy Princess! Alaric was very lucky, that's all I'll say.'

Posie was thrown, disorientated by the flattery and by the association from the past, but then she made herself remember Richard, and the home they had created together as the Lovelace family, and the children they shared. These things were tangible and real, not fleeting memories.

She was steely in her reply. 'How interesting, Mr Lorkinsson. But you are right. Time *has* passed.'

She held her left hand up, rather combatively, actually, for her. 'I'm married now. I have young children.' She said the words as if they were armour, and she were plating herself up against attack of some kind.

'Congratulations.'

The man didn't turn from his white roses, whose scent was almost overpowering. A small handwritten sign was pinned to a stake. It read: 'ULTIMATE SIN'.

Posie forced herself to remember Anouk Sinne's direct instructions about studying the guests: *Watch and see if any of them are behaving oddly.*

Well, it could be argued everyone here was behaving oddly.

But this man, Lorkinsson, had effectively stormed out of the 'reveal' at almost exactly half-past four, muttering curses, and he still looked like he was out of sorts.

Posie knew she needed to be charming now, full of flattery, perhaps. She focused on the roses.

'These white ones are beauties,' she said, burying her face in the blooms.

She moved right up close to Gordy Lorkinsson and dropped her voice to almost a whisper. 'And the credit is all yours, I believe? Miss Sinne told me, in confidence, about the "arrangement" in place.'

Lorkinsson raised an eyebrow. 'I'm surprised she admitted that.'

'You're obviously very good at what you do.'

'Thank you. Tea-roses are my speciality; creating new roses unlike anything which has come before. I grafted everything you can see here myself, and many of these flowers are brand new scions. This one included.'

'The "Ultimate Sin"? This was the one used in the new perfume, wasn't it?'

Chatter and laughter suddenly broke through the afternoon slumber of the garden, and the French Duchesse and Dolly came down the garden steps, full champagne flutes held aloft. The young Count followed, looking bored, checking a handsome wristwatch pointedly. Dolly was giggling hysterically, and behind them came Hubert Pring with his wife, both silent.

There was no sign of the Princess, or of Mr Van Dusen.

Posie turned her back on the giggles, tried to block the sound out. Lorkinsson was silent, but she saw how a nerve in his face twitched constantly. He was not a happy man, and Posie felt it had something to do with this special white rose.

'Could I have one, for my buttonhole?' Posie asked casually. She watched the man shrug, then reach into the masses. He cut a beautiful flower and then snipped at it with his tiny shears, making it into a corsage.

'It must be so rewarding,' Posie continued blithely, 'growing something which will become immortal. Part of a perfume. Wasn't it Shakespeare who said something similar?'

Lorkinsson passed the corsage to Posie.

'That's right. You English have an obsession with roses, and rightly so. Shakespeare mentions roses all over the place. I think you mean his quote from *A Midsummer Night's Dream*, Miss Parker, when he said: "*earthlier happy is the rose distilled than that which withering on the virgin thorn dies.*" Of course, he meant other things with that, but the description of the rose being used for perfume rings true.'

Posie didn't reply, let a small silence stretch out between them, not uncomfortably.

Posie felt – as often happened with perfect strangers – that this man was on the verge of telling her something else which was important and he couldn't be rushed.

And she was right. After a moment Lorkinsson spoke.

'It *is* professionally rewarding, working here. But it's been tiresome, too: I've grown so many hybrid tea-roses over the last two years on Anouk's orders, all as possible scents for her next perfume, but it never seemed that anything was quite right. She wanted something strong, yet fresh. And then I created *this*. Finally, she was ecstatic, and so was I.'

A beat of silence.

'You're not ecstatic anymore though, are you, Mr Lorkinsson?'

He didn't reply. Instead, he moved on down to another area of roses, further away from the house, where pink-and-orange blooms reigned. These were marked 'TALISMAN'. He started snipping, rather ferociously, Posie felt.

'As I said, it was a lot of work, getting the exact sort of fragrance Anouk wanted. I thought the rose was going to be used alone. Not violated. Not used as a heart note, to give way to a base which was so foul.'

Posie remembered Lorkinsson's words as he had fled the room a few minutes before, but she tried to sound casual: 'I heard you, Mr Lorkinsson. In the drawing-room. You said it was "*devil's work*." What did you mean? That strange bitter scent which made everyone so uncomfortable?'

'Absolutely.'

'Well, what was it?'

'The scent of death.'

'Oh, come! Isn't that a bit dramatic?' Posie tried to laugh, but she found the laugh had died on her lips. 'Tell me what it was.'

'It's not my place to. But it wasn't Anouk's place to use it. Never. Only a fool would try. All I will say is that it's a dangerous game she's playing. She got it right though, didn't she? A scent which was supposed to smell like the fall from grace, or being thrown out of Eden? Pah! Well, it was exactly that.'

Posie's thoughts were racing. Was this upset of Lorkinsson's nothing more than some horticultural tiff? And, if so, it was of no importance to her at all. A complete dead end.

She changed tack, remembering Anouk's assertion that she and Lorkinsson had once been more than just colleagues.

'Do you know Miss Sinne well, sir?'

The big man shook his head. 'No. She is many things to many people.'

His blue eyes clouded over. 'There was a time when I knew her a little, but it was a big folly, part of our youth. Hard times in which she seemed to sparkle for me, briefly.'

'I see.' So, whatever had passed between this pair, years back, had not been special. And the Icelander's use of the word 'folly' made Posie feel slightly sad.

Countering this, she now reverted to the topic of danger. Posie wasn't sure if the Icelander knew about the blackmail notes and she decided to find out.

'Are you worried about Miss Sinne? You mention she's playing a dangerous game. What game is that? Does she have enemies?'

Gordy Lorkinsson turned at last, and in his hand was a 'Talisman' bloom.

'This is not my own. But I love it anyhow. See how it smells of pear-drops? Of sugar candy.'

He came very close to Posie now, *too* close. Up this close Posie could see where the man had quickly shaved this morning, missing bits here and there, and she could see how intensely blue his eyes were, a beautiful cornflower blue; more vivid than anything he might ever grow or graft.

This close he smelt of the earth itself. He gave her one of his rare transforming smiles. For a second, Posie felt like her heart might explode, out of aching for him.

Get a grip.

He indicated to her buttonhole. 'Can I exchange it?'

'Of course.'

He leant in. His thick, powerful fingers, ingrained with years of dirt, ripped away the 'Ultimate Sin' white rose. He replaced it with the pinky-orange bloom.

'This one is so much more *you*, Miss Parker. And take my advice: if Anouk has given you any of that new perfume she has just created, tip it away. It does not, and will not, become you in the slightest.'

He stayed close, met her gaze. 'Look, I stay in the garden, Miss Parker. Simple as that. And in answer to your questions, I have no idea if Anouk has enemies. But I'll tell you this much for nothing: *something is wrong here*. Something has been wrong for two years; during all the time Anouk was trying to "create" this latest fragrance. Usually she's much quicker between releases, but these last two years she's been angry, careless, distracted, without direction.'

Lorkinsson laughed, but it sounded hollow.

'Poor Hubert, the man is a saint! Sometimes I've thought that Anouk is ill. Dying, maybe? Did you see her today, trembling? I didn't know whether to say something, but in the end I stayed quiet. Or maybe it's drugs that are her problem? You must have noticed her eyes? But that's new; I've never seen it before. Pah, she's a fool! But I'll tell you this: the last couple of weeks have been especially dreadful. She's been completely on edge.'

Posie realised that what he was saying made sense. Hadn't it been just these last two weeks that the blackmail demands had started arriving?

But it seemed as if this gorgeous man had no idea about any of that.

Lorkinsson was so close to Posie that they both stood within the shade of his tatty gardening hat.

'Things have changed, Miss Parker, and not for the better. Normally the initial "reveal" has been limited to just me, Hubert, and the staff. A kind of "thank you" for our work, I suppose. Often Maria, the strange French Duchesse, has come along, but who on earth are all these extra hangers-on today? That rich American? That famous Princess? The press? That drunk slip of a Countess? And you? Tell me: *why are you here, exactly*?'

Posie opened her mouth to loyally defend Dolly but then she realised that actually, the Icelander was giving a pretty accurate description of her friend right now.

Instead, she focused on something which had seemed hardly important in all of the diatribe, but which struck her as incongruous.

'Why do you say the French Duchesse is "strange"? She seems a model of respectability to me.'

Lorkinsson shrugged. 'I'm not saying she isn't respectable. But something doesn't sit right. She's a Parisian, isn't she? Anouk goes on and on about some fancy town house she has somewhere…'

'In Versailles, Paris.'

'That's right. But our Duchesse knows almost as much as *I* do about gardening. I swear it. I've seen her. She was down here before it got light this morning. Dawn.'

'But why were *you* here so early? Is that normal?'

The man shook his head. 'I'd dropped in early to check on some of my new hybrid tea- roses. I'm doing an important talk this evening about the future of roses at the Chelsea Flower Show, and I needed to decide which to take with me. I need them to be absolutely perfect and this hot weather has been unkind for roses. I needed to choose my samples early on.'

'I see. Go on, please.'

'I slipped around the side of the house, and there she was, the Duchesse de Poilac in her long white nightgown, with a knitted shawl over the top, picking flowers over near the lily pond, nosing about in the hedgerows, looking suspicious. I left as soon as I saw her in the garden; I went back the way I came, unnoticed. I didn't want to embarrass her.'

'That was nice of you. But how strange!' Posie shrugged. 'Maybe the Duchesse simply likes gardens. And this one is so very special. Maybe she loves the scent of flowers growing? Doesn't get enough of them in her hot dusty town house back home?'

'No. It was more than that. She was moving about like an expert. She had the touch, the knowledge. She was clipping things like she was going to be growing from them.'

'If you say so. Although if it was half-dark, I'm surprised you could see anything she was doing at all.'

Beyond the end of the garden, over near the hedge, Posie saw a sudden blur of blue, of gold mournful tail feathers.

She pointed towards the hedge. 'Maybe the Duchesse likes peacocks? Maybe she thought she'd give the resident peacock something to eat, for breakfast? Or are there a pair of them? I've only seen one so far.'

'Peacocks? What on earth are you talking about, Miss Parker?'

The Icelander looked completely confused, rubbed the back of his lightly grimy hand across his face.

'There are no animals here, Miss Parker. That awful hairless cat would never stand for it. Anouk hates birds, and animals. She's only got that cat because it has no hair, so it can't moult, and it doesn't smell. Didn't you realise?'

'Actually, I haven't had the pleasure yet of meeting the cat.'

'Mmmm. That's a point: I haven't seen him about the place today. But I can assure you there are no peacocks here. Quite apart from the cat, Julius, they'd end up dead pretty quickly. You know that Anouk's garden runs up hard against the Chelsea Embankment itself? It's a busy old road most of the time, full of carts and horses and motor-cars, and any bird would probably slip out and end up under a set of wheels. So, I'm afraid you've been given the wrong information, Miss Parker.'

Posie looked about again, but the blue glimmer had now disappeared. Had her eyes been deceiving her, after all? But on *two* occasions? Or was this a runaway bird, escaped from another nice garden? Although there weren't many gardens this beautiful, or this big, in London.

Apart from...

'You work at the Chelsea Physic Garden, don't you? Are there any peacocks there?'

But Lorkinsson shook his head slowly, as if slightly worried about Posie's state of mind.

She shrugged the glitch, the anomaly, off.

'Oh, well! I daresay you're right. I must have heard wrong. So, she's staying *here*, is she? The Duchesse de Poilac? Is that how she was able to get into the garden before dawn?'

Lorkinsson nodded. 'That's right. She's staying here. There's a guest flat, above Anouk's own flat, up on the second floor. The Duchesse always stays here, rather than in a hotel, and this time she has her son with her. They arrived yesterday, around noon. I was heading up here to do some extra work and I was coming along the pavement at the front, aiming to go around the side of the house to reach the garden, when they drew up in a dark-green motor-taxi.'

He frowned at what he recalled. 'And that was very odd, too.'

'Go on.'

He glanced over to the people on the lawn.

'Anouk was on the doorstep to welcome the Duchesse and her son. That in itself is unusual. Anouk barely gets up before midday these days, let alone actually dressed and ready to greet her guests in person. And then she did something even more bizarre. She carried two large, heavy black bags towards the green motor-taxi. One bag in particular Anouk seemed reluctant to let go of: I swear she was almost talking to it! And then Anouk instructed the driver to take the bags away. Anouk gave the cabbie a tip. A big one. She looked furtive and fearful, all at the same time. It was very strange.'

'Black, like a sports bag?' Posie asked, curious. 'Canvas, with a zip? With the House of Sinne emblem in white on the side?'

'Both of the bags were like that, yes.'

It sounded much like the same bag which Anouk had shown to Posie earlier. The one containing all that money. The one which had, presumably, been dropped off at Victoria Station by now. Was it possible that Anouk had lied to Posie and had already dispatched heavy bags filled with money out to her blackmailers, but on the previous day? And that this, today, was a second, later top-up?

But why lie?

Or Anouk Sinne could – and this seemed the most likely explanation here – have been simply sending her very precious and secret new perfume on to the big Department Stores who would sell it? Or perhaps she had been sending bottles on to the Embassy Club, for the launch tomorrow? Both options would have involved secrecy and planning, hence the furtiveness.

Posie made a mental note to ask her hostess about the bags she had dispatched when she next spoke to her, inside.

Just then Posie heard Dolly calling her across the grass. Her voice and her stance were both very unsteady.

'Coo-ee, lovey! Posie darlin'! There's a call for you in the house. The hallway. Urgent apparently!'

Posie felt Gordy Lorkinsson's acute embarrassment beside her, and she didn't need to look up into that sun-weathered face to see its flush of sudden red.

'I'm very sorry, Miss Parker. I had no idea you knew the Countess well, or at all, in fact. Of course, I should never have spoken of her like that just now. Please do accept my apologies.'

'Actually, as it happens, you were spot on, Mr Lorkinsson. Unfortunately.'

And as Posie turned towards the house she saw Dolly lose her footing in the grass on her yellow heels, almost collapsing into Count Anatole de Poilac's embarrassed embrace.

She tried to ignore Dolly as she ran past her.

'And while you're there, Posie darlin', can you get us all a top-up of the bubbly? The butler is all over the place, and Anouk Sinne, our hostess, seems to have disappeared off the face of the earth! Some party this is turnin' out to be, innit, lovey?'

****

Seven

Posie grabbed up the receiver in the entrance hallway, and indicated to Jenks, who hovered in the background, that he could leave. The time was exactly ten minutes to five, and she felt sure this would be Sergeant Fox reporting back.

She was right.

He sounded breathless. Like he'd been running.

'Miss Parker? Fox here.'

'What's going on?'

Posie kept her voice down, and deliberately didn't mention the Sergeant by rank, mindful that Anouk Sinne might walk through at any minute, and she was acting in direct contravention of her client's instructions not to involve the police.

'And *where* are you?'

'A public telephone-booth in the lobby of the Grosvenor Hotel at Victoria Station, Miss.'

'You didn't get far then. What happened?'

An exasperated sigh. 'Textbook drop-off, Miss. I stood in one glass telephone-booth in a row of them, unobtrusive like, near the lockers; pretending to make a call. Oof! It was boiling there under all that glass! That slip of a blonde girl arrived dead on four-thirty, all alone. She looks like the wind might blow her away, doesn't she? And she looked like she was struggling with the weight of the bag full of cash.'

'What did it look like?'

'What, the bag? Black, with a fancy white sort of logo.'

'Fine.' *Better make sure what Posie had seen leave was the same thing which arrived. Especially with all this talk of similar bags being shifted around town.*

'Well, Miss, this blonde girl strode across the forecourt like she did it every day of her life; a real brave-looking lass, she was. But then, when she'd deposited the bag in the right locker, and double-checked the number on it at least three times, and checked the door was left ajar, she crossed back the way she'd come, and I could see she was nervous; shaking all over, in fact.'

'Righty-ho.' So Lucy's part in the blackmail story so far seemed genuine enough. It didn't seem that she was engaged in double-crossing her employer or taking part in a charade.

'The girl posted a letter, too. In a pink envelope. She posted it at the postboxes right by me, on the concourse, and she seemed flustered. She looked behind her a couple of times, back at the locker, but then she disappeared out the side exit, where the cabs wait.'

'And then?'

'Then I stayed on, Miss. Didn't have long to wait, actually. A minute or two, maybe. And then this lad appeared. I reckon he'd been in one of the telephone-booths, like me, watching it all. He had a grey felt homburg hat on, pulled well down, and a grey flannel suit. Clever outfit for the chappie to wear, as he was able to blend right in while still looking smart and professional. No jacket though; just shirtsleeves with these smart little gold bands as sleeve-holders. Like those Americans you see in the movies. Very jaunty, he was.'

'And?'

'There's not much more to say, Miss. He looked all

about him, a three-hundred-and-sixty-degree turn, cool as a cucumber. He pulled out that black bag and tucked it under his arm easily, like a carpet-seller. Then he moved off.'

'You followed?' Posie said this last bit in a whisper.

''Course, Miss. I 'ad him, too, but he realised it. Quickly, too. He was very calm, but fast, and he led me a twisty path all the way through the railway station, which was getting busy with commuters. I lost him right by the Grosvenor Hotel. I even wondered if he worked here, or was a guest, so I came in and I've been in the bar, asking discreet questions. Nothing doing, and nobody has seen anything. The man with the cash has disappeared.'

Posie felt defeated. She'd learnt nothing from Fox, and it seemed Fox had gleaned nothing of the man at all which might make him traceable. She tried to ring off with a good grace. Fox had been doing her a big favour, after all.

'If you think of anything at all which seemed unusual, Fox, let me know.'

'Right you are, Miss. I might well get back to you later. I tried to employ something I'd learnt on my observational skills course recently. But it has mixed, uncertain results. Oh, and you take care, Miss, won't you? I think there's something funny about all this, but I can't put my finger on it.'

You're not the only one, Posie thought to herself, perturbed.

And where was Lucy Reeble now, anyhow? If the blackmailer had been giving Fox the run-around at Victoria Station and the secretary had turned tail and left again at four-thirty, she ought to be back, if she'd taken a motor-taxi. But Posie hadn't seen her.

Feeling like a real Nosy Parker, Posie wandered off along the white-tiled staircase, down to the bottom of the house.

And here she found Lucy, not in the laboratory, which was, as usual, closed and sealed up, but next door, in the small and clinically neat office.

Lucy was at the desk, laboriously checking the numbers on the bottom of some bottles of the new perfume, 'The Ultimate Sin', and transcribing these numbers onto a form.

So, Lucy *had* come back in double-quick time, and had probably been working all the while Posie was chatting away to the handsome Icelander in the garden outside, and then to Fox on the telephone.

Posie felt a flutter of sudden guilt at questioning the girl's whereabouts.

Lucy had been very busy. She'd obviously spent part of her day packing up bottles into beribboned turquoise boxes. Most of these small boxes were already stacked carefully inside two big black canvas zippered bags. Lucy was on the very last batch, a few open turquoise boxes on the desk beside her.

Posie stared hard at the black bags with the white emblem of the snake stitched on them.

So Anouk had lots of these identical bags.

Lucy looked up and caught Posie's eye. She looked weary. 'Can I help you, Miss Parker?'

'I won't keep you. I'm looking for Miss Sinne, actually.'

Lucy smiled a tight, watery smile. 'I hope she will come past *here* soon, Miss Parker. I need her signature on this consignment form before it all leaves today. I expect she's still out in the garden, isn't she?'

'I haven't seen her out there.'

The secretary frowned. 'I didn't check. I just came straight down here as this work is urgent. Perhaps she's still speaking to some guests in the drawing-room?'

Posie thought of Mr Van Dusen suddenly, of his white, white smile and dead black eyes.

That shark.

Posie thought of the man standing up and posing for photographs with Anouk, with the beautiful, captive, prancing Princess at his side. He had seemed strangely proprietorial over both the Princess and the perfume, come to think of it.

Was the man something to do with perfume himself? Posie's thoughts were running ahead of her as she tried to make things fit.

What if he was a representative tasked with taking samples of Anouk's perfume back with him to America? Some kind of expansion, perhaps, of the House of Sinne?

An idea was forming in Posie's mind, but it hadn't taken root yet, not properly.

'Are these two bags destined for America, by any chance, Miss Reeble? For Mr Van Dusen?'

Lucy sighed, slightly hopelessly. 'I honestly have no idea where these are going, Miss Parker. I was just instructed to make them ready. One hundred bottles as samples, with the correct forms.'

A hundred bottles?

As samples?

Posie stared. But hadn't Anouk said that only a small amount of this perfume had been made up so far? Only enough for today, and for the Embassy luncheon tomorrow.

There were no other bottles in the office. So where *were* the bottles for the luncheon tomorrow? Or for the shops?

Posie asked Lucy about the arrangements, and the girl looked blank.

Posie pressed on: 'Two big black bags, like these, were seen being given to a driver yesterday, at noon. Anouk Sinne sent them off herself. Do you think those contained the bottles for the shops? For the luncheon?'

'I cannot tell you, Miss, because I do not know.'

The secretary looked piqued for a second. And Posie realised that the girl felt embarrassed in front of her, and snubbed: almost certainly left out of her employer's confidence.

'Miss Sinne likes to hold her cards very close to her chest, Miss Parker, in case secrets are leaked. No-one wants to buy, or wear, old news, do they?'

'Quite. Well, I'm sure it's all in hand. Thank you anyway.'

None the wiser, Posie retraced her steps up to the main hallway, past the Tamara de Lempicka picture, and through the conservatory to loop down into the garden again. But before she did so she heard a hurried and angry whispering going on. A fight, almost.

It was coming from behind the closed door to the drawing-room.

Posie drew closer, then closer still.

She hated snoops. Hated those who hung about at doorways like cheap spies. And here she was, doing exactly that!

Need's must, Posie told herself.

And this was her brief, wasn't it? To listen to everything and everyone. And to see if anyone's actions or words could shed any light on the unnerving blackmail threats.

Leaning in to the very edge of the closed white door, what Posie heard was certainly very strange.

'How much longer will she be? That wretched woman!'

It was the Princess, the Maharani of Gwilim.

But she didn't sound very princess-like anymore: not regal, or polite, or charming. Not captivating. There was no tinkly laughter to be heard now. Instead, the Princess sounded bored and angry.

'It's unbelievable! She has the barefaced cheek to tell us not to go outside. Not to go into her oh-so-fancy garden. Not before or after the perfume was unleashed! What are we, Mr Van Dusen? Not good enough for her? Huh? *C'est incroyable*! We have to stay inside, here? Like prisoners?'

'Calm down, your Highness. We have done what we needed to, according to the contract. You have added your note of "mystique", and it's been captured on camera, as I requested. Soon we will be gone. I'm sure Miss Sinne is delayed for some completely understandable reason. Besides, your Highness, you will find that the door is not locked. You *can* get out. Try it if you don't believe me.'

Posie moved away quickly, worried the Princess might do just that.

Now she knew for sure that the second speaker was Mr Van Dusen, and he sounded exactly as he had earlier: sleek, unhurried, in control.

But what was he talking about? What contract? What had he wanted on camera? And why?

After a minute or so Posie leant closer to the door again and caught the tail end of Van Dusen's soothing words.

'Just relax, your Highness. It is not personal to you. Say, Miss Sinne didn't want *me* to go outside, either. I arrived earlier than you and I was told to wait in here for you to arrive: told not to go out in the garden. But I did actually have a stroll down there. I wanted to see this mythical garden, of course. You know, I expect Anouk Sinne has her own good reasons for asking us to wait inside. I am guessing there might be others here who are jealous of what we have managed to achieve, huh? Gee, perhaps Miss Sinne doesn't want to cause a scene, for *our* sakes. I've noticed that the English hate a fight. Hate confrontation of any sort.'

Van Dusen laughed, but Posie, outside the room, was frowning. What had Van Dusen thought he'd achieved?

And why had Anouk acted so strangely towards the man? Asking him to stay inside the drawing-room seemed rude. It was most peculiar. But Posie couldn't dwell on this much, as Van Dusen was talking again, and she listened hard.

'Her fame is justified, Princess, from what I've observed so far. It's a big talent that woman has.'

'You are kidding me, right?' The Princess sounded utterly furious. 'If you weren't taking me to Hollywood, I'd have thrown this stupid project overboard; stopped wasting my time with advertising a fragrance. And such a bizarre one, too. Actually, I didn't like it at all. *Zut alors*! It was horrible!'

Van Dusen's voice changed suddenly, and his tone was hard.

No longer playing along nicely.

'Say, I'd ask you to keep your opinions about the perfume to yourself, Princess. And keep *schtum* generally. This perfume is big news for all of us. We were lucky, I tell you, to be given this opportunity, and so late in the day. Only in the last two weeks! I'm telling you, your Highness, you'd better play along, or how else will you make it to Hollywood, without me?'

His tone had turned cruel, mocking, and he suddenly abandoned the use of all of Priyanka's formal titles.

'And how on earth would you pay for it all, little lady? With those chunks of gold around your neck? All of it cursed, eh? And your little boyfriends in Paris abandoning you because your past is catching up with you, eh? You'd better count yourself darn lucky to have landed *this* break, now. With me. You're lucky I took you on. *This* is your stepping stone. You'll need some fame behind you, and a bit of hard work, too, if you want to paper over the cracks of your life so far. And this perfume is going to do that for you.'

There was a lot of huffing, and the sound of flouncing footsteps on the parquet, and the pulling out of a chair, and Posie imagined the Princess, inconsolable in her rage and self-righteousness, sitting down, her back to Van Dusen, arms folded across her beautiful white linen jacket.

A can of worms, as dear darling Richard would say.

Posie's thoughts were jumbled.

Why did the Princess need to paper over cracks in her life? Why would this one, small 'reveal' make such a big difference to the Princess's prospects? To *his*?

It sounded very much as if Van Dusen had offered to act as an 'agent' for the Princess; that he had promised her the riches of America on a platter.

But for what in return?

After a couple of minutes of silence, Posie heard footsteps crossing the room, re-crossing it. Impatient stamping feet.

It was Van Dusen, his patience finally wearing thin.

Posie imagined the American checking and re-checking his wristwatch.

She heard him muttering. Losing his former cool. 'Time is not on our side... What on earth is Miss Sinne up to? Dang and blast her!'

'What's that you are saying now, Mr Van Dusen?' called out the Princess in a bored and sarcastic manner from her side of the room.

Van Dusen sighed audibly. His waiting, and his reassurances to the Princess, had all been for nothing.

'You know as well as I do that we need to get to Southampton tonight, your Highness, and we are already cutting it fine. It is almost quarter-past five. We should be outta here. Our boat sails at ten. We need to motor on down there. What is Miss Sinne *doing*? All she needs to do is hand over the bags with the samples and the certified documents. I don't understand it. The cheque has cleared, after all.'

What cheque?

But Posie felt a jolt of excitement, a self-congratulatory prickle which was a result of being right! The hundred bottles *were* off to America, and tonight by the sounds of it.

There was the sound of scraping chairs and Posie fled, sure that the unlikely and unharmoniously-matched duo she had been listening in on would now burst out of the room and start to search for their errant hostess.

Where was Anouk Sinne, anyhow?

The perfumier had struck Posie as odd, but extremely professional, and some carefully-arranged agreement of commercial importance seemed to be in the process of going very wrong here.

Posie ran to the top of the steps, where she was met by Dolly, completely drunk.

'Did you get that champagne, Po?'

Posie was about to turn and snap at her dear friend to bally well pull herself together and *behave*, but then her attention was caught by something else.

Something important.

It was something way down on the lawn, past the French Duchesse with her peculiar knowledge of flowers, on the arm of her handsome young son, and on past the Icelander, whose arms were full of roses, to take with him for his talk about the Chelsea Flower Show.

Posie stared past the blue peacock, which was back, strutting near the very back hedge, its tail feathers raised in a proud, high fan. In a kind of warning.

The sunlight was glinting full-beam on the lily pond, and the slices of reflected light were almost too bright to look upon, but Posie focused on something else that glinted there, and she was gripped by a sudden fear.

It was silver.

Silver stars embroidered on chiffon. A scarf without an owner.

A trailing wisp of a disaster.

****

Eight

It seemed as if time stopped still in that very moment, froze.

Posie was aware of a crush of movement at her back, and Mr Van Dusen and the impatient Maharani were stepping out of the French doors, squinting in the bright sunlight. Posie heard a sudden gasp behind her.

Princess Priyanka was clamping a long-fingered, jewel-laden hand to her mouth, jabbering wildly: 'I saw a PEACOCK! Oh, no!'

Posie, turning in an arc of incomprehension, looked at the girl, with Dolly staring on stupidly, and the Princess shook her head, horrified.

'In India the peacock, a *mayura*, is known as a holy bird.'

'How nice!' Dolly chirruped in her drink-addled state. 'Well, what's the problem wiv that, then, lovey? You look like you've seen a ghost! And *what* peacock you on about, anyhow? I can't see nuffink!'

'It was just there! You didn't see it, Countess?'

The Princess was pointing wildly, on past the scarf on the lawn. 'And you're right about ghosts, Countess. While Hindu mythology loves these birds, in *my* husband's dynasty, in the Princely State of Gwilim, the peacock is unlucky, associated with death. With a life taken too soon.

It's a ghost-bird. They are not allowed as pets! Very unlucky. Not allowed in gardens. No, not at all.'

Posie saw that the Princess's enormous amber eyes were almost wild with fear. She was stepping back slowly towards the house, whispering, but Posie could just about make out her anguished words to the American at her side.

'Oh! I had hoped not to see this again, Mr Van Dusen. I have seen it all too recently: five peacocks walking just like this, in front of my own burning home. A peacock for each of my family, all dead: my husband dead, my parents-in-law, my brother-in-law and also his wife. What does this now mean?'

Posie heard an embarrassed cough, and Van Dusen was laughing smoothly, cordially, averting a scene, offering the Maharani his arm.

'Come, your Highness, perhaps it is too hot, after all? Say, let's go inside and find Miss Sinne, or else, that helpful blonde secretary girl, huh? Perhaps she can get you a cold soda?'

Posie looked about her wildly, looking for a glimpse of the woman who had summoned her here today. But there was no sign of Anouk Sinne at all.

The fear which had arrived like a sudden crashing tide on seeing the scarf wouldn't shift, and Gordy Lorkinsson's recent words to her were echoing around Posie's head: '*something is wrong here.*'

Was she just being fanciful?

Imagining things?

The hot, stifling garden seemed to simmer and hum with a dreadful and heavy apprehension and, hoping against hope that she was wrong, Posie turned, yet again, searching for someone at hand whom she could trust.

Not Dolly.

Not today.

Posie found herself looking suddenly into the anxious blue eyes of Hubert Pring, a man she had yet to properly speak to, but who appeared so dependable that she found herself ignoring the cross looks of his wife.

Posie tried to keep her voice calm.

'Your Lordship? We weren't introduced: I'm Posie. Posie Parker. Could I ask you to please go, now, this minute, and call New Scotland Yard? You know my husband, I think; he's the Chief Commissioner, Richard Lovelace. He's at the Old Bailey today, but if you ask for his Sergeant, Fox, he'll get a message through to Richard. They both need to come here. *Immediately*. It's an urgent matter, my Lord. Tell Sergeant Fox to bring the doctor, too. He'll know who.'

Her face must have looked ghastly, for the Viscount Effington – Hubert Pring – took her seriously.

'A doctor, eh? Is it Anouk, Mrs Lovelace?'

'I still call myself Miss Parker.'

'Ah, right you are. But have you seen Anouk, Miss Parker? Where is she? By Gad! I *thought* something was bally well wrong with her. Nasty turn, what? I'll go at once. Clare, darling? Come with me. *Now*.'

Hubert Pring mercifully left his unanswered questions hanging in the air, and marched back through the French doors, his wife trying to keep up, and they almost collided with Lucy Reeble, who was struggling under the weight of the two big black bags in the conservatory, very red in the face, not at all her usual composed self.

And then within the house the telephone started ringing.

On and on.

'Ain't someone goin' to answer that?' squawked Dolly at Posie's side.

'What a place, eh? No servants, no nuffink! That odd-lookin' butler should be pullin' his weight! Keeps disappearing! Where is he? Shall we be gettin' on 'ome, Posie?'

But Posie had made up her mind.

Automatically, she kicked off her pink Mary-Janes and

she was running, moving faster than she had in a long time. Since before being pregnant with Kit.

She seemed to float over the hot grass of the long, long lawn, inhale the claustrophobic air with its heady halo of heavy pollen, to skim the borders of the prize-winning roses. She was aiming for that glittering scarf.

But then at her side, his cut roses abandoned, she found Gordy Lorkinsson, almost outpacing her. They came up sharp, together, right by the scarf, by the lily pond.

'Miss Parker?'

Lorkinsson was reaching down to pick up the gossamer-thin chiffon. 'Oh! This is Anouk's scarf. Well, she must have just dropped it. For a minute there I thought something was *really* wrong. An emergency. The way you were running…'

But Posie touched his arm, panting.

'Wait, sir. Did you see Anouk come down this way? You left the drawing-room at exactly four-thirty, and she followed you out here just afterwards. Was she in the garden, near you? Before *I* came to speak to you by your roses?'

The blonde giant shook his head. 'I haven't seen Anouk since I left that dratted room.'

He looked puzzled. 'I suppose she *may* have come down here, but why would she? Her guests were all in the house. Besides, if she came out here specially to look for me, it's very possible she missed me.'

'How?'

The gardener waved his tiny secateurs and tapped his gardening belt. 'I don't carry this stuff around with me normally, you know. I have a small shed, a lean-to really, at the very side of the house, in the alley, and I keep everything there. When I left the drawing-room I went to the shed first, picking up all of this, before tending the roses. If Anouk walked down the lawn immediately, she would have missed me.'

'I see.'

'What's the problem, Miss Parker? You look anxious.'

'Anouk Sinne is missing. She's been absent for more than forty-five minutes. Almost one hour. And she's needed. So yes, I am anxious.'

Lorkinsson shrugged. 'Anyone checked her bedroom? Her flat upstairs?'

Posie looked about her, ignored the well-meaning gardener, who obviously thought her at worst fanciful, and at best, hysterical.

Was she just being ridiculous? Would she look a complete fool soon when Sergeant Fox arrived with Doctor Poots in tow? And then again, later, when Richard turned up?

Would Anouk Sinne simply appear from wherever she had been, and angrily tell them all to clear off? Would she tell Posie to leave, for failing in her assignment? For involving the police?

But what had Posie's assignment *actually* been? She still didn't understand the task at hand. *What had Anouk Sinne wanted of her, anyway?*

Posie bit at her lip, trying to look casual, but a memory of Anouk recounting her dreams earlier in the laboratory came into her mind.

'*My murdered self. Here in my garden. Half-hidden in the undergrowth and the seeping water from the lily pond.*'

She stared at what she could see of the pond. But there was no-one there. Nothing odd at all. Apart from that scarf.

Posie was about to turn tail and start to search for the perfumier up at the house, when she saw that the Icelander was frowning, and she followed his gaze. Had that bad-luck symbol of a peacock returned, causing mischief? Made real for the gardener, at last.

But no.

At first there seemed nothing to see. A beautiful thick

beech hedge, its leaves blocking off the busy road at the very end of the garden, whose traffic, this close, made a considerable noise. Then Posie saw a gap in the hedge.

And that was where Lorkinsson was staring.

'What's through there, then?' she asked, trying to sound normal.

'I shouldn't tell you this, Miss Parker. But Anouk grows plants behind there which are all for herself. It's her private garden *within* this main garden. But she'd get into big trouble if she was found out.'

'"Found out"? Recreational drugs, you mean? Stimulants?'

She was thinking suddenly of Anouk's hugely dilated pupils, which could have been caused by some kind of home-grown atropine preparation, perhaps? A drug which could cause all manner of side-effects. Most of them bad.

The gardener shrugged. 'I really don't know. I asked Anouk about that area once and almost had my head bitten off. Me and old Tom Bowley, the regular gardener, have always been banned from going in there. But of course, I've had the odd peek when Anouk has been away. All I know is that Anouk has actively cultivated those plants, which is downright illegal.'

He swallowed unhappily. 'Most of the plants there are poisonous. Deadly poisonous, in fact.'

'I see. I'll go and have a look. I think I must.'

'Be careful, Miss Parker. It's best not to touch anything. I won't come; the space is very small. Too small for two people. But I'm sure there's no need for you to go through, is there?'

Was he protesting a bit too much? Posie wondered. Had she perhaps been blindsided by his handsome looks, and perhaps relied on his apparent honesty a bit too much in her investigations so far?

'I'll be just fine.'

Posie held onto the thin chiffon scarf, wrapping it around her lower exposed arms and her hands.

She stepped stocking-footed through the entrance in the hedge and found herself standing in a space of perhaps only two feet wide, bordered on one side by the hedge, and the other by a solid-looking high wooden fence which faced onto the busy road of the Chelsea Embankment. A secret 'strip' of hidden garden.

Plants were almost rampantly wild here, in complete contrast to the tended neatness of the main garden itself. Thick sweaty fronds and tendrils of blue-green plants seemed to compete for space, growing in thick clumps, and clinging, sucker-like, to the fence.

The only colours were the beautiful but dangerous pinky-mauve foxgloves, their bell-shaped trumpet blooms abundant, growing tall.

There was almost no room to move, and Posie felt horribly claustrophobic.

Just focus.

The ground underfoot was wet, despite the heat and the strong sun of the day. This was not a pleasant, refreshing place at all.

But there was no-one here. She chastised herself. *Well, thank goodness for that, of course. That will teach me to be silly and jump to conclusions!*

The fear began to ebb a little.

Posie turned quickly. 'I'm coming out. You were right, Mr Lorkinsson. Nothing untoward here!'

But then Posie saw that this hidden garden ran on right behind the beech hedge, in a very long row, and that the water underfoot seemed to be connected with the lily pond beyond it.

She forced herself to walk further along the strip, careful not to let her skin come into contact with any of the plants, keeping the brim of her hat well down around the nape of her neck and the borrowed scarf over her skin.

Her feet started sinking in the mud as the water got deeper, as the plants got thicker, wilder. Almost waist-height here.

This must actually be the very edge of the pond, Posie decided. *Perhaps its source was here? Or else some sort of tank associated with supplying the pond was located here?*

It smelt bad behind the hedge in Anouk's hidden garden.

There was a sort of rotting smell, like meat or fish left out too long. Or cat food, more like. Distinctly unpleasant.

Posie tried to blot out the bad smell. *It's just some stinky, horrible plants*, she told herself quickly.

Nothing more interesting than that.

She was about to edge back through the undergrowth when her stockinged foot brushed up against something very sharp, and Posie cried out in pain.

'Oh! Ow!'

She looked down and saw the very high heel of a shoe, a black patent Mary-Jane with silver grosgrain bows.

It was sticking out unnaturally from the fronds of a fern-like plant, which was decorated all over with a bloom of white confetti flowers.

A fist of horror pressed itself into Posie's throat, almost making her gag.

'Oh, my gosh!'

Her heart was beating madly, but Posie, scarf around her, knelt down and tried to prise away the undergrowth, batting away the flies and gnats swarming there.

And here was the body.

Revealed.

You never quite got used to it – death, and corpses – and this one was particularly horrible.

As Posie peered down into the undergrowth, she saw Anouk Sinne's cold, dead face. Saw the woman's surprised-looking dark eyes already filmy and clouded over, staring up unseeing at the impossibly hot and cloudless London sky. Her face was a mass of amber-coloured blisters, huge and pearlescent in their awfulness.

Anouk had, in her final death throes, flung an arm

across her face, and it too was red and sore-looking with the same blistering scabs all over it. Posie saw how Anouk's fingernails were no longer immaculate and silver; they looked muddy and broken, like she'd been digging in the earth.

'But *why*?'

Beside her on the ground was an un-stoppered turquoise bottle of 'The Ultimate Sin'. There seemed to be nothing left in the bottle.

Odd, the details one noticed at times like this.

'Come out now, Miss Parker!' called Lorkinsson, testily, impatiently, from beyond the hedge. 'It's dangerous for you in there.'

'It was dangerous for Anouk Sinne, too,' whispered Posie to herself. 'But why did she come down *here*, of all places? Was *this* the place in her dream? What was she looking for? Or was this the only place she could be private? Did she know she was about to die?'

She got up.

Anouk Sinne was beyond her help. And Posie knew in her heart of hearts that she had failed this odd woman.

But what kind of death was she looking at?

An accident? Suicide? Or murder?

Had that professionally-dressed blackmailer whom Sergeant Fox had chased through Victoria Station earlier managed to keep to his horrible promise after all? Taken the money and snuffed out the perfumier, regardless?

Too much here didn't make sense, and Posie was the first to admit that this time, she was out of her depth.

She edged out and ran right into the worried arms of Gordy Lorkinsson.

'Miss Parker? You look like you have heatstroke. What is it? *What?*'

In the bright sunlight of the lawn, Posie stood gasping for air, and she found herself absolutely lost for words, unsure what to say to the big man at her side.

So she didn't say anything.

But, as if by magic, Posie saw the very welcome, tall, gangly sharp-suited figure of the blonde Sergeant Fox appearing on the steps of the house, shielding his eyes against the sun. Behind him was the smaller, shorter, darker figure of Sergeant Smallbone, wearing an inappropriately-hot beige trench-coat, a Scotland Yard staple.

They must have left Scotland Yard the instant Hubert Pring had rung, Posie realised, and she'd never felt more thankful in her life.

Suddenly she saw the diminutive, tubby figure of Doctor Poots, Scotland Yard's most eminent Pathologist, coming into view, replete today, as ever, in a black bowler hat and a smart dicky-bow-tie above his immaculate city three-piece tweed suit.

He wielded his huge black doctor's bag before him like a weapon, as if to divide the group of people who were starting to throng onto the steps of the House of Sinne.

Posie turned her best beaming smile on the Icelander. 'You see the man in the trench-coat? His name is Smallbone. Can you show him where the drawing-room is, and tell him to get everyone gathered in there? The staff too? It's very important. *Please.*'

The Icelander stared at Posie for a second too long, his blue eyes narrowed, serious, but not panicked.

'Fine.'

And then, after the blonde man ambled off, throwing her a couple of confused looks over his shoulder, Posie waved urgently – but not, she hoped, desperately – at Sergeant Fox and the Pathologist.

She wanted to make light of things, without causing any alarm to the guests, while indicating that they should get here.

Now.

And step right into the heart of the poison garden.

* * * *

Nine

After showing Fox and Doctor Poots behind the hedge, Posie loitered. She realised suddenly that her hands were shaking, as was her whole body.

It was with a massive lurch of relief that she saw her husband appear at the top of the now-empty steps.

Here was her dear familiar Richard, tired and slightly creased-looking in a dark un-summery suit – his usual Court wear – with his best homburg in his hands and his summer-weight trench-coat folded over his arm.

He saw his wife and grinned, the late afternoon sunlight catching and reflecting off his thick dark-red hair, cut very short at the moment, but his smile vanished as Posie started to run towards him, throwing herself into his arms.

'Darling? What on earth? What is going on? And what are *you* doing here, of all places? I got the urgent message when I returned to my office. Luckily the court case ended today and we all finished early, thank heavens! I came here with a police driver, as fast as I could. But, oh, I say! Where on earth are your shoes, sweetheart? Why are your feet wet and covered in mud? What the blazes–'

'There's been a death, Richard. A suspicious death. At the bottom of the garden, behind that hedge. It's Anouk Sinne. You know? The perfumier? Sergeant Fox and Doctor Poots are there now. Oh, it's simply too awful for words.'

'Try to find the words, my love.'

And, as succinctly as she could, and trying not to cry, Posie gave him all the details: Anouk Sinne and her strange summons; the involvement of Dolly; the blackmail threats, and the manner in which one thousand pounds had been paid today by Lucy Reeble into the open locker at Victoria Station, watched by Sergeant Fox.

She told Richard about the 'reveal' of the new perfume, the scent of which had seemed to unnerve the guests attending, and she listed aloud who exactly the guests were, and also the staff.

Trying to keep it short, she described the workings of the House of Sinne and explained Hubert Pring's involvement. And lastly, she told him of Anouk Sinne and her weird behaviour: the dilated pupils and the shakiness; her bad dreams which seemed to haunt her; her bolt from the drawing-room.

And then Posie explained that Anouk had gone 'missing', despite having guests on the premises and business matters to sort out.

Throughout this summing-up, Posie started to feel calmer. She realised she was still holding onto Anouk's scarf. She put it down carefully on the grass.

'I still don't know why she called me in, Richard. Only that she wanted me to "watch" what went on here today, and to attend with her tomorrow, too.'

'Tomorrow?'

Posie explained about the Embassy Club in Mayfair.

'She agreed that policemen should come along tomorrow. I think she was genuinely worried that her life was in danger from the blackmailer, or blackmailers. Whoever they might be.'

Richard was looking at Posie in consternation. His green eyes, quite his best feature, were full of real anguish. He bit at his lip, and Posie saw him dig in his inside suit pocket for his battered cigarette case. All of these were signs of worry. Soon he'd be cracking at his knuckles, and that really was a bad sign.

'*You* found the body, love? Of course you did. Why do I even bother asking! And it looks suspicious, you say?'

'I don't know.'

'So it could be something, and it could all be nothing, eh?'

'I'd err on the side of "something".'

Richard Lovelace fumbled with a cigarette, went through the rigmarole of lighting it up and shaking the match out, inhaling the first breath of smoke deep into his lungs.

'Oh, darling. You know what I'm going to say, don't you?'

'That this is "a mare's nest"?'

'Uh-huh.' He exhaled slowly. 'Ah well. I've just finished one big case, and I've time to take on another, I suppose. And this sounds like it has the makings of a "big" case. Did I hear you correctly when you said that the famous Princess from India is here?'

'That's right. She's here with an American businessman. Sam Stubbs was here earlier, too, taking what seemed like thousands of photographs, adding to the strangeness of the thing. He left though, before anyone realised Miss Sinne was missing.'

Lovelace smoked a bit more, thinking hard. 'What do *you* think is going on here, darling?'

Posie shrugged. 'I feel like I'm looking at this whole thing through a smeary, bleary window, where nothing is quite as it seems. The blackmail thing is odd. Why did Anouk cave in today, and pay up after so blithely ignoring the first two threats? What secret was she desperate to avoid coming out? Because there was no secret mentioned specifically in these notes by the blackmailer. Not even alluded to!'

She passed the postcards over to her husband who read

them quickly, eyebrows raised quizzically, before handing them back to Posie.

'Whatever it was, we'll find it. I promise.' Richard ground out his cigarette under the heel of his polished black Church's brogue. 'What else have you found out?'

Posie bit at her lip. 'What I'm piecing together is that things hadn't been going well for Anouk Sinne for a couple of years – for whatever reason – and that this new perfume was big news.'

Posie reached again into her carpet bag and brought out the turquoise bottle the woman had given to her earlier.

She fingered the gold letters as if looking for a clue there.

'What I've also been picking up is that simply bally *everything* happened in the last two weeks. Anouk Sinne started getting the typewritten blackmail threats, but she also finally hit on the perfect, secret ingredient to make her new perfume work, even though she'd been trying to "create" it for yonks. It was a secret base note, apparently.'

Posie shook the bottle, watched the clear liquid bubble slightly.

She threw it carelessly back into her carpet bag before continuing: 'And Miss Sinne only involved the Indian Princess in her project two weeks ago. Same thing with the American gentleman who's here with the Princess. This man, Mr Van Dusen...'

Richard had been preoccupied watching the hedge beyond, twitching with movement, and he'd been rustling impatiently with another cigarette, but now he snapped to attention.

'Sorry, darling, did you say "Van Dusen"? As in *Archie Van Dusen*?'

'Er, who? I have no idea who you are talking about. And this fella wasn't properly introduced to me, so I've no idea as to his first name. He's smart, in his fifties. Snappily dressed with an enviable suntan. Oh, he looks like a shark.'

'Uh-huh. A big fish. The biggest.'

'You know him?'

'I know *of* him. As does pretty much everyone in America. He's a millionaire, and may be so several times over. He's the owner of Van Dusen's Department Store on Fifth Avenue in New York. And that's just for starters.'

Richard picked up Posie's left hand, kissed her ring finger, tapping the orange-blossom shaped diamond cluster ring there, the one he had given her on their engagement.

'In fact, your little Traub ring here was purchased from Mr Van Dusen's Department Store, by an American colleague of mine. Do you remember you'd seen the adverts in some American magazine of Dolly's? And I thought I'd surprise you, as they don't sell the rings over here yet.'

Lovelace lit his next cigarette quickly. 'And Van Dusen didn't just stop at the one store either: he owns smaller Department Stores right across the United States.'

'Is he a shady fella?'

'No, although he's known to be a canny, opportunistic businessman. He couldn't afford to risk his reputation over something like this mess you're talking about here. He's a very important man. A magnate. Blackmail and murder are hardly the tools of his trade. It's not his fault if he looks like a shark, is it, darling?'

'Mmmm.'

'We'll go in and talk to everyone in a minute. Hopefully this is all just some ghastly accident, eh?'

At that point Doctor Poots emerged from the hedge, his black bag wielded before him, his whole person bristling with excitement and fervour. Fox followed, looking green about the gills, like he'd just been sick.

'What-ho, Chief Commissioner!'

'Good evening, Doctor.'

'Not for that poor lass in the hedge there, it's not.'

Poots came right up close, and Posie could smell that dreadful cat-foody smell again, the rotten stink.

The Pathologist sounded excited: 'Goodness me, Chief Commissioner! I haven't had a case like this in years. *Years!*'

Doctor Poots pushed his tortoiseshell-rimmed glasses up on the bridge of his nose, a tic all his own.

'Send for the cavalry, Richard! The lot! We need the Forensics boys to come and crawl all over the place, under my supervision. I'll organise for this poor woman's body to be taken back to the Scotland Yard Mortuary and I'll conduct a full post-mortem later tonight. Although I can already give you the brief, potted version of cause of death, and that won't change.'

'Go on.'

Poots morbidly rubbed his pudgy hands with their short, hairy, clever fingers together. 'Hemlock poisoning! Never seen a case as bad. She's been dead about an hour.'

Hemlock!

Posie caught her breath, trying to make sense of it all, while her husband chattered on. 'Hemlock? The plant?'

'The very one. There's quite a bit of the stuff growing back there, behind that nice tidy hedge. Covers a multitude of sins, that does. Although someone has obviously been busy chopping away at the stuff, and recently too.'

Richard Lovelace looked gobsmacked. 'I've never dealt with such a thing in all my years on the force, Doctor.'

'No, well, me neither, Chief Commissioner. Not like *this*.'

'What do you mean, "not like *this*"?' cut in Posie, rather shrilly. 'Was it an accidental overdose, do you think? Isn't hemlock used as a sedative sometimes? Could Miss Sinne have taken it in error?'

But as she said this, Posie was aware of her words not ringing true.

Hadn't the perfumier earlier admitted to Posie that she never took sleeping tablets, or anything like that, for fear of ruining her precious 'nose'?

Doctor Poots grinned. 'You are right, Miss Parker, of

course. The drug *can* be used as a sedative, but it is usually used in a derivative industrial form, and then only in the tiniest, tiniest microscopic amount. *Naturally* occurring hemlock, like this, is one of the most poisonous things on earth. Certainly in England. All parts of the plant are poisonous; even a microscopic amount can cause death if ingested.'

Posie heard a pleading, but illogical tone to her voice: 'Could it have been suicide, Doctor?'

'Absolutely not. Hemlock poisoning is a dreadful and slow way to die. And, if contemplating suicide, you would choose a far less painful manner of death. No: this is murder. My expert opinion is that the hemlock was administered to the deceased sometime in the last twenty-four hours, perhaps with dinner, or a cocktail? It was an incredibly strong dosage. Hemlock is tasteless, so it could have been placed in just about anything, which obviously makes your job harder, but it usually smells pretty strong. Golly, I'm surprised the woman lasted as long as she did!'

'Oh!'

'Posie? What is it? Darling?'

Posie was remembering Anouk's weird behaviour which had been in evidence since their meeting in the laboratory.

'Miss Sinne had these enormous, dilated pupils, so *that* must have been the hemlock, then, Doctor Poots? And she kept trembling. She was thirsty all the time, too. Oh! Oh, my! How awful!'

Posie clapped a hand to her mouth, horrified.

'And all that time, she was dying, right in front of us?'

Doctor Poots nodded and seemed quite satisfied at this recounting of events.

'That sounds about right, Miss Parker. Those symptoms fit. And that's just what you could *see*. Imagine how she must have felt! She'd have been hallucinating too, and her legs would have felt numb, then her arms, and her heart would have been beating crazily. And those blisters, oof!

They would have come right at the end, all over. You know poor old Socrates was poisoned by hemlock, don't you? It was a nasty trick those ancient Greeks had perfected: poison a prisoner and let him die, very slowly, aware of everything.'

Poots addressed Lovelace: 'By Gad, I hope you catch the rotter who did this, Lovelace. No-one deserves to die like that.'

Lovelace nodded grimly. 'We'll turn this place – the house and the garden – upside down in searching for any clues which will lead us to the killer.'

He turned to his Sergeant. 'You got that, Fox? You run and call a back-up team; as big a group of bobbies as you can muster, and get them searching the place, inside-out.'

'Oh! I nearly forgot!' Doctor Poots was digging in his inside breast pocket. He pulled out something fine, gold, glinting, full of jingling and glimmering metal keys. 'I took this from the body. It's the only item I removed, but it looked important.'

It was Anouk Sinne's clever little bracelet, and Posie explained its function quickly.

'Thanks, Doctor,' said Richard. 'The keys to the kingdom, eh? Here, Fox, these are for you.'

Fox took the bracelet and lolloped off, glad to be somewhere away from that blistered wreck of a body.

Posie, Poots, and Lovelace walked up the steps, and Posie saw that her husband was cracking the knuckles on his right hand. She didn't blame him; she felt wretched herself.

She tried to be practical and she pointed out the side entrance of the house, where Poots' men could easily enter the garden with the stretcher for their grisly cargo, unseen by the guests in the house.

'Thank you, Miss Parker,' said Poots gratefully. 'I will go and use the telephone apparatus. In the hall, I think? But, you know, what beats me is why the lady was down there at all. Behind the hedge. There was no reason, was there? She'd have been better off calling a doctor. Still, the mind does curious things. Especially when it's half-starved of oxygen. Anyhow, until later.'

Posie stood on the top steps, watching the hedge, which hid horrible secrets. Secrets she still couldn't fathom.

A dead woman who had somehow envisaged her own death out here.

And peacocks which seemed to vanish into thin air.

All in a Chelsea garden.

* * * *

PART TWO

Another Murder

Ten

Posie and Richard stood outside the closed door to the drawing-room.

Inside was a very low murmur of chatter, like the buzzing of bees.

Lovelace bit at his lip. 'Let me get this right, Posie. In here, we have Mr Archie Van Dusen, one Indian Princess, an English Viscount and Viscountess, one French Duchesse, one French Count, and one English Countess? All as potential suspects?'

'If you mean the English Countess is Dolly, then yes. But since when did you set such score by titles? There are others too, equally important. Pretty cramped in, I'd say. With poor Smallbone keeping order.'

It was past six o'clock. 'They've been in there half an hour now. Not knowing what on earth is up.'

'Mmmm.'

Richard toyed with his hat uneasily. *He's wondering how best to play this*, Posie thought.

But any such planning was interrupted by the sound of the doorbell. Three insistent pulls of the handle.

'That's too quick for any team of mine to have got here from the Yard. Better see who it is, as the butler is locked in, so to speak.'

Lovelace turned tail, and walked out into the empty white entrance hallway, Posie following. He drew back all the bolts on the front door in the vestibule and looked out quizzically.

A middle-aged man in blue overalls stood there, with a soft cloth cap on his head. He was holding a wad of forms in his hand. Behind him, in the road, where Dolly's driver had earlier parked up, was a van with royal-blue canvas sides and a big crest painted on it. Two other men, dressed similarly in blue overalls, stood by its side, aiming for a bit of shade in the hot street.

The man on the step tipped his hat at Lovelace. 'Awwright, Guv'nor?'

'What's your business, man?' Richard crossed his arms, askance. 'And I am not your "Guv'nor".'

'Awwright! Awwright! Me boss said he would telephone the lady of the 'ouse, sir. In advance, like. A Miss Sinne, is it? He called but there was no reply. Who *are* you, sir?'

'Never you mind. State your business. Rightaway.'

'Can I speak to Miss Sinne, sir?'

'That you cannot.'

'Awwright.' The man looked crestfallen. 'Looks like we'll be goin' home empty-handed, then, eh?'

'What are you on about, man?'

'We're 'ere to pick up a painting, sir.' The man rustled his paperwork, then read aloud: 'It's a LEM-PICK-A, says 'ere. It's called *Woman and Cat*. A painting! A big one, an' all!'

Posie came forward. 'A Tamara Lempicka, you say?'

The man consulted his wad of forms again. 'Yeah, that's right, Miss. We was supposed to be comin' tomorrow, all by previous arrangement. But, by chance, we finished early today and we were in this same area, London SW1. My boss said he'd telephone Miss Sinne, and if she said yes, we'd remove this 'ere painting today. Kill two birds with one stone, save us a repeat journey. Valuable daubs of paint 'ere, innit?'

'I wouldn't know,' said Richard coldly.

Posie tugged at her husband's sleeve. 'I think this is some arrangement with the National Portrait Gallery, a loan, or for some temporary exhibition. The secretary told me.'

She indicated with a nod behind her to where the huge, imposing painting was mounted on the wall so dramatically.

'I see.'

Richard thrust his hand out towards the man. 'You'll not be taking anything today, man, over Miss Sinne's dead body. She's not here to give me her consent to the taking away of her property. But you give me this paperwork right away and we'll see this arrangement is honoured. It means a return journey for you, I'm afraid, my man. Come back tomorrow at four-thirty, eh? And don't worry, I know your big boss, anyhow: Sir Charles John Holmes? If necessary, I'll speak to him; make sure you're not in any trouble, eh?'

The man in blue looked flabbergasted for a second or two, but then recovered himself and instantly stuffed the forms inside a creased-looking envelope, passing it over.

'Right you are, Guv'nor. See you again tomorrow. Who shall I say I handed this 'ere docket to?'

'The caretaker,' muttered Lovelace, closing the door smartly and bolting it again and then stuffing the envelope, contents unread, into his inside jacket pocket.

'Good grief! Whatever next?'

Back at the drawing-room door, Richard didn't hesitate any longer. He simply flung it open, Posie hot on his heels. But what hit them both on opening up the room was the intense heat and the overwhelming stench.

It was the perfume from earlier, but it was as if it was concentrated, a hundred times over.

Around the table people were wilting, and the Princess actually had her head on the table, as if she were asleep, and Smallbone was standing sentry by the door, red-faced and sweating.

Next to him were grouped the 'staff', standing by the wall: Jenks, who seemed to have very recently injured himself and had wrapped a bandage around his right hand, prodding at it constantly, and Lucy Reeble, at whose feet were the two black bags Posie had watched her packing up earlier.

'By Gad! Sergeant Smallbone! Are you mad, man? Open the sash windows! Posie, throw open the French doors! Get some air in here. Quick! People are almost half-dead. And what is that strange *smell*? Smallbone, what were you thinking?'

The young, usually tip-top Sergeant looked cowed, his small eyes glinting nervously below his rather feminine black curved brows, and he patted at his dark Brylcreemed hair nervously.

'I didn't want to risk anyone running away, sir. Or of anyone getting *in*, sir. We didn't know what was happening outside, or what the danger was exactly. Therefore, I thought it prudent to contain the situation.'

'Roast people, more like.'

Richard was taking command, introducing himself in deliberately played-down terms, referring to himself as simply an 'Inspector' from Scotland Yard, rather than as its Chief Commissioner.

He dipped his head in a small token bow and glanced about the table. 'Your Highness, your Graces, your Lordship and Ladyship, and ladies and gentlemen, I am afraid something highly irregular has happened here at the House of Sinne. But I'd like you all to have some refreshment. It seems necessary.'

He ordered Jenks to leave the room, to go and get coffee, tea, and water.

Then he turned to the still-immaculate secretary, Lucy, who looked like she might cry at any second, and he smiled gently.

'Could you see your way to getting sandwiches for us

all, Miss? If there isn't anything suitable on the premises, call to Harrods around the corner for it, please. On the double. We have some very eminent guests here. Then see your way to helping the butler set up the refreshments in that hallway, eh? We'll have a bit of a change of scene. Stretch our legs.'

'Of course, sir. I say! Is Miss Sinne okay? Has there been an accident? We saw the doctor with his big black bag. What's happened?'

'I am afraid she is *not* all right, Miss Reeble, but I will explain everything later to you. Now do as I ask, and things will be fine.'

The young girl gulped and almost ran out.

Lovelace turned back to face the room. 'I regret to inform you all that I have bad news. So, brace yourselves.'

And now Lovelace strode over and sat down in the seat which had earlier been occupied by Anouk Sinne, at the very head of the table.

Posie shimmied over to the seat she had previously occupied, at the other end of the table, and she noted that the air was flowing freely through the room again, and that every pair of eyes was fixed on her husband, alert faces turned, like sunflowers, towards him. Even Dolly's.

'Anouk Sinne is dead. She died sometime around four-thirty this afternoon.'

Amid the resounding gasps and exclamations, Lovelace explained succinctly that murder was suspected, and that every person in the room was now a potential suspect.

He hadn't pulled out his policeman's notebook, but he got out his cigarette tin, banged it hard on the table, as if to open a faulty catch, although Posie knew the tin's lid worked perfectly and that this was a technique her husband employed from time to time to effect casualness.

'It's almost certainly a case of death by hemlock. Poison.'

'Hemlock?' Posie heard Lorkinsson whisper, almost under his breath, but almost in terror. 'Oh, no! I knew this would end badly.'

What was he talking about? *What* would end badly?

But Posie was intently engaged in watching the varied sweep of other reactions to Lovelace's news: Dolly's surprise, verging on delight; a tight, frightened horror stealing over Hubert Pring's face, and, beside him, something like a scandalous indignation flushing his wife, Lady Clare's, pudgy powdered cheeks.

Posie stared at the Maharani of Gwilim and saw that the Princess looked furious, and not at all sad. *But then, why would she be?*

Posie saw that Mr Van Dusen was shaking his head in annoyance, his fingertips restlessly tapping the tabletop.

The French mother and son were different, however. Posie saw how the Duchesse, Maria de Poilac, wide-eyed and visibly shaken, had thrust her arm out instinctively and covered her son's long bronze fingers with her own. Squeezed them, as if for reassurance, in sympathy. But the Count shook his mother's grip off impatiently, irritated.

What on earth was their part in all this? Posie wondered.

Richard was reeling off the formalities: 'I am afraid that while I make initial enquiries, none of you can leave the House of Sinne. You will – as soon as possible – be escorted by one of my men to your home or to your place of accommodation, and again, special measures apply. You cannot leave that place until I give you the order. Until this mess is all cleared up. Understand?'

Gordy Lorkinsson called out anxiously: 'But I'm supposed to be giving a talk.' He clutched at his big leather gardening belt with all its tools and implements still in it. 'An important one.'

Lovelace gave a pained smile. 'One of my men will telephone and send your apologies. I am afraid that in a murder enquiry nothing is sacred. All of normal life, all normal commitments, go right out the window. You are Mr Lorkinsson, I presume? The famous gardener?'

A nod. An incredulous tremble of the big man's shoulders.

Tap, tap, tap, went Lovelace's cigarette case, on into the silence.

Posie knew Lovelace was letting those assembled have the opportunity to take over, to clamour in some way; to trip up and perhaps give away their own secrets. For there were many secrets here, that much was certain.

Then the silence in the drawing-room was broken.

'Say, Inspector!' Mr Van Dusen made an effort to smile, those neat white teeth all on display, dead eyes glinting.

Shark.

'Mr Van Dusen, isn't it?'

Tap, tap.

'Yeah. Well, say, this is darned awkward, Inspector. And what a dreadful shock, Miss Sinne dying on us like this, a real shame. But darn, you can't hold me. Nor the Princess either. We need to leave! We have a boat to catch, to the States, tonight! The *Pride of Boston.* Bound for New York. You can't hold us. Before today I'd never so much as *met* Anouk Sinne, although we'd been in correspondence, of course, over a shared commercial interest. Why on earth would I want to murder the woman? I'm telling you, she was worth much more to me alive than dead.'

Richard Lovelace splayed his hands apologetically. 'You can't leave, Mr Van Dusen, and that's the end of the matter.' But Richard was obviously enjoying himself enormously. He pulled out a cigarette, shook his match out, not hurrying over it.

The atmosphere in the room changed instantly, and the place was flooded with tangible relief as everyone scrambled for their smokes, desperate for the nicotine.

'Oh, thank Gawd! I was dyin' for a ciggie! It's been hours,' gasped Dolly, her Sobranie already clamped between her lips.

Next to her, Posie saw Gordy Lorkinsson fumble inside his gardener's belt, bring out a pouch of tobacco, Rizla cigarette papers, and start to roll a smoke with a trembling hand. 'My God! If Anouk could see us all, lighting cigarettes in her scentless house. Pah! What would she say?'

The young Count, Anatole, was playing with a packet of Turkish cigarettes, Mughals, which he'd pulled from his inside jacket pocket. He lit one of the long, thin, cigarettes calmly, languidly, as if he were in a club or lounge. He offered one to his mother, but she declined, her face ashen.

Posie saw that Hubert Pring had not taken out any smoking apparatus.

From his place opposite the American and the Princess, the Viscount seemed to suddenly be coming back to life, colour rushing into his handsome fair face, the image of a man who has been underwater fighting for life, and now emerges, gasping into the air, the light.

Anouk's death has floored him, thought Posie with certainty. *He's only just taking it all in.*

Hubert Pring stared at the American, his chin up, combatively. '*What* commercial interests are you talking about, Mr Van Dusen? And why on earth was Anouk worth anything to *you*?'

The way he said 'you' at the end of his sentence was delivered as an insult, and it reverberated deliberately around the room.

Lovelace was smoking, very casually. He watched this all play out as he'd hoped it would.

Van Dusen drew himself up, crossed his arms defensively across his fancy suit. 'I don't really see what business that is of *yours*, Viscount. But, if you must know, I'd been on at Anouk Sinne to create a perfume for my Department Stores – an exclusive, if you like – for *years* now. When she suddenly, out of the blue, agreed to it, a couple of weeks back, I dropped everything in my agenda to make it here on time to collect the stuff in person.'

He nodded his head in the direction of Priyanka Lashari, who was also smoking a very long, thin white cigarette, in a golden holder. 'I'd already signed up Her

Royal Highness, Princess Priyanka, for some other work at my stores and it seemed suddenly right to combine the two: that the Princess could advertise Anouk's perfume.'

The Princess didn't say anything. She blew a perfect smoke ring instead, focusing on the ceiling throughout.

Golly, this all went a bit beyond merely trotting samples back to the States, thought Posie, quite caught by surprise.

Everyone was staring intently at Hubert Pring, who had gone very red, his hands balled up into fists on the table, like he might punch someone, preferably Mr Van Dusen.

But he spoke in a quiet, restrained, measured voice, not turning at all to help his wife, who had erupted in a fit of wheezy coughing at his side. 'Am I to understand you correctly, sir? That you believe the new perfume, "The Ultimate Sin", is *yours*? For American purposes? For your shop?'

'Sure thing. For my *stores*. That's exactly what I mean.'

Pring was reaching into a battered brown leather briefcase now, drawing out documents, slapping them down on the table, heavy as a truth. He pushed them across quickly to Van Dusen, who gave a slight sneer.

'Say, what in heaven's name are these, Viscount?'

'Just about everything which proves that whatever else Anouk was in terms of a "nose", not a single thing in this place – including that new perfume – belongs to anyone but me. Anouk would have told me if she'd gone into a venture with a new business partner! Why ever wouldn't she? A big American deal would have suited us both. It would have been wonderful!'

He pointed at the documents which, so far, the American was deliberately ignoring.

'If you are interested, Mr Van Dusen, these are the house deeds, and the company documents, and the wages roster. And I think you will find that whatever deal Anouk entered into with you, it was made either under duress or by sheer mistake, or else, as I am inclined to believe, you are lying about this whole thing.'

Van Dusen's face was riven with a searing fury. 'Say, Viscount, who you calling a liar?'

He was now reaching into an inside pocket of his grey jacket, pulling out a few thick cream pages, held together with a fancy pin.

From where she was sitting Posie could see the snake-like symbol of the House of Sinne printed as a letterhead on the first page. The letter itself was handwritten in a looped, scrawling hand. From across the table, Pring's face went deathly white again.

This is the real deal, thought Posie. *Pring recognises Anouk's writing; knows the American millionaire is not bluffing.*

Carefully, methodically, Van Dusen flicked through the letter, and then moved on to a typed-up contract fixed to the back, and he jabbed his finger at it smugly.

'You are welcome to look at our contract, Viscount. I will simply draw your attention to these points. On receipt of the sum of three thousand pounds, Anouk Sinne would hand over all rights to her newly-created perfume "The Ultimate Sin". Exclusive rights would then belong to me. Me alone. This to include one hundred bottles of real, physical perfume, by way of samples, together with the exact formula, so my lab-rats can re-create the stuff back in the States.'

Van Dusen grinned with self-satisfaction. 'You will note the name "The Ultimate Sin" is to be retained, and Anouk's name as "nose" or perfumier is to be credited, but only in the small print. And the "House of Sinne" as an entity was *not* to be mentioned. Instead, the perfume will be produced with the "Van Dusen" name on the new bottle. The contract also stipulates the agreed "use" of Princess Priyanka. Note also that the contract specifies I will collect the perfume samples and its formula, in person. *Today*. Which is what I happen to be doing here. I was waiting in this darn room for Anouk Sinne to give me these things. I had no idea she had gone and died on us.'

He said this as if Anouk's death were some kind of inconvenience to be worked around, and he pushed the contract across to the Viscount, who was now absolutely deathly silent.

Even from her seat at the table, Posie could see that the contract had been signed in the same loopy scrawl – Anouk's presumably – as the covering letter.

A suffocating hush fell upon the room as Hubert Pring read the covering letter and then the contract.

The Duchesse de Poilac had let go of her son, and she was fingering the cheap-looking jagged heart locket at her throat, muttering in an undertone: 'I don't believe it! *Non, non.* Anouk would never treat Hubert in this way!'

In the background Posie heard the doorbell ringing again, a sharp insistent pull, and then she heard Doctor Poots' voice in the hallway, and the low, frantic buzzing energy of male voices. The Forensics team, she supposed.

At last Hubert Pring put down the paperwork and pushed it back to its owner. 'Might I ask,' he said in a very level manner, 'if that money has been paid out yet?'

'Of course it has,' drawled Van Dusen, beaming again, on the home straight. 'I wired the money as soon as that contract was signed. It should have cleared by now.'

Hubert Pring looked like a man watching his future drain away, but he kept a lid on his emotions, although anger underpinned every word.

'By Gad – if Anouk was here, I'd have serious words with her – what was she thinking? The deuce! A mere *three thousand* pounds! For two years' work? For all that investment? Wages? Materials? For my maintaining her "lifestyle" while she dreamt up her latest creation! A bally ridiculous amount, Mr Van Dusen. And you darn well know it. You must have been laughing! Did *you* suggest the sum, or did she? Anouk was never good with money, but not even she would undersell something so spectacularly!'

The Viscount shook his head in disbelief. 'I wonder if Anouk had lost her mind? Perhaps we can claim so in the Courts of Chancery? Why, running costs per year at the House of Sinne exceed three thousand pounds! This perfume was our livelihood! I, *we*, I mean, needed this perfume to work! But it makes no sense. Anouk was all gearing up towards the big luncheon party tomorrow, in London, at the Embassy Club, to officially launch the perfume to the public. Why on earth would she do *that* if she'd sold the perfume exclusively to you? To take back to America?'

Hubert Pring fished in his brown leather briefcase again and pulled out a smart black-and-gold embossed party invite. 'See?'

Van Dusen read the card and looked foxed for perhaps the first time.

He gnawed at his lip slightly, but only for a second.

'It pains me to say it, but you're right, Viscount. It doesn't make sense. I sure don't know anything about an event at the Embassy Club. The only "reveal" Miss Sinne insisted upon was here, today, for her friends and supporters. She said she owed them that. Wouldn't be swayed. I agreed, but it was one of my terms that *I* came along too, although Miss Sinne wasn't crazy keen on the idea. I think she wanted me to just pick up the products and leave! But I insisted on a newspaper covering the event, too, and again, Miss Sinne wasn't exactly jumping for joy about that, either. She only agreed if she had control over *who* the journalist was, and *when* the copy went out. I thought it would be good to get the publicity machine rolling, even just a small piece in the British press is better than nothing, and I hoped the photos could be sent on to New York, to whet people's appetites for the new scent; get a buzz going. The big publicity event was to be in New York, in around one month's time. Miss Sinne said she would definitely come over for it.'

But then the American's dark eyes seemed to clear, as if he'd hit upon something illuminating. 'Say, I'm guessing Miss Sinne ordered these invites before she decided to switch the deal and come over to me, hey? When did you receive this, Viscount?'

Pring shook his head helplessly. 'I don't know. Clare, dear? Do you know? When did we receive this Embassy invite?'

The woman at his side was visibly fuming. 'We got it about two weeks ago, I think. More or less. Oh, that wretched woman! I could quite cheerfully kill her myself if she wasn't already dead!'

Lovelace raised an eyebrow. 'Careful what you say, Lady Clare. Words are dangerous, and they form evidence. As does this little mound of paperwork about the perfume. So, gentlemen, hand it all over. My Sergeant here will keep it very carefully in our standard evidence bags: have no fear on that score.'

Reluctantly the men pushed their various documents towards Smallbone, who darted forward, happy to be of some use, buff-coloured evidence bags already at the ready.

Out of the corner of her eye, through one of the open sash windows, Posie saw several motor-cars draw up out on the road. All dark-blue, all police. Uniformed policemen, at least twenty of them, began to swarm out of the cars and mass on the pavement. This must be the team Fox had assembled for the search of the house.

Several of the police obviously had instructions to go straight around the side entrance, and Gordy Lorkinsson stared at the garden, his face ablaze with worry, watching the bobbies starting to push and weave through his roses, searching.

Beyond, down by the hedge, other men – from the Forensics team, or maybe Mortuary Men – were moving about furtively in the hot evening.

Posie turned back to the room, her thoughts buzzing.

What game had Anouk been playing here? For this double-dealing was surely the reason why the perfumier had specified to Van Dusen that he could not come out into the garden, either before, or after the event.

Anouk Sinne had wanted to keep Van Dusen and Hubert Pring apart. She had been afraid of their meeting and their common interest becoming known. And, until now, the dead woman had managed just that.

Had she really signed up to a financially-disadvantageous deal with this American millionaire who could so obviously have paid out much, much more? And why?

Why on earth had Anouk Sinne arranged and hosted such a complicated and risky 'reveal' at the House of Sinne today, for a perfume which she had – ostensibly – promised to two separate men? Both of whom would be in attendance.

And why had Anouk Sinne treated her faithful sponsor, Hubert Pring, so shoddily? Had something happened between them?

There was a sudden flutter of white at the doorway.

It was Lucy Reeble, looking anxious. Her blue eyes were red and puffy and she'd obviously been crying.

'Inspector, sir? Tea and coffee are laid out in the hallway. There was no need to call Harrods. We've put out some Quiche Lorraine, purchased from the French bakery in South Kensington, which was left over from Miss Sinne's supper last night. There is also some fruit, and enough fondant fancies for everyone. Miss Sinne adored them.' Lucy sniffed sadly. 'We kept boxes of them here, at all times. Madam liked the lemon ones, especially.'

Lucy Reeble looked like she might cry again, and to Posie she suddenly seemed very young.

'A veritable spread, then. Excellent. Couldn't be better.' Lovelace clapped his hands together, breaking things up: 'Lead the way, Miss Reeble, eh?'

But Lucy shook her head. 'Sir, I know now that Miss

Sinne is dead. Your Sergeant – Fox, is it? The blonde one? – told me and Jenks, the butler, in the kitchens.'

'Oh, yes? I was going to speak to you both in a minute. Well, it goes without saying, I'm very sorry about the loss of your employer.'

A small nod. 'I couldn't help overhearing, sir, waiting outside...'

'Go on.'

'Only that Mr Van Dusen was talking about collecting a hundred samples, wasn't he?'

'Yes. What of it?'

'Well, that's what I've been carefully packaging up, but Miss Sinne hadn't told me who they were for, or why. But they *must* be for him, mustn't they? Exactly one hundred. Miss Sinne told me they would be collected in person. That was all. My instructions were simply to enter the correct number for each sample on the docket for travel, for tax and excise purposes. There was a pink envelope too, which had to go in with the docket.'

The girl pointed at the two big black bags over by the wall. 'It's all in there. I just wanted you to know I had done my job, and that these should probably go to Mr Van Dusen.'

Lovelace raised an eyebrow. 'I admire your thoroughness, Miss Reeble. Very commendable. But just at the moment, *I* will be keeping hold of these so-called samples. And the docket, please?'

'Wait. It's here, sir.'

Lucy Reeble, a flush of pride at Lovelace's compliment still showing on her face, dug inside the topmost black bag, and brought out a big white envelope. She was about to pass it to Lovelace but Mr Van Dusen grabbed it from her, ripped at it impatiently. Lovelace raised his eyebrows again but sat calmly, the old waiting game.

Within the big envelope were the documents Posie had seen Lucy completing down in the small office, and Mr

Van Dusen sat nodding to himself, satisfied. There was a small pink envelope, too, with 'FORMULA' written on it in that now-familiar black looping writing. He grinned happily.

'Oh, well, say, *that's* a relief! That contract and my three thousand pounds are worthless without the knowledge of how to formulate the stuff in the future.'

Van Dusen ripped the pink envelope open and pulled out a piece of matching pink notepaper.

Everyone craned their necks to see how very complicated this perfume was: how exactly one of the most famous 'noses' in the industry had transcribed her peculiar masterpiece.

It seemed to Posie that Hubert Pring and the French Duchesse, more than anyone else, sat very still, almost frozen, riveted.

But now Archie Van Dusen was waving the pink paper angrily, turning to Lucy Reeble. 'Say, little lady! This has gotta be some crazy, sick kinda joke, huh? Or an accident? Is this your fault, Missie?'

The page was completely blank.

And Hubert Pring threw back his head and laughed.

* * * *

Eleven

'Ten minutes for refreshments!' called out Lovelace calmly, tapping at his watch.

'Mr Van Dusen, and Viscount Effington,' he looked pointedly at Hubert Pring, 'I would rather you keep apart, gentlemen. This perfume sale – or *non*-sale – will have to be addressed later. We are, right now, dealing with a probable murder. A crime, of the most heinous sort.'

'Of course,' agreed Hubert Pring, leading the way to the entrance hall. Lady Clare, her face a closed wall of anger, followed. She was still clutching at the black-and-gold Embassy luncheon invite and her fuchsia-coloured nails were scratching at the gilt embossing.

The butler, Jenks, had set up a trestle table in the entrance hall, and the group moved towards it slowly, as if in a trance.

Posie noticed that one of the newly-arrived uniformed policemen was guarding the door, and she presumed that all the exits were covered. She hung back a little, watching.

She saw how Lady Clare was loading up her plate with quiche and a stack of fondant fancies, how she was stepping aside, alone, eating as if she was famished.

Dolly was chatting in low, thankfully now sober, asides to the French Duchesse. Neither of them was eating anything at all, both smoking and drinking black coffee from cups without saucers.

The young Count, Anatole, was also smoking non-stop, standing apart, back very straight, staring out of one of the long sash windows onto the street.

Mr Van Dusen and the Princess had both been escorted by a newly reappeared Sergeant Fox to make telephone calls in the office, to sort out their hotel arrangements for the night, and to get their luggage taken off the steamer leaving Southampton.

Hubert Pring stood stalwartly at Richard's side. Pring's voice was low, but Posie caught the words.

'You can check the bank statements, of course. The company account and Anouk's personal account are both at Haggerty's, on the Strand. There's nothing to hide, I can assure you. Oh, and I can vouch for the staff, of course. I'll get their full references sent over to you.'

'That would be kind, my Lord.'

'But rest assured, they had nothing to do with this. You will remember, Chief Commissioner, one of my little projects is to find employment for wounded servicemen, and Jenks applied to that scheme. I must admit that I had a vested interest in getting Jenks a good position, although he's obviously not really top-notch butler material: he was my eldest son Peregrine's wingman in the Great War. Poor fella still has the shakes pretty badly, as you can see.'

'Ah, a wingman. Better than a guardian angel, eh?' said Lovelace pleasantly. 'I had one myself, in the trenches. Rhoddy Brown, lovely fella; he was my best man when I married Posie. I'd do what I could for him, too, if he ever needed it.'

'Quite. Well, Jenks is an honourable sort of chap and has plenty of medals, but medals don't put food on the table, do they? And he's got a young family to feed.'

Pring paused, frowning, anxious not to leave anything out.

'Oh, and there's old Tom Bowley, who left before any of this happened today. He's a plain old fellow who comes in for a couple of hours a day to do the garden. He was full-time at Kew Gardens for years, but his rheumatism is bad and he can't do it anymore. I was happy to pay him over-the-odds for his expertise.'

Hubert Pring galloped on, seemingly desperate to exonerate anyone who had anything to do with him from any guilt. 'And lastly, that lassie, Lucy Reeble, she's also from one of my projects: finding employment for children in Catholic educational institutions. *Her* name, together with several other girls' names, was passed to me about a year ago. It coincided with a time during which I had noticed Anouk was getting more and more erratic, so I thought someone to come and help on a daily basis, with administrative matters might be good. Lucy was the best of the bunch by far: loyal, practical, excellent references, too. Poor Anouk was always prickly, not wanting others to "get involved", and Lucy understood that from the beginning.'

'That's all very informative, my Lord.'

'As I said, I'll send you what I have. Needless to say, I'll keep paying their salaries until I can find them alternative employment.'

'Jolly decent of you, your Lordship. And what about Lorkinsson? Did he get paid too?'

'Good grief, no! I never paid him a bally cent. I can't even remember how he ended up here, actually. But it was a good deal: we got a lot of raw materials for free, and also his expertise. If the fella gets a few roses out of it for the odd talk, who am I to protest? Fella keeps himself to himself. *Foreign*, you know.'

'Mmmm.'

Through the white doorway came Sergeant Fox with Van Dusen on his heels, who took a coffee wordlessly from Lucy Reeble. The Princess sauntered in afterwards, frowning and walking to the very centre of the room. She started to look fixedly at the huge and unusual painting on the wall: the Tamara de Lempicka.

Posie took the opportunity to move towards Priyanka Lashari, whose gaze was still entirely held by the painting of Anouk Sinne.

'You like this painting, your Highness?' Posie smiled.

Princess Priyanka turned suddenly, as if woken violently from a bad dream. She stared at Posie. Up close the girl looked like she was made of some exquisite porcelain, but she was so heavily scented with Anouk Sinne's new perfume that it made Posie almost recoil. That last, strange lingering note was so wretchedly strong.

'Who *are* you, anyhow?' the Princess asked curtly, looking Posie up and down and making her feel like a bit of grizzle squashed underfoot.

'Actually, I'm with the police,' Posie said, almost truthfully. 'My name is Posie Parker.'

'A policewoman? Plainclothes?' Priyanka pointed one heavily-jewelled finger at Lady Clare Pring in her identical pink dress. 'Is *she* a policewoman, too? Is this your summer uniform?'

'No, that's just...'

'An unfortunate fashion "mistake"?' the Princess snapped. 'Yes. On both you, and her. Although *you* manage it slightly better. *Just*.'

Posie smiled on, ignoring the beautiful woman's stinging words. But then she saw the Princess was staring again at the painting. As if a riddle was etched there.

'A powerful painting, isn't it?'

'Mmmm. It's the cat I'm interested in. You have many here, like this one, in England? It is fashionable to have such a funny cat?'

Posie was thrown for a second, but shrugged. 'I don't think so. In fact, I've never actually seen one – not even *this* one – in real life before. I think they are extremely rare. This one is a bit of a mascot. Always seen about London with Miss Sinne. He's called Julius.'

'Yes, that's right.' The Princess stared for a bit more, then seemed to recover her manners. 'You want a coffee, Miss Parker?'

Posie didn't, but she followed the Princess anyway over to the trestle table, where the Princess was handed a cup poured from a coffee-urn by Jenks. Lucy Reeble was looking nervily at the whole operation, and you could see her willing the man not to drop coffee all over the Maharani in her immaculate white outfit. Posie was passed a similarly-shaking cup.

Princess Priyanka took a sip of the coffee and grimaced slightly: 'Where *is* that cat, anyhow? Julius?'

'I've no idea,' Posie replied truthfully. The coffee was lukewarm, too strong, and it made Posie think of her own secretary, Prudence, whose coffee-making skills left a lot to be desired.

'Lovely coffee,' Posie lied to Jenks, who was fussing with his none-too-clean-looking bandage.

In the street outside, a motorcar's skidding wheels were suddenly heard tearing around a corner, and this proved a convenient distraction for everyone.

It was a very dark red motor which had pulled up, and a smartly-dressed driver in burgundy stepped out with a matching peaked cap. He reached into the back seat and took out a small wicker basket.

Posie followed the Princess to the open window, where she placed herself familiarly right next to the Count. Posie hung back.

The Princess seemed to be uttering a few words to Anatole, but the words were indistinct – *was she speaking French?* – and the young man wasn't speaking a word in reply, just smoking, his back rigidly tense. He said something at last, then turned his face away from the stunning woman at his side, stuck his chin up, defiant in his rebuffing of her.

Posie watched all of this.

The man outside with the burgundy peaked cap checked a piece of paper, then ran up the steps to Number 11, ringing the bell, all the while holding the basket warily away from him.

The policeman on guard went out onto the steps to meet the visitor.

Posie saw how Gordy Lorkinsson, smoking another one of his home-rolled cigarettes, was at the next long sash window, also focusing on the motorcar. The cigarette he was smoking seemed peculiarly strong, almost peaty in its intensity.

The Princess, rejected by the Count, and slightly flushed with embarrassment, had moved across to Lorkinsson's window, and Posie darted forward to stand next to the young Count, listening intently to the conversation starting up at the next window.

She heard the Princess laugh, joke a little, watched her pluck at the Icelander's creased linen sleeve.

'I left my cigarettes in that awfully hot room. I'm desperate for a puff, would you mind awfully if I took yours from you?'

The Princess was flirting so extraordinarily that Gordy Lorkinsson was obviously taken aback, and simply handed his half-smoked cigarette across, more out of surprise than any desire.

'Er, yes, of course, your Highness.'

'Thank you.'

The Princess was chattering away loudly between inhaling and exhaling puffs of his smoke, all in that extraordinary accent, which, when heard over time, certainly sounded French.

'A terrible business, all of this. Very unusual. Was that perfume woman a friend of yours? Everything here seems so topsy-turvy. And the policewomen, why are they dressed in those awful cheap-looking pink dresses?'

All the while the Princess talked, Gordy Lorkinsson

had been playing nervously with a strange-looking black bottle on the window-ledge – smoked glass with a black liquid within it, and full of little sharp-ended sticks – and suddenly Posie realised that *this* was the focus of the smell she had thought was his cigarette. This was the carbon scent that had been pointed out earlier as being the only perfume permissible in the place.

Gordy Lorkinsson's big hands played with the tiny sticks and Posie couldn't hear any more of their conversation.

'*Mon Dieu!* That woman is very dreadful,' muttered the young Count at Posie's side, directly into her ear.

'Not a real sophisticated woman at all. Not like some others.' He looked down at Posie appreciatively for a second too long before looking out of the window again, taking a drag on his Mughal.

'And she is a Princess! *C'est incroyable!* Unbelievable, huh? I have seen pictures and even *moving* pictures of her, and she is like a dream come true in those pictures. A potential screen goddess! I was ready to idolise her. But not anymore. Goddesses must be good, no? I think that those who loved her were taken for fools.'

He came even closer to Posie, lowered his voice again. 'You know, I have heard stories that she has not acted like a Princess at all: that she is a criminal. In fact, I could not bear her at my side. It was like a poison. Especially with that smell on her of Anouk's. Oh, *Mon Dieu*! The scent of death, ah?'

Posie turned in surprise and looked up into those endlessly deep green-grey eyes of his, which burned down at her with an intensity she had not expected.

The boy, for he was much younger up close than she had at first thought, gave off an energy which buzzed of new ideas and daring courage.

If I was younger, I would have fallen badly in love with him, thought Posie with a smidgen of surprise.

I used to love bad boys. Boys who never promised anything except the here and now.

Although I've never cared a fig for titles.

But this boy suddenly made Posie feel sad, and old: this boy who had been too young to fight in the Great War, too young to be hurt by it all. What would his life, and all his bravura, be *for*?

Another generation is coming, Posie realised with a jolt. *And this is it.*

Another generation pushing up roots behind the bands of shallow fools who masquerade as Bright Young Things and throw themselves around town with such nihilistic abandon.

Posie forced herself to concentrate, to press the Count for more information. 'The scent of death, Count Anatole? What do you mean?'

She remembered Gordy Lorkinsson's similar words earlier about the new perfume, out in the garden. What did these two men know which she did not?

And what had the Count meant about the Princess? How had he seen her in moving pictures when she hadn't yet starred in any movies?

'Do you know the Princess, your Grace? From somewhere else? Is she French, as well as Indian?'

But just then the uniformed bobby came back into the room, carrying the basket.

'It's the driver from the local Veterinary Surgery,' he explained to Lovelace, while everyone listened in. The bobby set the basket down on the floor rather gingerly. 'And this, apparently, is Julius, who has been staying with them.'

The small rattan cat basket was emblazoned with the name 'JULIUS' on its top, the letters picked out in sparkly stones. The basket looked much scratched and gnawed at, and everyone was staring at the wire door to the basket, where a pair of blue eyes could be seen, gleaming angrily.

'The fella from the vets says he was promised money,' said the bobby, sourly. 'He's waiting for payment outside.'

'Oh!' A flustered Lucy Reeble almost dropped the

teapot she was holding. 'Of course. Miss Sinne had told me. Yes, I had the money all set up; it's in an envelope on the office desk.'

'Let me go, Miss Reeble,' said Jenks quickly, anxiously, and he limped off down the tiled corridor. Meanwhile, Lucy had gone over to the basket and was unlatching it, speaking in a smooth, calm voice.

'Here, kitty-kitty! Here, kitty-kitty! Welcome home. Are you feeling better?' Then much quieter, breathlessly almost: 'I'm afraid your mummy is no longer here to look after you. But you'd better get out.'

The secretary stood back quickly, as if unleashing a lion, giving the cat space to walk out of its basket.

Everyone was watching the cat, and the creature really was extraordinary.

Its ears were huge and pointed, much bigger than a normal housecat; his eyes were like blazing blue opals; his hairless skin was a lustrous sheeny pink, full of wrinkles, and his long hairless tail was held proudly erect.

The cat seemed fearless, but as the butler crossed the hallway jerkily with an envelope in his hand, the cat hissed in the man's direction, spitting and grimacing, and Jenks almost ran.

The Princess, still next to Lorkinsson, was staring at Julius, and then staring from the painting of the cat back to the real thing, and then she was looking at the cat basket with its gaudy letters, and she was throwing a glance out of the window, where the driver was once more getting into his red motor.

'Perhaps I was wrong,' Posie heard the Princess mutter.

The cat stalked its way through the room, and Posie watched as it went up to Dolly, who was blowing an immaculate smoke ring, looking bored out of her mind.

People had lost interest in Julius by now, and Posie heard normal conversation resume. Jenks and Lucy Reeble were muttering together in low voices, dashing about collecting up cups, taking away the empty cat basket.

Doctor Poots was coming up the hallway, holding onto some sort of report which he was discussing with one of his Forensics team.

Posie also heard Richard's voice, clipped, giving instructions.

'Smallbone, get back to the Yard and get every bit of information possible on our murder victim herself. Oh, I nearly forgot! Hubert Pring's wife, Lady Clare, has asked us to call the Embassy Club and to cancel tomorrow's luncheon. Can you do that? Apparently, the club itself sent out the invitations – she ascertained that from Lucy Reeble – so ask them for the full guest list and then we will have to telephone each and every one and fob the guests off with some untruth. We are not going to let this story break yet.'

Lovelace made an exasperated groaning noise. 'Oh, and talking of stories, Sergeant Fox, get onto Sam Stubbs at the *Associated Press*. Tell him to hold fire on any publication: wave the threat of criminal prosecution over him if he protests. And then, Sergeant, think about the blackmail pick-up again. *You* were at Victoria earlier, lad. See if we can get any other witnesses to come forward, eh?'

'I've got better than that, sir. I hadn't got around to telling you or Miss Parker yet, but…'

But the rest was drowned out by Dolly's sudden and heartfelt exclamations of surprise.

'Coo-ee! Lord love a duck! Look at this little baldy cat!'

The eerie-looking cat had obviously decided it was going to make a special friend of Dolly and was rubbing itself up against her silk stockings. Dolly, who was not a cat person, or an animal person at all, picked up Julius and it nuzzled into her yellow dress, like a strange type of oversized, spooky baby.

'Well, I never! I reckon he's taken a right shine to me! Maria, *regarde moi*! *Le petit chat doux!* It seems he has very good taste!'

The Duchesse, at Dolly's side, laughed. But it was the Princess whose beautiful, exotic voice now cut through the room.

Priyanka was pointing slightly accusingly at the creature in Dolly's arms. 'You know, something is odd here. With this cat, you know. I recognise what I am seeing here . . .'

But whatever it was that she had recognised, or which was odd, was never voiced. For suddenly the Princess screamed, howled.

'Ow! Oh! I've been stung! In the neck! Oh! How it hurts!'

Beside her Posie heard Count Anatole de Poilac snort in derision, and Gordy Lorkinsson ran over. 'Can I help, your Highness?'

The Maharani was raising her hands to her slender neck, delving under glossy pearls and gold chains.

She slapped at her neck on the right-hand side and drew her hand away, and sure enough, there was a patch of blood there.

'What kind of English insect does this?' Priyanka almost spat. 'A bee? A wasp? A…'

But these words were lost to eternity, because all the light in those beautiful amber eyes suddenly died and went dim, and the Princess crashed to the ground.

A swirling, whirling spiral of white linen and the most expensive of jewels, all in a heap on the cold, cold floor.

****

Twelve

They were all immediately herded back inside that stuffy, perfumed room again.

It felt claustrophobic.

Although they were not quite sure how badly ill the Princess was, things didn't seem to be going well tonight.

Doctor Poots was with the Princess, and they all waited for news, restlessly, fearfully.

Richard Lovelace paced the room nearest the French doors, clicking his knuckles continuously, while Fox and Smallbone loitered near the door, standing, their long task-lists temporarily abandoned.

Dolly sat on a chair languidly, the cat in her lap. She smoked one cigarette after another. The two House of Sinne staff members sat together, watchful, scared, whispering occasionally.

Everyone else drank tea. All except Mr Van Dusen, who sat with his head in his hands, elbows on the table, very much alone.

Lovelace was so much on edge that every creak and footfall around the house had him jolt like a marionette. Posie hated watching him like this.

Her stomach too was a mass of dreadful nerves, butterflies flitting about in a sick sort of dance. She was, like the others, desperate to leave, to run home to her babies in Museum Chambers, right now probably being bathed and dressed for bed by Masha the Housekeeper.

Gordy Lorkinsson stared out miserably as all his blooms were washed with the clear silver of the Chelsea seven o'clock twilight.

Lovelace suddenly marched up to his men, a decision made. 'Smallbone, get on with the tasks I gave you. Whatever the outcome with the Princess we need you to make those urgent calls. Go now.'

'Right, sir.'

'And Fox? We'll start labelling up these ruddy black bags. You've got evidence forms on you, I take it?'

'Of course, sir.'

Taking comfort in doing something routine and practical to pass the time, Lovelace walked over to the two black bags with the perfume samples inside and kicked gently at one.

'We'll fill in one evidence form for each black bag and we'll state it applies to all the contents. But we'd better check the contents, eh, Sergeant? We need to check the perfume is exactly that. One bottle of the stuff will suffice.'

Everyone turned in their chairs to watch Sergeant Fox, kneeling on the floor, wrestling with a zipper. Eventually he had a black bag opened, and Posie could see the fifty perfumes packed neatly and carefully, beautiful inside their turquoise boxes. Fox counted them carefully.

'Fifty exactly, sir.' Fox then took a box out at random, nodding at Lovelace, who was completing the evidence form himself.

Fox unwrapped the grosgrain ribbon and opened the lid. Inside was a small bottle.

'I confirm this is a two-thirds of a fluid ounce bottle of the perfume, sir. It's sealed with a blob of wax, with the impression of the House of Sinne and the snake of their logo stamped into the wax.'

Fox broke the seal and pulled off the glass stopper. It made its resounding, pleasing little 'plop' as he did so. He bent his lean, closely-cropped blonde head right down, took a good long sniff. Pulled a slight face and shrugged.

'It takes a good minute, you know,' drawled Van Dusen. 'That's the magic. It steals up on you. We were all sitting here for a few moments before we smelt anything at all, and then it hit us. It was magnificent.'

'Actually, I think it is a scent you need to apply to your person, or at least splash about,' advised the French Duchesse from her side of the table. 'In its little bottle it just sits and sulks, *n'est-ce pas*? It needs movement.'

'Quite right, Maria,' said Hubert Pring in agreement. 'You have always been so in tune with Anouk's perfumes, so appreciative. No wonder she counted you as one of her best friends.'

The French woman wiped a tear from her eye. 'Thank you, Hubert. And what a rock you have been…'

Fox scowled slightly, but then obediently splashed the perfume onto himself, on his wrists. He did it warily, as if he might burn himself.

'Nope,' he said, after perhaps half a minute. 'Nothing. I'll shake the bottle and splash it around again. Just in case.'

He smelt the perfume on his wrist, licked at it, then shook the bottle again, and poured almost the whole bottle out over the floor.

'Fox? What on *earth*…?' Lovelace was outraged, but not as much as Van Dusen, who was now up on his feet.

'What in hell's name are you doin', Sergeant? That is worth a good deal of money. Heck, it's *mine*.'

But Fox was ripping open another turquoise box, as quickly as he could, as if he had lost his mind. He pulled out another bottle, broke the seal, pulled off the stopper, shook the liquid all about him, then poured it on the floor again.

Everyone was now up on their feet, open-mouthed, shocked.

Lucy Reeble had her hand clapped over her mouth, her employer's precious work lying in worthless puddles on the floor.

Fox shrugged. 'It's just water, sir. I swear on my life. On all I hold dear. Let's get the Forensics lads to test it, but there's nothing in here which hasn't come straight out of a tap.'

Lovelace was almost barking at Lucy Reeble, asking her if she had helped Miss Sinne to fill the bottles up with water.

And Lucy Reeble was on the edge of tears again. 'I was never given access to the laboratory, sir. *Never*. The bottles were given to me like that, already sealed up. Miss Sinne kept the special wax seal with the snake on it in her laboratory, sir, so I couldn't have switched the real perfume for water myself, either. Not without breaking the seals, could I?'

Hubert Pring was calling out calmly, 'Relax, Lucy: no-one is accusing you of anything. Are they, Lovelace?'

'That's right, my Lord. Just seeking information. That's all.'

Posie stared on in bewilderment.

Water? Like those sample bottles on Anouk's presentation shelf, so fancily lit up? So had Anouk Sinne's bottle which was used at the 'reveal' today been the *only* sample of the new perfume in existence?

Surely not. But where were the other bottles?

She thought suddenly of her own present, the bottle Anouk had given to her. That too must be water.

Posie remembered the perfumier telling her not to try and open it, to save it for later. No wonder!

It had been an empty present. A trick which couldn't yet be unveiled.

Was this case all about tricks, then? Everything in layers and layers of wrappings of make-believe?

So far there had been water dressed as perfume, and

empty pages dressed as perfume formulas. So, what did that make the blackmail delivery of a thousand pounds today?

Into the uncomfortable silence of the room came the sudden wildly inappropriate sound of laughter. Turning, Posie saw it was Lady Clare Pring, and tears were running down her face.

'What's so funny, Viscountess?' demanded Mr Van Dusen angrily.

Lady Clare laughed again, rather spitefully.

'You know what? Anouk Sinne was never my favourite person in the world, but I can actually say, hand on heart, that I admire her style. She managed to get *you* to come all the way over from America, and to pay her three thousand pounds, which is not a small amount, for *nothing*! For a formula which is a blank page, and for perfume which is mere water. It's perfect! Like the "Emperor's New Clothes"! It jolly well serves you right, too. For thinking you could cross my husband and take away any hard-earned profits. *Our* profits.'

Lovelace was just about to intervene, when there was a soft knock upon the door, and Doctor Poots stuck his head around it.

'Chief Commissioner, out here please, a matter of urgency. *Now*.'

And then Posie, and pretty much the rest of the room, knew the Princess was dead.

Murdered, most likely.

Because what, really, were the chances of two healthy, not-old women dropping dead at the House of Sinne today?

Posie tried to stay calm. She was staring down to the garden again, thinking of the out-of-place peacock, who was nowhere to be seen.

What was it the Princess had said earlier on the steps? '*The peacock is unlucky, associated with death. With a life taken suddenly, too soon.*'

Well, certainly the lonesome peacock – wherever it now was – seemed to have been a sort of portent of the worst sort today.

It had been unlucky in the extreme.

* * * *

Thirteen

When Lovelace returned, it felt like more than ten minutes had elapsed. Ten minutes of total silence.

He came into the room and his stance was of a man tired of the news he must bear.

He was carrying two waxed brown evidence bags, and he slapped them down on the oval table, together with a policeman's notebook in a leather casing, and then he threw himself hopelessly into his chair.

Fox slunk at the doorway.

Posie felt she could almost read the Sergeant's mind: *Double murder, not good.*

Double high-profile murder, even worse.

Richard cleared his throat. 'I regret to inform you all that the Princess Priyanka of Gwilim is dead. I am informed she died almost instantly, so that is, at least, some consolation.'

It felt as if all the air in the room had been sucked out, and no-one dared breathe, let alone gasp. Maria de Poilac wiped away a silent tear from her eye.

'Someone's gonna pay for this accident,' Archie Van Dusen barked, and he opened his mouth again to start up a torrent of questions, but Richard shook his head smartly.

'I am afraid, Mr Van Dusen, this was no accidental

tragedy. We all heard the Princess complain of a bee sting to the neck, but I am afraid she was killed very deliberately, with a murder weapon.'

Astounded looks followed Lovelace's every move, as he reached out for an evidence bag and opened the flap.

Lovelace took his own handkerchief and with it he shook out a thin bamboo twig about the length of a pencil, but much slimmer, the girth of a knitting-needle. One end was very, very sharp, the other blunt-ended.

'The deuce! What the devil *is* that?' asked Hubert Pring, askance. 'Something from India? From Gwilim?'

Lovelace gave a weary smile. 'No, your Grace. It is from this very house. I believe it is House of Sinne standard stock, your Lordship. A product your company sells.'

'I don't recognise it at all!'

'Well, in the manner it was used it is a poison dart, my Lord. Our murder weapon. In daily life, I believe it is a perfectly harmless item of home decoration: it sits with about twenty such identical sticks in a glass contraption with a soft foam insert, loaded up with perfume-oil. Some sort of carbon scent?'

'Oh!' Lucy Reeble exclaimed, almost in relief. 'Yes. It's from the diffuser in the hallway. They sell in great numbers, actually. But…' The secretary's pale face was pleading. 'The bamboo sticks are never stored upright like that; it would be very dangerous. The pointed ends are designed to stick into the sponge, to adhere better.'

'Well, today they stuck in a Princess's neck. And she might have survived, if perfume had been the only thing this little beggar had been infused with. But unfortunately, the thing is soaked – literally doused – in poison. As were *all* of the wooden spikes in that glass pot. The perfume-oil was completely toxic, and they had absorbed it all. Twenty dangerous weapons, just sitting there, ready to go.'

The Duchesse de Poilac clapped her hand to her mouth. '*Sacre bleu! Mais pourquoi?* Why? What poison was used? And why was the Princess targeted like this?'

Beside her, her son Anatole pulled out his Mughals again.

He gave a scoff as he lit up. 'I expect there are hundreds of reasons the Princess could have been targeted, *Maman*,' he said slowly, carefully. 'The Maharani of Gwilim was a totally detestable woman with no morals at all. I am thinking she had many enemies, but many of them, like her, are now dead.'

Lovelace stared at the Count in surprise. 'If you have any concrete information, your Grace, perhaps you could share it with me. Or is this merely idle gossip you have heard? Was the Princess known to you?'

Anatole shrugged, looked away. 'I hear things. As do most people in my circle of friends. And was she known to me? Well, I had no idea she was going to be attending today. We were not on friendly terms, *non*.'

Hubert Pring was shaking his head. 'It doesn't make sense, Chief Commissioner. None of us here knew the Princess. Most of us didn't even know she was coming here today. My wife and I certainly had no idea!'

'Hmmm. Well, that's as maybe, my Lord. But Doctor Poots has examined the body and feels it was a deliberate aim. A bally good shot. Unfortunately, the perfume-oil which coats these sticks means that anyone who touches them leaves no fingerprints: like a ghost. Which is jolly handy when you want to go undetected.'

Lovelace made a show of putting the pointed bamboo stick away, folding the handkerchief slowly. Posie wondered what might be in the next evidence bag.

'We do not yet know the reason the Princess was killed. We are aware of the Princess's tragic background in India, and also, as Count Anatole has alluded to, there are indeed some rather unpleasant rumours beginning to circulate about her.'

Posie saw a shadow cross Van Dusen's face, then saw him shrug it away. Whatever those murky stories were which concerned Princess Priyanka, they were no longer his concern.

Posie remembered his harsh words to the Princess earlier, when he'd been alone with the Princess in the drawing-room. '*You'll need some fame behind you...if you want to paper over the cracks of your life so far.*'

Had there been too much 'papering' on the horizon and not enough reward?

Was the beautiful Princess becoming not just an asset but rather a lead weight about Mr Van Dusen's neck? Had Alfie Van Dusen killed the Princess? Or organised for someone else to have done so?

Because this certainly seemed to have been a professional job.

But how was it possible to kill a prominent woman in a room full of people, with a poison dart? Could it have been someone standing outside that open window? Shooting in? That driver with the burgundy cap, perhaps? A fake 'placed' policeman? Posie's mind started that old mad clamour of questions all over again.

She struggled to remember the timing and place of everyone in the entrance hallway at the moment the Princess fell. It had been a chaos, with that cat stalking through; the open window with gritty London air coming in; the peculiarly alluring young Count at her side; the Princess flirting with Gordy Lorkinsson who had been toying with those very sticks.

'Oh! Golly, I say!'

Lovelace looked over. 'Posie?'

'Nothing.'

No, she wouldn't give Lorkinsson away. Not yet. The sight of him playing with those sticks...

'Oh? Well, as I was saying, we don't know the *reason* the Princess was killed. But we have our suspicions – and evidence, in fact – as to *who* exactly here did the killing. And the killing of Anouk Sinne.'

A murderer among them? Here?

Everyone gasped.

'Yes,' continued Richard calmly. 'Once we have made our arrest you must all give your fingerprints, but then you are free to go. Forensics have done a wonderful job. I heard everything when I stepped out of the room. They have confirmed that Anouk Sinne died of hemlock poisoning, but more specifically, hemlock from *this very garden*. They have also conducted an initial search of Miss Sinne's perfume laboratory, and interestingly, they have discovered that hemlock was being distilled there, although whatever was distilled has long since gone.'

Hubert Pring looked over at his staff, at Lorkinsson, including them all in his next statement: 'I speak for all of the staff here when I say that Anouk never let anyone in to her laboratory. Not a soul. She was famous for it. It follows that none of us could have got in and taken distilled hemlock. I paid for the special door to be installed, from the Sargent & Greenleaf Safe company, at enormous expense.'

Lovelace smiled. 'So, my Lord, are you suggesting that Anouk Sinne distilled the hemlock to use on herself? That she committed suicide? Because what else was she using it for?'

Hubert Pring shrugged, beaten.

Gordy Lorkinsson shook his head in disbelief. 'Anouk would *never* have killed herself,' he said with certainty. 'Not at all. But I must tell you something else, Inspector. Something important.'

Everyone turned and stared.

'Go on,' commanded Lovelace patiently. 'Please.'

'Well, I think I am right in saying that Anouk was attempting to get this latest perfume right for ages, wasn't she, Viscount Effington?' Here the Icelander looked to Hubert Pring for confirmation.

'That's right, Lorkinsson.'

'And while I am a humble gardener, and no expert on perfumes, or hemlock, I know that what I smelt today was pure hemlock. Anouk had distilled hemlock and used it as her base note for the new perfume. I know it *can* be done; the smallest amount of hemlock can temper sweetness, add a sourness. But, in my humble opinion, this was overkill. Anouk had added far, far, too much. It was a kind of shocking fragrance, and one which went too far: too close to the bone.'

Posie suddenly understood the Icelander's comments about '*the scent of death*'.

She saw how everyone else in the room looked surprised, and uncomfortable too.

All except the French mother and son. Well, Count Anatole had obviously known what the scent was, hadn't he? He'd used the same damning words about that perfume earlier, on the skin of the Princess as she stood next to him in the hallway.

But how had he known what the scent was, exactly?

Perhaps his mother, with her supposed gardening wisdom, had shared that information with him? *And did their knowledge matter, anyhow?*

Lovelace had been noting down Lorkinsson's explanation.

'Very useful information. I must say, Mr Lorkinsson, that contrary to your protestations, you do seem very well-read on the subject of hemlock. Why is this?'

The Icelander splayed his hands. 'What can I say? In my profession it is important to know what is poisonous and what is not. Much of that knowledge is based on scent. I attended a Horticultural College, too: we learnt it there, of course. And this is not secret knowledge, after all.'

Lovelace opened the second waxy evidence bag and brought out a single sheet of paper. From Posie's seat it looked nothing special: a thin sheet covered in a child's red dense scribble of wax crayon. *What on earth was it?*

'I said we do not know why Princess Priyanka had to die, but we believe we know why Anouk Sinne died. And *this* is the evidence. Anouk Sinne seems to have been one of those individuals who leaves virtually no documents behind them. It's possible she burnt everything quite recently. But one of our lads had a lucky break: noticed an empty block of writing paper and thought he would see if he could "lift" an impression off the block with wax crayon, of what was last written there. And he struck gold.'

Lovelace waved the red scribbled page. 'This is a letter dated with today's date from Anouk Sinne to *you*, Mr Gordy Lorkinsson. Telling you that your time and skills in this garden at the House of Sinne were no longer required. She says that things are changing here. Your last day in the garden is listed as being today.'

'*Today?*'

Posie turned to look at the Icelander. He stared down at the table, confused and utterly mute.

Gordy Lorkinsson hadn't mentioned any kind of dismissal in their chat by the roses earlier. Posie looked over at Hubert Pring but this was obviously unexpected news to him too.

Lovelace replaced the red-crayoned evidence. 'I assume you got this letter this morning, Mr Lorkinsson? Probably sent first post, eh? At your flat in...' He checked his notebook. 'Chelsea Cloisters, isn't it?'

The Icelander looked up, blue eyes burning with anger. 'That is where I live, yes. But no, I didn't get that letter, Inspector. If it arrived at my flat today, I wouldn't have got it, as I left at dawn and I haven't yet been home. The contents are new to me. But I must confess I am not surprised. I knew something big was coming; I could sense it.'

'I propose to you that you knew your garden here would soon be forbidden to you, and you had a big row with Miss Sinne about it. You decided to poison her with hemlock. A cruel death in retaliation for Miss Sinne's cruel action in banning you from the garden. Perhaps you slipped it in a coffee, or water? And then, later today, Princess Priyanka found out about this, or guessed at the truth? She confronted you with it, perhaps when you two stood smoking together by the window? Why else would she have chosen to speak to *you*? You were nothing to her! And there's more: you were actually observed playing with the diffuser and its sticks. One of my lads at the door saw you. Presumably there came a moment when you realised you had to kill the Princess at your side, to stop her from blabbing about your first murderous crime.'

Gordy's face was pale under his sun-burn. 'You can't be *serious*? This is mad! You want to accuse me of murder based on this one copy of a letter I haven't yet read? Which might not have arrived? Which might, after all, not have been sent? Because I was seen holding some sticks from a perfume pot for a couple of seconds?'

Even Posie, loyal as she was to darling Richard, felt the Icelander had a point. The case, and the evidence, seemed based on dangerously slim pickings.

'I have more,' said Richard Lovelace, smugly assured.

'Our evidence is *not* just this letter. The poison in the diffuser with the sticks was actually industrial-strength pesticide. Sodium arsenate in liquid form. In fact, it's the exact same stuff we have found in your shed here, in a big cannister. You use it for your roses, don't you, Mr Lorkinsson? To control pests?'

'Why yes, but…'

Richard sailed on: 'You also usually carry some with you, don't you? In a small metal atomiser around your belt? You will release that belt to me now, sir, as formal evidence. The murder of the Princess was ingenious, sir, but hardly difficult. You simply had to tip the contents of that atomiser into the diffuser while everyone was distracted with the cat.'

'But this is ridiculous!' yelled Lorkinsson. 'Sodium

arsenate for gardeners is available at every pharmacy in London! And as for my shed, it's never locked, so that Tom Bowley can go in and use the equipment freely. It's possible that *anyone* could have got in and taken some of the sodium arsenate!'

Lovelace raised an eyebrow, disbelieving. 'Possible, yes. Likely, no. Fox, do what you need to.'

Several incredulous gasps ran around the table, and Posie felt a slight flush of shame creep across her face at Richard's heavy-handedness. Especially as one of the gasps of outrage had come from Clare Pring, a complete non-detective if ever there was one, who also seemed to think that Richard was way off the mark here.

And then Gordy Lorkinsson, that big man, that force of nature, who belonged so very much to the outside, was being handcuffed and taken away, his belt with the atomiser on it being pulled from him. Everyone at the table stayed deadly quiet – even Archie Van Dusen.

And Posie, for the first time in their marriage, felt a terrible sense of disloyalty as a wife towards Richard Lovelace, because her professional instincts told her that her husband was wrong.

All wrong.

And now there were two deaths to avenge and the wrong man nabbed for both, and Posie would have to sort this out all alone.

Well, she said to herself as she watched the others teem out of the room, *alone was fine.*

In fact, there was nothing new there.

* * * *

PART THREE

The Lost Story of Hattie Synnes

Fourteen

It was almost eight o'clock as they sped homewards in the big, stuffy police car. Well, not quite homewards exactly.

Big Ben, his old face a slanting bronze shimmery mass of evening sunshine, was about to strike the hour as they drove through Parliament Square.

They had to stop at a traffic light, and Posie looked out. The grass of the big square was bleached a blonde, frizzled honey-colour, and was in desperate need of the rain which, like in the rest of the country, never seemed to come.

There were fewer protesters than usual, but the odd motley crowd of injured ex-soldiers remained, with big, time-worn banners declaring: 'HELP NEEDED FOR HEROES!' and 'MORE JOBS! LESS TALK!'

Newspaper boys were still walking up and down, despite the late hour, laden with their sandwich boards, which screamed: 'DIBBLES BRIDGE DISASTER LATEST!'

This was a sad story from just a few days ago, when a tourist bus on route to Bolton Abbey in Yorkshire, a popular sightseeing spot, had sped down a steep hill and toppled off the Dibbles Bridge. Many tourists had been killed and the figure was growing daily. It was a holiday-disaster scenario which had gripped the nation somewhat morbidly, but to be fair, there was little other news.

Black-bowler-hatted men in hot, heavy dark suits, heads down, newspapers rolled under their arms, were still coming out like hundreds of black ants from the nearby government buildings, scurrying along the pavements, anxious to get home, aiming for buses and Underground stations.

Here was the thrill of it all. Busyness, action, life.

London.

Posie rolled the window down further, sniffed the air, on which floated the scent of frying fritters.

Her stomach growled noisily.

Beyond the balustrade was Westminster Bridge, and that old woman of mischief again, the light-flecked River Thames, here as in Chelsea, blue-green and glittering and unknowable as the sea.

The car lurched off again and they drove along the Embankment, right past the huge red-brick crenelated monstrosity which housed the country's Police Headquarters, New Scotland Yard, and Posie thought suddenly, sharply, of Gordy Lorkinsson, in one of those small, dark, bleach-scented cells.

Not a flower in sight, let alone a tea-rose.

Ahead, in the front passenger seat, Fox directed the police driver to stop, and then he jumped out on the pavement, talking to Lovelace through the open window.

'I'll check on where we've got to, sir.'

'Jolly good, lad. Telephone to Sam Stubbs and get him to develop his photographs from earlier, and bring them along to us, tonight. Tell him to come at nine. You too.'

Sitting between Posie and Richard Lovelace on the back seat was Dolly, and she was still clutching the Sphynx cat, Julius. He was purring very loudly and was obviously enjoying himself, lying on the folds of Dolly's dress. The cat's basket was stuffed uncomfortably into the footwell.

They set off again.

Dolly hadn't said a word so far on the journey. It was all most odd.

Posie frowned slightly, remembering people being escorted away from the House of Sinne half an hour ago, when Richard had instructed everyone to go home, but warned them to expect the police to call later that evening.

This was no idle threat, as uniformed bobbies had already been dispatched to the homes of everyone who had been present at the House of Sinne 'reveal' today.

Lovelace's instructions to these bobbies had been to search for anything suspicious, and – where relevant – to question neighbours as to the occupant's behaviour in recent weeks. To leave no stones unturned.

At least on this he was being thorough.

After this warning had been made, Posie had watched the French aristocrats saunter off upstairs, to their guest flat. She'd seen the staff being dismissed, and noted a very subdued-looking Archie Van Dusen being put in a police motor-car, Ritz-bound. Hubert Pring and his wife had disappeared down the steps of the House of Sinne.

But Dolly had sat on, as if rooted to the spot in the drawing-room, stroking the cat. Fussing over it more than she ever did over her own three children.

Richard, who had looked bone-tired, had smiled wearily at Posie.

'Shall we go, my darling? I'll get a car to send you home. I've called Masha already and told her to put the children to bed. I'll have to go to the Yard. It will be a very late one for me tonight.'

Suddenly Sergeant Fox had entered the room, all in a rush, his face a study of confusion, clutching an open police notebook. 'Just had Smallbone on the telephone, sir.'

'Oh, yes?'

'He's doing everything you said, but he's drawing a lot of blanks. Unusual blanks, sir.'

'Go on. This sounds ominous.' Lovelace had sighed, taken out a cigarette, and lit it almost lethargically, perched on the edge of the table. 'Nothing here is easy, is it?'

'No, sir. I'm wondering if our deceased Miss Sinne was a trickster about more than just perfume, sir. It's her own, personal records, sir. Smallbone says there's absolutely nothing coming up!'

But just then Hubert Pring had entered the room again, a picture of unexpected excitement.

'I say, Chief Commissioner, I had the devil of a thought while I was helping my wife into the car there! I had to raise it with you, urgently.'

Lovelace had stayed calm, puffed at his smoke unhurriedly. 'Please, your Lordship. Tell me.'

'After all this guff with the new perfume apparently having disappeared, I wondered if Anouk had constructed the thing as she did to simply defeat Mr Van Dusen from getting his hands on the stuff. I wondered if the real thing, the *actual* perfume we all smelt today, plus its formula, is in the main House of Sinne safe? Sitting waiting for me?'

Lovelace had flushed slightly for a second, obviously annoyed that he and his men could have missed such a thing. 'Let's check, shall we? You know the code, do you, my Lord, or do we need to call a safe-breaker?'

'Oh, I know the code all right. I'll never forget it! It's *4-06-13*. Shall we go together and look? I also had in mind that I should remove the back-catalogue of scents: the previous formulas and their corresponding samples. I don't want Mr Van Dusen getting his hands on that lot! I'll take them home, to my own safe.'

'That seems fine. I have no problem with that, my Lord.'

'I wondered too if I should go to the laboratory and take away the very valuable ingredients there?'

But Richard Lovelace had continued, reassuring. 'I am sure we can rely on Doctor Poots and his team to have locked up properly, my Lord. The ingredients stay here, sir. I will make an exception for the contents of the safe.'

And then Lovelace, stubbing out his cigarette in a saucer, had looked up at Fox. 'Oh, Sergeant, you mentioned unusual blanks in Miss Sinne's personal records. Perhaps the Viscount might point us in the right direction? What were these "blanks"?'

Fox had flicked his attention to his police notebook.

'We are missing lots, sir. There is no "Anouk Sinne" listed anywhere on the birth registers at Somerset House. There is no "Anouk Sinne" listed as having applied for a passport, ever, and yet we are sure she has travelled before. To Paris, certainly, according to the Duchesse de Poilac and her son. There is no physical passport to be found anywhere. Was there another name Miss Sinne went by, your Lordship?'

The Viscount had shaken his head. 'How odd! There is no other name I can think of. None! I am sure you will find her passport. Your men should look properly. It *must* be here, in her flat probably. I had her recorded on the property deeds, with her name as "Anouk Sinne", so she could live here for her lifetime. She'd have said something at that point if it was incorrect. Surely?'

From her standing position, Posie had noted how Dolly was staring at the scene playing out with hollow-looking eyes, as if she was sleepwalking; not quite there.

Fox had been courteous, but firm, slightly angry below the surface. 'With respect, sir, our search-team have looked upstairs in Miss Sinne's flat, turned it over: made it even more of a mess than it was already, I mean. There is nothing to find. But perhaps this safe might hold some useful information? Where is it?'

It had turned out to be in a place Posie should have realised all by herself.

It was behind the Lempicka painting, which Anouk Sinne had hinted at, hadn't she? '*The real, original fragrances, and instructions for their composition are normally kept in my safe, under my own watchful eye.*'

And Anouk Sinne had loomed at them all from the wall, her blazing, dark, watchful eyes now only alive in oils and pigment.

The painting, when pushed at the right-hand side, could move smoothly along to the left, like a sliding door, on tiny in-built runners. A small, neat Sargent & Greenleaf safe was set into the white wall behind.

'A beautiful painting,' Posie had said, softly. 'A real treasure.'

'What's that, Miss Parker? Well, yes, I suppose so. I paid for it to be painted two years back, when Anouk created her last perfume. I paid for my wife to have her likeness done, too, by Miss Lempicka. Can't say it was anything like so successful, though. Very odd: gave poor Clare what looked like a big piggy head. She refused to have it up. Still, both have proved to be an investment, and that's all that counts.'

'It's yours, then, your Lordship?'

'Of course it is, Miss Parker. Like everything here. Now, young fellow, open the safe.'

4-06-13.

Fox had entered the numbers carefully, manipulating the safe mechanism this way and that, and then the door had sprung open.

But then all hell had broken loose.

* * * *

In the awful discovery that the safe was completely empty, with not one thing inside, Dolly had laughed manically, and then rushed past the policeman on duty at the front door – cat still in her arms – and she'd stood scanning the street, and then waved to a car parked further down.

Posie had come out behind Dolly, just in time to see the Cardigeon Rolls-Royce pull up.

'Golly, has your poor driver been outside all the time?'

Dolly had shrugged. 'I told Paul to wait, didn't I? At least this way Rufus has had the blimmin' inconvenience of *not* havin' a car at his beck and call all afternoon. I expect I'll get into a frightful old row at home. Which is why I'm not goin' home.'

'Dolly?'

The driver had got out and given the bald cat a quickly-disguised look of utter disbelief.

'It's all right, Paul lovey.' Dolly had dug around in her bag, opening up her purse. She had counted out five very fresh pound notes. 'This is for you. Sorry you were stuck here all afternoon. Just tell the Earl that you were ferryin' me about town, shoppin' today. Will you? And by the way, I'm not comin' home wiv you.'

'I'm sorry, my Lady?' The driver, caught off guard by the extravagance of his tip, and thrown generally, had looked confused. As well he might, Posie had thought.

'I'm goin' to stay at Posie's tonight. I'll call the Earl in the mornin'. Can you pass that message on to him, Paul?'

When the car had motored off again, Posie had looked at her friend without smiling.

'What on earth is going on?'

Dolly had taken out a bullet-style lipstick, filled with the peculiar fluorescent yellow greasepaint she was currently favouring. She had applied it with gusto, without using a mirror, perfectly; a skill honed with long years of practice.

'I suppose I should tell you all about Anouk Sinne, Posie lovey. And I know a good deal. But I'm not goin' to do that here. So, it will have to be at your place. Your *office*, I mean. On Grape Street. And I'm afraid it's goin' to have to be tonight. There's no other time. Your old man, Richard, had better listen in. With his little notepad, if he likes.'

Inside the House of Sinne there had been much shouting going on, and all of it was being done by Hubert Pring.

Dolly had looked adamantly away, down the street again.

'I want to get far away from this place. Away from old Hubert Pring in there. He makes my skin crawl. He's a bad man. And a terrible liar.'

* * * *

Fifteen

Which is how they were heading, without much other explanation, for Grape Street, in Bloomsbury.

Regarding Dolly's request to speak at Posie's office, Richard Lovelace had thought the proposal was actually quite sound: it would prove a good neutral rendezvous for now, especially given the high-profile status of the murder victims and the need to keep the story from breaking.

And so they were driving along the Embankment, the almost-midsummer evening light meaning the usual bright, pretty fairy lights which hung in ropes between the trees were not yet switched on.

All the while Dolly looked out at the Thames, absent-mindedly stroking the cat in her lap, which slept.

The boom-boom of the blaring horns of the river ferries filled the air, with the lower, more melancholy bass sound of the horns from the barges making a veritable medley. The river was always busy. Day and night, summer, and winter.

Richard had closed his eyes, and Posie focused on her friend instead. She was remembering Dolly's strange words from earlier, also uttered in a car, about Anouk Sinne. '*Things have a habit of turnin' out badly when she's involved. I have a bad feelin' about this afternoon.*'

Well, it seemed that finally they were going to learn the context of those words, and, as to the premonition itself, Dolly had been absolutely right, hadn't she?

The police motor-car was cutting up through the shadowy gloom of Northumberland Avenue, heading away from the river and out onto the wide sweep of the Strand, passing the huge lions of Trafalgar Square on the left-hand side, where throngs of tourists were packed together.

Dolly was avidly watching everything going past, turning her head from side to side, almost in wonder.

Posie had the strange sensation that her friend, a Londoner born and bred, was seeing the city as if for the first time, with fresh eyes. Perhaps that visit to the cold, windswept North of England had taken its toll on Dolly in some way?

As the police driver signalled left and moved into the Aldwych, Dolly hammered on the thin glass partition and the driver reached back to flip the divider open.

'Yes, Miss?'

'Lawks! Don't drive us up the borin' old Kingsway, lovey! We'll be lucky if we see a few wizened old lawyers heading home at this time of night. Everythin's closed. Imagine! All of London laid out before you like a glitterin' bit of a necklace and you have to drive us up *here*.'

'I wasn't aware this was a sightseeing tour,' mumbled Lovelace softly from next to Posie, but he half-smiled when the driver slowed the car down, uncertainly.

'Drive whichever way the Countess wants, man.' He closed his eyes again.

'Very good, Chief Commissioner. And where would the Countess like me to drive?'

'Take a left. Be a good fella and drive up through Covent Garden, would you? Try and hit Long Acre, and then get us up past the Seven Dials, then you're practically on top of blimmin' Grape Street, aren't you, dearie?'

'Very good, your Ladyship.'

The glass flipped back, and Dolly continued to stare out.

At one point Posie thought she saw a tear trickle down Dolly's cheek, but before she could say anything Dolly had pulled her yellow cloche hat further down over her face, and besides, they were at the chaotic juncture of Cambridge Circus now, in a long line of shiny black motor-taxis and with a few buses chugging through slowly.

Black motor-taxis.

Posie's mind was whirring. *What was it about these black cabs which made her think of something odd, an anomaly?*

But before she could make the connection, she was interrupted by Dolly, leaning across the almost-asleep Richard and tapping on the glass on the far left-hand side.

'Look! There's the Palace Theatre, Posie. And there's your *No, No, Nanette*! Look at all these people, enjoyin' themselves. London at its finest!'

They had come to a virtual standstill and were able to have a good look at the crowds on the pavement outside the big theatre, smoking and holding glasses of brightly-coloured cocktails.

It was obviously the interval.

The huge billboards above the theatre entrance, in lurid purple and yellow, featured a stylised girl in a flapper's outfit, dancing as though her life depended on it.

Posie touched her friend's arm, anxious not to wake the sleeping cat.

'Shall we go together, Dolly? I'm sure that between us we can pull some strings. They say there's never been such a hit musical comedy before in London!'

Dolly pursed her yellow lips in a moue of regret. 'I've already been, lovey. Didn't I tell you? Sorry. Right when it opened, end of March. You'll have to go with someone else. I'm sure Richard would like to see Binnie Hale. She's properly gorgeous, beltin' her little heart out in "Tea for Two".'

Richard opened his eyes, and grinned. 'Binnie Hale?

Oh, go on, you've convinced me. What's the storyline about, Dolly?'

Dolly looked away from the theatre, distracted by a pop of colour on a dress in the crowd. 'Storyline? Oh, golly. Er, well it was complicated, Richard lovey. It wasn't a love story, not really. It was a face-savin' exercise, I think. A blackmail plot which wasn't really that at all.'

Posie's thoughts were scrambling, but then the car moved off, heading jerkily onto Shaftesbury Avenue with its long row of theatres and cinemas, one after another, with Dolly's eyes as big as saucers, taking them all in.

It's as if Dolly thinks she'll never see any of this ever again, Posie thought with a twist of sudden surprise.

As if she is going somewhere.

And then they were pulling up at the corner of Grape Street, with the overflowing bins and shabby paintwork on the buildings all around lending the place an unglamorous feel.

And when Posie and Dolly – and the cat – and Richard, with his notebook, were all settled in the client waiting room, fortified with a pot of strong tea and a brand-new packet of the much-advertised new chocolate biscuits from McVitie's, Dolly began her tale.

And what a tale it was.

****

It had been the autumn of 1906, and Dolly had been twenty-four.

Both her parents were dead, and she'd been living on her wits for a good few years, moving from job to job in the East End of London, near Shadwell, then Poplar. She'd been born in the Limehouse Cut, where her mother had been a can-can troupe dancer in the Music Hall, and the family had never moved far.

At this time, in 1906, Dolly was happy enough: taking in a bit of sewing here and there, walking dogs, looking after babies. Working in a fish-and-chip shop proved to be her longest-running, most regular job.

'A fish-and-chip shop?' asked Posie, rather eagerly. This was Posie's favourite meal and one she'd always been unable to get her friend to partake of. Perhaps now she understood why.

'That's right,' Dolly answered. 'Nice little logo it had, a fish wearin' tap shoes! It tickled me to see it every time, reminded me of the theatre in a funny sort of way, I suppose.'

She lit one of her cocktail cigarettes, taking a deep pull.

'I lived in a flat two floors above the fish bar, too. Worked there about a year. Couldn't get the smell out of my hair and nails for months after I left. And of course, I wore my hair long then, like all the girls did; waist-length, in a plait. So it was even worse for smells. And with tight whalebone corsets and frothy long white skirts and no way of washin' it all regularly, you can imagine I probably stank.'

Dolly laughed bitterly at the memory. 'I'd never worked so 'ard in my life. The boss was a lovely man, but we were all hands to the pumps, me and him. His wife was ill, consumptive. We were so busy: big queues out the door, night after night. All the Scandinavian dockers would come. They'd want cod and chips, but also these 'orrid herrings. Raw, they ate them! With chopped onions, in buttered rolls! I had to do all that too, and that made the smell on me even worse.'

'Golly.'

'But you know me, I was always dreamin' of the theatre. It was in my blood. Tuesday nights I had off, and Sundays. I lived for those times.'

And Dolly Price had spent all of her earnings going

up to the West End of town on her precious nights off, on open-topped horse-pulled buses, come rain or shine.

She'd seen every show going. Musicals, variety, straight plays: it didn't matter what it was, Dolly watched it. Loved it all.

And it was in one of the intervals of a show at the Holborn Empire that Dolly had found herself talking to another young girl, also alone, looking for something else in life.

'Was that Anouk Sinne?' asked Richard. He was trying to stop himself from looking at his watch, aware Sam Stubbs would be arriving in about half an hour. He shook out a gasper instead and held his nerve.

'Nah, don't get ahead of yourself, lovey. Truth be told, I can't remember the name of the girl I met that night, although – it's odd, innit? – meeting her was one of the pivotal moments of my whole blimmin' life. How's one to know a thing like that at the time? Mousy little thing, she was.'

But the 'mousy little thing' had convinced Dolly to attend a meeting with her later that night, in Bloomsbury, of the Women's Social and Political Union, the 'WSPU'. They met every Tuesday.

A group called 'the Suffragettes'.

'It was like the scales 'ad dropped from my eyes that night,' explained Dolly quietly, lost in the mists of time. 'I heard Emmeline Pankhurst talk about the way we should, as women, be able to vote like men at the age of twenty-one. And I joined up straight away.'

Theatre trips into town on Tuesdays were replaced by meetings of the 'Waspy', and gradually, Dolly got friendly with lots of the other regular attendees. They were women from all ranks of society, about two hundred of them; keen to organise the peaceful demonstrations which took place a few times a month.

'Anouk Sinne was one of the women I met there, of course,' said Dolly, taking another puff.

'Only she wasn't called *that*, then. Her real name was Harriet, or "Hattie". And her surname was Synnes, pronounced like "signs". So you can probably trace her under those names, Richard. I know she was born in London, too. But it was a very different London from mine. Her father was a diplomat, very high-rankin'.'

'Thank you, your Grace. That's been very helpful.' A look at the watch, an uncrossing of legs. The story, and interest over.

'I'm not done, Richard. Not by a long chalk.'

'Ah.'

Posie took another biscuit, pushing one towards her friend, who was watching the cat, Julius, busy scratching at the wooden legs of the client settee.

Posie nudged slightly at Dolly's silence: 'So you got friendly with Hattie Synnes, then, did you?'

'No. I was never friends with her.'

Dolly ignored the biscuit.

'But out of those two hundred women, Dolly? That's a lot of women! *Something* brought you together, didn't it? So what was it?'

Dolly blew a smoke ring.

'A language, Posie. French, of course.'

She tapped off the ash in her saucer. 'Oh, and extreme violence.'

****

Sixteen

Dolly spoke as if in a trance, staring out of the window at the twilight dancing through the leaves of the plane trees, her cigarette burning down, forgotten.

She spoke of Christabel Pankhurst, who, unlike her mother, Emmeline, was disillusioned with peaceful protests.

'Christabel was a firecracker,' said Dolly, clearly but flatly. 'And in 1906 she was lookin' for like-minded women.'

'Christabel Pankhurst? Oh, my giddy aunt!' muttered Richard, his hand briefly shading his eyes in disbelief.

'You got in with *her*? *That* crazy woman? She's still famous at the Yard: known as "Queen of the Mob". Caused us endless sleepless nights until she moved to America, thank goodness! I say, does Rufus know about any of this?'

''Course not!' Dolly shook her head angrily. 'And it will stay that way. Why do you think I didn't want to tell this story back home? It would finish me. This stays strictly between *us*.'

Posie threw a warning glance at her husband. *Don't speak, or judge. Don't ruin this, darling.*

Dolly shrugged. 'Christabel wanted to try tactics which would get us into the newspapers. Around the time *I* joined the group – in the early autumn of 1906 – she'd decided *actual* violence was the way forward. Hattie Synnes was very much part of Christabel's inner group of pals. They were both clever girls and I was terrified of them both. But pretty soon I was invited into it. It was mad. We had this crazy feelin' we could do anythin' in the world. Christabel was a sort of magnet: ridiculously beautiful; crazily clever; brave like a lion. She directed blimmin' everything.'

'You don't say!' muttered Richard, but fortunately Dolly didn't hear.

Dolly was busy explaining how Christabel Pankhurst had realised she spoke fluent French, and this was the key which had led to Christabel putting Dolly and Hattie together.

'As it turned out, Hattie Synne's mother was also French! Although about as different as it was possible to be from my poor mama, who had come over as a troupe dancer with the touring branch of the Paris Moulin Rouge and then never left.'

Dolly laughed and made a tra-la-la gesture, indicating exaggerated snobbery.

'Hattie's Parisian mother was posh and had met Hattie's English father when he was stationed out in Paris. But, on the surface we both sounded French. And that's what Christabel wanted. For us to walk together, chatterin' away, for all the world like two nice French tourists. To walk into whatever madness it was that Christabel had planned, so people would never guess we were actually part of it all.'

Richard had been lighting a cigarette, but he paused, genuinely shocked. 'You were used as a *decoy*?'

Dolly nodded. 'Yep. And by December 1906, it escalated. We were told to cause trouble, basically.'

Dolly recounted the start of 1907 – the freezing January. There was a Suffragette raid on the Houses of Parliament, with Christabel's friends attacking Members of Parliament with sticks.

'We got hauled up for that. There was a trial in the February.'

'You got *caught*?' Richard looked horrified.

'That's right, there were ten of us up before the Magistrates' Court, including Hattie and Christabel Pankhurst herself. Christabel made a big nuisance of herself, shouting in the dock, and so she was imprisoned, and she was cock-a-hoop about the publicity, but the rest of us got off with a warning. And that was mainly down to Hattie.'

'How did she manage that?' asked Posie.

Apparently, Hattie had been very easy on the eye.

'Not like now,' said Dolly, slightly spitefully.

'She was very slim back then and had long dark hair. Same captivatin' eyes, of course. I don't know why some women are created as they are, but Hattie Synnes was pure catnip to men. She loved perfume, even then, and she seemed to shimmer in a cloud of different scent whenever you met her. Hattie was clever, too: her parents had encouraged her to train as a lady pharmacist and she worked in the Hospital Pharmacy at St Thomas' Hospital in central London. Hattie could cast a spell over men like it was the easiest thing in the world. And that's what she did from the dock in that Magistrates' Court: convinced them all – one in particular – that we were all dear, sweet innocent girls, led slightly astray.'

'Lucky you,' said Lovelace, in relief. 'Prison – and a sentence on your record – is no laughing matter.'

'I realise that, Richard love, don't be a bore.'

Quite, thought Posie. She was remembering something Anouk had told her earlier.

'*Hubert and I, well: we go back a long way.*'

Yes. That would work.

'Was Hubert Pring, Viscount Effington, the Magistrate, that Anouk – sorry, Hattie – had this effect upon?'

'*What?*' yelped Richard, but Dolly was grinning, grinding out her smoke.

'Too darn right, Posie my love. You know what? You should get yourself a job as a Private Detective.'

'Funny. So did they become lovers?'

'I'm not a hundred per cent sure,' said Dolly. 'As I told you, Hattie and I weren't friends. She never confided in me about anythin'. We had only ever met for these WSPU assignments, where she made it obvious what she thought about me: regalin' me for my "bad" French; my stink from the fish bar. She thought my job was hilarious: as if I did it for fun!'

Dolly shook her head in disbelief.

'Hattie even came out to visit the fish-and-chip shop once. It must have been October or November, 1906. Came all the way out to Poplar Dock in a hansom-cab from town, just to laugh at me. I suppose Hattie thought it was somethin' which she could use to hold me in my place, if she ever needed to.'

'What happened, Dolly?' asked Posie, intrigued.

'Not much, lovey. It was a busy Friday night and Hattie queued among the crowds, ordered a helpin' of cod and chips. Of course, she stuck out like a blimmin' sore thumb there, in her fancy clothes, with her pretty face. She held her nose the whole time I was servin' her. I wanted the ground to swallow me up. It was horrible. Embarrassing.'

Posie remembered Dolly's words earlier that afternoon, in the car on Embankment Gardens. '*She's always been a funny one for smells, has Anouk.*'

Dolly laughed shrilly. 'But I observed *her* from then on, too. And what I observed was that Hattie had several men on the go at once. Why, when we were waitin' for that Magistrates' hearing, up in Camden in February 1907, we were all placed in small single cells in a row. And Hattie had plenty of visitors. *Male* visitors. One was a doctor from St Thomas', from the same laboratory where she worked. One was a friend of the family, who obviously hoped to be more than that, and one was a Scandinavian man. Big, blonde. I knew his kind, of course; they were all quite alike. I met them most nights when I was servin' fish. But this man I watched through the bars of my cell was exceptional. A beautiful man.'

'Scandinavian? You're sure?' Posie's eyebrows knit together. 'Not…'

'Icelandic?' asked Dolly, not laughing anymore. 'Was he Gordy Lorkinsson? I asked myself that, today, as it happens. It's been almost twenty years. But I don't know. I can't be sure. Nah, I don't think so. This fella was rough-looking, somehow. Tattered and oily and dirty, but beautiful underneath all the grime.'

Richard intervened. It was now quarter-to-nine. 'Even if it *was* Lorkinsson, as you two ladies seem to be suggesting, I don't think it clears anything up, does it?'

'Perhaps not,' Posie answered.

She wasn't sure where the conversation was going either, but sometimes the beam of truth cast its strange light into even the darkest and most remote corners of people's experiences.

'What else did you observe, Dolls?'

'That after the February court case, and as the months passed, Hattie barely came to the WSPU events. There was some gossip among the girls about a love affair with a married man. Perhaps that *was* Hubert? Who knows?'

Dolly poured herself more tea, and walked to the window, looking out at the darkening sky. 'Hattie stopped comin' midway through that year, 1907, and Christabel, once out of prison, found others to help her. Fortunately, without my French "friend", I was dropped, and I moved into more peaceful pursuits again.'

'I'm relieved to hear it, Countess.' Richard's eyes almost twinkled. He had only written one or two facts down in his notepad, and he slammed the heavy leather cover over the whole thing, in a final sort of gesture.

But Posie had a sense of some kind of darkness coming.

And now she thought about it, she remembered Dolly telling her, years before, when they'd first met perhaps, about some kind of incarceration; a blight on her employment record which had led to Dolly finding it hard to get work both before and after the Great War.

She studied Dolly's slight, graceful back.

How complicated our lives are, Posie thought to herself suddenly.

How brightly we blaze, but for such a short time.

And for those whose lives are based on a pack of lies, or fragile understandings – as Dolly's seemed to be with Rufus – how precarious an existence could be.

'Unfortunately, the peaceful times didn't last for me,' Dolly said, flatly, picking the cat up, her back still to them.

'Hattie came back. It was 1909, and it was a different Hattie. Harder, crueller. She looked different, too. The beauty was gone. We found out her parents had died in an awful car accident, somewhere in France. Hattie was an only child and had taken their deaths hard. There was talk of a breakdown. Hattie hardly laughed anymore. Apparently, she'd given up her job at the hospital pharmacy and was livin' as a kept woman. But the main difference was that by 1909 she was willin' to do *anything* for Christabel, and the game had changed completely. Before, we just attacked government buildings, but now the idea was to attack things in public life, no matter if the public got hurt.'

Lovelace shook his head angrily. 'I remember. We never knew what was coming next. Acid-attacks on innocent bobbies, nail bombs in letterboxes. Bombs left all over London. Awful devices. Inhumane things.'

Posie remembered reading about this in the broadsheet newspaper her father took, at the vicarage up in Norfolk, where London had seemed far, far away.

Like another country.

'It was a bad time,' said Dolly softy. 'I tried to stay out of most of it, but once or twice a year I'd still be roped in, in the old "French girls" trick. Hattie and I, droppin' off parcels in churches, in shops, on buses.'

'My God, Dolly!' Posie gasped.

Richard looked sickened. 'Well, fortunately, only a small proportion of those hideous devices ever actually went off. But even so.'

Dolly turned at last; stood very still. 'I live with this truth every day, and let me tell you, it doesn't get any easier. Nuffink helps! If it's any consolation to you, it was Hattie who made up pretty much all of the chemical weapons, and, with other women, the bombs. She must have used her pharmacy knowledge and former contacts to get the ingredients, but it took nerve. We worked together on and off for a few years, and the last time was in March 1913. It was one of Christabel's last planned attacks, but this time it was arson. The Tea Pavilion at Kew Gardens. And again, we were caught.'

Richard groaned. 'I remember that. That was *you*, Countess!'

Dolly shook her head. 'No. It was Hattie and me. *Together*. And the Tea Pavilion was empty: I'd never have done it if there had been anyone inside. Of course not! We were working on instructions from Christabel Pankhurst. But, you see, there was a big difference in what happened afterwards, at the trial, in 1913. It wasn't like back in 1907. I was framed.'

Posie and Richard were looking intently at their friend, whose eyes were narrowed and whose mouth was an angry thin line.

'"Evidence" was found at my little bedsit. By 1913 I'd moved jobs and accommodation several times since I had first met Hattie. I had a small bedsit in Russell Square and was workin' as a seamstress from there. My bedsit was searched, and, miraculously, they found exactly what they were lookin' for: matches, stupid things like maps of Kew Gardens, a Suffragette scarf covered in petrol. All "placed". And at the trial, Hattie was given the most wonderful lawyer. He went on and on about her excellent background; her esteemed and sadly deceased parents; the way she'd been led "astray". By me!'

'By *you*?' Posie scowled at this untruth.

Dolly laughed at the memory. 'I couldn't afford a lawyer to defend me, and the WSPU didn't send one. I was made mincemeat of by the Counsel for the Prosecution. He made much of my lowly status, my bad job, and he even laid into my poor dead mother. He painted her as a French harlot, who had given me no sense of morality, when actually she was the loveliest person imaginable. When he finished speakin', I knew, without doubt, I was gonna be convicted, and Hattie would walk free in a cloud of one of her exotic, expensive perfumes. And when I looked up into the public gallery and saw Hubert Pring sittin' there, that Magistrate from years before, winkin' at the lawyer he had paid to defend Hattie so well, I knew it was all over before it even began. I reckon Hubert had paid to plant the evidence on me, too. I took the blame so his beloved little Hattie didn't have to.'

What Dolly was saying was incredible, but such things happened, didn't they?

Posie felt the shadow of the loaded scales of 'justice' from that Courtroom in 1913 flicker over their lives here, in this room, over a decade later.

Those days from before the Great War, which had ripped out the hearts of many a sister, mother, lover, wife, and given those same women jobs and legal rights they could never have imagined before.

It had been the Great War which had made the increasingly dangerous tactics of the WSPU obsolete. Women had got the right to vote. Because of war, not because of the Suffragettes. An awful sort of trade.

'What happened next, Dolly?'

But Posie knew the answer.

Because Dolly carried the devastation of those days with her still, in her quietly-closed-off sadness, her brave bright face turned to the world.

Dolly moved to the coffee table. She picked up her yellow cloche hat and jammed it on her head. Over by the unlit fireplace was the glittery pet basket she had brought from the House of Sinne, unused until now. She carefully moved Julius into it, clicked the wire door closed.

'Holloway Prison,' she said, softly, straightening up.

'Worst six months of my life. I can never tell anyone what happened to me in there. But afterwards was hardest. Unlike some, such as Hattie, I wouldn't change my name. I stayed as Dorothea Price. I wanted to atone for what I had done, so I studied nursing, paid for it all myself. Couldn't get a job, though, until later in the Great War. They needed us nurses then, didn't they? I managed to get packed off to the Western Front and did my bit. Life was tough, but that's what I deserved.'

Dolly explained that she had been aware, through a couple of ex-WSPU friends, that Hattie had changed her name, emerging phoenix-like from the arson at the Tea Pavilion. She'd become Anouk Sinne, the fashionable perfumier, running her very own perfume house.

'"Anouk" was her mother's name,' Dolly announced. 'I remember her tellin' me. And "Sinne" just sounds better than "Synnes", doesn't it? Catchier. Darker. But the House of Sinne must have been Hubert's doin', eh? A gift to Anouk,' said Dolly, buttoning up her coat.

'So he was lying to you in that drawing-room this evenin', Richard, when you asked him if he knew if Anouk had any other identity.'

Dolly sniffed pointedly. 'After all this time, I still don't understand exactly *how* Anouk Sinne managed to keep a man like that.'

Dolly laughed suddenly, but there was no humour in it. 'I suppose he loved her, didn't he? Must have done, poor man. Held onto her story for himself, as if it were special. Like that wretched blimmin' code to the safe! I didn't know whether to laugh or cry when I heard that number read aloud.'

Richard frowned, confused. 'What was so special about it, Countess?'

Dolly wasn't laughing anymore. 'It was a date: *4-06-13* is the fourth of June 1913. It was the day we got the verdict in the Kew Gardens Tea Pavilion case: the day Hattie walked free and "became" Anouk. Probably with his help, eh? For me it was the day my life changed forever, with a prison conviction. But most people remember it for an entirely different reason, also connected to the Suffragettes.'

'Go on,' encouraged Posie.

Dolly shrugged sadly. 'It was the date poor old Emily Davison threw herself under the King's horse at Epsom. Remember? She died four days later. She was the first martyr for the Suffragettes. I heard snippets of the news when the jury was out. The date has always stuck in my mind. Seems like it stuck in Hubert Pring's mind, too. Wretched man.'

Richard sat back, thinking, and locked his fingers behind his head.

'We will look into all of this, Countess. But tell me: did Hubert Pring recognise you today? Does he know that the beautiful and well-dressed Countess of Cardigeon is also the Suffragette terrorist, Dorothea Price, who took the blame for Anouk Sinne's crimes all those years ago?'

Dolly shrugged, hardly caring. 'I dunno, Richard lovey, but I'd wager not. We never mix in the same social circles. Last time he saw me properly was in that Courtroom. But I looked different then. Like any other poor London girl, underfed and under-nourished. Besides, I don't smell of fish and chips anymore, do I? Even though I only worked there for a year, it was something Anouk never forgot. In fact, I'm surprised she didn't mention it today. She talked about it even when we did the Kew job together, years later. It was a constant theme with her.'

Dolly suddenly lifted the cat basket up.

'Besides, I expect Anouk never told Hubert I was comin'

today; the invite was very last-minute. I think I'll go now. I know how busy you both are.'

Posie was on her feet. There was so much – *or so little?* – to deal with here. But there must be something else.

'Dolly, did Hattie – sorry, Anouk – have any weaknesses during those years you knew her? Any strong dislikes, or likes?'

Dolly was already at the frosted-glass door of the office. 'Apart from men, lovey? And buyin' perfumes? There is somethin', though, yes. In the years after her disappearance, she loved playin' cards. But it was more than that. It was gambling in general. Blackjack, and Roulette. In fact, I reckon she'd have bet the sun wouldn't have risen tomorrow if anyone had given her good enough odds. After 1909 I think she'd usually go on to a casino after she'd been at a WSPU meeting. I was never invited. I suppose it was Hubert Pring's money she was blueing?'

'That's useful, Dolly.'

And Posie was thinking hard, running snatches of what she had just heard together, disparate elements which seemed to stand out oddly from the awful tale.

French, France, French girls.

'Dolly, the Duchesse de Poilac, Maria, whom you spoke to earlier? Tell me: did *she* have some connection with those years, with the WSPU?'

This was now a frantic, crazy race to put pieces of this half-missing jigsaw puzzle together and it was so far proving completely futile.

'Nah, lovey. I never clapped eyes on Maria until today, nor her gorgeous boy. Coo-ee, what a lovey, eh? Wants to be a doctor, apparently: doesn't give a fig for his title or the aristocracy in general. Maria told me Anouk doted on that boy. The Duchesse was dead nice. *Too* nice for Anouk, who I haven't ever forgiven. In fact, I hated Anouk Sinne and I can't pretend to you that I'm sorry she's dead. You know, I even had it in the back of my mind that she might have felt regret after all this time; wanted to apologise to me today. But, no. Not at all.'

Dolly bit at her yellow lip. 'If it helps you, I think I understand why Maria de Poilac got on so well with Anouk.'

'Why?'

'Maria told me she'd trained as a pharmacist when she was younger, in Paris. She loves flowers, too. She's a dab hand at gardenin' and reads big books on botany for fun! She told me she'd spent all mornin' today at Kew Gardens, lookin' at somethin' special: I forget what. They were birds of a feather, see? Same background. Although Maria is much, much nicer. Anouk was only ever a snake in the grass.'

'Interesting.'

So, Maria de Poilac would know all about hemlock then, wouldn't she?

With her training in pharmacy and her knowledge of plants, she'd know exactly how much was needed to kill a person.

But why would she have wanted to kill a woman she got on so well with? And in such a terrible manner…

'And when were the French supposed to be leaving, Dolly?'

'This trip to London was short, Maria told me. They had planned to leave tonight. The late flight to Paris. From Croydon. And talkin' of leavin'…'

Dolly opened the door out onto the hallway. Outside the hot linoleum stank of heat and dust, and downstairs the entrance bell had started to ring.

Sam Stubbs, no doubt. Or else, Sergeant Fox.

'Oh.' Dolly's eyes widened. 'Somethin' funny, Posie. I quite forgot. You know that dead Princess, from India?'

Posie's heart pounded. Was this something to get Gordy Lorkinsson out of the frame of suspicion?

'Did you see something?'

'Nah. But I *heard* somethin'. When she was talkin' to

Anatole. The Princess spoke French, lovey. Like it was her mother tongue. Better than me, actually. Odd, huh?'

Posie was slightly disappointed. *Was that all?*

'What did you hear them say, Dolly?'

'It didn't make much sense. Anatole told her he was shocked to see her. And the Princess was sayin' to Anatole that she'd done nothin' wrong and that the stories were untrue. That he should stop holdin' a grudge; it was very unfair to her. That was all.'

Posie had no idea what any of this meant, but now Dolly was kissing her, turning for the stairs.

And, had she but known it, one day Posie would look back on this moment to truly appreciate her best friend for who and what she was.

'You've always been good to me, Posie,' Dolly called as she started off down the stairs. 'Don't judge me, will you, dearie? Nothing changes because of what I did, *then*. And I was proud of a lot of it, too: bein' a Suffragette, you know?'

Dolly swung the cat basket a bit too high, and Julius went wild, clawing and tearing at his wicker confines, his blue eyes angry behind his bars.

A dark-green-and-gold label marked 'Q- PETS. INJECTED!' suddenly fluttered to the floor from the basket and Posie darted down the stairs and picked it up.

'What's that?' asked Dolly, on the next landing. 'Oh, just a vets' label? Oh, Julius! You'll settle in a minute.'

And as Posie stood there, hearing the yellow heels clack-clacking down the cheap metal-trimmed steps, she couldn't help but feel that Dolly had not been telling the truth to her just now.

'*Nothing changes*,' Dolly had said.

But right now, everything felt like it had changed.

And forever.

* * * *

PART FOUR

Shards of a Whole Picture

Seventeen

Posie stood on the darkening landing, and random, completely unconnected thoughts occurred to her.

Black cabs, and bags being handed into cabs.

French girls, and France.

Hubert Pring and his ardent sponsoring of Hattie Synnes, who had become, because of him, an expert perfumier, rather than a woman with a bad past.

The past.

A past which threw shadows over the present, over the future. A past which had thrown shadows enough today to kill two women, not yet ready to die.

She remembered Gordy Lorkinsson's description of Anouk Sinne: '*She is many things to many people.*'

Well, that was as may be. But what had she been to Hubert Pring, all these years?

A lover, certainly.

That must have been the case. Anouk had been beautiful. But being a lover, somewhere in the far-off past, didn't usually mean obligations were created going forwards into the future. Why had Hubert always believed in Anouk, as she herself had so proudly told Posie earlier that very day?

And then, all of a sudden, it came to Posie, as clear as day.

The reason he had supported Anouk Sinne all these years.

'Oh! Golly Gosh! I'm such a fool! Of course!'

'What is it, darling?' Richard Lovelace was out on the landing with his wife. He'd pressed the entrance buzzer inside the office, admitting their callers, and now there were men's voices down in the grotty entrance hall, several flights below.

Posie wanted to scream aloud with excitement, just managing to tamp it down. 'I know why Hubert Pring has done everything for Anouk all these years. It *must* be, although of course, I have no proof.'

'Oh?'

'It's obvious when you think of it.'

'Nothing is obvious to me here, darling.'

She was about to explain but here was Sam Stubbs, puffing up the last flight of stairs, a sheeny sweat beading his face under his bowler hat. He had a big manila folder under his arm, and he stopped for breath at the last step. Behind him was the angular figure of Sergeant Fox, also carrying a manila folder. He was not puffing at all, and looked strangely pleased with himself.

Richard smiled politely at Sam. 'Nice of you to join us, Sam.'

'Evening, Chief Commissioner. What's the hurry? What's going on? Like you asked, I've developed all the photographs from the perfume event. I had to do it myself, completely alone, as that was one of the conditions Miss Sinne set me. I had a bit of trouble with the developer; I haven't developed photographs in years! It's a bit of an art, actually–'

Fox broke in, grinning. 'Talking of photographs, sir, I have something to show you myself. . .'

'It will have to wait, Sergeant. Step in here with us, Sam. Eh?'

And without offering drinks or explanation, Lovelace

asked Sam Stubbs to lay out his photographs from the 'reveal' across the waiting room floor.

There were about twenty good ones. Richard Lovelace walked up and down, looking, but Posie got down on her knees and searched each one for any tell-tale sign of the horror which had been about to unfold.

It was the backgrounds which interested Posie, of course. *What was going on there*?

Sam Stubbs was biting at his fingernails nervously, quite justifiably puzzled. 'What's this all about, Chief Commissioner? I've done nothing wrong; I swear! Has Miss Sinne complained about me?'

'Not at all, Stubbs. Tell us about your brief.'

'Well, Chief Commissioner, Miss Sinne asked me specially to turn up alone, and I did. She was being very cagey about everything, and didn't really seem to want me there, but I've worked for her before and she's a funny old bird, but we've always got along, and had good results. So, I ignored her prickliness this time around: after all, she promised me complete exclusivity, on condition I published tomorrow night. Which is what I'm going to do.'

That was as she had figured, Posie reasoned. Sam Stubbs had been seen as a 'tame' journalist by Anouk, someone who would do her bidding, even if the photographs had not been her idea, or what she wanted.

Posie heard Richard sigh. 'I'm very much afraid you can't publish, Stubbs. There's been an event – *events* – which alter things.'

'Oh?'

But Posie was still busy scanning the faces, the glances around the oval table earlier at the 'reveal'.

Here was Hubert Pring, anger and resentment in his eyes, staring at Van Dusen. Here was Anouk Sinne – in the throes of dying, although none of them, not even she, had known it at the time – with those great black dilated eyes, throwing a glance towards her French guests, a smile on her face. A genuine smile, it seemed.

Sam Stubbs had taken another snap with Lucy Reeble in the background, her smart blonde head angled down, checking her watch surreptitiously, about to leave with the blackmail money.

Next to Lucy was Gordy Lorkinsson, not looking at either Anouk or the Princess, but smiling at someone else, out of range. In the very back part of the photograph Jenks was looming at the door, laden with the money bag.

Posie picked up another snap, showing the young French Count, his arms crossed, one eyebrow raised, giving a dazzlingly glamorous, seductive smile. *But who had been the recipient of that smile?*

And in the background of the next photograph was Hubert Pring's shoulder, and Lady Clare, trying to disguise a slight, secret, soft smile which lit up her big face, making her look almost pretty; a split-second's worth of shared understanding with someone else in the room.

Captured mercilessly and forever.

Secrets. Secrets everywhere.

Posie held on to the picture of Lady Clare, and picked up its matching pair from the photographs, slotted the jigsaw together.

'Oh! I say! This puts a different spin on things…' Posie announced to herself in a whisper, sitting back on her haunches. 'But does it have an impact on what happened today?'

Sam Stubbs was gibbering away, incredulous at the news Lovelace had just given him about the fates of the two most important people in his photographs.

But he was calming down, thrashing out a deal with Lovelace whereby he could – exclusively – publish the news of the deaths the following evening.

Richard was wrapping up: 'I'll be in touch, Sam, but don't you dare publish any of these without my say-so. And I'll keep this set for now.'

'Right you are, Chief Commissioner.'

Posie stood and after she had heard the newspaper editor going down the stairs, she turned to her husband, 'Do you have any Arrest Warrants on you, darling?'

'Of course I do. Who for, my love? *What* for?'

'Lady Clare Pring,' she answered simply.

Fox stood by, open-mouthed, goggling.

'Fill it in, Richard darling, and sign it. And then, if it's all right with you, Sergeant, go to Mayfair to her home and wave it under her nose. Tell Lady Clare to come and speak to us urgently, tonight. Here. And on your way, Sergeant, could you possibly call at Kettner's and get some fishcakes? Chips too, if they've got any. Or croquettes. I'm positively starving. You both must be. And now, if you don't mind, I'm going into my own office to make a telephone call.'

* * * *

Posie, waiting for the operator to make the connection, heard another man's footsteps coming up the stairs, bursting into the main office.

It was Sergeant Smallbone, his low, clear voice explaining that Gordy Lorkinsson was saying nothing in interview at Scotland Yard, but, apart from that, was being a model prisoner.

Through the slightly-open door of her own office, she could see Sergeant Smallbone unzipping his leather messenger bag, and starting to pull out papers, and she could hear her husband, running the tap in the tiny office kitchen, putting the kettle on for more tea.

Posie thought briefly of her little red-haired son, Kit, three months old and asleep now – hopefully – in the yellow-painted nursery he shared with his beloved adopted sister, Katie, who was almost one year older but whose efforts to fall asleep were always longer and more fractious than his own. In her mind's eye Posie scanned the nursery, seeing little Phyllis, aged four – Richard's daughter from his first marriage – tucked cosily into bed, her line of teddies nearly taking up more room on the pillow than she did.

'Putting you through,' the operator announced crisply, interrupting her thoughts. And then there was a familiar woman's voice on the end of the line.

'Posie? How lovely to hear you. You don't normally call!'

The woman was speaking from a laboratory in Cambridge. The Department of Botany. It was a dear voice. A not-quite-family voice, but a treasured one nonetheless.

This was Evangeline Greenwood, mother of Posie's unofficial nephew, Harry. Posie had tried calling Evangeline at home, but the Housekeeper there had informed her that the Mistress was still at 'work'. Evangeline lived a difficult life, for many reasons, with many facets to her existence. One of them was 'running' the University Department of Botany as a glorified secretary, this respectable 'front' covering the fact that Evangeline was a world-class botanist in her own right. Evangeline's husband, Harold, was also a university botanist, but, unfortunately, he was also a first-class brute and couldn't bear his wife to have more acclaim professionally than he did.

Posie's long-dead brother had been a paramour of this wonderful, beautiful, remarkable woman, and the two women had kept in touch.

'Is everything all right, Posie?'

Evangeline was half-Indian. The daughter of a British Ambassador and an Indian Princess, she'd come down in the world since marrying her husband, Harold, whom she'd met .at Cambridge when studying there. Posie knew Evangeline kept in touch with her now-dead mother's family back home in India. Two of her sisters had married into other Indian royal dynasties.

'I'm quite all right, thank you. And Harry? Where is he?'

'It's half-term. Harold has taken Harry up to Scotland, fishing. I miss my boy dreadfully, but he'll be home at the end of the week. I'm here catching up on my own research. While the cat's away, and all that … I hope to publish again next year. In my own name if I can. All of this has to be done in secret for now.'

'Gracious. Good luck. I *do* admire you. I'll come to the point: I'm calling as I need your insider knowledge.'

'Plants?'

Posie laughed, although there was nothing humorous to be found in any of this strange situation. 'No, not today. Although I am, weirdly, working on a case which involves plants. But this is more a gossip-based enquiry. You've heard of Princess Priyanka, of Gwilim?'

There was a sharp intake of breath. 'Yes, of course. Gwilim is the neighbouring Princely State to that of my mother's family. What has happened there is a tragedy.'

Posie tried to blot out Princess Priyanka's strange words from earlier, resounding in her head: '*Five peacocks walking … in front of my own burning home. A peacock for each of my family, all dead.*'

'Is there anything you can tell me about the accident at Gwilim, Evangeline? Anything you might have heard from your relations? In their letters?'

There was a beat of silence. 'Well…'

'Please, Evangeline. I wouldn't ask if it wasn't necessary.'

A deep sigh. 'I've heard that maybe it wasn't an accident. Priyanka Lashari has always been controversial. She married into the Gwilim dynasty; you know. She isn't of royal blood herself.'

'Oh? Was there a French connection at all?'

'Absolutely. Her father was a French doctor working in India; he met Priyanka's mother – who was from a rich merchant family in Delhi – and after a couple of years they moved back to France where Priyanka was born and raised, in Paris. She only went back to Delhi a few years ago, with her mother, on the death of her father. Priyanka has always been ambitious and set her sights on the young heir to the Gwilim dynasty, despite his family's reservations. They married quickly, a couple of years ago. But being a Maharani hasn't been enough for Priyanka Lashari. She really wants to be an actress. When it was made clear to her by her husband that acting in India wasn't an option, not in her position as his wife, she said she wanted to try abroad. The French movie world, or even Hollywood. Well, she *is* fantastically beautiful.'

'And?'

'I'm not sure of the exact details, Posie. It's just shards of a whole picture. I've heard Priyanka was offered the chance to do some screen tests back in Paris. She went, did the filming, but was summoned home by her husband and ordered never to leave again. A radical group at a university in Paris had met her and supported her when she was in the city. They later got hold of the film reels and somehow became involved: said they wanted to "free" the Princess and help her with her dream of becoming a French movie star. Love-struck boys, probably, with too much time and money on their hands.'

Evangeline paused for a few seconds before continuing: 'I heard that, with the help of these French radicals, Priyanka got out, about a month ago, but, on her own initiative, she then set fire to the Gwilim fort while every generation of her husband's family slept there, supposedly safe in their beds. A wild act of revenge. But it's now being spoken of as arson, and murder. Who knows? Perhaps it really was an accident from which she was a truly lucky survivor?'

Posie twisted the telephone cable and stared out.

It was still half-light in the ugly, grey courtyard outside, its sides formed by the steep backs of buildings, all rising to blot out the London evening sky. The usual row of pigeons sat huddled along Posie's window-ledge, living their usual lives, roosting among the tatters of human existence.

What a mess this all seemed to be.

'Do you believe the story about the arson, Evangeline? Is it well-known in India?'

Posie could imagine her friend – her beautiful dark hair carefully braided into a thick, waist-length plait, ruby earrings glittering at her ears, sumptuous-coloured dresses in layers of silks beneath the white lab coat – rubbing her forehead anxiously, worry blurring the lines of her lovely face, her purple eyes half-closed.

'I was shocked you even mentioned it, Posie. It is *not* well-known. And what has got out has been hushed up. My sister told me, in a letter I received just two days ago, from Jaipur. I gather Priyanka has fled. Aided by contacts in the movie world, or perhaps, the French radical group who have supported her. Although my sister said there are rumours that Priyanka has now spurned Paris, setting her sights higher, in favour of Hollywood. Whatever the case, she will not be returning to India. She would face almost certain prosecution here.'

No. Princess Priyanka would not be returning to India, that much was certain.

Without telling *why* she was asking for this odd information, or giving anything of the case today away, Posie promised to be in touch soon, and to visit Harry, and she rang off.

What was it, Posie thought to herself briefly, *with all these clever, brilliant, beautiful women?*

Women such as Anouk Sinne and Princess Priyanka and Dolly Cardigeon and even Evangeline Greenwood: they were linked together by their ambition and marked out by the secrets and the desires they had to hide in order to get on in life.

Although, of course, there were degrees of 'getting on' in life.

Princess Priyanka's ambitions may have been admirable, but if she *had* indeed committed murder and arson back in Gwillim, then this was nothing short of terrible.

It seemed almost certain that Mr Van Dusen had supported the Princess in bringing her over to England, before taking her on to America. But what about Count Anatole?

Had *he* been part of that French radical university group who had hoped to sponsor a future French screen goddess? It seemed very likely. In which case his comments earlier about having seen the Princess in some moving pictures certainly made sense.

Had Priyanka's conduct fallen foul of what Anatole and his friends had set out to do? Had the Maharani spurned their help and chosen another path, right at the end? Anatole had certainly judged her harshly earlier: '*I could not bear her at my side just now. It was like a poison*.'

Poison.

Well, the Princess had met her death by poison, hadn't she? Some kind of fancy pesticide.

But was Richard Lovelace wrong to think that the Princess's murder was incidental to Anouk Sinne's? Or was it – in its own right – important? Had perhaps Mr Van Dusen or the very young Count wanted or needed to get rid of the Princess? A woman whose past had suddenly proved too much to deal with?

Baggage which was too heavy, and dangerous by its very association.

Posie shrugged to herself and then she walked out into the main office, and fortified herself with some of her husband's particularly horrid-looking stewed brown tea.

* * * *

Eighteen

Having reported the story about Princess Priyanka, Posie was met by a silence.

Richard Lovelace sighed heavily.

'This is the kind of thing which is almost impossible to verify, darling. But interestingly, we have the same sort of stories coming out of Paris; leaked and hushed-up stories to a newspaper there, *Le Jour*, by a group of students at the Sorbonne. They claim that Priyanka Lashari started that fire in Gwilim: that her conduct was reproachable, criminal; that they wash their hands of association with her. But it could just be sour grapes that the Maharani chose to pursue her dreams in America, eh? Now, let's stick with facts. Smallbone has been very industrious so far, good lad. Tell us what you've got…'

Smallbone *had* been busy that evening. All his information was spread across the coffee table.

'I'll start with something strange, sir.'

It was about the Embassy Club, where the big launch of Anouk's new perfume was planned to take place the following day.

'I called them, sir, hoping to do them a favour, and let them know ahead of time that the event would be cancelled, and to ask for the guest list. I'd already prepped a small team at the Yard to get ready to telephone the guests. We were going to blag and say Miss Sinne was sick.'

'Wise.'

'But it wasn't necessary. The Manager of the Embassy Club told me he knew the event was cancelled! Seemed very calm about the whole thing. I presumed that Lady Clare or the Viscount had got ahead of me, fearful of losing still more money, but no. Can you guess who had cancelled the luncheon?'

Both Posie and Richard shook their heads.

'Miss Sinne herself! She'd called them two weeks ago, needing to hire the whole place for two hundred and fifty guests. She'd asked the Embassy Club to send out their specially-printed invitations right away, but then, a couple of days later, she cancelled the whole shebang! What do you make of that?'

Utter stupefied silence met the question.

Posie broke it at last: 'Did you manage to contact all the guests who'd received invitations? Or had the Embassy Club done that themselves, two weeks ago?'

That had been the funny thing, Smallbone explained. Because, having asked the club to send out invitations, Anouk had given the Manager only *one* name: promising the Manager a follow-up list by post which had, in the end, not been needed.

Posie was remembering the black-and-gold Embassy Club invitation which Lady Clare had toyed with.

'So you're telling us that Hubert Pring's was the *only* invitation sent out?'

Smallbone looked annoyed to have had his moment of glory snatched away. 'That's right, Miss.'

Lovelace was dismissive. 'Sounds fairly typical to me of the chaos which was allowed to go on at this perfume house. Slap-dash, eh?'

Posie stood up quickly and looked out of the main window, watching the traffic with unseeing eyes.

It doesn't make sense. Any of it.

Anouk Sinne had told Posie only earlier today that she'd need her tomorrow. At the Embassy Club.

Had *someone else* called the Embassy Club two weeks ago, pretending to be Anouk, cancelling the event, to make trouble?

Had someone deliberately *not* sent them the guest list and sabotaged the whole thing? Who was in that position? Lucy Reeble, as secretary? Or the butler? Or Hubert Pring, as the financial backer of the whole project? Perhaps *he'd* executed the perfect double-bluff by holding onto that single, printed invite?

Or perhaps his wife had cancelled the thing out of spite, two weeks back? Lady Clare's attitude to Anouk Sinne had been (by her own admission) frosty, to say the least.

But Lovelace had moved on to other matters, asking about Anouk Sinne's personal bank account, and the company bank accounts.

'Useful, are they, Sergeant?'

'Yes. Quite useful, sir. We knew Miss Sinne got two thousand pounds a year as a salary. But her personal account shows us she took it all out, every month, in cash. Must have spent it.'

'What, *all* of it?' stuttered Richard, his eyes wide.

'But that was a colossal sum! More than thirty-five pounds a week! Most clerks earn six or seven pounds! And she was living rent-free in that huge place in Chelsea, so what on earth was she doing with it all?'

'Dunno, sir.' Smallbone shrugged, rather disgustedly. 'She's also been living in a big overdraft, sir. Four thousand pounds in the red! Been like that for two years now.'

'I say!' muttered Richard, askance. 'And the bank never called it in?'

'No, sir. The company bank accounts are also interesting. Notably, the House of Sinne hasn't been doing very well. There's not much coming in. There are monthly incoming payments from all the Department Stores for the sales of the older lines of perfumes, but it's not a fortune. The House of Sinne desperately needed to make money with this new perfume, sir. I noticed that the staff were due to be paid two weeks ago and they *weren't* paid, as the balance was too low. Poor chumps! The whole affair looks like a badly-patched ship, rolling in the deep.'

'I'll say!' replied Richard. 'Interesting how the Viscount didn't own up to any of this mess, eh? And Van Dusen's money? That *is* real, I take it?'

'Oh, yes, sir. Van Dusen's money from America has arrived, sir, but of course, it came too late for the staff payroll to be met. It's just sitting there. At least the Viscount can pay the staff now, I suppose. And keep on paying them, as he was so keen to promise you he would!'

'Let's hope so.'

Posie slurped at the nasty tea. 'What about the one thousand pounds Anouk sent to the blackmailer today? I *saw* that money with my own eyes. Does it show up anywhere as a debit on either of these two accounts?'

Smallbone checked his notes. 'No, Miss. There's no entry for the removal of one thousand pounds. Unless that was part of the monthly monies Miss Sinne was taking out? Maybe she was siphoning it off, as a rainy-day fund?'

'Mmmm.'

Posie didn't think Anouk Sinne had been the sort of person to have a rainy-day fund, but the policemen had moved on again.

'Our lads checked all the houses of the people at the perfume "reveal" today, sir. Well, "houses" might be going a bit strong, actually. Matchboxes, in the case of many of them.'

Smallbone detailed how Gordy Lorkinsson's small studio flat in nearby Chelsea Cloisters had been searched; a veritable 'matchbox' if ever there was one. But the place was immaculate, the sort of flat a person merely slept at.

A letter in a pink envelope had been found on the mat, still sealed. The bobbies had opened it and, sure enough, it had been the letter Anouk had written to Lorkinsson today, about stopping working in the garden of the House of Sinne.

Smallbone checked his notebook carefully. 'The lads made some enquiries of the neighbours at Chelsea Cloisters, sir. Both sets tell that Mr Lorkinsson is a model gent; quiet, clean, respectable. One of the neighbours mentioned a frequent lady visitor.'

'Oh?' Richard was busy lighting a cigarette. 'Who was that, then?'

'No name given. Tall, though. Fancy clothes.'

Posie chipped in casually. 'It was Lady Clare Pring.'

Richard almost choked on his first pull of the cigarette. '*What?* The deuce! Posie, did you *know*?'

Posie shrugged. 'No. Not when we were there today. But I saw something – a shared glance – in a couple of Sam's photographs just now, and I joined them up, and then I wondered.'

Smallbone raised an eyebrow in interest, before producing lists with professional references for Lorkinsson.

'We checked the references of the other staff, too. That butler, Jenks, he was definitely Peregrine Pring's wingman in the Great War. Our lads checked in on him tonight at his house in the Pimlico slums. His family were eating their evening meal, already delayed, and were surprised at being interrupted.'

Smallbone told how the place was searched but nothing found, and the visit had ended with Jenks' harassed wife, a big, formidable woman, shouting at the policemen to: '*Get the wages my husband is owed…and we don't care where it comes from!*'

Despite the debilitating effects of shell-shock, Smallbone reported that Jenks lived a full life outside his job. He was active in the local church and played ping-pong locally. His two small children had been polite and excitable, trying to show the two bobbies a new pet out in the yard, which was attracting envious attention from the other children in the neighbourhood.

Smallbone moved on to the secretary next. He explained that Lucy Reeble had been at home, too, in a tiny doll-sized studio on Sloane Avenue, also in Chelsea.

She'd been crying, apparently, and had been circling the personal adverts in a borrowed copy of *The Lady*, already looking for another job. Lucy had wanted to offer some coffee to the policemen who had called, but she'd been so upset when she got home that she had burnt her own coffee on the stove; scorched the cafetière right through, and the memory of this had made her cry even more.

Lucy's references had been checked. The Convent where she had been educated had been more than happy to supply details of how she had come their way.

Lucy had been born to a Danish labourer and his wife, Lenne and Lotte Fisk, and all had been blissfully happy. They'd lived among a community of Scandinavians in London.

But then, in a double-handed dealing of tragedy, first the wife died, and then the father couldn't cope alone. Lenne had abandoned his daughter.

And the baby, who was called 'Dorte', ended up in the big London Orphanage at Great Ormond Street. Blonde-haired 'Dorte Fisk' became 'Lucy Reeble', named after the Orphanage Principal's favourite grandmother, and, at age seven, she was taken in by a community of nuns at Reading, where she had thrived.

The nuns of Reading were happy to supply references and described Lucy as an efficient, reliable, likeable girl.

'They are all more than happy for Lucy to return to the Convent, sir. They told me they'd welcome her back with open arms if no other work was to be found for her, even though they still have other young women in their care.

One of the sisters who runs the place, a Sister Ignatia, was very effusive in her praise of Lucy.'

'That's good to know, Sergeant. Good work.'

Smallbone now spoke about the Prings.

Richer pickings had indeed been had in Mayfair.

The bobbies had not been able to enter Hubert Pring's house on Berkeley Square when they had turned up about half an hour after the Prings had returned home.

'The street was full of removal vans, sir,' said Smallbone incredulously.

'Our lads made some discreet enquiries and found that the Prings are in the process of moving out. Only going round the corner, mind, but to a much smaller place. A flat, actually.'

'Money troubles?' asked Richard, still puffing away. 'The Viscount didn't mention a move earlier, did he, Posie my love?'

Posie shook her head. 'Well, would you? He must be embarrassed.'

'Make enquiries, Sergeant.'

''Course, sir.' Smallbone took out his notepad. 'I'll check the property deeds. I've also ordered up the property deeds for the House of Sinne itself. They will come first thing tomorrow. I'll look at both.'

Smallbone explained that something else odd had happened at Berkeley Square when the bobbies had turned up earlier.

A young man, red-haired, very fashionably dressed, complete with several suitcases, had been standing outside on the pavement, yelling wretchedly up at the Prings' townhouse.

He'd been visibly upset, was shouting about being 'turned out', and was possibly drunk. He'd jumped into a big dark-green motor-car which had pulled up outside and sped off in it.

Richard Lovelace rolled his eyes: 'Sounds like one of

the Pring sons. Misbehaving? Now, what about the two Frenchies?'

There had been precious little to report on the Duchesse de Poilac and her son, Count Anatole, from the French Embassy in South Kensington. Smallbone brandished the letter-headed paper.

'The information they've provided is very short. The Embassy just gave their dates of birth and told us that the Duchesse is a much-respected resident of Versailles. She also spends part of the year in Cabris, in the South of France. And Anatole is a well-liked student at the Sorbonne. Studying medicine. First-year. This all seemed a bit bland, so I telephoned through to the University itself.'

Smallbone had struck lucky, getting through to the Deputy Vice-Principal of the Sorbonne, who was an Anglophile, and happy to talk.

Smallbone read from his notes:

'Anatole de Poilac is a clever student, apparently, but last year his attendance was patchy and he started getting into trouble: lots of warnings were given. He was on the edges of some groups wanting to question the establishment in general: a lot of campaigning for human rights, and women's rights, that kind of thing. But it seems it was love which got him into real trouble.'

'Oh, yes?' Lovelace tapped the ash from his smoke, interested.

'Yes, sir. Last year the Count took to spending time over here in London, apparently. There were weekends which went on a bit too long. He was also seen a couple of times in Paris in the company of an older lady who was *not* his mother. Laughing, joking, hugging. The woman had short, shorn dark hair. Silver lipstick and nails.'

Richard had been about to stub out his smoke, but he let it burn down right to his finger now in shock. He swore as it burnt his skin.

'The deuce! *Anouk Sinne?* Those two were lovers?'

Smallbone snapped the cover of his notebook back in place. 'Sounds about right, sir. No sightings recently though, sir. And his studies have picked up again. He's recently been seen in the company of a local nurse in uniform. Pretty little blonde thing, but a good deal older, too.'

'Good Lord! But Anatole is young enough to have been Anouk's son!' said Lovelace, shaking his head as he looked at the paper from the Embassy. 'He was born in November 1907! He's only just turning eighteen!'

Posie reeled. 'Not yet eighteen? But he looks so much older.'

Smallbone was looking sanctimonious. 'It takes all sorts, sir. Look at our Prince of Wales. They say he has a "sort" and that's just it, sir. Count Anatole too, obviously…'

'Well…'

Posie was remembering the Count's words to her in the hallway earlier. He'd been damning of Priyanka Lashari; had talked of the Princess as '*not a real sophisticated woman at all. Not like some others!*'

Posie had, rather vainly and stupidly, it now turned out, thought he might be actually flattering *her*. But perhaps he had been describing his much older lover, Anouk.

Had his own mother, the Duchesse, known about the affair? And if so, how on earth, even if she was very open-minded, could she have thought it a good thing?

Posie remembered, with some confusion, the Duchesse putting her hand over Anatole's hand, as if to comfort him, when the news was first broken of Anouk's death.

How complicated it all was! Particularly as Anouk's relationship with the French boy had seemed, from afar, to be so wholesome.

Posie remembered how Dolly had told her, not an hour before, that Anouk had doted on the Count, and she remembered the fond gaze of Anouk that afternoon, when she had pointed to Anatole in the garden.

'I think of him as the son I never had.'

Posie was suddenly desperate to change, to get out of the dotted pink dress, the same dress Lady Clare might still be wearing.

In her own office she always kept a spare set of clothes. A plain, well-cut black wool dress, as suitable for a Court appearance as a smart dinner. There were also a few jolly necklaces and belts, and a tube of bright-pink lipstick.

She left Smallbone telling Lovelace that any searches of Van Dusen's new suite of rooms at the Ritz were downright useless, as the American had checked out earlier in the day in anticipation of sailing on the steamliner, the *Pride of Boston*. Instead, his packed luggage had been given a good going-over by the Southampton police, who had efficiently got it off the boat, but nothing untoward had come to light.

As Posie passed the coffee table she accidentally knocked over the French Embassy's note with the information about the de Poilac family on it. She read it again.

A date stood out.

November 1907.

And the details of the two de Poilac homes. Versailles, and Cabris.

Smallbone was gathering up his things, and Lovelace was giving him Anouk's real name, Harriet Synnes, to investigate.

'We'll meet here again, first thing tomorrow, Sergeant. Eight-fifteen sharp. I want this kept low-key for now, but we'll have to get our ducks in a row by tomorrow. I'm afraid it's going to be a late night for you tonight, Smallbone.'

Posie then added to Smallbone's list of tasks. 'Could you contact the International Operator, Smallbone? About Anouk's house line? Can you find out if there were any international calls placed *by* her, from the House of Sinne around two weeks ago?'

'Of course, Miss.'

'Oh, and talking of *international*, can you find out what

the French aristocrats were up to at Kew Gardens today, Smallbone?'

'Of course.'

He was almost out of the door. Posie was taking down the black wool dress from its hanger on the back of her door, thinking of the times she used to keep more exciting things here to wear. Skimpier, silkier dresses. Sassier for sure, with panels of lace and sequins; more suited for clubs and theatres, and dancing.

For places of entertainment.

Places where you could go and seek reckless abandonment.

Clubs. Theatres.

Casinos?

She stuck her neck around the door. Just caught the Sergeant.

'One last thing. Anouk Sinne had a tendency to gamble, years ago. Normally gamblers don't change, and nor do their habits. Can you make enquiries, Smallbone?'

Smallbone's bright enthusiastic keenness seemed to be ebbing away, but his smile didn't falter.

'Of course. It's a pleasure, Miss Parker. Always a pleasure.'

And he almost managed to sound convincing.

* * * *

Nineteen

Posie changed into her black dress in about two seconds flat. And her speed was timely, as Sergeant Fox was back, with Lady Clare Pring in tow.

The woman's angry, petulant voice could be heard in the entrance hall below.

'What *is* this wretched place you've brought me to?'

'Well, it's not Scotland Yard, my Lady, is it? But, happily for you, it's not a cell. We do have some questions to ask you, and we thought you'd appreciate the discretion. If you would like to consult the details of the Arrest Warrant, you will find that we can question you wherever we wish.'

'The timing is not exactly convenient, that's all.'

Fox was bluffing well, Posie realised as she applied her lipstick very quickly. Fox, bless him, had no idea why he had been ordered to fetch this woman, and actually, Posie didn't have a very clear idea herself yet. But Lady Clare had something to add to this sorry tale, she felt sure.

She went into the waiting room and joined Richard.

As she heard the double set of footsteps on the stairs, she grabbed up the relevant snaps Sam Stubbs had left behind. In her hand too was the French Embassy report. She glanced at it quickly again.

That date...

November 1907.

What was it about that year?

What if…?

Posie was conscious suddenly of excitement pulsing through her every nerve, every sinew.

What she had suddenly tumbled across would make an odd puzzle-piece, but it would make a mad sort of sense. *Wouldn't it?*

Richard smiled at Posie from his position over by the window.

It was almost ten o'clock.

'Remind me again, sweetheart, what's your plan here with Lady Clare?'

'I thought she could give us some background on Anouk Sinne and the Viscount. One is dead, the other has actively lied, and won't ever talk. But Lady Clare might. And I want to play this *my* way, darling. A woman's touch, and all that.'

Richard laughed. 'You just need me to bring you in some tea?'

'Exactly. Golly, I'm hungry, though. I hope Fox ordered something. Otherwise, there's an emergency tin of Edward's Desiccated Soup in the kitchen. You might have to make me a cup, my love. Failing which, Bovril …'

And here was Lady Clare Pring, looking all about her with incredulous eyes, at the cosy waiting room with its newspapers and plumped-up cushions. The tea-pot and biscuits.

She whipped off a severe plain black skullcap and tucked her red hair behind her ear. The very short, shingled bob did not become her, and would have been better suited to a younger, leaner face, as Tamara de Lempicka had no doubt found to her cost when painting Lady Clare.

'Where *am* I? Chief Commissioner? I say, what is the meaning of this? An *Arrest Warrant*?'

'Good evening, Lady Clare. The Arrest Warrant is only

a speculative one. It is more a request for information. And this is my wife's place.' He indicated to Posie, who smiled politely. 'You met each other earlier, of course.'

A slight nod. 'So, what is it you want from me?'

'Perhaps you would be good enough to speak to my wife?'

Posie indicated through to her own office, and Lady Clare followed.

Posie had left her desk light on, and now that the light outside was dying, this small intimate circle of light seemed to focus things. 'Please sit down, my Lady. Would you like some tea?'

'Good heavens, no!' Lady Clare removed her dark brocade coat. She too had changed out of the polka-dot affair from earlier into a smart black dress, very similar to Posie's own. Lady Clare sat down gingerly. If the woman had been less prickly, Posie might have tried to make a joke about their similar ongoing wardrobe choices.

But no, better get to the point.

Posie had out one of her notebooks, with a pencil atop it, but she didn't touch it just yet. It was like a threat lying there, necessary, tangible.

Instead, she placed one of Sam Stubbs' photographs in front of Lady Clare.

It was of the woman herself, looking misty-eyed and tenderly across the table during the 'reveal'. Lady Clare looked momentarily unamused and took out a pair of half-moon spectacles from her shoulder bag.

A shrug. 'What of it?'

Posie fished out the other, 'matching' photograph which had captured the very subject of Lady Clare's glance.

When Posie spoke it was very gently, quietly.

'He's your lover, isn't he? Gordy Lorkinsson? More than that, actually. I think you love him. I think this has been going on for years. Perhaps...' she took a chance here, a leap of faith in her own abilities, '...perhaps since 1907?'

There was a horrid silence.

Lady Clare took off the half-moons, bit at one of the handles unattractively.

'Does your husband know?' Posie hated doing this; hated the element of threat behind it.

But I need to know what's going on.

The silence stretched on.

Posie blew out her cheeks in exasperation. She'd have to use the slim snippet of knowledge she *did* have, which was actually not even proven. Richard would have a blue fit if he realised how patchy her 'evidence' was.

'There's no point denying it, Lady Clare. We have a witness, in Mr Lorkinsson's block of flats, who will attest to having seen you attend on him there. Regularly.'

'Attest? Attest *where*?' For the first time a real flicker of fear lit up those steely grey eyes.

Then there was a break in the resolve. 'But we were so *careful*! For almost twenty years.'

Posie was sympathetic. 'Careful is as careful does, I'm afraid. In my experience, nothing is ever watertight. Someone, somewhere is watching. All the time.'

Lady Clare was rifling through her handbag, searching desperately for something. She found a silver case of cigarettes and struggled to open it. Posie saw how much she was shaking, almost in convulsions.

This was horrible.

'Look, Lady Clare, I'm not going to tell anyone about your affair with the Icelander, and neither is my husband, as long as nothing criminal has occurred as a result of it, of course. Nothing relating to the murders today, I mean.'

'Of course nothing criminal has occurred! Those dreadful murders? I'm innocent of all of it, and so is Gordy, poor love. He's a gentle giant. It makes me sick to think of him locked up tonight. By Gad! I'd give anything to get him out of there.'

'Help him then, my Lady.'

'How can I?'

'Tell me the truth. What am I not seeing here? Tell me about your relationship with Anouk Sinne. More to the point, I want to know about your *husband's* relationship with her.'

'A trade of information?'

'If you like.'

A slim Turkish cigarette was lit, and Posie pushed a pink glass ashtray towards the older woman.

Lady Clare sighed resignedly. 'You're right, Miss Parker, although God knows how you got the date right. I suppose you really must be good at your job, as people say. Yes, I met Gordy first in 1907. It was a very cold February.'

Posie had realised that it fitted.

She was remembering Dolly's recollection of a very tall, very blonde man, visiting Hattie in 1907, at Camden Police Station.

She watched Lady Clare smoke and relax a little.

'Hubert was a Magistrate at the time. Made him feel important. For some reason I was in that part of town, and I decided to wait for him to finish at Court that day. It was an important case: lots of newspaper men waiting outside. A case with Christabel Pankhurst, the Suffragette. A big crowd. That's when I met *him*. Gordy. We were both standing outside the Court, shivering. Gordy was smoking, and I asked him for a light, even though, back in those days, it didn't really "do" for a woman to smoke. I was looking for an excuse to speak to him. He was like some sort of blonde God. So physical, with his rough, cut and burnt hands and his tatty, ripped overalls; the opposite of Hubert. Even now, the memory of him…'

The woman exhaled for a long breath.

'Turned out, we were both miserable. He'd been involved with some pharmacist, and she'd finally told him they were over. She had been very dramatic, apparently: heartless. Well, that pharmacist turned out to be the woman we later knew as Anouk Sinne.'

'And you? You were miserable too, Lady Clare?'

'Of course I was. I was young, but I already had three sons. The boys were hard work, troublesome, and even though I had nursemaids, and money, I felt trapped. I felt unattractive, too: I'd put on a good deal of weight having three babies so quickly, and Hubert had always had a roving eye: lots of women. That was a feature of our marriage I'd grown used to. But Gordy made me feel like a princess.' Lady Clare smiled for perhaps the first time since sitting down.

'He still does.'

She explained quickly that it had been *she* who had had the money. How her father had been from the entrepreneurial Alladice family from the north of England, confectionary-makers, owners of huge factories.

'Sweet, cheap, teeth-spoiling treats for workers, but my father grew colossally rich on it all. He was a millionaire. And I was his only child, his only heir. My daddy was from a family of social climbers. Where titles meant *everything*.'

Posie didn't say anything. Once, she had met some members of another branch of the Alladice family, out in Venice. They had been equally red-haired, and equally preoccupied with titles. But she didn't admit to any of this; didn't want to break client confidences, or to interrupt this strange tale.

Lady Clare tapped off some ash.

'Somehow my daddy was put in touch with Lord Henry Pring, Hubert's father. The Pring family were virtually penniless, despite their history going back centuries. They were also heavily in debt, mainly due to Lord Henry's gambling habits. They had this huge great country pile, Effington Hall, simply haemorrhaging money, and it was agreed that my father's money would go to them, in exchange for Hubert marrying me. They were Roman Catholic, which was handy, as so were the Alladice family.'

Lady Clare laughed cynically. 'Although that was

about the only thing Hubert and I had in common. It was ridiculous, looking back. I was eighteen, and I went along with it all because I knew nothing else. I became Lady Clare Pring, and our wedding day was probably the happiest day of my daddy's life, which proved to be almost at an end, as it turned out.'

The money had poured into the Pring family coffers, and Lady Clare was left with no special settlement of her own.

'My daddy trusted Hubert. Thought he would always provide for me. Saw Hubert as a good, upstanding man. Which he *is*, actually. And he's a well-meaning man, but he's foolish, with no business sense. Just after our wedding, Hubert's father, Lord Henry, had a stroke from which he never recovered. He's still alive, but he's unable to direct how the Alladice money is, or was, spent. So it was left up to Hubert, whose first act was to patch up Effington Hall, which he should have sold, of course. And then he started spending money as if his life depended on it.'

Lady Clare shook her head in disbelief.

'From the beginning Hubert was a sucker for a sob story. He set up all these schemes: to reform the criminal system; fund the Suffragettes; help find jobs for people who were struggling. But it turns out his schemes haven't helped *him*. Or me. I've had to watch helplessly, over the years, as the Alladice money has been frittered away. Lord knows what my father would say if he could see it now. See *me* now. In my tawdry shop-bought dresses, like today.'

She looked up at Posie, suddenly horrified: 'Oh! Oh, I didn't mean anything against shop-bought dresses. I mean, *you* looked perfectly wonderful in that pink thing; the men couldn't take their eyes off you, could they? And no wonder. I'm not stupid enough to not realise that it's the woman who makes the dress, not the other way around. Forgive me.'

'The dress was a bold move for both of us, I think.' Posie smiled genuinely. 'There's nothing to forgive.'

Lady Clare took a last drag on her cigarette. 'I had some diamonds, though. From my father. A set with a tiara and a matching necklace and earrings, a parure. Worth a fortune. I was clever enough to have them valued and have paste replicas made some years ago. Then I arranged a sale of the real things with Sotheby's and I put the money in a bank account, just for myself. Still have it, thank the Lord.'

Another cigarette was lit and a small silence stretched as Lady Clare took a long pull.

Then another.

'Gordy was a compensation, I'll admit. He begged me to leave Hubert, again and again over the years; to marry him. But while Hubert lives, I can't marry again, can I? I'm Catholic. And there were my three sons to consider. My difficult boys. All blessed with the Alladice ambition but combined with the ineffectual business brains of the Pring family. I've tried my best for them, but I fear I have failed.'

Posie pushed on: 'And Anouk? Or "Hattie" as she then was? She entered your lives at the same time as Gordy, I think?'

I need to understand this past, Posie thought to herself with some urgency now. *Because the past has fingers which are possessive, long-reaching, inescapable.*

Lady Clare threw Posie a shrewd look. 'Yes, indeed. "Hattie". Well, if only she could have stayed as Hattie, eh? Not morphed into this dreadful blot on all our lives.'

Posie heard the door outside in the waiting room bang, and then Fox's voice, speaking to Lovelace. There was the sound of plates clattering in the kitchen, and there was the unmistakeable smell of fishcakes.

Her stomach growled hungrily.

Focus.

'You mentioned your husband had many other women, Lady Clare? But Anouk was special to him?'

The woman finished her cigarette regretfully. 'Hubert must have thought all his Christmases had come at once.

She was one of the girls up before him in Court that day. I saw her when she came out, and she was tiny, dark, sparkling, despite a night in the cells. Of course, Hubert convinced his fellow Magistrates to let her off, along with a few insignificant others.'

Posie didn't move, thinking of her friend, Dolly, described as an 'insignificant' other. Perhaps Dolly would have laughed merrily if she'd heard this description of herself, but Posie couldn't laugh.

No-one was insignificant, and every story was important. Wasn't it?

Lady Clare stared past Posie, out of the window, past the black outlines of the buildings there. 'I don't know how exactly it moved on from that day, only of course it did. It was the affair of Hubert's life. I didn't see him for a couple of months. I didn't care: I had Gordy to keep me going. All I knew was that Hubert was giddy with happiness. I saw them sometimes; they'd pull up in a motor-taxi outside our house, and Hubert would get out, hardly able to rip himself away from Hattie. She was like a fire, a blaze in the dark for him.'

'But something changed, Lady Clare, didn't it? Sometime in the late summer of 1907? This blaze in the dark? It went out?'

A silence, then a nod.

'It was earlier than that. Early summer, perhaps. May, or June? Anouk – or Hattie, as she was – went away. It was over, as suddenly as it had begun. And Hubert never really recovered. There were – *are* – other women, of course. But she was everything to him.'

Posie waited, but in vain this time. She pressed on: 'But something *more* than lust, than a blaze, bound Anouk and Hubert together, didn't it? It was a debt of guilt, wasn't it? And without this indebtedness, the House of Sinne would never have been set up. You see, I *know* that Anouk Sinne has made your husband pay for what happened to her back in 1907. And you know why, too, don't you, Lady Clare? What it was which bound them?'

A baby.

There must have been a baby.

A silence, then the woman gave a slight shrug.

'He never told me, of course; I pieced it together myself. The timing fitted. Her "vanishing". The way she came back two years later, completely changed, like some kind of succubus. The grip she had on Hubert was all-consuming. At first, she just wanted him to "keep" her, in a nice flat in town. Then, later, after that big trial about the fire at Kew, she forced Hubert to buy that huge house and garden in Chelsea and set up the perfume house.'

Yes. It all fitted.

'There was a child, Lady Clare, am I right? Anouk was pregnant with Hubert's child, wasn't she?'

An illegitimate child, which would spell ruin for the Catholic Viscount, and ruin of a different kind for Hattie.

A child which would have to be given away.

A child whose very existence would create a bond between its parents which could never be broken, or surrendered. A shared heartbreak, lasting forever.

Lady Clare gave a very slight nod.

'I think so. Yes. Born in the autumn of 1907, I suppose. Anouk must have gone away to give birth, then became ill. That was the only explanation.'

The secret as to why Hubert and Anouk had been bound together had come to Posie just after Dolly had left, earlier.

Now it seemed obvious.

Like it had been staring them all in the face all along. Teasing them.

'Do you happen to know the baby's name?' Posie asked. 'Or where this child ended up?'

'Of course not.' Lady Clare sounded outraged. 'Hubert and I have never spoken of it. How could we? He was bound to me by the money, and by our religion. There was never a question of divorce.'

Posie pushed a sheet of paper towards Lady Clare, who read, then shrugged.

'I don't understand. What's this?'

The Viscountess read the sheet again carefully. It was in English but with French crests and a French heading.

Posie reached over and tapped at the paper with her pencil. 'See the date? November 1907? The date fits, doesn't it, my Lady? Nine months after Hattie and Hubert met...'

Lady Clare gasped, slapping her hand across her mouth in horror.

'*Anatole?*'

And suddenly there were silent tears, a convulsing as she rocked to-and-fro.

'Anatole de Poilac is Hubert's son with Anouk? Oh! Oh, my days. No, it can't be!'

Posie wasn't certain, but it seemed a likely hypothesis. She remembered Anouk mentioning that Maria de Poilac had been quite old when she'd become a mother. That Anatole had been 'a gift'. *What if she had meant it literally?*

And hadn't Anouk drawn to Posie's attention the fact that the Count looked nothing like his mother.

Posie remembered Anouk's words earlier: '*I think of him as the son I never had.*' Well, what if he was the son she *had* had? And been forced by circumstance to give away?

What if the recent meet-ups between Anatole and Anouk had been wholesome affairs, after all? A re-discovery of each other as mother and son?

But was this all enough?

Posie shrugged. 'I don't know for sure. But it would make sense that Anouk packed her baby off to a French contact of hers, far away, wouldn't it? A childless contact, I suppose. Wealthy, titled, with all the best things to offer. And married, respectable. It makes sense.'

Lady Clare had gone very pale under her powder. 'Oh!

But I'd always assumed… I always thought the baby would have been a…'

'A what?'

'No matter.'

Lady Clare sniffed. 'So, their child was under our noses all this time? And Maria de Poilac did the good deed, did she, taking the boy in? Well, I've always had a lot of respect for that woman, she seems so sensible and kind. But I wonder… I wonder if Hubert *knows*?'

'I have no idea, Lady Clare. I just happened on this idea before you arrived here.'

The woman was shaking her head. 'I don't think he can know. Hubert would have found this impossible to keep secret. He always wanted a son he could be proud of. And Anatole would have made him proud!'

She snorted, keeping down a hysterical bark of laughter. 'I feel dreadful saying this, and I misjudged her, obviously, but I thought Anouk Sinne might actually be having an *affair* with Anatole. I knew her tastes ran to very young men, you see. I always thought there was truth in the rumours about her and the Prince of Wales, actually. And then there is the case of my *own* son.'

Lady Clare was reaching for her coat now; she shook it on over her shoulders.

'Your son, Lady Clare?'

'Peregrine. My eldest. He's twenty-five now, so not that young, but a full twenty years younger than Anouk. He's a wretch of a case. Went off to the Great War in 1917, got shelled senseless and never recovered. He uses drink and drugs to numb the pain, but he also – I think I mentioned – has the curse of the Pring family. Gambling. Peregrine gambles to forget who he is, what he saw. It must be in the blood.'

Lady Clare suddenly put her face into her hands. 'It seems Anouk couldn't leave my family alone, Miss Parker. Not content with bleeding us dry financially, in the last couple of years she has often taken Peregrine with her on her little "jaunts". Very unsavoury.'

'Gambling, you mean? More?'

A nod. 'I began to suspect Anouk and my son were having an affair early this year. Two weeks ago, I listened in on a telephone call he made to Anouk. It was pitiful. Peregrine was pleading with Anouk to see him, to come into town. But she wouldn't. She'd given him the flick: told him she had no time for him and that she wasn't going out at all anymore. Thank the Lord! It was the only good news I'd had in weeks, although Peregrine has been badly affected.'

Posie had grabbed at her notebook.

'Do you know *where* Anouk went to gamble?'

'Oh, yes,' Lady Clare said bitterly. 'Mayfair. I suppose the Curzon-Alhambra. That is certainly where Peregrine has come undone.'

And then it all came out.

How Peregrine, nerves shattered, had gambled away his own allowance, and then that of his brothers, and been bailed out by his father. Over and over.

Over the last two years, along with Hubert's vast spending, especially on the House of Sinne, Peregrine Pring had whittled away the Alladice fortune and rendered it to nothing.

The family was now in a bad way.

'I may as well tell you this, as Hubert won't,' said Lady Clare, very softly. 'He's in denial. But you will find out anyway. The Alladice money is gone. We were actually moving tonight, to a flat. We've been forced to drop most of our staff, and the three boys – who still live at home – were informed they would all have to share a bedroom again. Or else, leave.'

'I'm so sorry. How has Peregrine taken this? And the news of Anouk's death?'

Perhaps Peregrine Pring should be questioned too? If

he was, as seemed likely, a recent paramour, or at least a companion, of the dead perfumier?

But Lady Clare was shaking her head. 'Peregrine has spent today packing up to leave England. He's taken the split badly, and our financial ruin has unhinged him, too. So we decided not to tell him of Anouk's death: there seemed no point. Not yet.'

'Leaving England? Where is he going to?'

'He's gone already. It was horrible. Probably witnessed by your policemen. Peregrine was shouting and blubbing, blaming us for his lot in life: off his head on a cocktail of drugs. He told us he had enough money to get to Berlin, says that's where "life" is happening right now. He wants to make his way there as a photographer, and, I suppose, it will make or break him. One of the cars from Croydon Airport collected him earlier. He'll make the late flight.'

'I see.' Posie saw the woman opposite her, weary, tale told, checking her watch, pushing back the chair a little.

One last push.

'Do you know why Anouk Sinne, and the Maharani died today, my Lady? *Why* they were murdered?'

Because you, you of all people, have told me how much you hated Anouk Sinne, Posie was thinking.

How she tore a hole through your marriage and has taken money – your money – steadily throughout the years.

How she has perhaps corrupted your own son and has made him unhappy.

Lady Clare shook her head. 'I admit I hated her, Miss Parker. And she treated me detestably, but I bore it all because through her – incidentally, I suppose – I have met Gordy, who is the love of my life. And so I tried to make the arrangement work for all of us. Take the benefits of it, too.'

Lady Clare smiled in a satisfied way. 'It was *I* who insisted on Gordy being able to use the garden at the House of Sinne, just after Hubert had set the perfume house up for Anouk. Gordy had moved into gardening work by then, after he'd attended a Horticultural College down in Kent, paid for by me. By this stage he wanted a garden of his own. I told Hubert I had found a good man, who could help out supplying Anouk with specialised flowers for no salary, and Hubert jumped at the chance. I wasn't there when Gordy met Anouk again, just before the Great War, but it must have been an odd encounter. Wretched, in a way, but both were tied into it. I *do* know she wouldn't speak to him for weeks; that she was horrified with the *fait accompli* she'd been presented with.'

'Golly, but weren't you worried that the two of them would get together again?'

Lady Clare shook her head. 'I have always been utterly convinced of Gordy's love for me. Besides, by this time Anouk was becoming famous, and her tastes ran to much younger men than Gordy. I don't think he was ever that important to Anouk, anyhow. It became, over time, as I had hoped, a workable arrangement. After a while Anouk took to treating him like an employee, rather disdainfully. Look at the way she apparently wrote to him today, dismissing him! He wasn't hers to dismiss!'

The woman rose and clicked the clasp on her bag together.

'I didn't kill Anouk Sinne, Miss Parker. We are in financial difficulties, but Anouk Sinne's death makes no difference to that. If she had lived, she would have been turfed out of that expensive house, and it would have been sold. With her death, the result is the same. In some ways, the awful woman has done us a favour: Number 11, Embankment Gardens has been protected from Hubert and from Peregrine. It can now be sold and we can try and dig ourselves out of this current hell-hole. They can also sell that impressive painting of Anouk, which I suppose is worth more than the one of *me*. And if the formula for that strange perfume today is found, it will provide an income. A good one, hopefully.'

If Mr Van Dusen doesn't contest the ownership, which he probably will, Posie thought, but didn't say.

Standing at the door of Posie's office, Lady Clare Pring pulled on her dreary black skull-cap. Posie hadn't expected to like this woman, or to feel sorry for her, but she felt both of those things now.

'What will you *do*, my Lady?'

'I'll wait for this to blow over, Miss Parker. Then I'll make sure that Hubert and the two younger sons at home are fine enough, and then I'll leave. I'm fed up doing what people expect me to do, all my life. I want to live. For *me*. I'll start afresh somewhere, paid for with my secret diamond parure fund. I'll take Gordy with me. Somewhere roses can grow. Don't you think?'

'It sounds perfect, and well-deserved. Oh, one last question, Lady Clare.'

'Go on, please.'

'Did you see a peacock in the gardens today, at Chelsea? Or do you have any knowledge of a peacock there?'

The woman blinked slightly, shook her large head. But she didn't laugh, or look surprised.

'I didn't see a peacock, Miss Parker. No. But, you know, Anatole de Poilac wears a signet ring with a peacock on it? And I'm sure his mother, the Duchesse, always wears a cameo with a peacock on it. It must be a family symbol for the ancient de Poilac dynasty.' She half-laughed. 'My daddy would have loved all that, of course!'

The two women walked through the client waiting room, and in the lit-up kitchen Posie could see Richard and Sergeant Fox standing together companionably, washing up. She saw that, rather sweetly, a place had been laid for her at the tiny table, an upside-down tin plate covering her hot dinner.

She called for Fox to see Lady Clare down to the waiting police car. Posie stretched out her hand, and Lady Clare took it, pressed it, as if for strength.

'I hope I was helpful. I know now how good you are, Miss Parker. Find out who did this, Miss Parker. But get my Gordy out; that's the most important thing of all.'

And then she was gone.

* * * *

Twenty

Once she'd repeated the conversation she'd just had to her husband and to Fox, Posie sat down to eat. She listened to their chatter in the next room, their disbelief.

'A baby? Wrong side of the blanket, eh? So old Pring has been under the thumb screws ever since…'

'We should have thought of that, sir.'

'But where's the *evidence*?'

One thing she hadn't shared had been the detail about Anatole de Poilac being the illegitimate son.

Posie didn't know why she didn't share this information.

Perhaps something didn't sit right for her about the whole thing? And where indeed was the evidence, other than Anatole's handy date of birth – nine months after Anouk and Hubert had first met?

And there was something else which was nagging at Posie: something in the story Lady Clare had just recounted had struck Posie as being crucially important, but whatever it was, it was escaping her. The more she tried to remember, the harder it was to grasp.

She listened instead as Sergeant Fox telephoned through to Sergeant Smallbone at the Yard, instructing him not to lose time researching Hubert Pring's finances, but instead to look into Anouk Sinne's activities at the Curzon-Alhambra Casino, in Mayfair.

Then the two men were quiet, and there came the sounds of paper turning, then Richard's questioning voice, his ready laughter.

He was, Posie had no doubt, a good boss, just as he was a good husband and a good father.

She was lucky, she knew; she thought of Lady Clare, motoring now through Piccadilly, heading back to a husband whose love and dedication had always been for another.

Posie ate without much enjoyment, despite her hunger. The fishcakes she normally loved seemed tasteless. Perhaps they had only ever been delicious when she had Dolly with her, at the restaurant, to enjoy them with.

She stood up, running lukewarm water from the cistern over her greasy plate. She thought of Dolly, stepping out into the night, with that wretched Sphynx cat, similarly locked into a marriage which didn't seem to be working.

All these women, fleeing from themselves.

Posie stood briefly at the kitchen window and fingered the old red velvet curtains she'd hung there almost five years ago, when she'd been accompanied on this crazy little London venture by no-one at all, only her father's old Siamese cat, Mr Minks. She'd installed these curtains specially for him; this office had become his playground, his domain, and he'd run up and down the velvet drapes here merrily, even though he was quite an old cat, swinging from them with abandon.

Posie looked out into the darkness, remembering the time, three years back, when Mr Minks had vanished. Stepped out of his life, into the darkness of eternity.

The last link to her life with her father in Norfolk, gone.

She'd been more upset than she'd thought possible.

Cats.

She wouldn't have another. She'd decided there and then. It was too upsetting when they died.

Anouk had obviously been devoted to her cat, too. At

least Julius was going to be well-loved, and by Dolly of all people!

Posie put her forehead against the cold, misted-up glass and closed her eyes. She was tired. But in moments like this she just wanted to walk, rather than to sleep. To escape.

She turned back into the main room and saw that Sergeant Fox and Richard were now poring over a set of photographs on Prudence's desk. But not those taken by Sam Stubbs. She marched quickly across.

'My Sergeant has surpassed himself.' Richard grinned, indicating the photographs. 'Poor lad has been trying to show us these all evening and he's only just managed! This is your blackmail assignment from earlier.'

Posie scanned the photographs, some of which were very blurry and badly developed. The good ones – of which there were about nine – were fantastic.

'Goodness! You took a *camera* with you? You actually photographed the blackmailer? This is wonderful stuff, Sergeant. But, oh, I say! You were supposed to be discreet. You promised. How on earth did you manage it?'

Fox patted towards his chest rather smugly. On a loop of twined black string, hung a small metallic device designed to look like a plain cigarette tin, but of the travel-sized variety.

'*That's* the camera? It's tiny!'

'Isn't it?' purred Fox proudly, as if he had had a hand in designing the thing. 'We have a few of them at the Yard: work a treat. The beauty is that I don't need to raise the instrument to my face. I just snap away at chest-height, so no-one is any the wiser.'

'I expect Len would love one of those! Goodness, in his field of work that would come in most handy.'

But now Posie was checking through the photographs, taken from Fox's position among the telephone-booths at Victoria Station.

They had been ordered sequentially.

The drop was exactly as Fox had described. Lucy Reeble, smart in her blazing white outfit, carrying the heavy black bag with its white logo on it, full of money. Then placing it in an open locker, the number 56 marked clearly on the metal door.

Here was Lucy, turning, biting her lip, willing herself on. Forcing herself to walk away from the locker without looking back.

Here was another snap, where she'd stopped next to a postbox, the open locker still in view. She was captured pulling out an envelope from her pocket, her back to the camera. There was another snap of her posting the envelope.

'Has anyone asked her what she was sending?' asked Posie.

'Yes. Apparently, it was the letter to Lorkinsson, telling him to clear out tomorrow. Miss Sinne instructed Lucy to send it today, second class post. To get there tomorrow. The Royal Mail messed up; they were too efficient and it got there too soon.'

'I see.'

And here was a snap showing the man who had come to collect the money. Exactly as Fox had described. His very modern sleeve-bands which caught the sunlight sparkled brightly in the snaps, slightly gaudily.

There were shots of him walking away with the black bag, which he carried with ease, and then, obviously realising he had someone on his tail, shots – blurry and almost useless – of what had obviously turned into a chase.

Posie was about to speak, but at that very moment they all heard a key in the lock of the frosted-glass office door, and the three of them stiffened, watching the black silhouette framed there. Lovelace instinctively covered the photos and placed an arm across Posie protectively.

'Oh!' Posie breathed normally again. 'It's only *you*, Len!'

Len Irving grinned, his handsome face lit up mischievously as he took off his black felt hat, ruffled his curly dark hair. 'Wotcha! Yep, it's "only" me, Posie. That's a jolly nice welcome! I'm just back from a job. What you lot up to in here, anyhow? It's almost eleven o'clock at night!'

Len was a shadower; known to be the best in the business. He was highly sought-after by lawyers whose clients were seeking divorces; who wanted proof of adultery and other types of bad behaviour from errant spouses. In many of these high-profile divorces, only an attestation of adultery supported by a clear photograph in Court would do, and Len's were usually the photographs which were submitted.

He worked mainly in the evening and at night, haunting clubs, and hotel lobbies, peering through windows with long-range lenses and an appetite for destruction which, personally, Posie found very unsavoury.

In fact, the very nature of the work made her shudder, always had, and yet it was surprisingly lucrative, and had kept the little Detective Agency afloat on more than one occasion. Therefore, she couldn't complain. Not too much anyhow.

He had come in to drop off a film which he'd take for processing in the morning, apparently.

But Posie realised that of late, Len seemed to be spending less and less time at home with his snip-faced wife, Aggie, and their growing brood of children. Around the same time Kit Lovelace had been born, back in March, Aggie had given birth to a surprise pair of boy twins, Terence and Desmond, and, if Len's un-ironed shirts and drooping eyelids were anything to go by, chaos ruled at home, and there was very little sleep to be had for anyone.

Posie had come to suspect that Len might be sleeping at the office, for whatever reason. And perhaps that was why he was here now? Hunkering down for the night?

For a couple of minutes Len and Sergeant Fox waxed lyrical over the brand-new tiny camera, while Richard started to stack up the photographs into a neat pile.

But then Len saw one of the photographs in Richard's hands, and his manner changed.

He froze.

'Can I have a gander at that, sir?'

'I suppose so.'

Len took the pile, peeled off the top photograph: a clear one, showing the blackmailer sauntering up to the locker at Victoria.

Len flicked through the others, then he turned to Posie, his face white and horribly sheeny. 'What's all this about, Posie? Who's this? And why are you on his tail?'

Posie knew Len well, and she realised he was gripped with worry. 'Do you know this man, Len?'

He didn't answer the question, but bit at his lip instead. 'What's he supposed to have done, Po?'

Posie threw a glance at Richard, who shook his head just perceptibly.

'I can't say, Len. But it's serious, I'm afraid.'

'I don't believe you. You lot have got this all wrong.' Len sank down into Prudence's chair, head in his hands.

Posie marched around and tugged at his sleeve. 'Len, tell me. Do you know who this is? You *must* tell us.'

There was silence.

Richard Lovelace got out his cigarette tin, lit his cigarette and shook out the match languidly. 'I suggest you either tell us who this fella is, Len, or else find him and tell him to come to us. I must congratulate you, though: your timing is spot on. I was about to send Fox here straight over to the *Associated Press* with the best snap in this packet, and get it splashed all over the front pages of tomorrow morning's edition.'

Len rubbed at his eyes with the balls of his hands.

'Oh, Gawd! No, don't do that. You'll break him. Blimmin' 'eck, what a mess! What's he got into? Bitten off more than he can chew by the looks of things!'

Len stabbed his finger down forcibly at the picture. 'He's like me. He relies on being discreet.'

Richard sounded unsympathetic, cold. 'Well, this time he wasn't discreet enough, was he? Who is he? Another shadower? Someone who got too big for his boots? Decided to try a bit of blackmail? Even murder?'

'Blackmail? Murder? *What?*' Len looked uncomfortable. 'I don't know what you're talkin' about. But he's not a murderer. No way! He's reliable and works hard; does what's asked of him. I'll go, sir, and tell him there's been a mix-up. Tell him you'd like to see him. Where? At the Yard?'

Len was jamming on his black hat again.

'Get him to come *here*. Tomorrow. Nine o'clock sharp.'

'Right you are, Chief Commissioner. I'll go now.'

'Probably best, Len.'

In the silence which followed the drumming of Len's retreating footsteps down the stairs, Posie's thoughts were whirring, blurring, meshing together. She was thinking of the blackmailer, a man obviously held in some esteem by Len.

'He's reliable and works hard; does what's asked of him.'

She spoke quickly: 'You know, Richard, I kept thinking tonight of that play we still haven't seen: *No, No, Nanette*–'

Richard rolled his eyes heavenwards. 'Can't this wait, darling?'

'Absolutely not,' she snapped. 'Dolly said the storyline was about a blackmail plot which wasn't really that at all. She said it was a "face-saving exercise". What if we are looking at the same thing here? What if Anouk Sinne's oh-so-scary blackmail plot was simply a carefully-constructed mirage, fabricated by someone who did what was asked of him.'

'But why, darling?'

Posie wasn't sure, and bit her lip. 'Perhaps it was to make it look as if Anouk needed protection? Protection provided by me, and the police.'

'But *why*, Miss?' Fox cut in, stupefied.

She sighed. 'I'm not sure yet, Sergeant. But we *do* know that Anouk Sinne was a master of deception, don't we?'

Richard took in a deep mouthful of smoke, breathed it in almost mournfully.

'Nah, darling. Most likely this cheeky young fella is some sort of low-level photographer who saw or heard a bit too much. You're quite correct that Anouk Sinne seems to have had many secrets. Well, let's wait and see what this fella has to say for himself tomorrow, shall we, my love? What we *do* know for sure is that two famous women are lying dead in the morgue at Scotland Yard, and I've got to return there before the day is done. Make sure everything is in order.'

The Yard.

Posie thought suddenly of the Icelander being held there. What was it Lady Clare had called him? '*A gentle giant*'? What scant evidence had led Richard to lock him up? It was ridiculous.

There were so many other potential suspects in this case.

'Darling, I really think Gordy Lorkinsson is innocent. Or, if not innocent, only as suspicious as the next man or woman in that room today. Gracious, even Dolly had a motive. A history of hate!'

'Perhaps. But what about the Princess? That death can only have been Lorkinsson, surely? He was *seen* with those deadly wooden sticks. It was *his* rose poison which killed her.'

'But *why* would he have wanted to kill her?' Posie shook her head angrily. 'It makes no sense. All I know is that nothing here is what it seems.'

'Well, we agree on that at least, my love.'

Posie was thinking hard again, back to the moment she had stood on the terrace with the Princess, earlier in the day.

Another odd thought occurred to her and she voiced it quietly, almost to herself: 'Another funny thing is that no-one else, apart from me and Princess Priyanka, saw that wretched peacock today. It's so odd!'

Was it her imagination or had Richard suddenly gone very pale?

Her husband spoke slowly, grinding out his smoke. 'Er, what peacock do you mean, Posie love?'

'Oh, didn't I mention it to you? There's been so much else happening…'

She rattled off a quick explanation and saw her husband swallow slowly. 'I'm sure it's nothing to worry about, Posie.'

'I'm not worried. Just puzzled. Oh! One last thing, Richard.'

'Yes, darling?' He was pulling on his trench-coat, still visibly paler than before.

'In your jacket pocket was the docket from the National Portrait Gallery. About that Lempicka painting? Remember? From those men who wanted to take it away? I won't lose it, I promise. Can I have it?'

'What? Oh, yes.' He scrabbled for it and passed it over. 'Here. If there's anything odd then I'll call Sir Charles John Holmes in the morning and sort out the details. Much too late now, of course. You should go home, darling. Try not to let this keep you awake.'

But how could Posie sleep? She'd rather be puzzling it all out.

Walking and puzzling.

There was just so much here which didn't make sense.

No sense at all.

* * * *

Twenty-One

Walking home, which was only three streets away, Posie purposely took a long route, drifting through the leafy, thick-as-tar London night. Past the shut-up offices lurking in their night-time stupor, and past small cafés packed with after-show diners.

Somewhere above her came a single off-key line from *No, No, Nanette*'s most famous song.

Tea for two, and two for tea…

And the sound of raucous, broken laughter.

Posie saw and heard all this in an unconscious sort of daze. She clutched hard at her carpet bag, and the discarded pink polka-dot dress, which she would drop off at the laundry the next day, probably never to wear again.

Ahead of her was the dark looming mass of the ship-sized British Museum, all its secrets locked within, ready for fresh rediscoveries tomorrow.

Secrets.

This was turning into quite some case.

It was unbelievable to think that only this morning, even at coffee time, Posie had had no case to work on: an empty diary stretching ahead and worries about filling her two days a week of 'work'.

Now she was struggling beneath a wealth of facts,

stories, and half-whispered rumours. And who knew where the truth lay in all the resulting mess?

Two women had died. And was that an end to it, with their deaths? *But why had they had to die?*

Posie tried to free her mind of it all. As she walked, she tried to review the first murder victim as if with fresh eyes.

Posie crossed the road on Great Russell Street and walked along the railings outside the British Museum, looking over the black, shadowy forecourt within.

Black and shadowy as the dead perfumier had been in her lifetime.

Anouk Sinne had been a woman who, in her mid-forties, had still been able to fascinate and attract even young men as lovers, or at least as companions.

Catnip to men.

Undoubtedly, she had been cruel, especially to other women. Her treatment of Dolly, especially in 1913, throwing her to the wolves while she escaped scot-free, had been dreadful, but her conduct even before this, at the WSPU, with the teasing of Dolly over the way she smelt, had also been beastly.

The trip out to Dolly's work at Poplar seemed especially mean. Checking out a poorer girl's lot in life, for no other reason than for simple amusement. And then to harp on about it, for years afterwards, seemed malicious.

Difficult. Complicated. Mean. Catnip.

You were all of those things, Posie conjectured.

But perhaps another truth is that you were a trail-blazing woman in a world where there are few, and you did what you needed to do in order to get ahead.

Including giving up a child you couldn't have brought up alone, as a single woman.

Posie was walking again, pounding the empty dark pavements.

Posie focused on the House of Sinne, convinced more than ever that what she had witnessed today was a house of cards, already blown down.

Or pushed down deliberately?

Eventually Posie stopped marching. She had walked in a large loop and was standing outside Museum Chambers.

Bells were ringing from nearby St George's Church for half-past eleven, and her flat up on the top floor looked to be in total darkness.

Posie hunted in her carpet bag for her keys. It was dark out here with only one dim streetlamp to see by. Her fingers brushed against the horrid blackmailing postcards she had taken from Anouk Sinne earlier that day, and then briefly touched the cold, smooth glass of the turquoise perfume bottle she had also been given, probably just containing water.

Tricks.

And then her hand touched the ripped envelope of the paperwork from the National Portrait Gallery removals men.

She'd been in such a hurry to leave that she hadn't read the thing yet, and Posie did so now in the lamplight.

And it was a revelation.

Like a bright, glaring spotlight being switched on in her brain.

'Oh! I see what you were doing, Anouk Sinne!' Posie exhaled slowly. 'Trickery again, and timing! But *why*?'

And then Posie turned her key in the lock of Museum Chambers, stepping back into her own domestic life.

She snapped the electric light on in the hallway and saw that Ted the Porter had left the residents' pigeonholes tidy and clear. There was no post for her or Richard; just a few circulars. On Ted's tidy wooden desk lay a dog-eared copy of that day's *The Times*. The same edition Posie had been reading before Dolly had called her up earlier that day, summoning her to Chelsea.

It seemed a lifetime ago.

Stepping out of the lift and entering her top-floor flat, she was met by Patsy the Yorkshire terrier, happy to see her, jumping up for attention. Posie picked up the small dog and cuddled her, kicking off her shoes. She then looked in on her three children, followed everywhere by the pitter-patter of Patsy's little feet.

All three children were sleeping peacefully, despite the heat of the room, with Phyllis curled around her bears, and Katie in her cot, looking beautiful and fractious all at the same time.

Kit, in the cot next to Katie's, had fallen asleep with his hand outstretched into Katie's cot, plucking at the coverlet there, his red hair glistening with sweat.

Posie smoothed his brow, pulling his blue cotton blanket up higher. She'd never thought of herself as a woman who needed to be defined by being a mother: hadn't expected this honour; this task. But now she had it, Posie couldn't imagine these children *not* being part of her life.

Stepping out of the room, she picked up Patsy again and wondered for a brief moment about Anouk Sinne and the child of Hubert Pring's that she had borne.

How had Anouk felt, if Anatole had been her son, knowing he was being brought up elsewhere? And what had happened in those two missing years of Anouk Sinne's life, between late spring of 1907 and her reappearance in society again in 1909? Had she perhaps been in France?

It seemed that, unless Hubert Pring – who might not even know the answer – talked, the answer would be lost forever.

In the stiflingly-hot living-room, Posie poured herself a stiff gin and tonic from the little walnut bar in the corner, and then she threw open the sash windows, letting the linen curtains flutter in the breeze which was getting up.

She dropped wearily into her usual armchair, the room still in absolute darkness. Patsy jumped up into Posie's lap and, despite the heat and the black wool dress, Posie didn't move the little dog, rather enjoying her companionship.

Perhaps Anouk Sinne would have been better off with a dog

than a cat, Posie thought to herself as she drank quickly.

Then she poured herself another.

She realised she was steadying her nerves. Her hands simply wouldn't stop shaking. It wasn't the best way of calming oneself; in fact it was a bad idea, but it had been one dreadful sort of a day, after all.

And then Posie fell into a half-sleep, waiting for Richard's key in the door. But it was far from comfortable, or restful.

In her mind's eye she was following a peacock, down to the end of a long, luscious English garden, but the bird turned suddenly, running into a dry, yellow field. Somewhere abroad. A smell of sunshine.

The dream jolted on and Posie found she was still following the peacock, but he had morphed into something else: a peacock on a ring, a brooch. And then Posie was turning, standing with Dolly again on the front steps of the House of Sinne. And Dolly was holding up Julius, enclosed within his glittery travel cage, his claws ripping at the wicker confines.

In Posie's dream a motor-car drew up suddenly. And past them both, hurrying down the steps, came Anouk Sinne, as she had looked just before she died. She was carrying two identical black House of Sinne bags, loading one straight onto the back seat of the motor-car, but hesitant about the other.

Posie heard Gordy Lorkinsson's words again, clear as a bell. '*One bag in particular Anouk seemed reluctant to let go of…*'

And then the car was driving off, Anouk had vanished, and Lady Clare had joined Posie and Dolly on the step. In the dream, Lady Clare was looking up and down the street.

'Where's the car?' she was saying. 'My son needs it. He's catching the last flight to Berlin. Tonight. Don't tell me Anouk Sinne is going to join him out there? In Berlin?'

Posie sat up suddenly, woken completely from her

half-dream, shocked, gasping, as if she had been underwater for a very long time, the remnants of the dream playing over and over in her mind.

'Oh! But what a fool I've been!'

She stood up quickly, forgetting Patsy entirely, and she apologised profusely as the little dog fell onto the floor. Posie fled into the hallway, where the crumpled pink dress was lying on the floor. She dug in a pocket and produced the tag which had earlier fluttered out from Julius' cage.

A dark-green tag.

'Of course! We've been looking at this all wrong!'

And then she was running downstairs, not bothering with the lift, breathlessly hurrying through the entrance hall, and lifting up the tatty edition of *The Times*.

Here was that story – old news now – right down low on the front page.

Posie read the caption: 'PERFECT PRINCESS PRIYANKA TOUCHES DOWN AT CROYDON!'

The beautiful and possibly murderous Maharani had arrived on Sunday, late afternoon. And here in the crowd of well-wishers was Mr Archie Van Dusen, his head almost cut off by the photographer's freeze-frame, but his dead shark's eyes were wide and thrilled-looking, hungry.

But now Posie understood almost everything and how everything joined together.

Everything except *who* the killer actually was.

And what their motive had been.

* * * *

PART FIVE

The Heart of the Matter
(Tuesday 16th June, 1925)

Twenty-Two

At eight-fifteen the next morning Posie found herself sharing the client waiting room of her Detective Agency with several of Scotland Yard's best policemen.

It was already boiling hot outside, and Posie had opened the windows as far as they would go, but little air came in.

Coffee and croissants were on the small table, but they had been polished off in less than two minutes flat.

Lovelace had grouped his men, consisting of Smallbone, Fox and – rather unbelievably, Posie felt – Inspector Oats, all around the coffee table. All had their notebooks out, and there were papers piled high on the table, and the mood was one of barely-contained excitement. There were plans to release details of the deaths that evening, with the *Associated Press* carrying the exclusive.

There were hopes of publishing Lorkinsson's name, too, in connection with the murders. Although so far, no formal arrest had been made.

Right now, Oats had a pair of very shiny handcuffs in his possession. He had put them on the table, among the crumbs.

Doctor Poots had come along too, albeit for a brief visit, as he was due to give evidence shortly in another murder case at the Old Bailey. He'd brought some toxicology results which had developed overnight and he'd wanted to see Richard in person.

He flapped around importantly with his blue post-mortem reports.

'No doubt about it at all,' he said excitedly. 'It was the pesticide which did for the Princess. Oh, and there's something else which might prove interesting: her lungs bore the tarry residue of having breathed in a helluva lot of smoke. As if she was trapped in a fire, a pretty big one I'd say.'

He cleared his throat dramatically, tugged at his bow tie. 'Oh, regarding the perfumier, an incidental detail I can disclose is that Anouk Sinne had had a child. Can't tell you *when* exactly, but it was a fairly traumatic birth, I'd guess. Twenty years ago? She underwent what looked like a caesarean section, and an emergency one at that. Bad scars, poor woman. Must have taken a while to heal, mentally and physically. Save for that, there's nothing new to report on either of the corpses.'

And once the Doctor was gone, taking a croissant or two with him, stuffed into his black velvet smoking-jacket pockets, conversation in the waiting room flowed thick and fast.

Posie, sitting in Prudence's chair, was slightly apart, trying to make sense of what she heard.

Smallbone, perhaps having worked all night, but fuelled by adrenaline and strong black coffee, had the most to contribute.

He addressed Posie first, flicking through his notebook for the outlines of a conversation which it was obvious he hadn't understood properly.

'You asked me to find out what the French aristocrats were doing at Kew Gardens, Miss?'

'Please.'

He jabbed his finger down at a page. 'They were in the hot houses mostly. Then they were looking at various types of camellias, apparently.' Smallbone said the words carefully, anxious not to get them wrong. 'Rare ones. Ones which can grow in intense heat. They purchased some seeds for planting and took cuttings too. It was a very expensive transaction, but all above board.'

'I see. Thank you.' Posie was writing this all down. 'That's most useful.'

'Is it? Oh, well…'

His face flushed with pride, Smallbone reported to Lovelace about Pring's finances. It was as Lady Clare had admitted.

'It's bad, sir. There's a Bankruptcy Order looming which will take effect soon, too.'

Richard bit at his lip. 'I see. Good work, lad. And you got the information from the Casino, did you, about Peregrine Pring? He'd run up big debts?'

Smallbone's eyes were furtive with the drama. 'I'll say! Scandalous, sir. He was a regular at the Curzon-Alhambra, as his mother told Miss Parker. The past two years have seen him there most weeks, on at least three evenings a week. Sometimes with an older lady – a dark, short-haired lady – who wore silver lipstick and was accompanied by a bald cat.'

'Miss Sinne, herself?' asked Richard, eyebrow raised.

'That's right, sir. Peregrine Pring and this lady were often – ahem – intimate, together. Slightly indiscreet. Peregrine settled his debts on a bi-monthly basis. But the amounts involved were shocking: five hundred pounds here, two hundred there.'

Inspector Oats whistled. 'Blimey! All right for some, isn't it?'

Posie tapped her pencil on her blank page.

She called out, happy to rock the boat. 'I bet not as shocking as the debts which Anouk Sinne herself ratcheted up, eh, Sergeant Smallbone?'

Smallbone looked a little thrown, then frowned, his

thunder stolen. 'I was coming to that. But you're right, Miss Parker. Losses going back *years*.'

'So that's where her salary was all going, I'll warrant,' muttered Richard darkly.

'I don't know about that, sir,' continued Smallbonne, shrugging, 'but the last two years have been a frenzy for her, sir. She won a lot, mainly poker. But she lost, too. The Curzon-Alhambra was kinder to her than Peregrine Pring, sir. They allowed her to settle her losses quarterly. And she's managed to keep paying, until about a month ago.'

Smallbone checked his notes quickly. 'The losses were staggeringly big amounts, sir. Last year she paid the Casino sums of two thousand pounds, and then five thousand pounds, and then another ten thousand. She was easily their best customer. Her own worst enemy.'

Inspector Oats' fishy blue eyes boggled and he perched on the edge of his chair as he processed the figures. 'Seventeen thousand pounds! In a year! Blimey! That's more than most people can imagine the King and Queen spending in a lifetime!'

Richard Lovelace was looking slightly panicky. 'Especially as she "only" earned two thousand a year. By Gad, where did she get this enormous amount from last year, eh, Smallbone?'

'Well, you won't believe this, sir…' he rustled with some paperwork, frowning, not finding what he was looking for.

Posie had half-suspected something dreadful had been wrong in Anouk Sinne's life, but she had not expected anything as dire. She felt a little queasy.

She thought suddenly and painfully of Lady Clare, sitting here stalwartly last night, putting all her hopes of financial revival on the unencumbered House of Sinne and the 'favour' Anouk had done the family, by holding an asset apart, safely.

Or not so safely.

She watched Smallbone with his papers. She examined

her lollipop-coloured nails carefully, then spoke aloud to the group.

'I think, no, I *fear*, that Anouk Sinne raised the money to pay her gambling debts by raising a fraudulent mortgage against the house: Number 11, Embankment Gardens. I suppose for nearly its full value, isn't that right, Sergeant?'

Gobsmacked, Smallbone held aloft some white letter-headed papers, waved them in the air, as if everyone would learn their contents that way.

'That's right, Miss. Yes.'

'Tell us, lad,' growled Richard. He had started to click and pull at his knuckles, Posie noticed.

Smallbone read aloud. 'She raised the sum of seventeen thousand pounds against the house last year, as a mortgage. The full value of the house is twenty thousand pounds. She got the sums in regular cash withdrawals from the Huntsman & Villiers Bank on the Strand, where she, and Mr Pring, are *not* personal customers.'

'But how?' Richard demanded, looking incredulous. 'Why did the bank grant her a mortgage?'

It was early for him to smoke, but Posie saw the tin emerge, its poor battered rim being struck against the table mercilessly. A Turkish was lit, and the silence which gripped the hot room was impenetrable.

What was a double murder was also now a dreadful – and massive – case of fraud. Almost unrecoverable.

'Here it is.' Smallbone was pulling a thick, cream, parchment-like document out. 'Land Registry documents for Number 11, Embankment Gardens.'

He flicked through, aware of all eyes on him. 'In these title deeds it says under "ownership", that the proprietor is Hubert Pring, Viscount Effington, and in the same box Anouk Sinne's name is also given.'

'But that's a mistake!' Posie was shaking her head. 'Anouk Sinne told me she was on the title deeds, but only as some kind of "sitting tenant". She told me she found it funny; but I think she found it insulting. She must have realised there had been a mistake in the drawing-up of the house deeds. Used it to her advantage. Realised that she could get away with playing a stronger hand than she had been dealt.'

'Some mistake!' Lovelace whistled. 'A mistake which made her look like a fully-fledged owner. How on *earth* did the bank think Hubert Pring had agreed to such a huge remortgage?'

Posie was remembering Anouk's odd words to her in the laboratory yesterday. '*When one is well-known, you find yourself in a peculiarly powerful position: on the receiving end of great generosity and trust.*'

'She conned her way in to this bank,' Posie said with certainty. 'A pretence built on top of an initial mistake. Perhaps she forged Hubert's name on some of the application documents? It seems to make little difference now, does it? The crime is done. The money is spent. Gone.'

Inspector Oats was shaking his head dismally from side to side.

Smallbone coughed politely. 'There's more, I'm afraid, Chief Commissioner. That was *last* year. This year she seems to have got along well, mainly winning. Until last month. She lost badly at Blackjack. Then two weeks ago the Curzon-Alhambra sent in a bill for three thousand pounds. It was outstanding until last Friday when she paid it back in cash. Sorted, just in the nick of time.'

'How did she pay this time?' asked Fox, confused. 'Her borrowing allowance on the house was all used up, surely?'

Into the silence which followed, Posie put the documentation given by the delivery men from the National Portrait Gallery onto the coffee table.

'This is how.'

Posie explained that the Tamara de Lempicka painting had been sold two weeks ago.

'*Sold?*' whispered Richard. 'But it wasn't hers to sell!'

'That's as may be, but according to this document, it was sold for four thousand pounds. Paid in cash last Thursday. Your fella Sir Charles has signed the bottom of the chit. One of Anouk's stipulations was that the painting be picked up, but only from *today* onwards. Those men should never have arrived yesterday; it was bad luck. But I should have had an inkling, I suppose. The secretary told me the picture was going to be taken away, but, in good faith, I thought she meant simply as a temporary loan to the gallery. To be fair to Lucy Reeble, I think that Anouk explained it that way to her, too.'

'What the blazes?' said Richard, incredulously. 'So she fraudulently sells the painting for four thousand, pays off three to the Casino, and then it leaves her with a clean thousand left over. For the blackmailer?'

'Yes,' agreed Posie. 'No wonder Anouk Sinne was on edge the last two weeks! She was under mounting pressure. The Casino was closing in for their money, but I think worse was yet to come, wasn't it, Sergeant Smallbone?'

Smallbone nodded. He picked up another letter-headed piece of notepaper, inscribed with a swirling Huntsman & Villiers Bank crest. 'Correct, Miss. The bank who'd granted the mortgage last year had written several times to Miss Sinne, about starting to repay the big loan, and I think she ignored it all. And so, two weeks ago, they sent *this* letter.'

Smallbone summarised quickly. 'They are going to foreclose on the loan. They will be sending in bailiffs and repossessing the property on Friday. This week. In three days' time.'

'By Gad!' gasped Richard. 'What a complete mess! I'll have to tell the Viscount, won't I? That his house, and that wretched painting, are no longer his.'

'A bad business,' muttered Oats from his armchair, obviously relishing it all. 'A right mare's nest if ever I heard of one…'

'Sir,' said Fox, eyebrows knitted together. 'Does this

new financial knowledge impact on our holding of Mr Lorkinsson as chief suspect for the murders? We haven't yet arrested him, and we have until six o'clock this evening to hold him. But apart from the manner of the Princess's death – the pesticide – I fail to see his motive. Sure, he was about to lose his garden, but what if word of this fraud with the house had got out, sir? What if Hubert Pring discovered it, and decided to kill Miss Sinne in revenge? Or his wife did? I've investigated her, sir. She's of Alladice stock: a ruthless family. Surely this financial fraud, if it was suspected, gives the Viscount and his wife a motive to have wanted Miss Sinne dead? Cases such as these are often all about money, aren't they, sir?'

Richard shook his head. 'Nicely argued, Fox, lad. But where's your evidence? And what about the Princess? No. The evidence points to Lorkinsson. We keep him, for now.'

Posie's brain whirred, but slowly, as if it needed more oil. Fox was astute, she knew that, and at least he was questioning Lovelace, but he couldn't possibly have a grip on all the information here.

What if these complicated financial affairs had got nothing to do with the murders at all? Were they just a distraction? A smokescreen?

What about the visitors to Kew Gardens, the French aristocrats? Where did they come in to all this? Did *they* have motives? Stronger than anything as dull as money?

One motive, Posie knew, from experience, was the strongest one of all.

Love.

And love could come in many forms.

Perhaps this was linked to Anatole himself, if he was indeed Anouk's child?

Had *he* killed her as some sort of mad act of revenge for the ultimate betrayal of himself as a baby? Out of a sense of thwarted, lost, abandoned love?

Or had the Duchesse, Maria, with her pharmaceutical

and horticultural expertise, killed her friend? Did that plump-faced sweetness hide an unhappiness at Anouk's developing relationship with her beloved adopted son? One she had sought to put an end to? A motive of jealous love? A motive of stopping a new, developing love?

Outside came the sound of keys rattling now, and two soft voices with cockney lilts.

'Ah, it's the thousand pounds,' said Inspector Oats happily, grabbing at his handcuffs and looking distinctly cheerier. Chipper, in fact.

'And our blackmailer. It's about time! Let's be havin' him, then!'

* * * *

Twenty-Three

The blackmailer's name was Larry Lively, and he was distinctly easy on the eye.

Pleasant, too, if very nervous.

He sat with Len next to him. Under his fawn-coloured homburg hat, his face, which hadn't been captured by Fox's sneaky little spy camera, was tightly-boned, handsome, with clever, deep-set brown eyes.

He and Len knew each other well. They drank together once or twice a month, compared notes, swapped tips, yearned after the same equipment.

Larry Lively was a Private Investigator who acted out of a small office in a basement under the Grosvenor Hotel at Victoria, who dealt mainly in following and capturing on camera errant spouses.

His work was essentially the same as Len's, but his reputation and his rates were both significantly lower.

Larry Lively had brought Anouk's black bag with him. He sat with it at his feet while Oats chomped at the bit, pulling at his moustache in frustration as the story spilled out.

It was a simple enough tale.

'I got a call from this woman, about two weeks ago. It turned out to be Miss Sinne. She said she'd pay me five hundred pounds – that's a huge sum to me, two years of wages – if I'd stage a bit of a stunt with her. I was to pretend I was blackmailing her. She said she wanted to make a man-friend of hers feel "caring" and protective towards her. They were stuck in a bit of a rut as a couple and she needed to jolt him up a bit.'

Oats harrumphed. 'A likely story if ever I heard one!'

'I swear on my life it's true, sir. The money was too good to pass up, I'm afraid. I 'ad no idea things would go this badly, did I?'

'*You* typed the notes?' asked Posie, calmly.

'That's right, Missus. Miss Sinne told me exactly what to write and I typed it up, postin' the cards from Victoria Station on pre-arranged dates. And I was told exactly what to do about collectin' the money, too.'

Richard indicated towards the bag. 'It's all there?'

'That's right, Guv'nor. It all played out fantastically yesterday, until I realised I had someone on my tail. It's usually the other way around; I'm on someone else's tail! I'm a bit of an expert. Your fella was good, though. He nearly had me once or twice! And I had no idea about the camera. Len 'ere says it's a good'un. I'd love to see it later, eh?'

Lovelace shrugged. 'Perhaps. But you said you were promised five hundred pounds, Larry. That's still in the bag, right?'

The man nodded.

Richard looked stern. 'We're actually missing a thousand pounds, Mr Lively. And the notes you apparently wrote refer to one thousand.' Lovelace crossed his arms, scowled. 'So where's the rest, man?'

Larry Lively was sweating now, but he shook his head defiantly. 'I ain't got it, Guv'nor. Never expected to receive a thousand. Lumme! I can't imagine that amount of money in me life! I know the typewritten notes made mention of one thousand, but I never questioned it. Just wrote one thing and accepted another. You've got to believe me! And, as far as I'm aware, there was no-one else involved. Miss Sinne was at pains to tell me no-one could guess the thing was a fake.'

Richard nodded. 'Fox, you check the bag.'

Fox obediently went and knelt on the floor, pulling out small, neat piles of new white bank notes. Pound notes.

Each packet was a neat bundle of twenty fresh pound notes. The stacks grew as Fox counted them. Pile after pile. Twenty-five piles.

'That's five hundred pounds there, sir,' said Fox, matter-of-factly. He delved further into the bag, and started to pull out plain white paper bundles, cut to around the same size as the bank notes. About twenty or more such piles. On closer inspection you could see they had been cut out of the notepaper bearing the House of Sinne letterhead. Obviously, Anouk had made these herself.

'That's what was making it so heavy for the secretary yesterday, sir,' explained Fox. 'It was stuffed out, weighed down to look like it held more money than it did.'

Oats was standing, the handcuffs gleaming. He was clearing his throat in anticipation of a pleasant duty looming.

Lovelace stood up quickly and put his hand on his colleague's arm. 'I know I called you in here, Bill,' he said softly. 'But what on earth are we going to charge this fella with? He's not even been aiding and abetting anyone. All he's been doing is following a set of instructions to the best of his ability. Trying to earn a livelihood. Which is all any of us are doing, eh?'

Fox was reloading the bag. Lovelace passed him an evidence form. 'Fill it in and tie it around the bag's handle, like we did with the fake perfumes. We'll need this lot as evidence. I expect, if we match it all up, that these bank notes will come from the very same consignment which the National Portrait Gallery used to pay Miss Sinne for the Tamara de Lempicka painting last week. We'll match the numbers up for sure.'

He turned to Larry Lively. 'You'll get this lot back, lad, fair and square. I promise.'

Relieved, a certain jauntiness back, Larry and Len left the office, chattering in low voices.

Oats was looking hot and bothered. 'Where's the rest of the money, then, sir? The missing five hundred?'

'Actually, Bill, for the life of me, I have no idea.'

Oats shook his head gloomily. 'You still need me, Chief Commissioner?'

'Perhaps later. You can help me announce the deaths this evening, if you like. Tell the world we have arrested the killer.'

You haven't.

Not yet.

And you have the wrong man.

Oats, looking rather more pleased, left, and Posie watched her husband and his men pack up.

Posie knew what she needed to do now. She needed to see past this financial mess.

She needed to join up the dots, and fast. And she'd need help to do it before the planned public announcement about the murders was made tonight.

'Richard, darling?'

Richard Lovelace looked over, smiled suddenly. And when he gave her his schoolboy grin, she was suddenly transported back in time to when she had first met him, when he was unattainable and out of reach, and she felt weak at the knees.

Like she wanted to climb into his lap and nuzzle against him: feel the world disappear. Forget that they were two separate beings, let the time unravel…

Even if he *was* wrong.

'I need you to call a meeting, Richard.'

'Oh?' The grin vanished immediately. 'Where? When?'

Posie checked her little red wristwatch. 'It's nine-thirty now, and I'll need a good portion of the day. I've got to get myself all around London and do some digging. Shall we say four o'clock?'

'Here again? It's hardly convenient, my love. We'll be announcing the deaths at five o'clock, before the run of the evening print presses.'

'No, not here. Let's meet at Anouk's house. We need the same people there as yesterday, at the "reveal". Can Sergeant Smallbone organise it? *Everyone*, mind. Even if Dolly is in a funny mood and refuses to come at first. And we'll certainly need Mr Lorkinsson.'

'Well, as I said, it's hardly –'

'This *is* necessary, darling.'

'Do you know a good deal you're not telling me?'

'I will do, by four o'clock. At the moment I just have hunches. By then I may even have some evidence. Besides, you don't want to annoy your contact at the National Portrait Gallery, do you? You told his men they could come along at four-thirty today to get that painting, didn't you?'

Lovelace groaned and ran his hands through his thick red hair. 'All right, all right. We'll do as you say. But *where* are you going, darling? And can we – the men here – help you in any way?'

'Oh, yes. Thanks. For starters, can Smallbone call a Left Luggage Department for me?'

Posie wrote something on a piece of paper in her notebook and tore it off.

She scribbled on another sheet, hurriedly. 'Smallbone, if they have the missing luggage, then organise for it to be collected, and get it opened up, right away. I need you to ask also about anything irregular which may have happened at this same place. On Sunday, probably. Perhaps a mechanical failure…'

Then she wrote down an entirely separate question.

She passed the second piece of paper across. 'Can you

get one of your bobbies to go to Gordy Lorkinsson in his cell and ask him this one question, please?'

'Of course, Miss, if it will help.'

'Oh, it will. And talking of bobbies helping, I need you to organise another search-team, and these fellas are going to get very mucky, I'm afraid.'

She scribbled again in her notebook, passed across an address to Smallbone.

Fox was edging nearer, wanting to get in on the action.

Posie stared down at her notebook. It was completely blank. She thought quickly, joining those dots again.

'I need *you*, Sergeant Fox, to do some telephoning for me. Use the equipment here. Two things need sorting. We need to locate a fella in a burgundy cap. Oh, and a good deal of this case is to do with girls, groups of girls. Women together, in solidarity. Can you track some girls down for me? Get some answers from them?'

She wrote details down on a slip of paper and passed it across.

'And then go to the French Embassy in South Kensington, Sergeant Fox. I need you to dig into some personal history for me. This might be quite meaty. Get whatever you can.'

She wrote down two names and pushed them across.

Richard was nervy. 'Darling, where are *you* off to? And is it dangerous?'

'Hardly, love. I'm going to be chasing peacocks.'

His face paled again and she saw his hands shook a little. *What was it when she mentioned peacocks?*

'I'm joking, sweetheart. I'm going to Fortnum's, actually. To the perfume department. I'll be approximately one hour there, and then I'll meet Fox, together with Smallbone, if he's finished with the luggage, in the entrance hall of the French Embassy, so we can compare findings.'

'But that will only take you until eleven-thirty. Twelve, at most. Surely?'

'Ah, well. I've then got to get myself right across town, see? More digging. I'm going to reach right into someone's past.'

'Really? Well, I hope you know what you're doing, my love. Would it help if I came with you?'

'Er…'

'I see. A "woman's touch" again, is it?'

'Something like that.'

'Well, that suits me fine. Something unexpected and not at all welcome has crossed my desk at the Yard and I need to give it my full attention.'

'I'll see you at four, Richard.'

'No doubt you will. Enjoy your busy day.'

And with that, and with a flash of that schoolboy grin again, he was gone.

****

Twenty-Four

It was just before four and Posie stood nervously in the entrance hall of the House of Sinne as people flitted through.

She felt, rather absurdly, like the host at some strange party, although there was precious little to celebrate here.

She'd sprayed herself liberally with her wonderfully reliable scent, the Parma Violets which had never let her down. And Posie took comfort in the feeling of familiarity the scent gave her.

She was really waiting for Dolly, who so far hadn't turned up.

The diffuser which had emitted the carbon smell had obviously gone, taken away as evidence, but the scent of that carbon remained, filling the place with its awful memories.

There were two bobbies at the door, and Scotland Yard men were everywhere, clustering in small groups in their dark flannel suits, sporting collective worried frowns. Posie had already seen Inspector Oats dashing about inside, which made her feel more nervous than ever.

Posie was dressed in the same plain black woollen dress as the night before, with a matching black satin belt, not wanting to risk looking too distinctive or colourful today, and to avoid another wardrobe clash.

She'd added a dark raspberry lipstick and, as usual, wore her favourite necklace, a string of pink Murano glass beads, given to her a lifetime ago, by a man who had been special.

She watched as Sergeant Smallbone directed the butler and the secretary, both in sombre, dark, non-work clothes, to bring in trays of coffee and plates of biscuits to the drawing-room. The sight of biscuits, for once, turned her stomach miserably.

She called over: 'You *did* leave a message for the Countess of Cardigeon at her home, didn't you, Smallbone?'

Smallbone, flushed, came bobbing over. ''Course I did, Miss. I called three times today. Their butler told me he would pass the message on.'

Posie felt nervous, her stomach uneasy. 'I think I'll try again, myself.'

Dolly had told her driver yesterday that she would be staying away from home overnight; had said she would stay with Posie. But, of course, that hadn't happened. So Dolly would logically have returned home instead. *Wouldn't she?*

But placing a call to Dolly's home address, Pavilion Road, did nothing to assuage Posie's growing fears. Recognising Posie's voice, the Cardigeons' butler confessed he had not seen the Countess all day; in fact, she had not come home last night. Nor rung to explain.

It was a first.

The Eleventh Earl of Cardigeon – Rufus – was going spare.

Posie came away from the telephone feeling worried, but she had to get on. She had a whole room of people sitting waiting for her.

Richard was beckoning her, tapping at his wristwatch. She saw he was dressed in his Chief Commissioner's dress uniform of darkest navy serge, the gold buttons and epaulettes and many medals glittering over the front of it, making him seem unreal. His dear, beloved face was almost hidden in the shadow of his jutting formal hat. These were the kind of official clothes to be photographed in.

There was a nervousness to his smile, and he seemed to be saying: '*Don't mess this up. I put my trust in you and you need to get this right.*'

Into the room again, windows and doors open wide, and here were the people she had asked to be gathered together.

They sat at the big oval table as before, but at the head of the table in Anouk's place was Richard Lovelace, with an empty chair for Posie beside him.

Next to Richard, on his right, was Mr Van Dusen, looking more resigned and quieter than yesterday, with the next chair left empty, where Princess Priyanka had sat. Then followed the butler and the secretary, and next was a sweaty-looking and mussed-up Gordy Lorkinsson, wearing exactly the same clothes as yesterday, his short-cropped hair needing a comb; released from his cell specially.

Dolly's chair was still empty, and in it sat Sam Stubbs, without his camera this time, but with excitement flushing his face. Then came Anatole, Count de Poilac, with his mother next to him. Both looked keen for things to be wrapped up. Maria, the Duchesse, was playing nervously with the odd little half-heart locket on its choker, this time worn alone, without the accompanying strings of pearls.

And last of all in the circle were Lady Clare, together with her husband, the Viscount, who sat next to Posie.

Lady Clare, as before, was right opposite Gordy Lorkinsson, although today she was careful not to even look in his direction.

Posie knew that Richard had managed to inform the Prings about the extent of Anouk's financial fraud and she had expected Lady Clare to be sitting here with a change of demeanour; anger or desperation making themselves evident. But, if anything, Lady Clare was the most composed Posie had seen her yet.

Hubert Pring, her husband, was less in control. The

assurance of yesterday, the easy-breezy English charm, seemed to have vanished overnight. In its place was a sad, creeping fragility, an incredulousness.

Posie marched to her seat.

She was all set.

In the doorway hovered Oats, and next to him, right up against the wall, like sentries, stood Fox and Smallbone. At Smallbone's feet was one of those now ubiquitous black bags. It looked to be absolutely stuffed full, zip straining.

Posie cast the Sergeants a quick grateful look: *I couldn't have done this without either of you.*

She saw Fox smile, nod, almost wink. *He would go far, that one, and probably soon.*

She laid out items in front of her: the dark-green cat label from the vets; a map, folded; a small, white glossy bag from Fortnum's; an unused printed paper bag bearing the words 'THE DANCING FISH' and a couple of pages of ripped-off notepaper, covered in Posie's curved, neat handwriting. And then she added a front page from a newspaper.

'Welcome, all of you,' said Richard Lovelace, in his calmest, most soothing voice.

'Say, what is this? Apart from a disgrace!' cut in Archie Van Dusen, impatiently. 'We spent most of our lives yesterday in this godforsaken room, and here you are, calling us back! It's really a darned scandal. What are we here for, *exactly*?'

Posie wanted to laugh aloud, quite inappropriately. She knew her husband actually had no idea why they were gathered together; only that he knew she believed Lorkinsson was innocent.

Truth be told, she was surprised Richard had given her such a free hand. It was as if he wasn't concentrating, which was odd. As if his mind was elsewhere.

'We are here,' smiled Richard, 'because I want you all to hear something very important. In the interests of justice.'

Oh, he was smooth. So good at these parts of his job, she'd give him that.

'And in those interests, I am going to hand over, for a short while, to my wife, Miss Posie Parker. Because she has some information for us all. Posie, please carry on?'

Posie's heart was beating very fast. For a bad moment she doubted the veracity of all she had discovered. Doubted the terrible truths she had uncovered.

But she *had* to do this.

Oh, how I wish you, Dolly, were here, too, she thought to herself. *You would have been so surprised.*

Where are you right now?

Posie cleared her throat, then addressed her audience.

'We all have secrets. All of us in this room. We all have pasts we want to escape.'

She looked pointedly at the empty chair next to Mr Van Dusen, to where yesterday Princess Priyanka had sat as the focus of a camera's lens.

'Some of us have left loved ones in burning buildings, and whether or not we tried to save them may be known only in our hearts.'

She saw Mr Van Dusen's face had darkened, and Anatole de Poilac's handsome features were twisted in anger.

Beside her she felt her husband stiffen perceptibly, caught off-guard. His first wife, Molly, had died in a house fire from which she could not be saved, but Phyllis, happily, *had* been rescued, and Posie knew the thing haunted him still. As did any talk of fires.

She moved on from the topic quickly.

'Perhaps it is for us, those of us remaining, to give those who are gone the benefit of the doubt. And move on.'

Posie looked about the table. 'Let us turn to Anouk Sinne, who was murdered in appalling circumstances yesterday. *She* had many secrets. But, on searching, these were readily discoverable: a Suffragette past, marked by violence; "her" perfume house, the House of Sinne, built up using another man's money to fund everything; and lastly, the debilitating gambling addiction which has caused the House of Sinne to come tumbling down in a staggering mass of debt.'

Posie watched the reactions around the table. The staff looking incredulous, gawping, and Gordy Lorkinsson with disbelief etched on his creased face. The Viscount and Lady Clare stayed silent. The French, straight-backed, composed, were already reaching for cigarettes.

But Archie Van Dusen was laughing. 'Say, what, Miss Parker? You've sure got this all wrong! This place was thriving. Anouk Sinne assured me of that!'

Posie smiled back calmly: 'Oh, I can assure *you*, Mr Van Dusen, Anouk Sinne had made a mess of things. Despite the fact that everything belonged to the Viscount, Anouk had fraudulently managed to raise loans against his assets, until finally, the bubble was going to burst. Two weeks ago she was given a notice of foreclosure on this house. It is scheduled for this coming Friday. She was forced to act. And fast.'

Ignoring the American's petulant expression of disbelief, Posie explained that within a two-week time frame, Anouk Sinne had gone into a kind of mad frenzy. She'd created the perfume Hubert Pring had been waiting for, for two years – 'The Ultimate Sin' – while selling it simultaneously to Mr Van Dusen.

Posie looked at every person around the table as she spoke again: 'Anouk was crazily busy in these last two weeks. She organised yesterday's small "reveal", to convince Hubert Pring, her sponsor, that all was well in the House of Sinne. She also took steps to organise another event, the big launch at the Embassy Club in Mayfair, planned for today, which has turned out to be a clever fake. All of this was designed to prevent anyone from thinking something was wrong.'

Mr Van Dusen's dark eyes stared at Posie penetratingly. 'Say, why did she involve *me*, then? It makes no sense.'

'Miss Sinne simply thought you represented a slice of easy money, Mr Van Dusen,' Posie replied smoothly.

'In this frenzied last two weeks Anouk Sinne has organised to generate funds wherever possible. And this included involving *you*, sir. Probably Anouk Sinne thought your three thousand pounds would be easily-earned money for work already done. She probably thought it would be very easy to pull the wool over your eyes. But, to give you your due, I think she 'bit off more than she could chew' with you! Your insistence on coming to England yourself, and attending the "reveal" was a pain; as was the attendance of Princess Priyanka, and a journalist. It made everything more complicated. But Anouk Sinne had signed up for that easy money and she couldn't get out of it, however hard she tried to keep you apart from the other guests yesterday. Her involving you in this mess was foolhardy, and showy, and, in the end, completely pointless. And she really didn't care.'

The American was pulling at his collar, a slight twitch at his temple. 'You're telling me I've had a wasted trip, Miss Parker? That Miss Sinne never planned on honouring her part of her contract? That I was *duped*?'

Lovelace was managing to keep a very straight face, but he addressed the American with great courtesy. 'I am afraid it looks that way, sir. This whole sorry tale has many victims, I fear. And you were one of them.'

The American got out a cigar, played with it quite calmly. 'Strikes me the woman was acting crazy, hey?'

Posie nodded. 'Anouk Sinne *was* acting crazily, because she was desperate. But what strikes me most of all is that in addition to generating funds, wherever and however she could, she was clearing out: she has burnt all her papers, cleared out her stocks of precious perfume ingredients and even emptied the safe of its precious contents.'

Lucy Reeble had been sitting with her mouth covered in horror, but now she spoke up, her voice wavering.

'But what about the blackmail? I've been wondering all night if maybe it was connected to Miss Sinne's death. Do you know who was behind it?'

'Oh, yes,' Posie confirmed.

Posie looked over at Gordy Lorkinsson, then at Lady Clare. 'Most of you do not even realise there was a blackmail element to this case, and, in fact, that was why *I* was called in yesterday.'

She turned and smiled comfortingly at the secretary. 'But rest assured, Miss Reeble, the blackmail plot was as fake as the bottles of perfume Anouk had left behind for Mr Van Dusen in a last act of the blatant disregard she held him in.'

Perhaps Anouk Sinne had, along with half of London, seen *No, No, Nanette,* and this had inspired the idea of a blackmail plot which was fake?

Of course, it was a load of nonsense. Flim-flam.

She recalled something Anouk Sinne had told her only yesterday, about London. '*I could give it up in an instant.*'

Well, Anouk Sinne had been about to do just that.Posie looked around the room, meeting every gaze.

'You see, it was *meant* to look as if Miss Sinne had been kidnapped or killed by a blackmailer. Because, as I realised very late last night, the truth is that Anouk was leaving. She was running away.'

****

Twenty-Five

'*What*?' Hubert Pring was incredulous, shaking with anger. 'But how could she leave us with all this mess?'

'Leaving? But where on earth *was* Anouk going?' asked Lady Clare, her voice smooth and firm, not a tremor in it.

Just at this moment there was a slight commotion at the door.

Inspector Oats bustled in, looking important. 'Chief Commissioner, there's a fella arrived to collect a painting. Can I tell 'im to go ahead?'

'Yes, Inspector. It's all in order.'

Posie cast a glance over at Hubert Pring, who had gone beetroot-red, his mouth a tight line of anger, and she saw Lady Clare gripping his hand under the table.

Posie smiled. 'I will tell you where she was going in a minute. But to do so, you need to appreciate a special relationship upon which Anouk relied. Sergeant Fox will explain, please?'

Fox grinned and shook out several official-looking documents. 'Research at the French Embassy today led us to become aware of a connection between the *mothers* of Anouk Sinne and the Duchesse de Poilac here. They went to the same school in the early 1860s.'

Everyone turned, bemused, to look at Maria de Poilac,

with her calm, inscrutable face. After a couple of seconds, she shrugged. 'That is not a crime, is it? *C'est vrai.* Our mothers were best friends, inseparable.'

Maria de Poilac's hands fluttered at her neck, at her velvet choker. 'When Anouk's mother left Paris for her marriage in England in 1878, my mother and her mother exchanged these gold lockets: silly little things, really, not even real gold. A half each, to remember each other by. Each side says '*Ne m'oublie pas.*' How you say, in English? '*Forget-me-not*'? My mother carried on wearing this, even after Anouk's mother died in a car crash, in 1908. On *my* mother's death a couple of years ago I took to wearing it as a keepsake.'

The Duchesse carefully lit a cigarette, placing it in its long holder, but her hands were shaking slightly. 'Our mothers remained in touch throughout their lives. We were not of the same age, we girls: Anouk was almost a decade younger than me, but our mothers encouraged us to write to each other. The "pen-friends", you call it? It was helpful, actually. Particularly later when Anouk decided to train as a pharmacist. I was able to give her advice, of course. *Mais c'est normal, n'est-ce pas?* It was a profession I had trained in myself, up until my own marriage. Anouk and I, we followed the same sort of path.'

'Ah, yes.' Posie nodded. 'Up until your marriage to the Tenth Count, Nicolas de Poilac. An interesting man, by all accounts: much, much older than you, your Grace. An aristocrat, and a botanist, too. He must be almost eighty-five years old now, is that correct? His family's ancestral townhouse is, of course, in Versailles. But he has a country place too, of course.'

Maria de Poilac smiled tightly. 'My husband *was* a great man, Miss Parker. Sadly, he died a few years ago.'

Posie checked her page of scribbled notes. 'I noted at the tax office of the French Embassy that your husband describes himself in his historical tax affairs as working with the famous French perfume houses of Carobonne and Verney-Depuis. In fact, your husband, Nicolas de Poilac, the Tenth Count, is still known today in the industry in France as a well-regarded "nose".'

The Duchesse blew a perfect smoke ring, eyes slightly narrowed. 'That is all correct, Miss Parker. *Mais, en réalité*, you are still using the wrong tense. My husband died. Please respect that. It is upsetting otherwise.'

'What was the year he died, Duchesse?' asked Posie politely.

The Count, Anatole, now spoke up, his fingers tapping at the table, his signet ring making a jarring, banging noise against the wood. 'I am sure you do not mean any disrespect, Miss Parker. He died in 1920, Miss Parker. Five years ago. I was just thirteen years old. It was sad, but he was already quite an old man.'

'Thank you, Count Anatole. Sergeant Fox, do you have anything to add to this?'

'Oh, yes, Miss Parker. *Much* more.'

The Sergeant obligingly opened an official-looking form, held it up for effect. 'You told the world, and your son, that your husband died, Duchesse. But the evidence of the current tax forms bears a different testimony. Your husband is returned here, very recently, only a month or so ago, as being an "*invalide*" and being cared for in his country estate; at the de Poilac castle at Cabris. He pays no tax, based on this apparently unfortunate health condition.'

The young Count, Anatole, turned to face his mother in a sudden burst of amazement. 'But, *Maman*, that is not true. You told me he was *dead*! When I came home from boarding school that time. There must be some mistake!'

Posie watched the Duchesse tugging at the heart locket even harder, looking as if it might snap, like the fragile silence around her.

'Perhaps, Count Anatole, you should take a trip out to your country castle, at Cabris?' said Posie softly. 'Soon? Your father is an old man, after all…'

Anatole turned to Posie, his grey-green eyes fierce, burning up with anger. 'Why would I do *that*, Miss Parker? Why would I go to Cabris? I never go there. It's a falling-down old place. My mother goes to study her flowers, where she keeps a big garden; that is all. It is useless, in the middle of nowhere.'

Posie picked up the map from her table, shook it out and showed it around. The South of France. She pointed at it.

'Cabris is actually not quite in the middle of nowhere, Count Anatole. It's near Grasse. Which is, apparently, the best place in the world for growing camellias, and for perfume making. It has become a centre of renowned skills. All of the major perfume houses have people working there. Your father is in the perfect spot for what he likes doing best.'

'*What?*' Anatole stared from his mother to Posie, his face a wretched mask of confusion. 'But why the secrecy? Telling me he was *dead*?'

Sergeant Fox was flicking through yet more documents. 'I may be able to explain. From the tax reports we can see that in 1920 a small perfume company was set up, based in the Castle of Cabris. It has reported its affairs to the French Tax Regime diligently, but it returns very small profits. No attention has ever been paid to it. But that will all now change. All the French Tax Commissioners will crawl over the details of it, demanding their due.'

'*No!*' The Duchesse was shaking her head, carefully extinguishing her cigarette. But there was a slight tremor in her fingers, a touch of panic about her eyes. 'This cannot be! It is a mistake, truly. *Une erreur!*'

Posie didn't look at Maria de Poilac; instead, she reached for the glossy white Fortnum's bag on the table.

Inside it was a small white box.

Posie took off the lid and pulled out a plain glass bottle. On its side was stamped a stencilled golden peacock, a match for the peacock on the cameo brooch worn by Maria de Poilac, and a match to the peacock on the ring of Anatole.

Richard, next to Posie, was staring at the box, but not in wonderment. In fact, he groaned softly: 'Oh, the deuce! Ruddy *peacocks*!'

Posie tapped the bottle. 'This perfume – "*Le Paon*" – or "The Peacock", is the signature scent of the perfume house of the same name, set up at Cabris by Count Nicolas de Poilac. The peacock is also the centuries-old symbol of the de Poilac family. This perfume was released about four or five years ago. The lady on the perfume counter at Fortnum's told me it has fast become their best-selling fragrance. It is the same story at Selfridges and Harrods: I have asked at them all. It smells of flowers in a sweet shop, apparently, with a salty-caramel base note. The Department Stores cannot get the stuff in fast enough. They are also hankering for a new scent from *Le Paon*, and it is eagerly anticipated. I imagine it is the same in France.'

'*Mais non*! This is complete nonsense!' said the Duchesse adamantly, but her face was burning red now.

Fox grinned again wolfishly: 'I would say that *Le Paon* in Cabris is turning over a very healthy profit. And it is odd that the Duchesse does not know anything about this, as she is recorded on the tax forms as being one of the Directors of *Le Paon*. Alongside her husband.'

He flipped to another form now. 'And this is a copy of the most recent paperwork, filed in Paris just under two weeks ago. It seems that another Director was added at that point. That person was Harriet Synnes, which is the real name of Anouk Sinne.'

Posie didn't know where to look: at Richard's disbelieving countenance; at the dark, flaring anger on the young Frenchman's face; at the hot, burning face of the Duchesse.

In the background somewhere came the sound of banging and tapping. Men laughing.

Hubert Pring looked sick as a dog.

In the event, it was Mr Van Dusen who broke the silence, reaching for Posie's plain glass bottle. 'Say, Duchesse, I'll see what this peacock perfume is all about, hey? Perhaps we can cut a deal, too?'

Richard batted the man's arm away.

'Later,' he growled. 'But Posie, this is all fascinating, particularly for the young Count, who may have gained a father where he thought he had none. But tell me, how does it help us, *now*?'

Posie had been expecting this. 'It gives us sight of where Anouk was going. She'd messed up here and, in her panic, she called her old friend. She needed Maria de Poilac's help with two things. Maria offered Anouk an immediate new career as a Director at *Le Paon* in Cabris, closed off from the world in a remote castle until the fuss in London had died down.'

Posie grinned, certain of her story now. 'And maybe there would be longer-term advantages for Maria de Poilac, too? While her husband is still the "nose", there will come a time when Nicolas de Poilac dies or becomes properly an "*invalide*". He's already slowed down. Indeed, there has been no new perfume at *Le Paon* for five years, and the wait for a new scent perhaps seems endless. All of Maria's pharmaceutical training and experience with flowers does not mean she is a "nose" herself, and it must be frustrating. I suppose the plan was for Anouk to become the new perfumier there. The person who would carry on making *Le Paon* a great perfume house. The plan ensured a future for both of these clever women.'

Hubert Pring called down the table. 'And you *seriously* thought it would turn out well, did you, Maria? That Anouk wouldn't mess things up like she did here?'

The Duchesse sat stiffly, head held high. 'I am much afraid, Hubert, that I was not given to understand the extent of Anouk's gambling habits. I am truly sorry for you, *bien sur*.'

'You've had a lucky escape, let me tell you.'

Anatole de Poilac looked to be on the edge of tears. 'But *Maman*, why did you keep all this a secret from me? *Pourquoi?*'

His mother rested her hands in her lap. Posie saw that the velvet choker had broken at last and the thing was balled up in her fists.

'Oh! You are a wonderful son, Anatole. But you are *not* discreet.'

The Duchesse sighed theatrically. 'We needed the perfume and any future perfumes to *pay* a great deal of money. We need the income. For your expensive education; for maintaining our town and country houses; for buying the expensive ingredients to make your father's perfumes. But we could not afford to pay the government's extortionate taxes, not at all. They would have taken more than half of all our profits.'

Maria de Poilac shrugged nonchalantly. 'The truth, *mon cher*, is that we thought you would give us away: blab to one of your little revolutionary groups, who all hate the aristocracy. Who would, in turn, blab to the authorities. Do you know, we even rent out parts of the castle's outbuildings and cottages to people who are willing to pay extraordinarily good prices? But we never told you that either, for the same reason. It is a sad fact, but we could not trust you to keep our financial secrets.'

'Good Lord!' Richard was muttering quietly beside Posie, scoring lines through his hurried notes. 'Poor lad, life is hard enough without your parents pretending to be dead.'

But Gordy Lorkinsson was looking at Posie, frowning. 'You said Anouk needed Maria's help with two things, but that was just *one* thing, wasn't it? What was the second?'

Posie nodded. 'Sergeant Smallbone has obtained the telephone records from the International Operator. On the same day as Anouk Sinne was warned that the bank was foreclosing on this property, giving her two weeks to get out, she contacted Maria de Poilac, by telephone, at Versailles. I think on that call, Maria suggested that Anouk join the perfume house at Cabris. But I think Anouk also declared she wanted to create a *final perfume* before she left here: she wanted to leave on a dramatic high note, a blaze of professional brilliance. She wanted to appear to have created the most wonderful perfume in the world, a legend, if you like, to be remembered by, after her fake 'death'. But the problem was that she had not managed to create it yet. She must have told the Duchesse that even Gordy Lorkinsson's perfect new white roses weren't enough to make 'The Ultimate Sin' work. She was stumped. Anouk needed a base note, as distinctive as the salty caramel of "*Le Paon*". And to do this she needed to consult another "nose". A genius.'

Anatole broke in, incredulous. 'You mean my mother told Anouk to call my apparently-dead father? To get his advice?'

'I *know* that's what happened,' Posie said with certainty.

'I think your father lives like a hermit, a virtual recluse, and that special permission is needed in order to make contact with him. And that is what your mother, the Duchesse, arranged. There's an extortionately expensive twenty-minute call recorded from here to the castle at Cabris, right after the call to Versailles. I think it was your father's idea to add hemlock, and in such a high dosage. It was just what Anouk needed. She finally had "The Ultimate Sin".'

The young Count turned to his mother, who was very still and silent.

'*When* were you going to tell me this, *Maman*? And this new arrangement with Anouk at Cabris? That would have compromised *me*. It would have been awkward. Crazy! Can you imagine our lives, going forwards? Because, as you know, she was my…'

But just at this moment there was another tap at the door.

* * * *

Twenty-Six

Posie recognised the sweaty, cheerful face of the man from the National Portrait Gallery, from yesterday. He sought out Lovelace, didn't bat an eyelid at Richard's formal uniform. Took it all in his stride.

'Beg pardon, Guv'nor. But the men and me had awful difficulty in moving out that picture, see? On account of it being on runners. Pleased to say we got it off eventually. But we found these five pink envelopes stuck behind the frame, Guv'nor. Very well concealed. I'll hand them to you.'

Posie recognised them. She had seen them in a stash on the desk in Anouk's laboratory yesterday. Although then, they had not had names scribbled on their fronts.

And even from across the room, she could see that one of the names was hers.

But Richard was shaking his head as he clutched the letters.

'One minute, Posie. You said Anouk was planning on leaving? Presumably before the "fake" Embassy Club launch today was exposed as being fake, and before the National Portrait Gallery men came for the picture today? And before Gordy Lorkinsson read that second-class mailed letter, also meant to arrive today, and before the foreclosure. So *when* was she actually going? It had to be last night, eh? And if so, where was her luggage and her passport? Her ticket? We never found anything in the searches.'

This was what had thrown Posie for a while.

Cabs.

Cars.

Dark-green cars.

It had been stupendously clever.

'It was very neat,' said Posie. 'Perfect, in fact. Anouk was booked on the late flight yesterday to Paris, leaving from Croydon Airport. She would have travelled with the Duchesse, and Count Anatole, not that *he* knew about the plan. Anouk Sinne was planning on leaving last night, once the last guests had gone. She would have walked out of here in just her normal clothes, alone, with no luggage and no passport, probably travelling by a normal motor-taxi to Croydon. No-one would have suspected she was leaving for good. It would have looked like she was going for a short walk, or for an evening out. It was perfect.'

Posie looked over at the staff, who were sitting, looking stricken. She spoke gently: 'I bet neither of you had any idea Miss Sinne was leaving, did you?'

Jenks looked very upset. ''Course not, Miss. She acted just the same as usual.'

Gordy Lorkinsson was almost laughing. 'I have to admire her! What a plan!'

'Yes,' agreed Posie. 'And it was you, Mr Lorkinsson, who gave me the clue as to how it was done. You told me a dark-green car had brought the French guests to the house on Sunday at noon, and you were amazed that Anouk had actually bothered to greet them. *But why had she made the special effort?* And the answer was because the very same car which brought the French visitors was also Anouk's vitally important way of escaping without being noticed.'

She ignored her husband's baffled expression, and looked across briefly to Lady Clare. 'Last night, Lady Clare, you told me that your son, Peregrine, had left for Croydon Airport in one of their specially-sent dark-green cars.'

The aristocrat looked bemused. 'That's right. But how is *he* implicated in all of this?'

'He's not. Not at all.'

Posie looked back at the Icelander. 'I realised that what *you* had seen, Mr Lorkinsson, when the French guests arrived, must have been the same thing as Lady Clare was talking about. The car you saw on Sunday was no normal London black motor-taxi. The Duchesse and her son must have come direct from Croydon airport, in one of the airport's fleet of dark-green cars. The plan was for Anouk to be ready and waiting, to put her passport and her own luggage -what she needed for her new life in Cabris- into the airport car, which would take those things away and store them for her safely at the airport until her flight. You, Mr Lorkinsson, saw Anouk putting two bags into that car.'

Smallbone had picked up the heavy black bag at his feet and placed it onto the oval table, unzipping it quickly.

'*This* is one of the bags in question, sent on ahead. It was being held at Croydon airport,' he explained. 'In their Left Luggage department. They confirmed it was Miss Sinne's, due to be put on the night flight with her last night. A flight she ended up missing. Because she was dead.'

He started taking things out hurriedly, flipping them on the big empty table. There was a passport, a small make-up bag, a diamond lead for the cat. There were also big, neat bundles of money, about two hundred pounds in all.

Smallbone struggled with a brown leather box which had taken up most of the room in the bag, like a big jewellery box. He forced it open and everyone stared, open-mouthed.

Glass vials of clear-coloured liquid were stacked inside, one after another, carefully, in insulating leather pouches. Tiny drawers, when pulled out, held sachets of dried ingredients; powdered finer than sand.

Posie saw Hubert Pring look momentarily wary, then suddenly furious.

'Those are the most precious ingredients from the laboratory!' he blurted out. 'That's *my* property! By Gad, Anouk was literally stealing every last thing she could from me! I don't know whether to laugh or cry.'

'Laugh, Viscount,' said Richard, leaning over the table and shutting the box up again himself. 'At least you'll recover *something* from this wretched mess, eh? The only other thing which hasn't been cleared out is Mr Van Dusen's three thousand pounds, which is still in the bank account from luck rather than by design. I expect Anouk was going to draw it down on her way to the airport, but of course she never made it…'

Gordy Lorkinsson had been following the conversation with worried eyes. 'But I saw *two* bags, Miss Parker. Where is the other one? Anouk surely needed more than this? What about clothes? To start afresh?'

Posie laughed.

'I reckon she'd planned to buy new things in France. And as for the other bag, let me turn to it in a minute. It's very important. In fact, it's the very reason why Anouk, and crucially, the Princess, died. And let me tell you, it's utterly, utterly ridiculous.'

* * * *

Twenty-Seven

But before she could explain further, Richard directed that the pink envelopes were handed out without further delay.

The butler and secretary were handed one each, and they warily ripped open the stuck-down flaps.

Inside each was a folded set of bank notes, totalling a hundred pounds.

'Good grief! Lucky blighters,' muttered Oats audibly, crabbily, as the staff sat, speechless, unsure whether to hand the money back, or whether to celebrate their good luck. 'At least that odd woman was good to her staff, eh? And that's where the rest of the National Gallery pounds went to, I'll warrant…'

There was one similar envelope, presumably with the same amount inside it, for the jobbing gardener, Tom. There was a slimmer one for Dolly, too, but Richard kept hold of that.

Posie ripped open her own pink envelope. Hers was a message. A shaky hand had given her instructions, and confirmation of something she had already guessed at.

She got up hurriedly, passed the note to Oats. 'Can you do as this says, Inspector? Get one of your lads to go into the garden and dig for me. But tell them to wear jolly good gloves, please.'

She came back to the table and sat again. Richard had taken off his heavy Commissioner's cap, and he was staring at her.

'*Dig*?' he hissed under his breath. 'Dig for *what*, darling? What the blazes is going on?'

But Posie shook her head, *not now*.

Sam Stubbs, quiet so far, but now almost jumping up in his seat, called down the table. 'Chief Commissioner, if Miss Sinne was staging her own disappearance, her own "kidnapping", then why did she end up dead? And what about the Princess? Where does she come into all this mess? Was her death just bad luck?'

'That's a fair question, Mr Stubbs,' said Richard pleasantly. He tapped at his notebook a couple of times. 'And the answer is–'

Posie cut in. 'The answer is because the biggest secret of Anouk Sinne's life got in the way.'

Hubert Pring had been sitting with his arms crossed. He gave a huge, juddering sigh.

'Is this something to do with me?' asked Hubert Pring, almost as if he had given up on life itself. 'My wife told me you had gathered some truths which might be a little, er, uncomfortable, for me, if they were made known. She wanted to warn me.'

Sam Stubbs was biting at his lips in excitement, his hands hammering nervously on the table-top, adding an extra level of tension. His beady eyes were glistening, looking from Hubert Pring and Lady Clare, and then back at Lovelace again, expectant.

Richard rapped his pen on the table. 'Mr Stubbs, and *all* of you here, I must warn you that anything said within the confines of these walls is strictly confidential. Do you all understand? Mr Stubbs, your newspaper will get its exclusive, as I promised. But *this* stays here.'

Nods all around. But wide, excited eyes.

Posie turned to Hubert Pring. 'Yes, Viscount Effington.

The biggest secret of Anouk's life *is* something which is to do with you. But, strangely enough, at the same time, it wasn't anything to do with you at all.'

'I don't understand.'

'Neither did I, until today, my Lord.'

Posie explained to the silent, watchful room very briefly about Anouk's Suffragette past, and her meeting with Hubert Pring at the Magistrates' Court, her affair with him in early 1907, and then her sudden disappearance for two years, between 1907 and 1909.

You could have heard a pin drop.

She turned to the Viscount again. 'This is delicate territory, my Lord, but we *do* know that Anouk's disappearance for two years must have been related to a pregnancy. We know, from the medical evidence, she gave birth around this time. My presumption, Viscount Effington – and your wife already knows this – is that Anouk told you there was a baby?'

The room seemed suddenly very hot.

Men's voices, raised and excited, could be heard at the bottom of the garden. Inspector Oats shouting in the background: '*Naaw! Give it some welly, lad!*'

In the quiet, awful silence of the room, Posie watched Gordy Lorkinsson roll a cigarette for himself, carefully, methodically, and she saw how Lady Clare watched his long, brown fingers greedily, possessively. Her husband got out his own gold cigarette tin and started to light up a good cigar. After he'd shaken off his match, Hubert Pring sat inhaling his smoke with a bitter, contained nervousness.

'I'm a ruined man already,' he said softly. 'So yes, I'll admit it. There was a baby.'

He blew out the heavy blue smoke. 'But Anouk didn't tell me at the time. I had no idea. We met in the February, and she was gone by the summer. When she came back to me, two years later, she told me there had been a child, and that she'd had to give it up. She said she thought about it every minute of every day. She said I'd ruined her life. That I would have to make it up to her.'

Posie scoffed loudly: 'I think that was a convenient thing to say, your Lordship.'

'What *do* you mean?'

'With respect, my Lord, it was how Anouk got money out of you. She was angry with you, sir. But it wasn't over the baby. No, what tore Anouk Sinne up was that she wanted you to step away from your wife, and marry her, but you wouldn't. I expect she asked you to marry her before she disappeared in 1907, didn't she? And then again, after 1909, but before you set up the perfume house. Is that right? I expect she was insistent, wasn't she?'

Hubert Pring almost choked on his cigar.

'How the blazes do you know that? You're right of course: she went on and on about it. Withholding herself from me, promising she would be mine again but only if I married her. I gave her everything I could: money, clothes, a flat, lawyers' fees when she needed them. And later, when she needed a new life, I gave her the House of Sinne, and all the documents which meant she could live as 'Anouk Sinne'. But it was never enough for her. Never enough to make her love me again, to pick up where we had left off in 1907. But, you see, Miss Parker, marriage to her was impossible. Even if I'd wanted it.'

He looked shame-facedly away from his wife and down at the table. 'And I *did* want to marry her. But my religion would not allow it. I thought Anouk understood that.'

Posie tried not to look at the flushed face of Lady Clare, still proud, unlikely ever to cry, even in the face of public humiliation.

'I know, my Lord,' Posie spoke gently now, tentatively feeling her way. 'But I don't think anything like religion mattered to Anouk. It was the one thing you wouldn't give her, and that was all she was after. She simply *needed* to be married. But behind it all – for *you*, sir – was the shame of that baby born in 1907, the guilt of giving him away. Anouk recognised you felt it all keenly, and so steadily, steadily, she bled you dry.'

A gasp, a choke on the smoke. '*Him?* I have a *son*?'

'Well...' Posie smiled. 'I'm coming to that. I decided to do some investigating, my Lord. It began with a name, a place I'd heard of. Where this story all began...'

A shop.

Posie remembered her friend Dolly's words: '*Nice little logo it had, a fish wearing tap shoes...reminded me of the theatre, I suppose.*'

Posie took up the paper in front of her, which featured a happy-looking fish, above the legend 'THE DANCING FISH'. She showed it around.

'I decided to go there, today, to this place. Sergeant Fox came with me, for company. What did you make of it, Sergeant?'

Sergeant Fox gave a low whistle of slight disbelief. 'Poplar Dock? In the East End, Miss? I thought we'd come to the wrong place at first. The area is rough as old boots. Grimy, dark, stinking of tar and fish, and worse. But this shop we'd come to see was really first-class: clean and unusually well set-up; new fat-fryers and expensive tiling on the walls; a fancy flashing light outside which must have cost a few bob. Nice fish lunch we both enjoyed there, didn't we, Miss? Nice older fella serving there, too. He was proud of his shop, been there more than thirty years. And he was chatty.'

Fox gave a laugh laced with irony: 'Well, I suppose he had to be, what with me waving an Arrest Warrant in his face. And after I had insisted he cleared the shop of his customers, so we could have a good chinwag. Cosy, like.'

They'd gone to the same place where Dolly had worked for a year, all those years ago, way before the Great War.

A fish bar popular with dockers, fishermen, shipbuilders, all the trades who clustered together in that huge centre of ship-building down on the Thames, where the river swelled and thickened before the estuary led out to the cold North Sea.

Posie flipped the fish shop wrapper around to its other side. It was printed with the same cheap tap-dancing fish logo but read: *'DEN DANSENDE FISK'*.

She held it up. 'See this? The place is especially popular, then as now, with Scandinavian workers.'

Posie pictured it again in her mind's eye.

The fish bar was on the corner of a side street near the entrance to the docks. Despite the hot day, the corner had seemed cold, whistling with a howling wind, with the angry, hungry ghosts of men who had sweated and worked their lives and bodies to a husk, making the huge boats in the yards there, cathedral-sized boats made of steel and blood.

It hadn't taken long to get what they had come for.

Dolly was mentioned, among general chit-chat. Then the year -1907 – had been thrown into the mix. And all the while Fox had toyed with the blank Arrest Warrant.

A quiet threat.

Posie took a deep breath and addressed the people in the drawing-room at the House of Sinne again. 'I asked the Proprietor and his wife if a young woman had gone there, in 1907, with a baby boy, seeking sanctuary? Or seeking *something else*?'

The whole room stared, confused.

'Whatever do you mean, Posie?' asked Richard, caught up in the story. 'You mean to say that Anouk Sinne took her baby boy to the fish-and-chip shop where your friend Dolly had worked? A place she had laughed at; ridiculed? She was famous for hating bad smells! Had a sensitive nose! Why the deuce would Anouk go *there*?'

Posie recalled how the Proprietor had clammed up, just goggled and stared, wiping his hands on his clean cooking apron, eyes bulging, watering. But fortunately, Posie had managed to get it out of the Proprietor's wife quickly, who was a typical cockney, and the type who loved to talk, albeit worried by a long shadow of a guilty conscience which had blighted her husband's life for many years.

Posie met Richard's gaze.

'The wife confirmed that Anouk had moved into the empty second-floor flat above The Dancing Fish with her baby. It was November 1907. The baby had been born in a Nursing Home somewhere off in the country, in difficult circumstances. But against the odds, Anouk had kept the baby: convinced the authorities at the Nursing Home she would be fine. I expect she used a fake name, a fake story about a husband in the services. She was always good with deception.'

Hubert Pring was red in the face, ashamed, angry. 'But what was she playing at? She could have come to me! By Jove, I'd have seen her and our boy right. I would have looked after them. My love for her never stopped. Never.'

Posie swallowed uncomfortably. 'I know that, my Lord.'

The Viscount was shaking his head. 'It must have been wretched! There are so many places in London to go. So why there?'

'Because she had been before, sir. And she was looking for something special there. Something she had lost.'

It had been easy enough to put this horrid little tale together, Posie reflected. *Hattie Synnes had been to The Dancing Fish once: to sate her curiosity, and to laugh at a girl she thought was beneath her.*

But that one visit had changed her life.

Just then Oats reappeared, through the French doors. He was carrying a small black box. He banged it down on the table in front of Posie, causing Archie Van Dusen to almost jump out of his skin. The American had been quietly in the process of removing the stopper of the peacock bottle of scent.

Oats was nonplussed. '*That* was what was there, Miss.

But beats me why it was worth all the effort, eh? It's just a lot of numbers inside, looks like lists to me. A mare's nest.'

'Thank you very much, Inspector.'

Hubert Pring was frowning, edging closer to Posie now, almost desperate to know the next part of her story.

'What did Anouk find in Poplar?' he asked, half-whispering.

Posie felt nervous. This was a hard tale in the telling.

She spoke directly to the Viscount.

'Well, sir, the first time Anouk went to Poplar she met a man in the queue of The Dancing Fish. It was very late autumn, 1906. He would go on to become her lover. And later, after she'd dismissed him out of a panicky horror at discovering she was pregnant, she realised she'd made a dreadful mistake. She had become *your* lover by then, but she was certainly already pregnant when she met you. Pregnant with her lover's child.'

Posie watched the Viscount's face freeze in confusion and pain, and she got no enjoyment in this tale at all.

'She thought you would provide her with a safety net, a cover for the pregnancy. But you refused to commit to marrying her, didn't you? So she left to have the baby, and after he was born, she concentrated all her efforts on going back to where it had all begun. Anouk went back to the fish bar to find the father of her child. We were told today by the Proprietor that Anouk lived in Poplar with her baby for six months; paying over-the-odds to rent the little flat, looking after the baby all by herself. In bad weather she looked out of the window, and in good weather she pounded the streets and dock-works with her baby in its pram, asking after the man she wanted to find. She knew his name, and that he was a riveter. That he worked with Danes. Not much more.'

Sergeant Fox broke in. 'It was a sad tale, Miss, wasn't it? The man was never found, and eventually Miss Sinne went loopy, couldn't cope. Had a massive breakdown.

The owners of the fish bar managed to get the details of Miss Sinne's parents, who hadn't seen her in months and had gone mad with worry, and they contacted them. The parents came straight away and took Miss Sinne away. Sent her off somewhere to get better.'

'This man she was looking for,' asked the Viscount, his eyes wide, jaw slack, 'the customer at the fish bar? *He* was the father of Anouk's baby boy? Not me?'

'That's right, sir,' said Posie, firmly, surely, hating this story.

'Anouk was tricking you again, sir, all these years. Like water for perfume, this was a baby which was never yours in the first place. You could have saved all that money, all that guilt. All that time.'

Suddenly Posie stared across the table, fixing her gaze on the Icelander.

Gordy Lorkinsson was looking aghast. He was, unconsciously, shredding his cigarette papers into nothing, into wretched confetti pieces for a celebration which didn't exist.

'Oh, no. No. Please, please don't say it was *me*,' he said very slowly, very softly.

He shook his head in disbelief. 'Anouk and I were together only a few short months. And she sent me away. I was heartbroken. But the timing fits. I *did* meet her in the autumn of 1906, where I was working with a lot of Danish shipbuilders. You sent me a policeman with a question today, Miss Parker, didn't you? Asking me what my trade was when I first came over to England?'

Posie nodded. 'Yes. You told him you were a riveter; you trained in Iceland and came over here to the shipyards. I should have guessed: there had been mention of your work overalls, your burnt and scratched hands.'

The Icelander shook his head in disbelief. 'I think it *was* in a fish bar where I had met Anouk initially, but I can't quite remember. It's all so long ago, and hazy. After she broke up with me my life changed direction. For the better. It had a new purpose. I left almost immediately.'

For a second, he looked across the room at Lady Clare, but he forced himself to look back at Posie again.

'I never set foot in Poplar again.'

He shook his head in misery. 'But Anouk never said a thing! Not in all these years since. Never said she'd looked for me. Never said there was a baby boy!'

Posie shrugged. 'What was she supposed to say? When you arrived here later, in 1913, it would have been obvious you had moved on. As had she. But it *was* you, Gordy, whom she searched for. And it was your baby.'

Posie opened the black box she had been given by Inspector Oats. Earth clung to it in little knobbly bits. It was what she had expected it to be.

She slammed the lid down tight, pressed her hands on top as if to stop magic escaping.

Bad magic.

Lorkinsson was frozen, shaking his head from side to side. 'But what of the baby?'

Posie reached for her last set of notes.

'Well, it came full circle. The baby was sent away, and it's only been in the last year or so that this grown-up child has come to know Anouk Sinne. A relationship was, at last, forming.'

Everyone in the room turned as one to look at Anatole de Poilac.

And he hung his head in shame.

* * * *

Twenty-Eight

'I am very much afraid you have got the wrong idea,' he muttered to the floor, before looking up again, gathering back his pride.

'Anouk was not my mother! She was my lover. And a very good one. I learned a lot from her. There! Now you know.'

He shrugged at the embarrassed looks from the others.

'Scandalous, I know. But enjoyable. However, it was all over. I met someone else in the early spring as part of my studies: a nurse, in one of the big Paris hospitals. The real reason I came here with my mother on Sunday was to tell Anouk that our affair was over. I thought she might be upset, but, when I explained, on Sunday, she hardly listened. She was rushing about crazily. Now I understand why: she had so much more to be thinking of. But I had no idea she would be coming back with us on that plane. My mother, and she *is* my mother, for all that we look different, keeps many secrets from me, it seems. Big secrets.'

Posie smiled. 'Thank you for your honesty, Count Anatole. And I must apologize.'

Posie had, she had to admit, got it wrong.

Very wrong, on a couple of counts.

And she hated being wrong. It was a kind of agony for her.

She bit at her lip regretfully. 'This is all *my* fault, Count Anatole. I made the incorrect assumption that, because of your convenient date of birth, you must have been the missing baby. It was handy, neat: you were born in November 1907, nine months after Anouk had met the Viscount. I didn't even think to consider that the baby could have been conceived beforehand! But, of course, that is what happened. So, I was not looking for a child born in November at all.'

Red herrings.

Loose ends which never tie up.

'Also, because, Count Anatole, your date of birth so neatly fitted, I simply and stupidly put it in my head that the baby was a boy. And I have continued with that fabrication in telling you all this tale today, to see where it would lead…'

Posie turned in Lady Clare's direction, whose face gave nothing away. 'Last night you told me you had always assumed something about the missing baby, and that was, unless I am much mistaken, that you had assumed it was a *girl*. Am I right?'

'It was just a feeling I had.'

'You were right.'

A baby girl. Not a boy.

A baby girl honoured with the name of another, feisty, sparky woman.

Posie read from her notes.

'We can find no birth certificates, or anything of the kind, but the fish shop Proprietor told us that the baby was a girl. And although Anouk and her baby arrived in November, the baby had actually been born in or around the end of August, and had been born very small, needing expert care. By the time they arrived in Poplar, the baby was already a couple of months old, and a lusty little thing. The baby was called Dorothea, and Anouk called her "Dolly."' Posie shrugged. 'It is my fancy that the baby was named after my friend Dolly Price, who had "brought" Anouk to Poplar in the first place. We were told that baby Dolly was a bonny little thing. But what happened next was a tragedy.'

Posie was almost surprised at the tremor in her voice, at the sudden rush of emotion bubbling beneath the surface of a tale which was not hers for the telling.

Come on!

She took a deep breath, willed herself on, but tears were pinching at the corners of her eyes.

Count to ten.

Sergeant Fox seemed to sense this.

He cleared his throat, taking over seamlessly. 'On Anouk's breakdown, her parents paid the Proprietor and his wife a huge sum to look after baby Dolly: become her "unofficial" parents. The Proprietor couldn't believe his luck. With the windfall of money from Anouk's parents he was able to improve The Dancing Fish no end. And that investment is what we can still see today, lucky fella! But the arrangement was especially heaven-sent for his wife, his *first* wife, who was sickly and childless and had always wanted a daughter. The wife, Carlotta, doted on Dolly. But it ended badly. The next year, midway through 1908, with Anouk still in an institution somewhere, Carlotta died suddenly. The Proprietor couldn't cope with Dolly alone, and the fella tried to contact Anouk's parents to get them to take baby Dolly away. But they never came.'

The Duchesse, who had been silent since the debacle over her not-dead husband, who hadn't even protested over the possibility of her son being Anouk's child, covered her mouth in horror.

'*Mais, non*! In 1908, Anouk's parents had died! In that car crash! There was no-one left. Oh! How terrible! I knew nothing of this. *Nothing*!'

'Exactly,' said Posie, briskly, recovered. She nodded at Sergeant Fox.

I've got this now.

'No-one knew, or could help. Which is how the Proprietor, who, I didn't mention before, is Danish, and called Leonard, or "Lenne" Fisk, found himself very unwillingly standing at the doors of the main London Orphanage, at Great Ormond Street, carrying little Dolly. She was one year old. All she had with her was her name, Dorothea, which in Danish is said "Dorte" – the name Carlotta had called her by – and a small locket on a necklace. It was described very clearly by Mr Fisk for us today, wasn't it, Sergeant? When he'd recovered his tongue…'

Fox looked at his notebook, threw a look over to the Duchesse.

'It was shaped like half a broken heart, and there were words on it in French: "*Ne m'oublie pas*". It was apparently hung around the baby's neck on a metal chain by her French grandmother, when they came to take Anouk away.'

The Duchesse was shaking her head, looking close to tears.

Posie checked her final page of notes.

'It wasn't a complete disaster. We know the baby grew and flourished, and that Anouk, mostly recovered from her breakdown, tried unsuccessfully, again and again, from 1909 onwards, to access her lost daughter. She was told she would only have a hope of being reunited with her if she was married, a respectable woman. She tried again with Hubert, and although he set her up as his Mistress in her own little flat, still he wouldn't marry her. The years wore on, and finally the baby, by now a little girl, was placed away from the Orphanage. And at that stage, Anouk finally lost her. And this was around the time of the start of the House of Sinne, and the Great War, and I believe that then, but only then, Anouk gave up on her daughter.'

Richard Lovelace was flushed dark red in the face, flicking through his notes, salvaging his own detective skills in front of his wife.

Posie sat back, exhausted. She felt like she had run a long, hard race, and that there was no happy ending to be had.

Let him finally make this connection.

Dorte Fisk, the girl who had been taken on by the nuns of a religious institution.

A capable, good girl, whom they would take back in a heartbeat.

A girl just turning eighteen, but with the poise and capabilities of a much older girl. A girl who could pass for being in her mid-twenties, easily. A girl whom, the nuns confirmed when Fox had asked, had had a birthday ascribed to her by the Orphanage as being August, 1907.

The secretary.

It was obvious when you thought about it.

Richard Lovelace turned to the blonde girl half-way along the table.

He spoke gently. 'So, *you*, Lucy, were Anouk's daughter? Did you know?'

The girl, so unlike Anouk Sinne to look at, today in drab greys and blacks, lifted her beautiful blue eyes to meet Richard's, and she nodded primly, without any emotion.

'Yes, I knew. But I didn't know Mr Lorkinsson was my father, though,' she whispered.

'But how on earth did you find your mother?' Richard was asking, baffled. 'Anouk Sinne had covered her tracks her whole life, hadn't she?'

But Lucy Reeble stayed quiet, had drawn into herself, oblivious to the penetrating glances of those around her.

Posie spoke again. 'Lucy is a clever girl. I suppose she had access, at age sixteen, to her records at the Orphanage. These would have led her to The Dancing Fish. And I know, from chatting to the second Mrs Fisk, that a smart, blonde girl called there a little over a year and a half ago, asking for her father, for Mr Fisk. Lenne Fisk was so terrified at the thought of coming face-to-face with little Dorte again that he hid in the back room and gave his wife a piece of paper to give to Lucy, with a scribbled explanation on it as to her grandparents' names.'

Posie got up, taking with her the black leather box which Inspector Oats had given her from the garden, together with her carpet bag. She walked to the French doors, to be nearer to a very pale-looking Lucy Reeble, to talk directly to her, but Posie was also desperate for air.

'From there on it would have been easy to unpick the history of the Synnes family. You tried to trace Hattie Synnes. And you succeeded!'

'Why did you come to work as her secretary?' asked Richard, interested. 'I am supposing you never got around to telling Miss Sinne of your true identity?'

Everyone stared at Lucy Reeble in astonishment. She tucked her white bobbed hair behind her ear unnecessarily, nervously. She licked at her unmade-up lips, and when she spoke it was faltering and hesitant at first.

'Miss Parker is quite correct in her explanation of how I found my mother. The desire to find her had been with me for as long as I remember. There was one nun who helped me especially. She encouraged me to go to Poplar, where I discovered the "truth" that the Orphanage kept in its files about me was all a lie. But at least the necklace, the pendant I had been given as a baby, made a sort of sense at last. I wasn't Danish, I was part-French! This nun and I, we traced the story of my mother.'

Lucy laughed suddenly, but it was a sharp little laugh, with no pleasure behind it at all. 'We traced her metamorphosis into the strange and awful creature that was Anouk Sinne.'

Her final words were stinging, censorious.

'You didn't approve, Miss Reeble?' asked Richard, slightly amused. He concentrated on lighting a cigarette, narrowing his eyes as the smoke billowed around him.

Lucy Reeble shrugged. 'You forget, sir. I have been raised

in a God-fearing place, of one kind or the other, for all of my life. And then I discover that not only is my mother famous, but she's scandalous. *Notorious*. Photographs with very young men in nightclubs; Princes even! Rumours of drugs and a dreadful cat on a diamond lead! Decadence, debauchery. I had wanted a mother, yes. But not *this* one. I was unsure what to do.'

Posie had imagined something like this. *Sensible girl*, she found herself thinking. *I think I would have done the same thing.*

'You applied for a job here instead?' Posie asked, approvingly. 'A year ago? To see what sort of a person your mother was? And I suppose this nice nun helped you again, did she?'

A nod.

It had been more than that, Posie knew.

The helpful nun had obviously done her research well, and found out that Hubert Pring helped Catholic-educated children get jobs. She had got five of her young charges, including Lucy, to apply to Hubert's scheme, asking for work as secretaries in a perfume house, specifying the House of Sinne as their preferred choice. But Lucy's was heavily weighted as being the strongest application by far.

Posie knew all of this as Sergeant Fox had gone through the staff files for the House of Sinne, locating all of the girls' applications, and he'd then telephoned the Convent at Reading, asking to speak to the four other girls involved.

Women together, in solidarity.

Tearfully, they had all admitted their parts in the subterfuge, attesting that they had simply been trying to 'help' Lucy get on.

The nun who had aided Lucy so much, Sister Ignatia, had also been questioned by Fox and she had been unrepentant of her actions: stressing, quite rightly, that nothing illegal had happened in the application process.

It had arguably just been a way for Lucy to get ahead.

Posie found the whole thing bittersweet.

'It sounds to me, Lucy, as if, in this nice nun, Sister Ignatia, you had already found yourself a mother-figure: a clever, caring, adventurous sort of person. Goodness, she sounds pretty amazing. I'd have loved to have a woman like that, batting for me, growing up! She told Sergeant Fox she'd even taken you to the best hairdressers they could afford in Reading, to have your hair cut in the modern style before you came for interview. And she scraped together all the resources at her disposal to buy you one or two good outfits, so you'd look the fashionable part. That is *real* support.'

Lucy pouted slightly, discontentedly. 'Perhaps…but the desire was still there. To find out.'

Gordy Lorkinsson spoke at last. 'So what *did* you think of your mother, Lucy? After having worked for her?'

Posie had been aware of him watching this girl at his side very carefully, almost slavishly, for the last couple of minutes. His face had been transformed in this time, and was picked out in light, in joy.

A daughter.

Lucy Reeble played with the pink envelope in her hands, folding and re-folding its gummed top, jiggling the money inside. She seemed to consider the question with all due seriousness before she spoke, and Posie realised that this was the very measure of the girl herself.

'I found things to be worse than I had feared, sir. I had no idea, obviously, as to the scale of Miss Sinne's debts and her gambling, but she was living in a crazy sort of mess. And the men! It was dreadful!'

Lucy flashed a look of pure venom across the table towards Anatole. She wrinkled her nose in scorn. '*He* was her lover! He's younger than me! It was disgusting. *Horrible.* I had to pretend I couldn't hear or see things, sometimes. It was a relief when she went away, to Paris, to see him. But when he visited her in this house, it made me feel sick.'

The Duchesse, across the table, almost laughed.

'*Mon Dieu*, love is not always conventional, Miss Reeble. You should learn that! Your mother certainly knew it. Life is very short and should be full of pleasure. Who cares how my son spends his time if he is not hurting others?'

'But there *were* others,' whispered Lucy acidly, throwing a glance heavy with meaning at the Viscount and Lady Clare.

'And some were vulnerable. Like *their* red-headed boy, crying about the war up in Miss Sinne's bedroom, and wanting a love my mother wouldn't give to him. He was just one of many, and they were all too, too young for her.'

'Did you plan on staying on here, Miss Reeble?' asked Richard gently.

'Yes,' Lucy replied certainly. 'My mother might have been embarrassing, but she was a kind of genius. I had decided to tell her who I was. I wanted to do it today, after the fuss had died down over the new perfume, after the big event at the Embassy Club.'

'I see.' Richard gave a gentle smile. 'And you honestly had no idea she was leaving?'

Lucy shook her head simply. She looked down at the table, quite devastated.

'Well, I am truly sorry for your loss, Miss Reeble,' Lovelace said kindly. 'I am only glad that once this murder is cleared up, you can move on with your life.'

Posie turned from the window, smiling at her husband's words. In the garden, the policemen who had been digging in the hemlock were now chattering away.

She pulled out of her carpet bag the pink note she had received earlier and put it, together with the black box, down on the table in front of Lucy.

'It's such a shame Anouk Sinne was murdered. She was not aware of you being her daughter, Lucy, but I'm sure she would have welcomed you, loved you. In her heart of hearts, she never forgot you, even if she had convinced herself of the futility of finding you. Look at this...'

Posie pushed the pink note in front of Lucy.

In a shaky hand, Anouk Sinne had written:

MISS PARKER,

YOU ARE TELEPHONING FOR A POLICE GUARD AS I WRITE THIS. WHEN YOU READ THIS, I WILL BE LONG GONE.

I'M SORRY FOR THE DECEPTION I INVOLVED YOU IN.

PLEASE FIND MY DAUGHTER.

I HANDED YOU THE ONLY REAL BOTTLE OF 'THE ULTIMATE SIN' A FEW MINUTES AGO. THE REST HAS BEEN THROWN AWAY.

PLEASE GIVE THAT, TOGETHER WITH A BLACK BOX I HAVE HIDDEN UNDER THE HEMLOCK AT THE END OF MY GARDEN, TO MY DAUGHTER, WHEN YOU FIND HER.

THE BOTTLE AND THE BOX ARE MY GIFTS TO HER, HER BIRTHRIGHT.

THEY ARE NOT FOR ARCHIE VAN DUSEN, NOR FOR HUBERT PRING, WHO HAS ALWAYS DISGUSTED ME.

A MAN WITH LESS COURAGE OR CONVICTION I AM YET TO MEET.

THANK YOU.

ANOUK SINNE

Posie tapped the top of the black box gently. 'I have checked inside this black box, and it contains *all* the formulas for all of the perfumes that Anouk Sinne ever created.'

Posie brandished the turquoise blue bottle she had been entrusted with. 'Including this one! With these, Miss Reeble, you stand in line to become a very rich young woman. So at least something good has come out of all this mess.'

Lucy stared at Posie, and tears were coursing down her young, white, porcelain-like cheeks.

A life-long search was over, finished in calamity.

A fragile child was suddenly being asked to bear the weight of her genius of a mother's legacy, and it seemed too, too much.

But then Posie did something very strange.

* * * *

Twenty-Nine

Posie grabbed up the pink letter from the girl's hands and snatched up the box.

She turned on her heel, and walked smartly back to her seat, carrying both things with her. She passed these over to her husband, turning to smile at Anouk Sinne's daughter.

'What a shame you will never see any of those promised riches, Lucy.'

Everyone in the room turned to stare at Posie, baffled.

As was Richard, at her side, who muttered darkly, 'What are you talking about, darling?'

But Posie sat down and addressed the room. 'I'm talking of something dreadful. Nightmarish. *Matricide*, the killing of a mother.'

'Eh, what? Darling…'

Posie stared hard at Lucy Reeble. 'You, Lucy, killed your own mother. And quite deliberately. And dreadfully.'

A horrified gasp resounded in the room, and Sam Stubbs had got out a notebook and was scribbling furiously.

No!' shouted Lucy Reeble, standing up suddenly. 'Why would I have done that? I was about to tell her who *I* was!'

Richard, at Posie's side, was grinding out his cigarette almost angrily. 'Posie?' he muttered. 'Are you sure?'

But Posie stayed calm, ignored the whisperings. Ignored Gordy Lorkinsson who was now also on his feet, putting out one hand ineffectually towards his just-found daughter, being batted away by the girl herself.

She saw Oats at the door, inching slowly towards where Lucy Reeble stood, and the Sergeants looking grim, forewarned.

'Please explain, Miss Parker,' said Lorkinsson, his voice sounding broken. 'Why on earth would my daughter kill her own mother?'

'Because, quite simply, she was being let down by that mother. Being abandoned, all over again,' said Posie.

'But I want to come back to *why* Anouk Sinne and the Princess died yesterday, and that is purely because Lucy learnt that Anouk was leaving, due to *one telephone call*. It was ridiculous. It was all about a cat.'

She got out the dark-green tag which had been dropped by Dolly from Julius' travel basket as she left Grape Street.

Oh, Dolly, where are you?

Posie looked over at the Icelander. 'Mr Lorkinsson, you mentioned to me you saw Anouk with *two* bags on Sunday?'

'What of it?' Lorkinsson shrugged, hardly caring, his eyes only on Lucy.

Inspector Oats was now pulling at his moustache in excitement.

Posie explained to the room that the second bag Lorkinsson had seen being loaded into the dark-green airport car, late on Sunday morning, had actually contained Julius, the adored Sphynx cat.

'You said, Mr Lorkinsson, that Anouk seemed to be talking to the bag. Well, I expect she was! I think she must have given the cat a sleeping tablet, and was calming him down, reassuring him. He was inside his usual basket, packed neatly into a black bag.'

Posie laughed slightly. 'Anouk Sinne had told her staff

that the cat had gone to the Veterinary Surgeon in Chelsea for a minor operation. It was a good bluff. Julius was, as we are now certain of, bound for Croydon Airport. He was supposed to be put on a mid-afternoon flight to Paris, that very same day, Sunday. Along with a whole load of other animals.'

Posie waved the dark-green tag with its big 'Q' on it.

'Julius was destined for the quarantine bin over in France. For a few weeks at least. When I found this, I thought this was a mundane vet's tag, but actually this is Croydon Airport's special "Quarantine" tag, in their trademark dark-green colour, attached to the baskets of all travelling animals.'

'What happened?' cut in Sam Stubbs, excitement getting the better of him. 'Something went wrong with the plan, eh?'

Smallbone, over by the door, grinned. 'I'll say! The Quarantine plane, loaded with all the drugged and sleeping pets, wouldn't start. It was grounded at three o'clock on Sunday. The next special plane for animals wasn't scheduled to leave Croydon until next week. So, all those animals had to be unloaded on Sunday. Each owner was called, sometime in the late afternoon. Croydon confirmed to us they had called here, telling the owner to come and pick up Julius.'

Posie spoke directly to the blonde, silent girl who had suddenly collapsed back into her seat, her head in her hands. 'But the problem was that Anouk did not take the call, did she? It was *you*, Lucy, who took the call from Croydon Airport. Wasn't it? You had come in during Sunday afternoon, to make sure all was perfect for the French guests.'

Everyone stared.

The girl said nothing. From somewhere in her pocket Lucy had pulled out a locket on a tarnished silver chain.

It was a half broken-heart, the exact match for the Duchesse's own.

Posie carried on: 'And, clever girl that you are, Lucy, you realised that something odd was happening if the cat was being sent away on a plane. You realised Anouk Sinne was leaving, didn't you? I don't think you realised the many-layered shams your mother had surrounded herself with; all you could see was that you were about to be denied your chance to tell her your news. You saw red. Decided that she had to die.'

'By Gad!' whispered Richard. He was neither smoking nor cracking his knuckles, just sitting very, very still. 'But she's not yet eighteen! To kill her own mother? What about the…'

'The *evidence*, sir?' asked Fox, still standing over by the doorway, looking slightly smug. 'There's nothing from Croydon in particular; they had to telephone so many animal owners they can't remember this one particular call, but we *do* have concrete evidence of another kind. From the Veterinary Surgeon in Chelsea.'

Richard shook his head, frowning. 'But Posie just said Anouk Sinne *hadn't* sent the cat to the Veterinary Surgeon?'

Fox grinned in an impressed way. 'It was clever of Lucy, sir. A double-bluff. Anouk Sinne had told her staff that Julius was at the vets, so he wouldn't be missed. And when the arrangement with the Quarantine plane failed, Lucy had to make sure that *Anouk* herself didn't realise that her own plan had unravelled. So the cat had to be kept away. And in order to do this, Lucy fell back on the bluff itself.'

Fox laughed. 'Lucy had dealt with the Veterinary Surgeons' driver a few times over the year. His name is Jimmie Minter. Lucy contacted him on Sunday afternoon, going to his home address, claiming to be acting on Miss Sinne's instructions. She asked Jimmie to go out to Croydon, collect Julius and then to look after him for the next twenty-four hours. He was told to bring the animal back on Monday, after the "reveal" had taken place.'

Richard looked confounded. 'But why would the man agree? It seems a strange request, surely?'

Fox laughed. 'Not if you are being offered a big wad of cash, sir. Jimmie Minter has told us he was given five pounds on Sunday, before setting out to Croydon, and he got another five pounds yesterday, when he dropped Julius off again, in front of us all. That's big money to a chap like Jimmie. And he's been in trouble with the law before, sir: when he saw my Arrest Warrant, he blabbed everything. Said how nice Lucy Reeble was, how clear and controlled her manner was.'

'I'll be blowed!' whispered Lovelace.

From her seat Posie stared at Lucy, who stared back, no tears now, eyes burning with a rather terrifying determination.

'I think you made the plans for the cat on Sunday immediately, and you planned how to get rid of Anouk that same evening,' suggested Posie calmly, as if she were talking about the weather.

'You had to think quickly and be resourceful. You had no obvious murder weapons here, and no access to Anouk's laboratory. In addition, you needed to make sure Anouk attended her precious "reveal" yesterday, and preferably, you wanted her to die during it. This would ensure there would be several suspects to choose from for her murder. You had seen how complicated Anouk's life was, and you realised your crime would probably go undetected if it was hidden in among so much oddness. And so you decided upon the cruellest murder weapon. *Hemlock*. It was a painful, dreadful way to die, but it was also apt, and suitably slow-working.'

'*Guð minn góður*! My God!' stuttered the Icelander. 'Are you sure of this, Miss Parker?'

'Oh, yes.' Posie didn't take her eyes from the young blonde woman opposite her.

'Perhaps, Lucy, you had seen your mother picking hemlock in the two weeks before she died? When she was following instructions from the Count de Poilac, that famous "nose". Maybe you'd recognised that distinctive smell? So, for Anouk, it was indeed "the scent of death".'

Gordy Lorkinsson was looking sick as a dog, but it was Hubert Pring who started fighting back, defending the blonde-haired girl who was not his daughter, but could have been, if destiny had been different.

'She's only seventeen! For goodness' sake!' he said, banging his fists down on the table.

'You must have this wrong, Miss Parker, and, Chief Commissioner, I must say I find this a disgrace. This young girl has been brought up in a Convent! What would *she* know of poisons?'

Sergeant Fox called across the room, and he had to contain the glee in his voice.

'Well, my Lord, listen to this!' Fox read loudly from his notebook.

'Sister Ignatia informed me that Lucy Reeble was a keen gardener while she lived at the Convent, showing an especial interest in plants and their medicinal uses. The Convent makes home-made soaps, salves and medicinal drinks, all for sale, and Lucy was involved in all these activities. Sister Ignatia told me that anyone who agrees to undertake such work is first given a course in the use of plants – which includes a section on which plants *not* to use – and their effects. One of these was hemlock.'

Posie bit at her lip. In her mind's eye she saw it all now, how it had happened.

The girl, as straight-backed as a pale river reed, slipping down that shimmering garden scented with hundreds of roses, to pick hemlock behind the hedge near the road. Perhaps by moonlight; certainly under cover of darkness.

The girl would have been careful to wear gloves, and to carry her quarry home to her nearby studio flat, a couple of streets away. Lucy had known what to do next, of course.

The process of distilling hemlock might have been new to her, but it would have been the same thing she'd done hundreds of times before, making salves or tinctures in the laboratory at the Convent with rosemary, thyme, clary-sage, peppermint.

Little equipment had been needed; just the small cafetière Lucy used for making her breakfast coffee.

And the fact it would be rendered forever useless was a small price to pay for the end result it would yield: the syrupy concentrated tasteless hemlock oil which was pure poison.

'I suppose you made her a cup of strong coffee, did you, Lucy? Or scented tea? Yesterday, when she woke up? Something very strong to disguise the slightly putrid scent of the hemlock oil?'

But the girl said nothing. Nothing at all.

Posie was trying to blot out the memory of the great black dilated pupils, the unquenchable thirst. She recalled the memory of Anouk's shaking hand on the poker which had been burning her last secrets on this earth.

A history of secrets.

Posie tried not to think about the effort it had taken Anouk to write that shaky pink note to her yesterday, detailing what she wanted Posie to do for her, in finding her daughter. Tried not to think of the poison in Anouk's veins, slowly killing her, as she shakily bundled up money for her staff.

Had she known she was dying?

'This is all just guesswork!' said Lucy Reeble suddenly, almost shrugging. 'You can't prove any of it. It's as fanciful as a fairy story!'

Richard was looking worried, toying with his big, useless, glitzy hat. 'Much as this is an interesting theory, darling, the girl is right. We cannot prove the case. There is not a single scrap of direct incriminating evidence, is there?'

But Sergeant Smallbone had picked up a waxy, bulky evidence bag and he waved it cheerily.

'Don't worry about that, Chief Commissioner! We found the cafetière you threw away, Miss Reeble. You should have been more careful, eh? Miss Parker instructed me to send bobbies to the communal rubbish bins on Sloane Avenue this afternoon and, after a very mucky half-hour, they found this, in a sack from last night. Dr Poots and Scotland Yard's best forensics team will start working on it straight away. And I'm certain they'll find your fingerprints, and traces of the hemlock oil inside it. So it is like a fairy story, isn't it? One in which the witch's cooking pot manages to trap the very witch who sought to harm others with it!'

And then Lucy started screaming.

It was a horribly shrill and unearthly sound.

She was suddenly running at Smallbone, grabbing at the bag he held up so jauntily.

'Give that to me! It's mine! You had no right! And I wasn't the witch! *That* was Anouk Sinne. I'm glad I killed her. She was dreadful.'

Oats had grabbed at the girl, pinned her arms behind her. She was like a cat herself now; like Julius must have been after being drugged for the flight and kept in his cage for too long.

It was the end, but not an insignificant one by any means.

There was a final horrid twist to this tale.

'There was a contingency plan too, wasn't there, Lucy?' Posie asked, politely. 'In case the hemlock hadn't finished your mother off in time, yesterday.'

Lucy Reeble continued struggling and didn't answer.

'You mean the sodium used for the roses?' cut in Inspector Oats, lips tight. 'Obtained from Lorkinsson's shed? Placed in that fancy diffuser with the sticks?'

'Exactly right, Inspector,' said Posie grimly. 'But, as it turned out, it was a contingency plan which was not needed. Not for Miss Sinne, anyway. Because she had already died, according to plan. But Princess Priyanka came a cropper with it, instead.'

Lucy Reeble had given up moving about, and stood,

face tight and impassive, staring at Posie with her blue, blue eyes which were actually, now Posie realised it, so much like her father's.

Although there was a madness there, dancing away furtively, which was all her very own.

Richard Lovelace had snatched on his weighty cap and was scoring through an Arrest Warrant card, scrubbing out Gordy Lorkinsson's name rather savagely.

'But *why* was Princess Priyanka killed?' piped up Mr Van Dusen.

Posie saw he had got the lid off the French bottle of perfume, had been sniffing it appreciatively for a good couple of minutes. 'Was it an accident? What did *she* do wrong?'

Posie turned over the newspaper in front of her, the front page she had salvaged from her own hallway at Museum Chambers last night. She held it up.

'Here's why.'

Sam Stubbs stared, then grinned excitedly. 'Princess Priyanka? That's *The Times*, Monday morning's edition, isn't it? But it's showing old news! I know cos I sent one of my best reporters out to get a similar snap of the Princess touchin' down at Croydon, from Paris. It was on the Sunday. Quite a crush of journalists, apparently. The Princess should have landed at four o'clock, but she was ten minutes or so late, and crucially, this meant none of the reporters made it back to file for the start of the evening print-runs. So the story ran the next day instead in all the newspapers. Is this important, Miss?'

'Yes, Sam. Spot on.'

Mr Van Dusen shook his head dismissively. 'But *I* was there to greet the Maharani,' he said casually. 'And nothing happened which was so extraordinary! Just a lot of press. Once Priyanka had got out of the plane they melted away. Gee, the airport – tiny little place – was quiet as the grave.'

'That makes sense,' said Posie.

'Because Princess Priyanka died not from some grudge Lucy Reeble bore her, or because of her own perhaps controversial past, but due to a simple case of unfortunate timing. You see, the Quarantine plane with the animals had failed to take off at three o'clock, and at ten minutes past four the Princess then landed. And then she would have walked through the airport, perhaps with you at her side, Mr Van Dusen?'

'Yes. But, gee, what of it?'

'Did you see anything unusual in the airport itself, Mr Van Dusen? In that tiny little place?'

'No. Of course not! We just got her landing forms stamped, and her passport pages stamped and...oh! Well, I say...'

'What was it?' Richard said impatiently. 'What did you see, sir?'

'Animals, Chief Commissioner. Lots of animals. Just brought in, stacked up. They were piled high all around the men who were doing the stamping. The men seemed pretty put upon, I must say, and the animals didn't look too happy either, making a helluva racket!'

Lovelace groaned. 'It was that wretched cat, Julius, wasn't it? Did you see it, sir?'

'That I did not.'

'But Princess Priyanka *did*,' said Posie firmly. 'The cat was so unusual that it stuck in her memory; both Julius himself and the unmistakeable special basket with his name on it in glitzy little stones. And then Priyanka's tragedy was that she recognised it the next day, in the entrance hall, right after Anouk Sinne had died.'

The Princess had recognised the cat first in the painting, and then in the flesh, when Jimmie Minter had returned the cat to the House of Sinne.

Posie had heard Priyanka Lashari muttering: '*Perhaps I was wrong*.'

But she had been right.

Posie collected all of her things up and threw them willy-nilly into her carpet bag.

'The Princess realised something wasn't right, voiced it aloud, and Lucy heard her, and knew it was only going to be a matter of time until the Princess blurted out about having seen the exact same cat at Croydon Airport the day before. And this could have led to Anouk's carefully-laid escape plan being discovered, and then her death becoming inexplicable. Lucy panicked. And so the Princess had to die.'

Richard nodded silently at Oats, who reached for his faithful pair of handcuffs.

But before he could attach them, Lucy was grabbing at something on the desk, throwing it wildly.

It was the half-heart locket, and Lucy had thrown it at the Duchesse.

'You might as well have both of them. It means nothing to me. Nothing at all! You can stick your riches and your perfumes and your long family histories. Stick all of it!'

Richard was standing, sombre-faced, indicating his Sergeants to accompany Oats out, together with the prisoner.

'The irony is of course, Lucy,' said Posie suddenly, 'that you seem such a clever girl. A girl with guts. And in that, at least, you are your mother's daughter.'

Lucy Reeble turned at the doorway and looked at Posie with dead eyes.

'I am *nothing* like that dreadful woman, Miss Parker. And I hate you, from this moment forwards. I hate you for everything you have done here today.'

Posie laughed, as if in relief. 'I'll take that as a compliment, Miss Reeble.'

And suddenly the room was swamped in a blaze of artificial light. It was Sam Stubbs, taking a picture with a teeny-tiny camera.

He grinned cheekily. 'You said I could have an exclusive,

Chief Commissioner, and I wanted to get the chance to use this nifty little camera belonging to Sergeant Fox. Very smooth. Now, if I leave right this minute, I'll just make my own print-run.'

As Lucy was led away, twisting and pulling, trying to stare back at everyone in the room, Posie noticed that the watertight black box and the bottle of 'The Ultimate Sin' were being watched eagerly, on all sides, by the remaining people in the room, and she wished wholeheartedly that Anouk Sinne had simply burnt everything.

Posie opened the box, took out the latest, newest formula and passed this, together with the turquoise bottle of 'The Ultimate Sin', to her husband.

'This will be fought over in a Court of Law,' he said quietly, confidently.

'But *this*,' Posie said, snapping the lid back down on all the other back-catalogue of formulas, 'belongs to someone who deserves a return on their investment, at last. Leverage for a new future, perhaps?'

To the astonishment of Hubert Pring, Posie passed the box across directly to Lady Clare, whose hands closed over it firmly, but whose face gave nothing away.

And then Lady Clare got up, but no-one accompanied her. Her husband sat, deflated, at the table, while her lover also remained sitting, head in hands, the picture of a broken man.

Posie watched as Hubert Pring's wife walked out of the French doors and down the steps into the long, long garden, whose roses blew in the wind coming off the river.

New people would move in here after the foreclosure, and things would be different, as always happens.

One generation replacing another, stamping their own mark – or scent – on a place, only to be ousted again in their turn.

Everyone has secrets, Posie thought to herself suddenly, ready to leave. She swung her carpet bag over her arm rather jauntily.

Secrets can define us.

But perhaps not acknowledging those secrets, and the histories of our past selves, is, after all, the ultimate sin.

She fingered the string of pink beads at her throat, her own secret from another time, and grinned down at her husband, who was still frantically scribbling on a form, which looked very boring.

'Shall we go, darling? Perhaps we can grab some tea at Lyons. I'm famished. And I think I can eat just about anything, but not fishcakes.'

'Just coming, sweetheart.'

And so Posie followed the noise of all the policemen out into the white, empty hallway, where there was no scent left at all, and where only bare white walls looked down upon them.

And she got out her own bottle of cheap trusty perfume, and she gave herself a good spray.

* * * *

Epilogue

It was the following day, Wednesday evening, ten o'clock, and Posie sat at the window-seat in the living-room of the flat in Museum Chambers.

After weeks of no rain, the heavens had finally opened.

She had the sash window up, and outside the rain was lashing down, running in torrents down the street, vast gurgling rivulets washing down through the grey expanse of Bury Place.

In one of those inexplicable London tricks which the city kept all to itself, the summer rain outside smelt of the seaside. Of being far away.

On holiday.

The children were all in bed, and Masha had retired to her room for the night. At Posie's feet Patsy lay huddled in her basket, not liking the sound or smell of the rain.

Richard had been late at work, dealing with the formalities of the Anouk Sinne Murder Case. He was just home and had brought with him the largest beribboned box of chocolates Posie had ever seen.

He'd also arranged to secure two tickets to see *No, No, Nanette*, at the weekend, and Posie was thrilled.

He came through now from the kitchen, still in his suit, but carrying a whisky for himself and a gin and tonic for Posie.

'Cheers, darling,' he said, smiling. 'This case was all yours, and the credit is all due to you, too. I think, actually, *you* should have my job.'

'I don't want it,' said Posie, clinking glasses. 'I wouldn't suit the hat.'

Richard laughed and they stared out at the rain together. Posie was often aware that it was *her* desire which had led to the family staying put, where there was no garden of any sort; not even a roof terrace or balcony, and she sometimes felt guilty.

She looked over at the blue vase on the main table, which was holding at least twenty pinkish-orange roses of the 'Talisman' variety, sent over to her by Gordy Lorkinsson, with no note.

'Has this case – the House of Sinne – made you hanker after grass and roses and a full-sized garden yourself, Richard, my love?'

'Good grief! No! Not likely! Not if it proves to be *that* dangerous.'

Richard smiled, taking a sip of his single malt. 'No. I'm a Londoner through and through, sweetheart. I'm happy with visiting the park and going to Lords occasionally for the cricket. Anything more would be excessive, perhaps a little greedy, don't you think? Just think of all that grass!'

He mock-shivered, but then he looked serious. 'I mean it, darling. *You* solved this case. It was hard, and without you that little slip of evil would have got away with the whole thing.'

Posie looked at Richard carefully. He sounded cheerful enough, but his eyes were clouded with worry.

There's something wrong. Something he's not telling me.

She tried to bat the anomaly away. 'Well, at least there was nothing *very* odd - no ghosts, or no unusual happenings which we can't explain - this time. Only that wretched peacock in the garden! I still don't understand. I *saw* it! I saw it with my own eyes, as did Princess Priyanka.

But no-one else did. I thought initially that Anouk Sinne must have seen the peacock just before she died, and that she tried to follow it down to the end of the garden, but then I realised that she must have wanted to retrieve that black box she had hidden there, to give it to me, to be *certain* I had it. She must have realised by that point that she was dying.'

'Perhaps, my love.'

The rain lashed down, and then the purple night sky was riven through by lightning. Patsy whimpered and Posie picked her up, calming her.

Posie chewed at her lip, distracted, preoccupied. She should have been happy, but something huge was worrying her, spoiling everything.

An absence.

'Look at this night,' she whispered. 'I keep thinking of Dolly, you know. How she left my office with that troublesome cat, and that was her way of saying goodbye. It's too much to bear! Didn't she realise how much we would all be upset by her just *leaving* like this? With no explanation?'

Posie rounded on Richard, whose fault none of this was. She was choking back tears which had come on rather suddenly.

'I keep thinking of that ride in the police car, Richard. When Dolly was looking out of the window, drinking in the London sights as if she would never see them again. You recall? And that story she told us about being a Suffragette and being imprisoned in Holloway, without which we never would have understood Anouk's story. Well, Dolly wouldn't have told us all that if she was going to carry on living her usual, normal life with Rufus, would she?'

'It *was* odd, darling.'

'Something wasn't right, Richard. But I'm not sure what exactly. Dolly was sad, and then drunk, and then sad again. Maybe it's Rufus, dallying around with someone else? Or maybe Dolly just feels trapped. It was all out of character. But now she's gone, and all hell's broken loose. What about the children?'

Richard sighed. He pulled the window half-down, leant his head against the cool glass. It had been a long day.

'She's only been gone two nights, Posie. There's a chance she's simply taking a break. Dolly wasn't born a Countess, was she? And perhaps, sometimes, it all gets too much. Give her time.'

Posie was shaking her head mournfully.

Her husband squeezed her arm, forced a smile.

'We know she was seen on the night train to Paris, on Monday night, Posie darling. We also know she arrived at the Gare du Nord yesterday morning. She speaks French, and she's a capable woman in her own right. And, when we talked about Dolly's disappearance to the French Duchesse, Maria de Poilac, whom she apparently spent a good deal of Anouk's party chatting to, the Duchesse said Dolly had spoken eagerly of rediscovering Paris, the city of her mother. Apparently, Dolly mentioned a friend there, Violette? Have you heard of her?'

'Oh, yes.'

Violette had been a young French nanny Dolly had employed a couple of years back, whom Dolly had got on with like a house on fire. The girl had been dismissed by Rufus, probably, Posie had thought at the time, out of sheer jealousy.

Richard sounded falsely-cheerful. 'So, perhaps she's gone to stay with this Violette, eh? Look on the bright side. Things will be fine.'

But Posie felt that unbearable rising sense of loss again, a pang of panic.

Dolly, a friend made in London, had brought colour and company and so much fun into her life that the thought of her being gone was more than Posie thought she could bear.

'I'll give it one month,' Posie declared suddenly. 'Then I'm going to look for her. Besides, I've got that letter Anouk left her. I see it as my duty to deliver it to her. Even if it is only one word. It will mean a lot to her, as will the fact that Anouk named her only child after her.'

Posie had taken the liberty of opening Dolly's pink envelope from the perfumier. A folded piece of paper inside had simply said 'SORRY'.

Richard didn't say anything.

He suddenly sat down, and reached inside his inner jacket pocket. A thick cream paper envelope was brought out, and he shook it in the air in a melancholy manner.

'Talking of important letters, you'd better sit down, Posie,' he said, and indicated towards the armchairs. 'I've had something on my mind, actually, darling. And I need to share it with you.'

'Oh? Sounds ominous…'

Here it came.

Once she'd sat down, Richard raked his hand through his hair, then shook out a piece of paper which featured an expensive swirling purple letterhead. The name 'REDON' stuck out. The letter was covered in black typewritten words, with many numbered points.

'I haven't had my mind on the job lately, sweetheart. Not since I got *this*. I picked it up on my very brief return to my desk on Monday, after Court.'

'What is it?'

Richard exhaled. 'Caspian della Rosa,' he said simply.

Posie sat up, her heart hammering loudly in her chest.

Caspian della Rosa had haunted and blighted Posie's early days as a Private Detective.

He'd been a Swiss aristocrat, but also one of the world's most deadly con-artists and criminals.

Caspian della Rosa, for reasons still unclear to Posie, had become utterly fixated and obsessed with her back in 1921, wanting to make her his wife, and plaguing her repeatedly on the subject.

In 1924 Caspian della Rosa had been grievously wounded in a gun-fire incident, and Posie had not, mercifully, heard from him ever since then.

A situation she thanked her lucky stars for frequently.

'What of him?' she asked now, in a soft, low, calm voice.

Richard shrugged. 'It's just odd, darling, that's all. I feel dreadful saying this, but I hoped that the man had died, after that shooting last year. And now it seems, on the surface, that I have got my wish. He has died.'

He shook the letter. 'This is from his Parisian lawyers, from a posh office high above the Champs-Élysées. It includes a copy of his Will, and an accompanying note. It seems della Rosa must have made his way to the South of France to recover from the gun-shot accident last year, and he's been renting a cottage in the grounds of a castle. In a place called Cabris.'

'*Cabris?* The de Poilac's family home?'

'Seems to be one and the same. Anyway, he died there. Apparently. Last Monday. His lawyers in Paris have sent on the Will to us first, at Scotland Yard, because there were so many criminal actions still open against Caspian della Rosa in this country, with many parties still owed money. The lawyers also sent us a list of della Rosa's assets. They have suggested the ones which should be sold first in order to meet all the lawsuits. Then there are some gifts which will need to be honoured.'

'This is interesting, darling, but how does this affect *you*? Why has this made you worry, unable to focus?'

'Because the wretched fellow has gone and left you two gifts. And I knew I had to tell you, obviously, but it worried me. And, ever since your mention of "peacocks", it spooked me. Here, there's a note. It's for you, from him.'

Richard thrust a short letter on plain white paper towards Posie. It was in a hand she was familiar with; had hoped never to see again.

The writing was shaky, as if the fingers gripping the pen

could only do so lightly. It was dated a week-and-a-half earlier.

She read quickly:

POSIE,

THEY TELL ME I DON'T HAVE LONG.

SO I WANTED TO WRITE TO YOU.

TO TELL YOU I FEEL THE SAME ABOUT YOU NOW AS I DID THE MOMENT I FIRST SAW YOU.

I HAVE NEVER GIVEN UP HOPING.

THE FACT I CAN TELL YOU THIS, THROUGH THIS NOTE, AND WITH MY TWO GIFTS, GIVES ME COMFORT.

I AM IN A PLACE OF GREAT BEAUTY.

I WISH YOU COULD SEE IT WITH ME. AN OLD CASTLE AMONG FIELDS OF FLOWERS.

THE VERY OLD MAN WHO LIVES HERE MAKES PERFUME. HE'S RENTED ME THE COTTAGE AND I SEE HIM BUSILY GOING ABOUT HIS WORK, MUCH ABSORBED.

HE KEEPS PEACOCKS. I LOVE THESE STRANGE, MOURNFUL BIRDS: SO BEAUTIFUL, SO CHARMING.

I WILL SEND ONE TO YOU. A GLIMPSE OF BEAUTY. THAT IS MY FIRST GIFT.

THE SECOND GIFT IS MY HOTEL. IT WILL BE YOURS.

THE *PALAIS DELLA ROSA*. YOU WILL HAVE TO GO TO MY LAWYERS IN PARIS IN ORDER TO GET THE DETAILS, THE KEY, THE DOCUMENTS, ETC.

YOU HAVE THEIR ADDRESS.

I WISH YOU FUN AND FROLICS AT THE HOTEL, OR, IF NOT THESE THINGS, A SUITABLE FINANCIAL RETURN.

GOOD LUCK.

WITH THANKS FOR ALL THE ADVENTURES; YOU CERTAINLY KEPT ME ON MY TOES.

C. DELLA ROSA

Posie looked up, swallowed. That awful word – *coincidence* – hung bleakly in the air.

She tried to make the best of it. 'Well, this isn't so bad, is it, darling? But the peacock…? I just don't understand. You can't think that the one I saw at the House of Sinne was something to do with *this*?'

Richard looked at Posie gravely. 'We *know* it was something to do with this. You remember Jenks, the butler, with his wife's fears over where their next meal was coming from?'

'Yes, of course.'

'Seems he was asked at the eleventh hour to facilitate the peacock's appearance. To receive it at the House of Sinne and then to let it out in the garden. Specifically, so *you* would see it. And then to whisk it away again.'

'*What?*'

But Posie remembered the butler's frequent absences at the 'reveal' itself, and his mucky, dishevelled appearance. It had all seemed rather odd at the time.

'But that's crazy!'

'Not really. Seems he was offered a nice fat wad of notes to make it happen. Apparently, a man contacted him by telephone just after one o'clock on Monday. The fella told Jenks he would bring the peacock in a cage at just after three-thirty, and then Jenks had to ensure you saw the bird in the garden, before disposing of it. The fella promised he would bring money along with the bird.'

Posie was frowning. 'But I don't understand. How did this fella who telephoned Jenks know I would even be attending? Dolly had only just called me up at one o'clock!'

'Exactly! We think your Grape Street office line was bugged. That Caspian della Rosa or his men were listening in to work out where and when you would be going out.'

Posie bristled: 'You make it sound as if Caspian della Rosa might still be alive, my love. He's dead! The lawyers told you so. And what did you mean that Jenks was asked to "dispose" of the bird? That sounds easier said than done. It was huge!'

Richard almost laughed.

'Jenks was given no exact directions. He stuffed it back in the cage it came in, with difficulty and great mess, apparently. It even bit him on the hand; quite badly actually. And hence the bandage he was wearing half-way through the event. And then, after everyone left on Monday, he took it home on the Underground with him to Pimlico. Let the kiddies play with it in the yard. Can you imagine? One of the bobbies who visited there happened to write down that he had seen a half-frightened-to-death peacock trying to escape out of Jenks' yard, cowering in the outhouse. I chanced upon the note and thought it worth investigating. I got Jenks into Scotland Yard today. Asked him a few questions. Put this whole sorry story together.'

Posie spoke calmly. 'What did the fella who dropped the peacock off look like? Did Jenks say?'

'Nondescript. Brown hair, brown eyes. Could have been anyone.'

'Hmmm.'

This didn't bode well. Caspian della Rosa was famous for his range of impersonations, his disguises, his ability to seem inconspicuous.

Suddenly Posie recalled sitting in the car with Dolly, outside the House of Sinne. She remembered seeing the butler, and a man delivering a huge black box of a parcel. He'd got out of a brown van.

Posie frowned at the memory.

That man had been nondescript, for sure.

Tobacco-coloured overalls, like all the delivery men in London wore, and a cap. Grey tweed. Much more suitable for winter than summer.

Yes: now she came to think of it, that had struck an odd note.

The cap would have been too hot to work in, but fine for a quick disguise. A slight glitch.

Posie felt slightly sick.

'It gets worse, my love. I may as well tell you all of it, eh? The *deuce*!'

Richard was shaking his head in disbelief.

'I've had the lads check it all out. The French police too. These lawyers, 'Redon', with this fancy purple embossed notepaper, who work for Caspian della Rosa – well: they don't exist. Although the address given for their office does. And the hotel, the *Palais della Rosa*, which he seeks to give you, also does not exist: not in France; not in Switzerland; not anywhere.'

Richard swilled his drink, took a half-hearted sip of the whisky.

'I fear this is a trap, my love. A bluff. And I very much fear that Caspian della Rosa is not dead. That he has recovered, like some wretched cat with nine lives! What I think is that Caspian della Rosa was never in Cabris, either: it is all a fiction. A dangerous one. I think that he and his team put this whole story together very quickly, but perfectly, including drawing up these immaculately-conceived supporting documents. It was designed as a way to draw you in, and to connect himself to the case you were currently working on. The peacock you saw in the garden in Chelsea is a sign from him. A "calling-card" if you like. A flicker of a starting-flag, a race to be run. All over again.'

A race to be run.

But she felt tired of running. Had thought that was all behind her.

Posie put down her drink. She saw a shadow flit across Richard's tired, lined face, saw how he set his mouth grimly.

She knew there was more to come.

What could possibly be worse?

'There's something else though, Richard, isn't there? Go on. Tell me.'

Richard got up, crossed his arms, and Posie saw him there, at the window, silhouetted black against the London night. So solid, so reliable. Her beloved man.

And she saw that he was trembling. It didn't happen often.

'The only contact the French Police have been able to make with anyone at this so-called lawyers' office in Paris is with a woman. She is hardly ever there, and when she is, her behaviour is suspicious, erratic. They suspect she belongs to the criminal underworld of Paris. Perhaps working for Caspian della Rosa, but they are not sure of her exact position. They are monitoring the "Redon" offices there for me, now.'

'And?'

'The woman's name is Violette.'

Posie closed her eyes and breathed hard.

The thunder and lightning had started up again outside and a wind blew through the room.

'There's something else, Posie. Dolly Cardigeon received a telephone call from the number of this so-called lawyers' office on Monday morning, just before she took a call from the House of Sinne. Whatever was said to her on that call, we think – *I* think – it must have been instrumental in her leaving London.'

Posie felt as if her world was spinning. She remembered Dolly saying something about taking calls, dragging up the past.

'We'd better go to Paris,' she said softly, although she felt terrified inside. Frantic, almost unable to breathe.

This will be the fight of my life.

'We need to get Dolly. Save her. Bring her back.'

'*If* she wants to come back, my love. People leave their

normal lives for all sorts of reasons, and many don't want to return.'

And then little Kit, awoken by all the noise of the rain, started hollering.

As she passed the vase with the 'Talisman' roses on the table, her heart heavy, Posie couldn't help but notice that all the petals, every single one, had fallen off in the last few minutes.

Blown by the weight of the incoming wind, a promise of so much, which, like safety and happiness, can never be taken fully for granted.

Kit's cries were getting louder.

'I'm coming, my love,' Posie called out quickly to her little son, who must have been sailing along on the thread of some nightmare, washed up on a craggy shore of dangers which couldn't yet be known.

And she was aware when answering him that she was somehow including Dolly – wherever she really was now – in her response.

'I promise, I'm coming to get you. You'll be just fine.'

Hold on.

I won't let you down.

Not now, and not ever.

* * * *

Historical Note and a Short Note on Money

All of the characters in this book are fictional, unless specifically mentioned below.

Weather, timings, general political events, and places (and descriptions of places) are historically accurate to the best of my knowledge, save for the exceptions listed below.

As in the other Posie Parker books, I refer to the First World War of 1914–1918 as the 'Great War' throughout, which is simpler for the modern reader, although it would not have been referred to in this way in 1925.

As ever, Posie's work address in London (Grape Street, Bloomsbury, WC1) and her home address around the corner (Museum Chambers, WC1) are both very real, although you might have to do a bit of imagining to find her there.

1. (Throughout) Please note that the famous Chelsea perfume house, the House of Sinne, as used for a location throughout this novel, is entirely fictional, as is the character of the perfumier, Anouk Sinne. The French and English perfume houses which Posie speaks to Dolly about (in Chapter One) are all correct as of 1925, as is Anouk

Sinne's reference to the House of Worth developing a violet-themed scent. This would come out much later, in 1932, and would be called *Je Reviens*.

Embankment Gardens in Chelsea *does* exist, although none of the houses in that terrace have (to the best of my knowledge) the sort of garden which Anouk Sinne possesses in this novel. The wonderful Chelsea Physic Garden which is mentioned in this novel (as being a nearby location) is also real and can be found and visited here: https://www.chelseaphysicgarden.co.uk/

2. (Chapter Two) The Tamara de Lempicka painting I describe of Anouk Sinne is, of course, fictional. Tamara de Lempicka (1898–1980) was, at this time, becoming very fashionable and collectable as an art-deco portrait painter. For something similar, see her *Self-Portrait, Tamara in a Green Bugatti*.

3. (Chapter One and then throughout, especially Chapter Seventeen) The entire character and history of the Indian Princess (or Maharani) Priyanka Lashari is fictional. As is her dynasty and the Princely State of Gwilim itself (including the ancestral home and fort). For more on the (fictional) character and story of the half-Indian Evangeline Greenwood, who speaks to Posie in this book at Chapter Seventeen, see *The Vanishing of Dr Winter: A Posie Parker Mystery #4*, by L.B. Hathaway.

4. (Chapter One) The devastatingly handsome Prince of Wales (the future Edward VIII), was, in 1925, at age thirty-one, London's hottest young bachelor (and perhaps the most famous man in the world). At the time this novel was set he was indeed on a tour of Africa. Highlights from this tour were featured often in the British newspapers as leading stories, but the story I mention in *The Times*, which

Posie sees, is fictional. He was famous for enjoying the company of and having love affairs with women much older than himself, most notoriously (for almost a decade) with (the married) Freda Dudley-Ward, which Anouk Sinne refers to in Chapter Three.

5. (Chapters One and Seventeen) The wonderful real-life restaurant Kettner's was trading in 1925 and can still be found in Soho, London. It is the fictional favourite restaurant of Posie and her friend, Dolly, Countess of Cardigeon (also mentioned in *Murder of a Movie Star: A Posie Parker Mystery #5*).

6. (Chapters One and Fifteen) The play *No, No, Nanette* which Posie refers to was actually playing in London at this time, having started on 11 March, 1925. It proved to be a roaring success, with 665 consecutive performances, catapulting its female lead, Binnie Hale, to stardom. It was later turned into a highly successful movie, with the well-known tunes 'Tea for Two' and 'I Want to be Happy' still known today. The Palace Theatre, at Cambridge Circus, was indeed its venue in 1925, and this is a short walk from Posie's office in Grape Street.

7. (Chapter One) The store (Garlands on London Street, in Norwich) where Posie orders her usual violet perfume, ceased trading in 1984, but it was a well-known and upmarket Department Store in Norfolk in the 1920s.

8. (Chapter One) "Blenheim Bouquet", as worn by Richard Lovelace, is Penhaligon of London's real-life longest-running perfume (and is still in production.)

9. (Chapters Two and Three and throughout) No wonder Hubert Pring is worried about losing the perfume ingredients in this novel! Some of the components Anouk Sinne would have used would have been the costliest of the time. Orange flower and Oud are still some of the priciest perfume ingredients used today, with orange flower (retailing at current 2021 prices) at around £11,000 per kilo, and neroli at around £20,000 per kilo.

10. (Chapter Four) The famous gardener Gordy Lorkinsson is a completely fictional creation, but the Chelsea Flower Show was (and is) very real. It is now one of the highlights of the London summer social diary, patronised by royalty and celebrities alike. Although it had started off as a show with various gardening exhibits all under one tent, by the time of this novel it was growing in size and popularity, with the 'Show Gardens' which are now a feature of the event becoming very popular. It was not until 1928, however, that a tent for just roses was featured, which is what Gordy is campaigning for here. The 1920s also marked the time of a move towards the Chelsea Flower Show becoming a social event in its own right, with tea-parties and music put on for the important guests who were visiting.

11. (Chapter Seven) The Grosvenor Hotel at Victoria Station is now named the Clermont.

12. (Chapters Nine and Ten) Mr Archie Van Dusen and his New York store on Fifth Avenue are not real, but Traub rings were.

    In the 1920s the Traub Manufacturing Company of Detroit became known for their 'Orange

Blossom' line of engagement and wedding rings which were (and are) highly desirable. These rings were mid-range, die-struck and sold in most of the upmarket American Department Stores, such as Mr Van Dusen's would have been. In *Murder on the White Cliffs: A Posie Parker Mystery #8* we learn that Richard has bought Posie one of these rings.

13. (Chapters Ten and Twenty) Sir Charles John Holmes (1868–1936) was indeed the Director of the National Portrait Gallery in London at the time this novel is set.

14. (Chapter Ten) Fondant fancies are mentioned as being Anouk Sinne's favourite cakes. These delicious Mr Kipling cakes, known first as 'French Fancies' were not at the time of this novel yet created. It is a culinary liberty (and indulgence) all of my own that I mention them.

15. The Dibbles Bridge tourist coach crash (as mentioned in Chapter Fourteen) was a horrific real-life crash caused by brake failure which happened on 10 June, 1925 near Hebden, North Yorkshire, in which seven tourists lost their lives with many, many injured. The crash was to have a dreadful sequel. A virtually identical event took place almost exactly fifty years later, on 27 May 1975, resulting in thirty-three deaths.

16. (Chapter Fifteen) The British biscuit company, McVitie's, did indeed bring out their famous (and still much-loved in the UK) 'Homewheat Chocolate Digestives' in 1925.

17. (Chapter Fifteen and Sixteen) There is no room here for a full-length discussion and explanation of

the Women's Social and Political Union ('WSPU') created in Britain by Emmeline Pankhurst and her daughters in 1903 with the motto 'deeds not words'. Briefly, members of the WSPU became known as 'the Suffragettes', although women had been campaigning for years for women's suffrage (the right to vote).

From 1905 sporadic violence became the WSPU's normal mode of behaviour, increasing in the years up until 1914, with serious and dangerous bomb attacks planned and effected across London and the country in general (notably London buses and the Underground trains of the capital city).

In May 1913 alone, there were fifty-two bombing and arson attacks carried out in Britain by the Suffragettes.

Christabel Pankhurst's activities in this novel (as a background device) are pretty accurate, but Harriet and Dolly's deployment as French girls to act like tourists by Christabel is fictional, as is Hubert Pring's involvement in the Suffragette movement in general and the trials the women attend in 1907 and 1913.

18. (Chapter Seventeen) The arson attack as described in this novel (by the Suffragettes) on the Tea Pavilion at Kew Gardens, London, really did take place, on 7 March, 1913, just before Christabel Pankhurst was forced into a year's exile in Paris. I have replaced the protagonists, who in real-life were Olive Wharry and Lilian Lenton, with my fictional Suffragettes, Harriet and Dolly. The punishment for such a crime, as Dolly experiences, was six months hard labour in Holloway Women's Prison.

19. (Chapter Eighteen) The story of the suffragette Emily Davison (1872–1913) is correct. She died while trying to (it is not clear which) either bring down the King's horse, or attach a flag with the colours of the Suffragette movement to the King's horse, which was racing at Epsom on 4 June, 1913. She died of her injuries a few days later and became something of a martyr for the Suffragettes. She represented (and still represents) the pinnacle of their activities as a violently-active political movement. It is still, after more than a hundred years, unclear if Emily Davison meant to commit suicide, but the balance of evidence suggests not, and that the tragedy was not meant to pan out as it did.

20. (Throughout) The dark-green colour of the cars sent from Croydon Airport is a fictional device of my own, as is the use of that colour for their signs, logos, paperwork, etc.

21. (Throughout) The Casino Anouk frequents, the Curzon-Alhambra in Mayfair, is fictional.

22. (Chapter Twenty-Four) The famous French perfume houses of Carobonne and Verney-Depuis, as mentioned by me in this novel, are completely fictional, as is the castle and perfume house of *Le Paon* at Cabris. Cabris itself is real and is near Grasse (in the South of France), which is famous (in 1925 and today) for being the premium centre of flower-growing and perfume production in the industry. Chanel's perfumes, including growing the famous camellias for the best-selling No 5 perfume, are created in Grasse.

* * * *

A Short Note on Money

It is always hard to try and convert money into meaningful present-day amounts. But the following may be of use:

a.) Regarding salaries, a trained legal or secretarial clerk in London in 1925 (as given as an example in this novel) would have earned around £6 or £7 pounds per week (therefore around £24 per month and £288 per year). It follows that the £2,000 which the perfumier Anouk Sinne earns as a salary per year is truly an astronomical sum. So too are the amounts of £1,000 (being asked of her in blackmail demands) and the £500 payment which Mr Lively receives.

b.) The 'House of Sinne' is located in an exceptional house and garden situated in Embankment Gardens, Chelsea, London. The value of the house (£20,000) is conjecture on my part as I can find no precise and exact evidence for such a house in that exact location in 1925. However, huge houses overlooking the Thames in fashionable Chelsea at this time must have been worth a great deal, and I am basing my figure on the 1910 Land Tax Valuations (the 'Lloyd George Domesday Survey') which gives a comparable house on Fleet Street in central London as being worth around £20,000.

c.) The gambling debts I give my characters are, obviously and appropriately, monstrously high.

Thank you for joining Posie Parker and her friends

Enjoyed *Murder in a Chelsea Garden* (A Posie Parker Mystery #12)? Here's what you can do next.

If you loved this book and have a tiny moment to spare, I would really appreciate a review or rating on the page where you bought the book. Your help in spreading the word about the series is invaluable and really appreciated, and reviews make a big difference to helping new readers find the series.

Posie's other cases are available in e-book and paperback formats from Amazon, as well as in selected bookstores and at Audible and other main audiobook retailers. You can find all of the other books, available for purchase, listed here in chronological order:

http://www.amazon.com/L.B.-Hathaway/e/B00LDXGKE8

and

http://www.amazon.co.uk/L.B.-Hathaway/e/B00LDXGKE8

You can sign up to be notified of new releases, pre-release specials, free short stories, and the chance to win Amazon gift-vouchers here:

http://www.lbhathaway.com/contact/newsletter/

About the Author

Cambridge-educated, British-born L.B. Hathaway writes historical fiction. She worked as a lawyer at Lincoln's Inn in London for almost a decade before becoming a full-time writer. She is a lifelong fan of detective novels set in the Golden Age of Crime, and is an ardent Agatha Christie devotee.

Her other interests, in no particular order, are: very fast downhill skiing, theatre-going, drinking strong tea, Tudor history, exploring castles and generally trying to cram as much into life as possible. She lives in Switzerland with her husband and young family.

The Posie Parker series of cosy crime novels span the 1920s. They each combine a core central mystery, an exploration of the reckless glamour of the age and a feisty protagonist who you would love to have as your best friend.

To find out more and for news of new releases and giveaways, go to:

http://www.lbhathaway.com

Connect with L.B. Hathaway online:

(e) author@lbhathaway.com

(t) @LbHathaway

(f) https://www.facebook.com/pages/L-B-Hathaway-books/1423516601228019

(Goodreads) http://www.goodreads.com/author/show/8339051.L_B_Hathaway

Made in the USA
Monee, IL
14 February 2022

91273485R00204